WHERE THE Stars BURN

Scottish Stars Series

ERICA MAE

Copyright Notice

This is a work of fiction. Any resemblance to real places, persons, or events is entirely coincidental.

WHERE THE STARS BURN

Cover Art by *Ink and Laurel*

Publishing History

First Edition, 2025

Paperback ISBN 979-8-9991833-0-9

Scottish Stars Series

Published in the United States of America

Books By Erica Mae

Scottish Stars Series

The Stars of Scotland

Where the Stars Burn

Standalone

Falling for Lemon Snowballs

Visit www.ericamae.net for more details!

For the sassy, big-hearted ones and the quiet ones, too, who are brave enough to recognize what real love looks like and fight for it. This story is for you.

Content Warnings

Thank you for reading *Where the Stars Burn*. This witty, opposite attract romcom is full of love, laughs, loss, adventure, self-discovery, sisterhood, and of course, happily ever after.

Where the Stars Burn also includes a scene with a miscarriage. Though respectfully written to give this topic the care it deserves, this topic may be triggering, so please read with discretion.

Chapter One

SMACK! SMACK! SMACK! ANDREA WHACKED THE chicken cutlet with a metal mallet. "Thanks for nothing." *Smack! Smack! Smack!* With a huff, she set the mallet down and grasped the wide-hipped wine glass, taking a long drink of the delicious red with notes of currant, cinnamon, and a sharp edge from citrus. But the wine didn't help. Anger, betrayal, and frustration still pumped through her blood. *Your dedication here has been immeasurable, and we thank you. Unfortunately, we're letting you go.* She gazed at the ivory walls of her Los Angeles apartment and punches of bold, colorful art with swipes of violet, red, and gold, highlighted by the afternoon sun through the single, rectangular window, and then at the stack of boxes along the far wall, readied for moving. She had so many plans. Her new townhome in Santa Monica would close in four weeks, but she was counting on her current salary to pay for the mortgage. Who knew when she'd find another job? What the heck was she going to do now? Setting the glass down, she flipped another chicken cutlet onto the parchment-covered board. *Smack! Smack!*

Her phone pinged, notifying her of a new notification

from Date L.A. *Rich sent you a message.* Placing a hand on a round hip, she opened the message and immediately snarled.

RICH

I don't date women over 120 lbs.

"Seriously!" She swiped the message away, then glared at the device as a new match notification popped up with a like. She promptly deleted the app. She didn't need a man, but she also couldn't fight the urge to sweep her gaze down, eying her full breasts and ample curves in the red, floral wrap dress. With a huff, she grasped the mallet. *Smack!* "Arrogant!" *Smack!* "Jerk!"

Ding! Her text chimed.

Seizing the device, she prepared to throw it across the room, then noticed the sender: *Brie Bestie.*

BRIE BESTIE

Sorry! I'm impatient. Tell me the good news already!

Andrea exhaled. She had to text her best friend because Brie couldn't come over. Brielle Finlay Fraser—single mom and bad-ass memoirist—had fallen in love with Scottish *Swords of Scotland* television star and kilt-clad heartthrob, Bryce Fraser, moved across the Atlantic with her two beautiful kids and away from her. Although Andrea was happy for her, she missed her best friend. She dialed.

"Did you get the promotion?"

She whacked the chicken. *Smack!* "Nope. And to top it off, I just got insulted by a jerk on a dating app."

"What? Andrea! They're out of their minds," Brie said.

They were. She'd earned the promotion to Chief Human Resources Officer with her more than seven years with the company. Hell, she'd filled in for the role since her superior left Tech Co eight months ago, focusing on strategy and growing

2

revenue with other executives, while continuing her own duties as VP of Human Resources, burning the midnight oil and sacrificing weekends. She excelled at her job. But no, the CEO laid her off, and what's worse, he promoted her subordinate who was three years younger and had less experience, and who, by the way, Andrea trained. She ground her teeth. "They gave the position to Valerie. Valerie!"

Brie gasped. "Why?"

"I don't know." Andrea pressed a palm to her chest where a fresh sear burned. They didn't want her. They used her and took advantage. When she felt the sting of tears threaten, she inhaled. She wouldn't give them the satisfaction of crying. Straightening, she eyed the chicken cutlet. *Smack*! "Fucking assholes." *Smack! Smack!*

"What ARE you doing?"

"Tenderizing chicken for Chicken Parmigiana. I might be an unemployed, date-less loser, but I'm eating well tonight." She laid the mallet down, swiped a curl off her forehead, and snagged the wine glass. She downed the remaining dark liquid. "And I'll be binge-watching Bryce's show the next few days, eating leftovers." Glancing at the television screen, she paused as Hamish Macrae swirled a larger-than-life sword in the air and took on nearly a dozen redcoats back-to-back with his fiery-headed cousin, Alexander James Mackenzie, played by Bryce. They vanquished the Lobsterbacks, and a weeping lass threw herself into Hamish's arms and kissed him hungrily. *Hell, I need some of that.*

"I wish I was closer," Brie said wistfully. "I hate you're dealing with all this alone."

Andrea looked through her glass at the bounty before her. "Don't worry, I'm not by myself. I'm with Cab, Parm, and Spaghetti."

"Well, in that case." Brie snorted. "Maybe it's a blessing in disguise? You can finish your book."

Crinkling her nose, Andrea glanced toward the corner desk where her laptop perched. The witty women's fiction book she started over a year ago hadn't progressed in months; she was stuck on page sixty. She wasn't inspired to write. Twisting toward the stove, she turned on the gas burner, set the wine glass down, and added a pat of butter along with a swirl of olive oil to the frying pan. "I haven't been in the mood to write. At least I can cook. I'll fill my days with decadent food, cooking shows, and bargain shopping, and, oh yeah, hunt for a job until I get to fly out to you for New Year's."

"What about your new house?"

Andrea thought of her pending townhome near amazing restaurants and a short walk to Palisades Park overlooking the Pacific Ocean. She *loved* that house. But now, she was jobless. Fresh bubbles of worry sprung up in her gut. "I have the money for the down payment, but I doubt being unemployed looks good. *Ugh*. I'll put some feelers out tomorrow."

"I have a fantastic idea! Since you're flying out to Scotland for New Year's, why don't you come early? How about Christmas or heck, leave tomorrow! We'd love to have you."

Excitement skittered through her like the sizzle of butter in the skillet. Why not go to Scotland early? She could have some fun with Brie and her family and forget about the corporate hangover. Of course, she'd research and apply for jobs, as well. But most importantly, she'd get out of L.A. and away from this layoff funk and model-obsessed men. She glanced across the room at the bold Glasgow skyline photograph she'd picked up during her last Scottish vacation, highlighted by the golden rays of the setting sun. *Hell, yes.* "I can't think of anything better! I'm in."

"Really? Yay! I'll tell Bryce and the kids. They'll be so excited."

"Me, too." Andrea smiled and selected a chicken cutlet, dipped it in parmesan, coated it with egg, and lastly dredged it in herbed bread crumbs. After a quick shake, she placed the cutlet into the hot pan. The chicken *crackled* satisfyingly, making her lips curl. "Since I'm coming early, I can help with your wedding to-dos." She still couldn't believe the press hadn't discovered Brie and Bryce secretly wed two months ago, but they'd get their photos at the formal affair next spring.

"I'd love that."

"Oh, and tell my favorite star, I'd love another set tour!"

"You got it!"

Andrea lifted her wine glass. "Scotland, here I come."

* * *

After a thirty-minute neck and upper back massage in the premier lounge, Andrea requested a margarita. Thanks to TechCo, she'd accrued loads of frequent flier miles and priority seating accompanied by a posh airport lounge after jet-setting. But now she didn't have to worry about HR, people complaints, manipulative executives, and work drama. *At least for a little while.* She'd set her social media status to *Open for Work*, contacted a few old colleagues, and applied for a handful of jobs the day prior. She'd put the ball back in motion. What better way to give the bird to TechCo, than land an even better job? Rolling her shoulders, she watched the bartender add margarita ingredients to a stainless-steel blender that matched the modern bar's decor with a shiny steel bar top, silver drop lights, and mirrored bar back, highlighting colorful alcohol bottles. The invigorating smell of fresh lime filled her senses. She was ready for the next stage of her relax-and-don't-worry-about-anything plan.

Her phone shrilled beside her.

Glancing over, she squinted at the name. "Perfect timing as always, mother," she muttered before answering.

"Darling, I'm calling to remind you about my annual

Christmas gala," Gloria Taylor said on the other line. "Cherish will send out invitations soon. Please tell me you're bringing a date this year."

Andrea pressed the heel of her left hand to her temple. "No, Mom. I won't be coming or bringing a date."

"You really need to get yourself a social life. Living to work is no way to live."

She rolled her eyes. That was easy for her to say, since Gloria was still living off of her ex's—all five of them including Andrea's dad's—alimonies. "Yeah, okay, thanks for the reminder, but I won't be in L.A. for Christmas. I'm on my way to Scotland."

"What? Why?"

Exhaling, she watched the bartender blend the liquid brilliance. "I was laid off, but I don't want to talk about it, okay?"

"Oh, Andrea. What did you do?"

"Do?" she sputtered. "I didn't do anything. They gave the job to...never mind. It doesn't matter. I'm going to Scotland and getting out of Dodge for a while to spend the holidays with Brie and her family."

"Well, that's the smartest decision you've made lately. Brie can introduce you to one of Bryce's co-stars. You never know where it might lead. Before you know it, you could be engaged and planning a wedding."

Andrea blew a curl off her temple. She'd attended all four of Gloria's weddings after her parents' divorce. The last thing she wanted was to walk down the aisle—it was all a façade, anyway. Marriage was nothing more than a way for Gloria to feel better about herself or a reason to buy a new dress, or redecorate her home. Andrea wouldn't give her the satisfaction. "That's the last thing I need."

"Oh, Andrea! Haven't I taught you anything?"

The bartender placed the frosty margarita on the bar top.

Grasping the glass stem, she toasted him, then slid her tongue across the salty rim. "Yeah, that men are replaceable."

"I beg your pardon."

"Come on, Mom. The last guy you married you barely knew."

"That's not true. We were perfectly smitten," she quipped, and a sniffle followed. "It wasn't my fault Mark and I didn't see eye-to-eye after we were wed, but we still maintain our friendship. In fact, we golfed together last week. It's a shame it didn't work out."

With a shake of her head, Andrea took a giant drink. Closing her eyes, she savored the sharp citrus, sour tequila, and salty notes.

"Are you listening?"

"Mmmhm."

"Marry well, Andrea, and you don't have to worry about HR anymore. Just look at me. I'm happy—"

"For now," Andrea murmured.

"I have a fabulous social life, attend incredible events and magnificent parties, meet fascinating people, and have wonderful friends. A man with connections is what you need, not a nonsensical job. Are you still on that diet I recommended?"

Sighing heavily, she looked through the margarita glass at the blurry world on the other side. A duo of women chattering happily brought her out of the Gloria-haze. Lifting her head, she watched them converse with their hands, smiles, and mouths, excited for their destination. Andrea was ready for hers. "My flight's boarding. Gotta go, Mom. Bye." Lifting the golden margarita, she cleared Gloria from her mind and toasted herself. "Cheers to one heck of a year-end!"

Chapter Two

ARRIVING IN GLASGOW UNDER A GRAY-AND-WHITE cloud-speckled sky, Andrea glanced at the rolling green-and-brown mountains with a grin and swiped on some hot, fire-engine-red lipstick and then added jet-black liner to her lids. Brie met a movie star the last time they arrived in Scotland and look how that turned out—*frickin' perfect*. But Andrea didn't need love—not like Brie—just a fantastic distraction. Yet, as she strolled off the passenger gate into the airport, no star awaited her. Just throngs of vacationers and locals coming home, wearing thick coats and fuzzy beanies.

Exiting the airport, she was hit by a blast of frigid air. "Brr!" She tugged her coat collar and spotted a woman with honey-brown hair, an oversized, white wool sweater, and a huge smile beside an SUV.

Brie shook a giant sign. "Andrea!" The next moment, she dropped the poster and sprinted toward her.

Andrea flung her arms around Brie. "Oh, my God. I missed you so much."

"Missed you, too!"

She held onto Brie, breathing in her light, floral scent mixed with syrup and some sweet baked confectionary. Embracing Brie was like stepping into a homey kitchen filled with warmth and life. "Promise me we won't go that long without seeing each other again."

Brie held out a pinky. "Pinky promise."

With a laugh, she hooked a pinky with Brie's. "Where are the munchkins and Bryce?"

Pressing the button for the hatch, she hauled the first of Andrea's luggage into the cargo area. "Bryce is finishing up some script work at the studio for the final fortnight of shooting, and Mimi is picking up the kids from school. They're so excited!"

"I can't wait to squeeze them." Andrea tossed her tote and second luggage piece into the SUV. "How about we surprise everyone with homemade pizza?"

Brie tilted her head, shuffling golden-brown waves. "But you just got in. You must be tired."

"I'm great! I just flew across the ocean to see my favorite people. I've energy to spare and tummies to fill."

"All right." Brie smiled. "We'll stop at the grocery store and grab a few things. Do you have the recipe?"

She tapped her temple as her lips curved. "Always."

Driving through the vibrant city passing giant, colorful murals and Renaissance-style as well as modern architecture, Andrea was transported. She didn't need L.A.—not for a few weeks, anyway. After stopping at the grocery store, they drove through suburbia until they pulled up to a private driveway lined with a wall of trees and in the front, an ornate, metal privacy gate shining with the last remnants of the golden afternoon sun. Brie entered the passcode, and the gate opened. They made their way down a short path to a circular driveway.

A two-story stone house with a white-and-coffee-toned

exterior, canopied entrance, and charcoal accents stood at the edge of the driveway, while various sized terracotta pots filled with pink and white heather, a plant with budding red flowers and shiny evergreen leaves, and another with dark green foliage and bright-purple berries added charm. Beside the main house, a guest house stood with a separate garage with doors below and windows above. Behind the house, pine and evergreen treetops pitched into the neon-pink and burnt-orange sky between puffs of clouds, while sweet notes of pine and grass filtered through her cracked window, filling her nostrils. She'd stayed for a single night nearly three months ago to attend Brie and Bryce's private home ceremony, then had to jet-set back to her pain-in-the-ass job. *Old job*. But the beautiful sight was welcome. "Fucking beautiful."

Brie smiled brightly. "We love it." She swung the door open and stepped onto the cobblestone. "Bryce is even putting in some sort of discovery swing set with a castle for the kids this weekend with some of his friends."

Shivering, Andrea rubbed her arms and gazed at Brie. She couldn't deny the tug of jealousy in her gut. "Seems like you've all settled in."

Brie's green eyes sparkled with happiness like glowing emeralds. "We have, although the cold is a completely different beast. The kids love the room to play and exploring with a quick fifteen-minute drive, but they're still getting used to the weather."

"Well, it was fifty degrees and raining when I left L.A. It's forty-ish here. That's not too big of a change, right? Plus, snow should be falling soon. What kid doesn't like snow?" She glanced at the yard where the grass had already taken on a brownish hue.

"Exactly." Brie skipped around the SUV and grasped one of Andrea's suitcases. "I took the liberty of setting you up in the guest house."

"Really?" Andrea lugged another suitcase out, then swiveled toward the picturesque guesthouse. "Fancy."

"I thought you'd like to sleep in a bit, well, at least the first few days while you catch up with jet lag. If you're in the main house, then the kids will be in your room at the crack of dawn. But if you'd rather have one of the spare bedrooms—"

"This is perfect." Andrea grasped Brie's arms. "Thank you!" With a quick squeeze, she swiveled and unloaded two grocery bags, then rolled a suitcase to the charcoal door. Tiny dark-eggplant and snowy-white flowers with waxy-green leaves perched in pots before the front door, creating a relaxing, cottagey feel. She opened the door to a quaint entry, noting the soft, forest-green accent wall on one side with a built-in closet complete with hooks for coats, a bench, and a cubby with woven baskets below. She set her purse on a hook, then removed her coat and boots and glanced at the opposite wall, which held a large, whitewashed wooden mirror beside a garden photograph with vibrant, blue thistle and another of tiny boots in black and white she knew immediately were Noah's and Phoebe's. Her apartment in L.A. was empty save for dusty rectangles where pictures once hung and a few wine stains on the cotton carpet, and her more than three dozen boxes and furniture were snug in a storage unit. She hoped she'd be moving into her new townhome the first of the year, but for right now, she'd relax and enjoy.

After hugging Brie with a promise she'd meet her in the main house shortly, Andrea climbed the short flight of stairs to the guest house suite. Flipping on the light, she roamed her gaze over the broad windows and the creamy-white interior accented by soft blues and warm greens, as well as natural wooden detail. In the corner, a kitchenette with bright-green cabinets, a porcelain-white sink, and charcoal two-burner stove drew a smile. She looked forward to cooking—one of her favorite pastimes—not to mention tasting the local fare. Once she settled in, she strolled to the main house.

In the living room, Phoebe played house with Brie's mom, Mimi, on plush, cream-colored carpet beside a six-foot Christmas tree dressed with multi-colored lights, an array of vintage ornaments, handmade picture frames with pictures in between, and strung popcorn. Her petite, three-year-old hands shot up in the air with a wooden doll flying around the mini play home, while Mimi arranged a tiny bedroom.

Big brother, Noah, meanwhile, with his soft fluff of sandy blond hair and blue jeans, built a vehicle opposite beneath the mantle where personalized, large knit stockings hung under green garland.

Joy rushed through her, flooding her chest with warmth. "Hey, kiddos. Hi, Mimi!"

"Auntie A!" Phoebe squealed and hopped up, arms wide, and sparkling in pink bedazzled sweats.

Noah pivoted. "Hi, Auntie A!"

"Oh, you're here!" Mimi rose, her short gray bob swishing, hazel eyes warm and welcoming, and whimsical tails of multiple scarves floating around her. "It's so good to see you."

"You, too!" She wrapped her arms around the kids who flung their arms around her chest and legs, then breathed in hints of dirt, lavender shampoo, and sweetness. "Missed you."

"Missed you, too." Noah squeezed her tight, then looked up with big blue eyes and floppy blond hair. "Can we have pizza tonight?"

She snorted. "Missed me or my pizza?"

Noah grinned mischievously, showing a gap where he'd lost a tooth.

When they separated, Mimi embraced her, swirling scarves over Andrea's wrists and searching her eyes. "Are you sure you don't want to relax?"

"I'm good, really," she insisted. "I had a catnap on the plane. There will be plenty of time to sleep later."

"Okay, then." Mimi rubbed her hands together. "I'm here to help."

"Thank you! Let me prepare the sauce and then the kids can help with the dough and toppings." She paused, remembering Mimi was a part-time art teacher and artist. "Wait, why aren't you still teaching? Is your semester already done?"

"Oh, the community college has a few weeks to go yet"— she fanned her hands—"but I took off early, which couldn't have made my students happier. They submitted their final paintings the week after Thanksgiving before I left. Besides, I missed my grandbabies."

Andrea glanced at Noah and Phoebe. As she watched them, she felt a smile tug at her lips. She'd never been around children much before meeting Brie, but being Auntie A added a layer of joy to her life she never expected. She was a member of this family, and she loved it.

While Mimi and the kids played, Andrea organized pizza ingredients. She knew the pizza sauce and dough recipe by heart, having been taught by *Nonna* when she was a teen. She treasured her patient hands, warm hugs, sharp tongue, and *Nonna's* zest for all things cooking. They spent a single summer together before she passed, but Andrea cherished every moment. Gloria stood by and watched, of course, with the 'messy dough making' as she called it. But when it was time to assemble the pizza, Gloria lent a hand, using tongs to place mushrooms, peppers, tomatoes, and other toppings alongside Andrea and *Nonna*. Reminiscing, Andrea separated garlic cloves, treasuring one of the few happy memories from her childhood.

Angelic giggles drew her out of her thoughts, and she refocused on the task at hand, chopping garlic and then adding it into a saucepan with olive oil to become soft and fragrant.

Next, she opened cans of bright-red crushed tomatoes and paste, grunting at the effort of the manual can opener—one of her least favorite kitchen tools—and added them to the pot, along with fresh basil and oregano and a pinch of salt and pepper. She breathed in the sharp, spicy notes and sighed. She loved cooking—she loved sinking her hands into a meal and stirring up magic, creating a dish on the fly, and most of all, she loved cooking for her family. With sauce simmering, Andrea swiveled. "Okay, pizza makers. Who's ready?"

"Me!" they caroled.

She arranged three separate bowls for the doughs. Soon, she and her petite helpers were arms deep in dough with Andrea giving directions and demonstrating, and Mimi and Brie assisting.

"This is hard." Noah gripped the wooden spoon with both hands, golden brows furrowed.

"Want me to take over buddy?" Brie asked.

"No, I've got it." With his lower lip tucked in his teeth, he held tight to the handle and stirred the dough.

"Can we eat it?" Phoebe stared at the mixture with round green eyes flecked with gold and golden-brown hair braided away from her face, then dipped a finger into the floury concoction.

Andrea snorted. "Let's save it for the pizza."

Phoebe stuck the flour-coated forefinger into her mouth. "Yum!" She scrunched her face.

"Ha!" They laughed together.

Swooping her hands under the dough, Andrea tucked and folded, helping Phoebe, while Noah rolled the dough into a giant, ivory blob. Once they had three dough balls, she drizzled olive oil in another set of bowls and transferred the dough to rest and rise.

"Now, what?" Noah asked.

"Now"—she ruffled his hair—"we prepare our toppings

and cheese." She eyed the large, firm mozzarella balls they'd bought at the grocery store. "We should really make our own cheese. I've always wanted to try it."

Brie gazed at Andrea over the rim of a water glass. "That would be fun just not today."

She tossed a mushroom at Brie. The sliced, spongy vegetable landed firmly on Brie's sweatered shoulder.

"Hey." Brie laughed and tossed the mushroom back, hitting Andrea square in the right boob.

"Watch the tatas!"

Brie snorted.

Just then, a pepperoni hit her in the middle of the forehead.

Noah grinned devilishly. "Bullseye!"

"You stinker! I'm not pizza." She flicked it back.

With a quick hop, Noah dodged the flying meat. "Food fight!" he yelled and flung ingredients at her and Brie.

Brie ducked and grabbed a handful of cherry tomatoes, tossing the bright balls into the air, while Mimi grasped eggplant slices.

Phoebe picked up a chunk of cheese and chewed happily, watching the show.

Between laughing and screaming, Andrea flung toppings and dodged them, enjoying every second. Within minutes, the counter and hardwood floors were littered with meats, shredded mozzarella, and vegetables, looking like an impressionist pizza photo, but smelled even better. She missed this—spending time with Brie and the kids—and creating joy with food.

An hour later, after they devoured the pizza with fewer ingredients alongside a movie, Andrea kissed her niece and nephew good night, then tiptoed downstairs. The hallway held beloved photos of Brie and the children that had graced her best friend's home in California, as well as new photos with Bryce. She inched toward one silhouetted in the vibrant rays of the sun.

Bryce held Phoebe's and Noah's hands as they strolled through bright-green grass—the large, gentle Scot with her niece and nephew.

She still remembered when Brie showed her the picture nearly five months ago now when she told her she'd fallen for the tall Scotsman. They had their trials of course, especially after Brie's ex-husband's girlfriend violated both her and Bryce's privacy when she leaked a photo of the two of them in Scotland, but that incident had brought Brie and the children back to Scotland. Although Brie and Bryce's relationship created a chain of events including the uprooting of Brie and the children away from her, Andrea could see how happy they were. She just wished she could erase the sting of sadness in her chest. She'd always be leaving.

* * *

Boom! Andrea jolted awake, blinking rapidly at the cottage's soft blue-green ceiling and rustic green-and-white chandelier. *Boom! Boom!* "What the hell?" Someone was dropping big-ass boulders in the front yard on a Saturday. She'd spent the day before in Glasgow with Brie, Christmas shopping, enjoying afternoon tea, and returning early because, well, jetlag sucks, and she passed out way before bedtime. But this was vacation —no schedule, no set plans, or alarms—and she would've loved to sleep in.

When she heard another loud *boom*, she groaned and flung the cozy comforter off, marching to the window. A large, box truck blocked the majority of her view, but she spied a lowered lift gate and long, rectangular boxes. Catching sight of two delivery men, Bryce, and a large man in a flannel jacket moving boxes, she peered closer, intrigued, as her warm breath made a foggy cloud against the cool glass. What were they up to? She roamed her gaze over the scene below until settling on a pair of dark eyes staring above a full, reddish-brown beard. A zap of excitement shot straight to her belly. Something about his eyes —serious and unwavering—under thick brows magnetized her. She couldn't look away.

Bryce yelled something.

The thick-built man turned. He and his rust-colored flannel disappeared around the truck.

"Sexy lumberjack at the Frasers." She grinned. With one last glance outside, she strode toward the bathroom to touch up her curls, then threw on her signature red beret along with a red cable cardigan sweater over formfitting, winter leggings, ready to investigate. Pivoting, she gazed at her shapely image and thrust her chest forward. She was curvy, sexy, single, and ready for a foreign fling. *Screw L.A. men*. A moment later, she swung open the guest house door and strolled toward the truck where a familiar copper-red head stood with his back toward her, talking to a mover. "Hey, you moving your television set over here or something?"

Chuckling, Bryce Fraser turned with a side grin, laughing crystal-blue eyes, and short, copper beard. "There she is." He enveloped her in a quick hug. "Welcome back to Scotland. Didn't mean to wake ye."

She fanned her hand. "Thanks! And, no big deal. I need to be up to enjoy my vacation, don't I?"

"Aye." He grinned, then squatted to lift a rather large, square box. "We'll be assembling the weans' playset today."

"Oh! Brie mentioned that. Though I didn't know that would take place today..." Flashing a smile, she glanced around Bryce. *Where did the mystery man go?* "Can I help with anything?"

"*Och*, no, we've got it."

And just then, the large man ambled over with a charcoal

beanie, reddish-brown beard, and beefy forearms bulging from shoved-up sleeves where an intricate black sword tattoo sliced along the interior of his forearm. He stood almost as tall as Bryce's six-foot-three inches, since she knew Bryce's stats as part of his fan club, and his broad chest and thick middle heaved with the effort he just exerted. Packed into snug jeans and solid workbooks with scuffs on the hard toes, he looked rugged and sexy. Andrea was used to the sharp-dressed, sleek, and yes, sometimes, slimy suit-wearing men at her office and professional events, even at her mother's galas. But he was different. And *all* man. Excitement swirled in her chest.

Bryce set the box down and jerked a hand toward the man. "Rory Cameron, Andrea Accardi."

"Well, hello." She smiled brightly. "Looks like Bryce brought in the big guns today."

Grinning, he extended a hand. "Aye. Pleasure."

"Pleasure's all mine." She gripped his hand, which was big, thick, and blunt-fingered like a frickin' bear claw. *Holy cow.* But as she gazed up, noticing those gray eyes like molten pools...he looked vaguely familiar. "Have we met before?"

He nodded. "We have. On the set of *Swords.*"

His eyes, which she now noted were like gray steel, stared unwaveringly into hers.

"Rory's our swordsmith," Bryce added and dropped to his haunches. A grunt escaped his lips, while he lifted another box.

She skimmed her gaze over his profile. "That's right. A man who can work with his hands."

He grinned slowly, beard tipping up.

"Rory, can ye grab the end, mate?" Bryce huffed.

With a quick tilt of his head, he squatted and lifted the bulky box.

Andrea had an ample view of his beefy butt and muscular thighs in those snug jeans. And, *boy,* was he wearing those jeans. "I'll let you men work and...go say good morning to Brie." With a whistle under her breath, she skirted toward the house with heaps of questions. A moment later, she glided through the kitchen entry where Brie shredded zucchini into a glass bowl. "There's a sexy swordsmith in your front yard."

Brie paused, stilling her hand and glanced outside. "Rory's here? Oh, he's so sweet to help out. I didn't know he was coming. I heard Hugh was dropping by, as well."

Andrea stopped mid-stride. "He's—wait." She slapped a hand onto the kitchen island, steadying herself on the cool stone. "Did you say Hugh Macrae?"

"The one and only." Brie continued grating the vegetable.

She fanned herself. "Wow. Two sexy Scotsmen."

Brie laughed. "Control yourself. And, there're three sexy Scotsman outside plus a couple delivery men who don't look too shabby."

With a wave, Andrea snatched a bag of semi-sweet chocolate chunks and dumped a couple into her hand. "Please, one's old enough to be my grandpa." She popped the chocolates into her mouth, crunching the rich, creamy morsels. "Of course, there are three, but Bryce is yours. I don't think of him like that."

Brie laughed softly and grasped the chocolate bag.

Noticing the quiet, Andrea glanced around. "Where are Mimi and the munchkins?"

"Gymnastics." She poured chocolates into a cup measure and added them to the bowl.

"Nice. What's up with the zucchini and chocolate?"

Brie smiled. "Almond flour zucchini bread. Bryce is still on his television diet, but he'll be exerting quite a bit of energy today with that playset build. And I want chocolate, so I'm dumping a few in."

Andrea made a face. "Almond flour?"

"Yup."

She popped another creamy chocolate into her mouth and plopped onto a barstool. "You're the baker. I won't argue."

As Brie smashed brown-spotted bananas into a bowl, she grinned. "Coffee's hot. I just made a fresh pot."

Andrea glanced over at the pot and two cups beside it. "Isn't it a little late for your coffee?"

"Well, yes. I already had a cup, but I didn't get much sleep last night."

Watching her friend's cheeks pinken, Andrea snorted. "I bet. Not when you have a toss-me-over-your-shoulder hot Scot in your bed."

Brie blushed deep crimson. "He's such an incredible lover."

"Don't rub it in. I'm in my longest dry spell e-ver," she drawled out the last word.

Brie cut a glance toward Andrea. "What do you think of Rory?"

Flutters filled her belly. Rising, she crossed to the coffee. "He's got that mysterious, sexy lumberjack thing going on, but tell me about Hugh. Is he single?"

"I think so? I never really ask. He's always got a girl on his arm, and of course, the tabloids love to flaunt him as the bad boy of *Swords*." She chopped walnuts and added them to the bowl.

Fishing her phone out of her pocket, Andrea gazed at the heroic Hamish aka Hugh Macrae on her screensaver in a blue-tartan kilt, then blew him a sassy kiss. "I think that's just what I need right now. A bad boy."

"You and Rory might hit it off. Hugh isn't exact—"

"Marriage material?" she interrupted. Seeing Brie nod, she set her phone down and poured herself a cup of rich, steaming coffee. "I don't need a proposal just a little adventure and sex. Hot, hot sex."

Brie swiveled, pausing mid-stir. "Are you sure you don't want someone with more substance?"

"I'm not the same as you, Brie."

She frowned. "I know, but—"

"Don't worry about me, all right? I'll just enjoy the...ride." She lifted the cup of coffee to her lips and hummed. Nothing said vacation like a bad boy romance in another country.

Chapter Three

RORY SHOULD BE FINISHING THE CUSTOM SWORD that rested in his vise. He still needed to shape the handle and complete the leatherwork. *Och*, but here he was standing in the Frasers' yard with massive boxes stacked beside him and a storm set to ensue. He could smell it—the hint of moisture in the air—and feel the brisk whispers of wind at his neck.

"Thought this would be a painless assembly." Bryce lifted a woolen cap to swipe a hand over auburn hair. He gazed at the boxes and then back at the delivery driver and two men appearing to be in their early twenties beside him.

"They've complicated them a bit since my weans were young." The driver grinned, lines deepening around his mouth, and handed Bryce the tablet for signature. He wore a faded, yellow-striped safety vest over his jumper, along with a multi-colored, green-and-yellow knit scarf tied snuggly around his neck.

"Oh, aye?" Bryce asked. "How many do ye have?"

"Four." He glanced at the scarf. "My youngest, in fact, knitted this herself."

"An artist," Rory acknowledged.

"That she is." He reached a hand up, peppered with sunspots and scattered with lines, and wove it gently around the scarf. "She's twenty now. They grow up fast. Enjoy them."

At that moment, a door slammed, and Rory glanced up to see wee Noah dart from the backseat of a four-by-four.

He raced toward them in blue sweats.

"Thank ye." Bryce shook the driver's hand. "Happy holidays to you and yer family."

"And ye. The lads here will help ye assemble." The driver nodded toward the men slipping razor blades between glossy cello taped boxes and waved to Noah before hauling himself into the cab.

"Wow! Where'd all the boxes come from?" Noah's big blue eyes scanned the mountain of packages.

"The shop, lad."

"Can I help?" His eager wee fingers pulled at the cello tape.

"Aye. I'll cut the tape, and you can pull it off." Bryce set a hand on his shoulder to pause Noah's action.

"I have scissors in my pencil box."

Rory chuckled and crossed his arms over his chest, while Bryce and his stepson discussed the grandness of the playset and proper safety he had to abide by if he were to help. Noah agreed quickly, brilliant smile spreading across his bonnie face. Rory, himself, could imagine building something like this with a son of his own one day. He supposed that's what his own Da wanted—for him to take over the family forge—just as he had from his father. But when Rory had attended the smith convention, he couldn't forget the craftsmanship of the swordsmith and the offer to learn another aspect of the ancient trade. Still, he stayed longer than he'd planned, and even after he left to train in the art of sword making, he returned to lend a hand now and again. But since his brother took over the forge, he hadn't returned, save for a holiday.

Rory reached for the cutting blade on his tool belt, pushing past thoughts of what once was and got to work.

Half an hour later, the large set was unboxed, and the lads from the delivery company had already laid out supports and beams along the grass, preparing for assembly. Thank Christ, the mossy tree house and wooden bridge came partly assembled, or they'd be at it all day. Like his own sword work, nothing brought more satisfaction than a finished product, and he was keen to begin. He withdrew a screwdriver from his belt and stopped mid-stride when laughter flowed from the house. Through the large, living room windows, he caught sight of Andrea, chasing a high-pitched, screaming princess with oven mittens. An expanding feeling flooded his chest and rose against the self-constructed armor around his heart. He wanted a woman, a family, and a domesticated life. Watching the interaction before him warmed his blood. When he'd glanced up at the wee cottage window hours prior and found her staring down with tousled hair and a grin playing at those rosy lips, he felt something stir within that had been dormant for some time.

"What do ye think of her?" Bryce asked.

Rory pivoted. "Who?"

A slow grin tipped at the corners of Bryce's mouth.

"Are we assembling this beast or standing here?"

Bryce chuckled, then squatted and hoisted a long, wooden pole. He stood it on end. "Assemble it."

With one last glance at Andrea, Rory attached a beam. He was keen to speak with her again, but hell if he knew what to say.

* * *

Rory pushed against another sizable, metal beam, sweat dripping down his forehead despite the nip in the air, while one of the lads stood atop a metal ladder, driving screws through pre-drilled holes.

"I see ye have started without me," a voice said from behind.

Craning his head, he swore under his breath as Hugh Macrae strolled into the yard with leather breeks and jacket. Rory pursed his lips and cranked the wrench a few more times.

"We'd freeze to death waiting on ye." Bryce strode toward Hugh and clasped a hand before drawing him in for a swift embrace. "Thanks for coming, mate. We could use all the help we can get."

"Happy to oblige."

"Ye might want to change your breeks. Wouldna want ye to tear them," Rory tossed.

Hugh smirked. "Worry about yerself, Cameron."

"Well, hello," a female voice all but purred.

With a glance over his shoulder, Rory rapidly straightened. Andrea approached bonnie in her red jumper and fitted pants, hugging those ample curves and knocking him in the gut with longing.

"Thought you hardworking men could use some refreshments." She held three beers and bottled water between her hands.

"Thanks." Bryce grasped a beer.

Rory nodded and accepted one, looking over the rim at her, noting the brilliant red polish on her nails, and thinking of what to say to the lass. Speaking to women was never his strong suit, and he was out of practice.

"Don't mind if I do." Hugh grasped an offered beer, then cracked it open and guzzled like he hadn't had a drink all day. "Thank ye." He leaned toward Andrea. "I don't believe we've formally met. Hugh Macrae."

She giggled.

Rory rolled his eyes.

"Andrea."

"Pleasure." He lifted a hand to his lips.

Wanker. Rory downed the rest of his beer.

"Stop fawning over Andrea, mate. We've a playset to build and a storm comin'," Bryce said.

"I'll let you get back to work. I'm off to the grocery store anyway to cook up something special...for you," she drew out the last line.

With a nod, Rory busied himself in the next task, but he couldn't fight the urge to glance back. He found Hugh staring at Andrea's disappearing backside, as well, and felt a wee spur of competition spark within. Hoisting another beam, he swung it around.

Hugh dropped to the ground like a feral beast. "Watch it, Cameron."

Rory grinned.

Four hours later, he gazed upon the play masterpiece and bobbing sand and brunette heads as the sun dipped low. But he'd lost sight of a certain brunette.

"It looks magnificent," Mimi commented beside him. Multi-colored-stones swung from her earlobes, while gray-and-light brown spirals twirled to her chin. "Thank you for helping today. I've heard such wonderful things about you, Rory."

"Thank ye." She reminded him of his mother—warm and welcoming—though with her own artistic flair. A drop of guilt settled in his gut. He hadn't visited Ma in some time, and he needed to remedy that, soon. Like the earrings she wore, the scarf around Mimi's neck was a symphony of colors like a painting, reminding him of something he'd learned. "Bryce told me about yer artistry, as well. Are ye visiting the Christmas fair?"

"I am. In fact"—she checked her watch—"I'll be heading out soon."

He nodded again, glancing above Mimi's head; yet, Andrea still hadn't re-emerged. "If ye want to tour some local artistry outside Glasgow, there are numerous art fairs and festivals in Inverness."

"Thank you so much. I've connected with a local artist in Inverness, thanks to Bryce, and will be heading up there in a few weeks. You were born there, correct?"

"Aye, I was. Ye'll enjoy yourself."

"I'm sure I will." With a soft pat on the arm, Mimi looked him square in the eyes. "I'll be sorry to miss dinner tonight though because Andrea"—she smiled brightly—"is a true artist in the kitchen."

His lips curved, and he smoothed a hand over his beard. He'd seen Andrea return with Brie hours ago with heaping bags of messages, and his interest piqued. He wondered if she was a chef. With a nod toward Mimi as she jogged to the weans, Rory turned in the opposite direction.

Hugh stood off to the side of the yard, yapping on his phone.

Rory supposed it must be a lot of maintenance, keeping up with that many hens. With one last glance, he ambled into the house in search of a certain bonnie brunette. Stepping into the kitchen, he had one thought: Andrea moved. Quickly, steadily with a precision he could appreciate, he watched her stir a pot, then pivot and flip vegetables with a flick of a wrist on the long arm of a pan. Next, she crossed to the double oven to crack the door and peered inside.

A pleasant, yeasty scent filled the air and merged with rich, meaty aromatics of a lamb rack resting on a rustic board atop the island. He breathed deeply. With a quick stroke of his beard, he strolled farther into the kitchen. "Can I help ye?"

Andrea swiveled, and her eyes widened. "I'm good. Controlled chaos, you know?" She flashed a smile, then tossed those rich curls before seeing to the meal preparation once again.

God, she looked good from where he was standing with the rich, red jumper neatly tucked around those generous curves, and dark, glossy locks around her shoulders. He hadn't noticed a woman in some time. Of course, women were always on set—crew, actors, extras, etc.—but he didn't mix business with pleasure. He keenly separated them, which was lousy for his social life, since *Swords of Scotland* kept him on set near twelve hours a day, then busy on his off days. "Are ye a chef, then?"

She tapped a wooden spoon on a pot. "No, I'm just fond of cooking—all the variety, discoveries, and of course, happy bellies. It satisfies, you know?"

He nodded.

With another quick tap, she set the spoon down, topped the pot with a lid, and swiveled. "I work in HR." She paused, pursing her lips.

He tilted his head and considered the acronym. *HR?*

"Human Resources," she clarified and scrunched her nose. "Well, used to. I was laid off. Anyway, my mother would have a field day if I took up cooking. She—you know what? We don't need to talk about her. Just focus on this fabulous feast, right?"

"Aye." He grinned. "Smells grand."

She smiled wide, sparkling her bonnie brown eyes with a light shimmer, then busied herself with the tasks at hand.

He knew plenty what it was like to have a parent disagree on a career move. He'd butted heads with Da for a handful of years now. But standing here watching the woman cook was like magic. He wondered what she did in HR and how anyone could've felt she was redundant. Of course, the production company had an HR department for the show, and he'd visited a time or two discussing set safety, but he didn't see the fiery woman before him sitting behind a desk. He wanted to know more. With a tug of his beard, he considered asking her how she grew to feel confident in the kitchen, or what was her favorite meal to prepare?

Swiveling, she lifted a brow. "Where are your swords today?"

He opened his mouth. He hadn't expected her to speak first. *Come now, Rory, you can talk to a woman!* Clearing his throat, he straightened. "Back—"

"I'm coming for you, you sashbuckler!" Noah's voice shot out.

He glanced toward the entry where young Noah wielded a plastic sword and paired it with a yellow construction hat and an orange-and-yellow safety vest.

Noah pointed the gray sword at Rory's stomach.

With a chuckle, Rory felt the pressure in his chest ease. "Sashbuckler, ye say?" He plucked the sword out of Noah's hands. "I *dinnae ken* what or who that is, but perhaps yer looking for a swashbuckler. In that case, ye've found him." He held the sword high.

Noah jumped up and down, dislodging the hat, which fell with a *plunk* on the ground. Noah pouted. "Hey, give it back."

"Aye, I would, but I've no weapon myself." Something hard rapped him on the shoulder. Rory glanced back.

Andrea held out a long, wooden spoon. "Here, have at it." She handed him the spoon and then bent down to Noah. "Get him."

Merriment moved through him.

Noah sprang up, seizing the sword, then took off like a rocket around Andrea, weapon drawn on the opposite side of the large, marble island. "Ready to meet your doom?"

"Never." He wielded the wooden spoon, slicing the air, while watching Andrea sashay to the stove.

29

With a quick step forward, Noah sprinted toward him.

They pretended to sword fight until Noah ran Rory clean through, or at least he thought he did with Noah's plastic sword stuck under his arm. "Ye got me." Rory fell to the floor.

"Now, Andrea!" Noah circled the island again, then stuck her square in the arse.

"Ow! You little booger." She seized a clean spoon from the utensil basket and swatted Noah's retreating figure. "You better run!"

Screaming and giggling, Noah raced out of the kitchen.

Rory pushed up to his elbows, laughing.

As Andrea danced in triumph, she spun and her elbow connected with a wide-mouthed saucepan handle. The pan *clanged* and tipped. "Shit!" She slapped a hand onto the base and the other on the handle, righting the pan on the burner. "Ah! That's hot. Hot." She swore and gripped the seared hand, while pain flashed across her face.

Rory launched himself up and in a few giant strides was by her side. "Let me have a look." He grasped her soft hand in his larger one, noting the strike of flaming red across her palm. He lifted his gaze to hers and felt his mouth go dry.

* * *

Concerned, smoky, gray eyes stared into Andrea's. Although the sear in her hand radiated, she could feel Rory's pulse beating steadily through his fingertips, splaying up her arm.

"Hold still." He twisted toward the sink. He grabbed a towel and ran it under the tap, then pressed the cloth onto her injured palm.

The cool towel immediately eased the pain. "Thank you." She puffed a breath. "That was stupid. I know better than to mess around in the kitchen."

"We've all made plenty o' errors."

She leveled her gaze. "You seem to have everything under control. I saw you out there, helping assemble the playset. You should add foreman to your list of trades."

He grinned, while his fingertips rested atop her hand and the other held hers.

"How's dinner coming?" Brie bellowed, entering the kitchen.

Andrea snatched her hand from Rory's. "Almost done. Just a little mishap."

Rory straightened.

Rushing to her side, Brie stared at her toweled hand. "Are you all right? Can I take over?"

"No." She shook her head, squeezing the cool towel. "This is a thank-you dinner. Plus, nothing I can't handle."

"You're our guest! There's really no need to do this all by yourself. Can you please let me do something?"

Andrea glanced from Rory—who watched her quietly with those smoky eyes—then back to Brie.

"E'scuse me." Rory strode out.

Watching him leave, Andrea had to admit he had that sexy, slow smolder going on. And she could admit, something was there—a tingle of interest and definite heat between them, plus a beefy butt she admired upon his exit. But what about Hugh? The Herculean Highlander was literally a few feet away outside...She could date them both, that is, if they asked. *Of course, they'll ask!* She was single, sexy, and available. But that could get messy, right? Hugh and Rory apparently knew each other from set...she didn't need messy.

"Did I interrupt something?" Brie glanced from Rory's disappearing figure to Andrea's.

"No...you didn't. He was just...checking my hand." She squeezed the cool towel once again, though she still somehow felt the lingering warmth from Rory's hand. "I'm good."

Brie looked at her with questioning, mossy-green eyes.

Pivoting, Andrea stirred the sauce with her good hand. "I'm fine," she lied. "Can you grab the finger food from the fridge and the bread? You can put that out to stave off the wolves a bit longer."

"You got it." She nodded, then added with her head in the fridge. "Oh, by the way. Eleana's on her way over, as well."

Andrea dropped the stirring spoon. Sauce splattered around her like a sparkler. "Eleana Evans?"

Brie reappeared with the tray in hand and a bright smile. "Yes! You'll love her."

Swinging down, Andrea snatched the wooden spoon, tossed it in the sink, and quickly wiped up the smear of sauce, feeling the sting of her burn. "Does she even eat real food?"

Brie guffawed. "Of course, she does. Probably no carbs though."

"Actors."

Brie winked. "Actors."

"Oh, is her fiancé coming? Should we expect one more?" She turned, remembering something Brie had told her.

"No, he's traveling." Brie exited with the platter of antipasto and cheese.

Blissfully alone in the kitchen again, Andrea inspected the rosemary-garlic rack of lamb resting on the cutting board. Under the foil tent, the main course was browned to perfection with dark char marks on the edges and a nice, finished sheen. She inhaled the savory aroma with notes of woodsy rosemary, then exhaled, tearing off a few extra sprigs of rosemary to line the serving platter.

Eleana was just an extra person, right? She puffed a breath, shaking her head. Eleana Evans *was* Eleana Evans—mega television and movie star with willowy long, romantic waves. Here Andrea was in the kitchen with grease stains already on her apron and hair stiff with extra hairspray to hold unruly curls. She wanted to thank the Frasers for inviting her to stay and also impress the single men at the table, but she worried Eleana would steal the show. After all, Eleana was used to the spotlight—she was an actress—and not just any actress, the lead playing opposite Bryce on *Swords of Scotland*. She had a fancy television award, and Andrea had a...? What the heck did she have? Exhaling, she picked up her phone from the counter and tapped the screen to check a recipe she'd saved and winced.

Dan - Loan Agent. Missed call (1)

"Shit." She'd forgotten to call him back. Since dinner was near ready, she'd have to call him later. But what would he say when he learned the news? He'd told her, 'Don't make any rash financial decisions like opening a new account, getting a new job, or buying a car until you're fully in your house.'

"Well, he didn't account for a layoff, either." Last night, she'd researched jobs and sucked up her pride when she applied for a few director-level and vp positions. But could she actually get hired within the month? With a huff, she stalked over to the blender and loaded the pitcher with fresh parsley, a few sprigs of rosemary, garlic, lemon zest, lemon juice, and olive oil, and pureed the *chimichurri*. She blended her frustrations away until the sauce was velvety and luminous. Sniffing the bright sauce, she sighed. She didn't have a job or a guaranteed new townhouse, but she had a hell of a dinner nearly ready.

Chapter Four

ANDREA STOOD AT THE HEAD OF THE LIGHT-BROWN rectangular dining table per Bryce's request with her food set out family style in large white and wooden platters. "This is just a small thank-you to Brie, Bryce, and the family for the fabulous holiday invitation. You're the best friends I could ever ask for. I love you. Cheers!"

"*Slàinte mhath!*" Bryce toasted.

She passed platters and waited for everyone to serve themselves, then scooped and slid the delicious creations onto her own plate. As she sliced into the lamb and took a bite, she couldn't contain the groan that escaped her lips. The roast was rich, meaty, flavorful, and fall-apart delicious. Even as a happy food dance happened in her belly, she stole a glance at Eleana Evans in a silky, pearl-white blouse and glossy, dark hair piled atop her head and Hugh Macrae seated beside her. One tasted and the other devoured the meal in quick shovels. Rory, meanwhile, sat across the table beside Bryce. She noted the way he bobbed his head and his beard turned up as he chewed in silent appreciation. Yet, no one said a word. Prickles of anticipation danced in her bosom, even as she speared an asparagus.

A moment later, Eleana set her fork down and dabbed her lips with a green tartan napkin. "Andrea, this is fantastic."

"Magic," Rory agreed.

Bryce concurred.

Andrea beamed. "I'm so glad you're enjoying it."

"I'd love the roast lamb recipe," Eleana added. "I don't cook much, given the lack of time with filming, but the holidays are upon us, and I'd love to make this for Miles."

"Of course." She bobbed her head, while happiness danced within. "Though I'd have to scribble something from memory. I search for recipes, then when I find one I like, I spin it my own way. I don't really write things down."

"But you should!" Brie added.

"Auntie A makes the *best* pizza," Noah piped in.

She winked. "Thanks, buddy."

"I love pizza!" Phoebe said with a full-toothed smile. "And cupcakes."

Laughter floated around the room and mingled with the musical sounds of forks and knives clinking and slicing— music to Andrea's ears.

"So, you're a natural cook?" Eleana asked.

She shrugged, though a smile teased her cheeks. "I love food. My *nonna* instilled her love of cooking in me when she visited one summer. Since then, I've dived in so to speak, discovering new cuisine and making my own recipes. It's one indulgence I allow myself with my busy work schedule."

Eleana smiled brightly. "Well, it shows. Thank you for allowing me to join you." She sank her fork into an asparagus.

Andrea couldn't contain her grin. Scanning the table, she noted her nephew had eaten almost all of his roast, a pile of mashed potatoes, a spear of asparagus, and a giant piece of garlic bread. Phoebe, meanwhile, had mixed everything together like a shepherd's pie and was happily still eating.

"So, Andrea, how long are ye in Scotland for?" Hugh asked.

At the strong burr of Hugh's voice, she whipped her head around. "Until the New Year."

"Ye'll partake in yer first Hogmanay then," Rory noted.

"Yes." She looked from him to Hugh and back again. "I can't wait, but what exactly is it?"

Rory opened his mouth. "'Tis—"

"The grandest celebration of the year!" Hugh toasted his wine in the air for emphasis. "People take to the streets with an epic street party in Edinburgh and ceremonies throughout Scotland. There're even torchlight processions the day prior. Some say the fire purifies the world by warding off evil spirits." He wiggled his brows at Andrea.

Warmth pooled in her nether region. He could stroke her fire anytime.

"After the Reformation of 1640, Christmas was banned in Scotland," Rory noted.

Andrea's gaze barely strayed from Hugh's sparkling one.

"Aye, and Hogmanay became the grandest celebration!" Hugh cheered.

Andrea's lips curled. "I've always loved New Year's. It's a time to try...new things."

Hugh leaned forward. "If ye like to bring in the New Year with some excitement, ye should join the Looney *Dook*."

"*Och,* man, and freeze yer bollocks off!" Bryce laughed.

Andrea glanced from Bryce to Hugh. "What is the Looney *Dook*, exactly?"

"A Scottish event that happens on New Year's. People dress in costumes and plunge into the bitter Firth of Forth in Edinburgh," Bryce added.

"A freezing swim?" Andrea cringed.

"Just a start to our adventures, right, mate?" Hugh toasted.

Bryce nodded. "Aye, I'll let ye freeze your bollocks off alone, but I'll climb Ben Vane wit' ye as planned the next day."

"You actually climb mountains in winter?" she asked with her fork in the air.

"Aye." Hugh winked. "'Tis a feisty, wee Munro in winter, but nothing we can't handle with some ice axes and crampons."

With a sharp inhale, Brie's eyes widened. "I didn't realize you were going hiking somewhere you needed"—she paused —"tools."

"'Tis fine, *mo ghraidh*." Bryce steadied a hand on Brie's shoulder and then pressed a kiss to her temple. "We've climbed it numerous times. Winter makes it an exciting challenge."

"I've hiked up there in the summer months. It's beautiful," Eleana added.

Pitching a brow, Hugh leaned forward. "Ye hike?"

She lifted her nose. "Yes."

"With whom did ye climb?" He inclined his head, swishing dark locks along his collar bone.

God, he's hot.

"With Bryce, Lettie, and George."

"So, Milo didn't join ye?"

She speared another asparagus and lifted her nose. "He was away."

Andrea noticed the annoyance in Eleana's tone, along with the bristle of tension in the air—like a buzzing of sexual energy —and for a moment, she wondered if they were ever involved. Dating co-stars wasn't abnormal in the television industry, according to tabloids. Still, she made a mental note to ask Brie later. "Speaking of celebrations, how's the party planning going, Brie?" She'd spent numerous fun-filled hours on the phone with Brie, discussing colors, dresses, and flowers. The wedding celebration would be held at a private, full-service venue in Loch Lomond. Plus, Brie and Bryce hired a skilled wedding planner who was taking care of the rest of the details and a discreet photographer and videographer known for their work with other celebrities. She couldn't wait to celebrate Brie and Bryce in full party mode.

"It's going...good." Brie rose, picking up plates and flashing a smile. "Everything's coming together."

Sensing there was more, Andrea stacked plates and followed Brie into the kitchen. "Hey. What's going on?"

With a sigh, Brie placed the dishes in the deep sink. "I'm already married."

"Yup. I was there. Maid of Honor, remember?"

Turning, Brie leaned on the counter. "I'm serious."

"Me, too. You had a small, private, and beautiful ceremony right here." She swished her arms around. "But you deserve to be celebrated at a star-studded, amaze-balls event."

Brie nibbled her lip.

"If it's not what you want, I'll help you break the news."

"I'd marry Bryce a thousand times, but I just feel like...it's my second marriage." Her lower lip wobbled, and tears shined in her eyes. "I had the big wedding the first time with Ryan, and Bryce and I are already married, though the public doesn't know it, yet. What will people think?"

Andrea crossed to Brie and grasped her hands. "Who the hell cares? It's not about them. It's about you and Bryce and those cute kids. If you guys want to celebrate your marriage with an inclusive event with friends and family, then do it. I'm behind you one hundred percent. Forget about everyone else."

"You're right."

"Damn straight, I am. That's why I'm your MOH." She wrapped her in a hug.

With a sniffle, Brie embraced Andrea. "Thank you." A moment later, she released her.

"Come on. Let's rejoin the dinner party." Strolling out of the kitchen, Andrea found the men standing in the archway between the dining and living rooms, laughing and smiling, while the kids pulled out games on the colorful rug with Eleana. The energy in the room was joyful, and she was glad her meal started the night off right. Now, if only she could snag a date with Hugh Macrae, the night would be perfect. A few inches taller and ten years younger, Hugh was the bad boy to Bryce's rugged good looks. Then, there was Rory—no, she didn't want to focus on Rory. Something about him flashed a red warning sign of serious. And she didn't do serious.

"Rory, come be on my team!" Noah beckoned.

Andrea couldn't help but grin when he strolled over to Noah and Phoebe's corner, then tucked his bulky body into a sitting position with effort.

His large frame took over two corners of the game's landscape.

Noah and Phoebe squealed.

The big, quiet man had a soft spot for children. She'd seen that a few times today. He'd make a good husband for someone. Definitely not her.

"That Rory—he's so good with the kids." Brie beamed.

Andrea bobbed her head. Yet, suddenly, Rory's gray gaze found hers. Even with the distance, she felt a little tug. She shifted quickly, ignoring the flutter in her gut and swiveled to where Hugh stood tall beside Bryce by the drinks, barking laughter at something he said, rich mahogany hair rippling with the motion. *God, he's gorgeous. Straight off the cover of a romance novel. A Highlander Casanova.* Not that she needed romance—far from it. She needed a good roll around the sheets, and Hugh was just the ticket. She caught his gaze and flashed him a smile, then sashayed to the couch. When she saw him pour two glasses of whisky and pivot toward her, she flicked her hair back and pretended to watch the kids; yet, her pulse buzzed. As Hugh's tall frame filled her view, tickles of excitement raced through her.

"Can I join ye?" he asked with two glasses of whisky in hand.

"Absolutely." Andrea scooted and accepted a glass, grazing her fingers not so subtly over his. He settled beside her, arm resting above her shoulders on the couch. A sharp, yet sweet, scent floated toward her, almost like the whisky in her glass, but with a little more bite. "So, Hugh what are your plans before you go back to work? I hear your final shoot of the season happens in a few days."

"Aye, it does. We have another fortnight of work, and then I'll be on a long-awaited holiday."

"I thought ye just stood there and looked pretty?" Bryce ribbed.

Brie elbowed him.

Bryce quickly squeezed her, causing giggles to erupt.

"That's your job with yer red curls."

"Aye, Moira does keep my hair lookin' fine." He flicked his head, tousling auburn hair that rested on his forehead and ears.

Brie giggled into Bryce's chest.

With a grin, Hugh tilted his whisky and settled a hand on Andrea's thigh. "I'm making an appearance at Laoch, a local brewery outside Glasgow, tomorrow. Ye interested?"

Anticipation danced and twirled in her stomach, and she leaned closer, clinking her glass with his. "Definitely."

"I'm their brand ambassador, so I can show ye a few... secrets." He rubbed her leg.

Heat emanated from his hand, and her body fired with anticipation. She needed this night to move faster.

"Hell, why doesn't everyone come? Make a public appearance."

"Aren't you always in public?" Eleana baited, gliding her long fingers in Phoebe's hair.

Hugh scowled.

Eleana crisscrossed Phoebe's glossy hair and weaved a braid. "You have a lovely time. I'll be visiting my sister for the next few days."

Unwrapping his arm from Andrea's shoulder, he angled his glass. "What about ye, Cameron? Ye in?"

Rory studied Hugh from across the room, then shifted his gaze toward Andrea. "Aye."

"Count us in, as well." Bryce lifted his glass.

"It's settled. Bryce, you'll bring Andrea and Brie, and I'll have the best whisky out." Hugh toasted.

At the announcement of bath time, everyone rose and meandered toward the entry, save for Hugh who strode through the foyer and out the front door with his cell pressed to his ear.

Disappointment settled in Andrea's gut. Where was he off to? She sighed. *Well, hell*. Marching toward the kitchen, she spied food lining the island. "Would anyone like to take any food home?"

Rory followed her into the kitchen.

She heard the *swoosh* of his movements as a faint smoky and woodsy scent wafted toward her. Something zipped and swirled in her stomach. *Gas. It's probably gas.* She pivoted, grasping the board with the lamb, then dipped to grab containers in the bottom drawer. When she stacked containers a few moments later in a bag, she glanced up and met his gaze. His gray eyes were so unique with pinpoint jet-black pupils etched with copper-orange like tiny, sunny flames that arrested and steadied at the same time. *I've never seen gray eyes like that.*

He cleared his throat. "Thank ye. Dinner was grand."

"My pleasure." With a smile, she handed him a bag of leftovers. Her fingers touched his briefly, and the connection sent tingles up her arm. She told herself it was just because she was all amped up from Hugh, but Rory was a handsome man—strong, sure of himself, and thicker around the edges with one heck of a beard—so different from Hugh and his playboy, warrior looks.

He rocked back on his heels. "Bryce has been mentioning how good 'tis to have ye here."

"It's mutual."

He nodded, while a smile tugged at the corners of his lips, curling his beard; yet, he simply stood.

Andrea waited a beat, then two as silence filled the room. She could hear the thump of her own heartbeat in her ears.

"Could I call ye sometime?"

She opened and closed her mouth. *I should say, 'no,' but he's Bryce's and Brie's friend. A number doesn't mean anything, right?* "Sure." She exchanged numbers.

"Do—"

The front door crashed open, and Hugh strode into the kitchen. "Off before eight like the weans, Cameron?" He shook his head, then strode closer, skimming a hand down her arm. "What about ye, Andrea?"

She felt Rory stiffen beside her, while her pulse quickened. She glanced from Hugh to Rory. "I'm not tired—I'm still on L.A. time."

"Ace, let's head out back." He strode out, hair flying.

Rory shoved his hands into his pockets.

Here she was stuck between the swordsmith and the highland warrior. But as she waited for Rory to say more, she caught the whip of Hugh's hair as he swung through the slider to the backyard patio. Hugh Macrae was waiting for *her*. Excitement filled her chest. "Well, good night." When she saw Rory simply bob his head, she flashed him a smile and rushed past him, ready to tangle with a sizzling, hot star.

* * *

Andrea cozied up beside Hugh on the spacious patio couch with a Scotch, while clouds drifted across the inky night sky. Although she felt bad for ditching Rory, she shoved the guilt away. The quiet man was interesting, but Hugh had a sexy star factor and a million-watt-smile she couldn't ignore. She brushed her breasts against his arm. "So, what do you like best about acting?"

"The physicality. I get to wield swords and slay redcoats. I never get tired of slaying those Lobsterback bastards." He grinned devilishly. "I get to fight and be paid for it."

"It sounds amazing. I'm sure you're naturally gifted, but did you also do any training for the show?" She swirled a fingertip over his sweatered arm.

"Oh, aye. Some weapons training with reenactors." He took a long pull of his whisky.

"What did you do before acting?"

His gaze hardened. "'Tis and that."

So, he didn't want to get personal. She didn't care; she was with Hugh Macrae for fuck's sake. "*Swords of Scotland* is my absolute favorite show. I've watched it since the very first episode."

"Dedicated, are ye?" He set the now-empty glass down and tossed those dark-brown locks back. Rotating toward her, he settled his opposite hand on her legginged thigh and stroked up and down. "You're fun, aren't ye?"

She leaned in as her inner thighs pooled, and her pulse pounded with desire. She was entranced by Hugh—his voice, his looks, and his touch.

"Watch yerself, Andrea. This one's known to be a rogue," Bryce called out.

With a groan, she swiveled and glared. *Seriously?* "Don't you have a new wife who's more in need of your attention?"

"Aye, just checking a few things." Whistling, Bryce walked around the side yard.

Hugh continued to rub her leg, ignoring Bryce, then nibbled her ear.

She was glad for the attention, but having Bryce nearby prickled irritation. When she thought she heard him leave, she pressed closer and slid her tongue over Hugh's lips.

Flash! A bright spotlight aimed from the patio.

"Christ Jesus!" Hugh shot an arm over his eyes. "Are ye seriously cock-blocking me, ye *tadger*?"

"Night, mate. Andrea." Bryce disappeared into the house.

"Away and bile yer heid," Hugh shot back and pushed to standing, swiping a long lock of hair over an ear. He grabbed the empty glass and strode to the outdoor bar, pouring himself another.

Chewing on her lip, she watched Hugh knock back the whisky—all tall and Herculean in tight leather with an edge of annoyance. The mood had shifted. Sure, she wanted a sexy night with Hugh Macrae. What single, sane woman wouldn't? Hell, she *needed* one. But she didn't want to be an ungrateful friend and houseguest either. The clouds had parted, and the stars now shined above them, in addition to the spotlight, like stage lights setting the scene, and she was his new leading lady. She should invite him to the guest house, but this was Bryce and Brie's house. Would Bryce really be pissed if she was with Hugh?

Chapter Five

Rory studied Andrea's phone number on his mobile under the glow of his kitchen lights later that evening. She'd given her number freely, and he felt pretty darn grand about it all until Hugh waltzed back into the Frasers' and turned her head. Hugh had too many hens as it was, or, so he'd heard and seen in the tabloids, so why did he have to go and dazzle one he was interested in? But Christ, Rory was out of practice. He could have offered to take her to a niche dessert shop he was fond of in the city. *Do ye like ice cream or crepes?* No, he simply stood there like a fool. *Eejit.*

Lifting his coffee cup, he took a long drink of the steaming rich brew, eying his tidy, empty kitchen with the scrubbed dining table, polished wooden worktops, and stacked dishes thinking of his next move. He'd go to the brewery. Andrea would see how Hugh's head turned easily. And he'd be there waiting when she realized she'd chosen wrong. He couldn't deny that spark—the ember—that had ignited between them the night prior. He'd felt it. And he was keen to learn where that spark would lead. Plus, Bryce and Brie trusted Andrea wholly, which wasn't easy to find in a lass—he knew that firsthand.

Thwack-thwack!

He glanced down into Maggie's dark eyes surrounded by golden fur. "Aye, girl. Let's head out. 'Tis time to get to work." He tugged on a jacket and boots.

Maggie pranced around the kitchen.

Opening the door, he looked out into his property, darkened by the deep indigo night, and the wee drizzle that calmed his soul. The crisp, winter air welcomed mingling with boggy earth and sweet pine. He inhaled, filling his lungs, then grabbed a beanie from his pocket, tugged it on, and strolled into the yard toward his forge.

Maggie bounded ahead in search of a squirrel and a place to do her business.

The dark, gray metal building stood strong with a large garaport in the front and lean-to on the side, illuminated by large dome lights. The forge held a sense of pride, as well as offered a sturdy structure for both work and storage of hand-crafted swords and other pieces. He'd expanded and brought in the large, metal structure after the incident. The simple, wooden barn he'd renovated prior had been part of the house's original outbuildings when he'd purchased the property, but it didn't keep those with loose morals out. Combing a hand through his beard, he glanced at the space. Memories rolled in like the clouds darkening above.

He'd returned home near midnight, following a night shoot. On the set of *Swords*, night shoots always ran late. Yet, he'd returned to find his gate open, even though he was certain he'd closed it. Even with wee sleep, he kept ahold of what was his. When he pulled into the yard, he found a large box truck parked in front of his humble forge shed with doors open wide. And there they were—thieves—making away with his blood and sweat. Then, he saw her. Her crisp crop of blonde hair flew back from her face, and he faltered, glancing from Jennifer to the two men beside her. His stomach turned and teeth clenched. How could she be a part of it?

They'd been dating for near a year. Although he'd noticed a piece would go missing a time or two, he blamed it on exhaustion. *Swords* had just begun with a low budget and long hours, but Rory saw the opportunities that lay ahead. He believed in the show. And they believed in his art. He still remembered when the directors came to his booth at an Edinburgh swordsmith convention. They'd told him they'd partnered with a historian who was bringing in historical artifacts, but they needed real-life replicas and new originals. Rory was given the job two weeks later. But the lass—his lass—had shattered his heart and pride. He'd marched across his property, boots tearing up the earth, and met the first, unsuspecting thief's face with his fist.

"Rory!" Jennifer shrieked, eyes wide. She sprinted around the men and jumped into the truck.

Meanwhile, another thief swung one of Rory's own cases, smacking him in the back of the head.

But Rory was no stranger to fighting and recovered well, blocking, then throwing an elbow and a jab.

When the truck's engine turned over, the thieves ran to close the back.

Rory slammed the door open and hauled himself inside, kicking metal boxes out of the truck as it rolled.

The truck pitched and lurched to the side.

Rory was thrown against metal, then out, tumbling onto gravel and earth. Watching the vehicle barrel down the road, he grabbed his phone and called the police. A few days later, he'd received a call they'd found the truck. *Empty.* He was glad he'd gotten a few hits in, but they'd taken his work and left a *craig* in his heart.

After that horrid day, he'd closed himself off to women for

years—that is—until last night. He'd felt a part of his self-inflicted armor crack when Andrea had spoken with him and a connection when her gaze met his. Entering the code at the main door, he waited for the locks to release, then entered. Though the night was *dreich*, the row of skylights highlighted his tools, work, and equipment. A sense of pride surged through him once again.

Buzz-buzz. His phone vibrated in his pocket with a new text.

Fishing it out, he clicked open the message from his younger brother, Collin. A picture appeared with an ornate iron gate with sword-like details at the tips.

COLLIN

Made some wee swords.

Rory chuckled.

RORY

I can see that. When are ye joining the art of swordsmith?

COLLIN

Ah, I can't abandon my heart in Inverness.

Rory sighed. Collin was happily married to his secondary school sweetheart with a sweet two-year old, lived a domesticated life, worked at the family forge during the week, went on weekend outings, fishing at the local loch, and more. Rory longed for something similar.

RORY

If you ever change your mind.

COLLIN

I know where to find ye. Come for a visit.

Rory added a thumbs-up icon to the last text. He didn't know when he would return to the highlands. He and Da still couldn't see eye-to-eye since he joined the trade and left Inverness for Glasgow and a brilliant new television series. Ambling through the forge, he entered the adjacent office, powered up the computer, and released a satisfied breath when he saw near a dozen new orders. He'd be busy, especially with Christmas a few weeks away, but the work would also keep his mind occupied and provide needed distraction until he could speak with Andrea.

Thinking of her, he opened a custom sword request from an American woman—*something strong, fierce, and feminine*—the order read in the Notes section. "American like Andrea," he uttered. He imagined an intricate sword design with a ribbon of gold plating weaving around the handle like a feisty curl. With the idea and her in mind, he selected a piece of drafting paper, a graphite pencil, and sketched.

Chapter Six

LATE THE NEXT MORNING, ANDREA STROLLED INTO the main house in search of her best friend. A chair squeaked from the interior—Brie's office. She hiked the stairs and poked her head in, scanning the soft pink walls, ivory rocking chair, and floral couch until her gaze settled on her bestie sitting at her white washed writing desk. "How's the writing going?"

Turning, a smile flashed across Brie's face. "Great! My new book is romantasy with some historical elements, too. Polar opposite from memoir, but it's been so much fun diving into characters and researching twelfth-century Scotland."

"That's great." Andrea grinned, though internally, she sighed. Of course, Brie was working on another genre, and it would be successful because her friend was an incredible writer, but what about her? She glanced out the window, gazing at the darkening clouds obscuring the tree-line. She'd given way too much of her time and energy to TechCo, but at least, she had a direction. Since they promoted Valerie and released her, she was ready to kick corporate life to the curb for a while, or, at least until her savings ran out. But shit, she had a townhome to pay for and a conversation to be had with her loan agent. She looked forward to that call as much as getting smacked in the head with a frying pan. She'd shot him an email last night, letting him know she was in Scotland and she'd be available in the morning PST.

"By the way, how'd things go with Hugh last night?" Brie asked.

Kicking a brow up, she strolled in. "Your husband played protective big brother and turned the spotlight on us, destroying the mood."

Brie's eyes widened, and her mouth formed an *O*. "He did not."

"Did, too." She flopped on the couch beside Brie's desk. "And you know what? It worked because here I am, jetlagged, horny as hell, and no highlander to have sex with."

"Hugh's actually from Glasgow."

She shot Brie a look that would sear a steak on a cool day.

Brie stuck her hands up.

"We all know I haven't seen action in months, well except my vibrator. But I couldn't exactly bring that on the plane now, could I?" She looked sideways. "Oh, you're with TSA? And you think you found a weapon in my luggage, do you? Well, let me clear the air: it's a vibrator. A vibrator. Tried and true toy for my lady downstairs. The only thing it's hunting is orgasms."

Brie waved her hands, laughing. "Stop. Stop."

"You started it. Well, you *and* Bryce. Seriously, I could've invited Hugh up to the guest house, right? I'm a grown-ass adult."

"You are."

Leaning her head against the headrest, she groaned. "*Ugh.*" She'd watched Hugh leave in a private car close to midnight. She was an idiot. He was right *there*. Ripe for the taking, but she was worried about what exactly? Disrespecting her friends? They had a healthy sex life. They knew how it worked.

Brie leveled her gaze. "I'm sure you'll have another opportunity. Plus, you'll see him at the brewery later. Rory will be there, too."

"I'm not having sex. I'm not dating. I'm not employed. I am a loser. A big frickin' loser!"

"No, you're not." Brie stood and walked around the desk, placing a hand on Andrea's shoulder. "Besides, your worth is not connected to a man, right?"

She straightened. "Right."

"And you made one heck of a dinner last night."

"Damn straight. I added a few new recipes to a notebook, thanks in part to Eleana asking." She thought of the flawless roasted rack of lamb and the accompanying chimichurri sauce. The topper, though, would've been a naked man in her bed. She gripped her hand and felt the soreness of the burn mark on the interior. Glancing down, she noted the red slash across her palm like a battle scar from a sword. Immediately, she thought of gray, smoky eyes, and the swordsmith they belonged to.

"How about we take a break?" Brie closed her laptop. "We can go to this fabulous Indian restaurant for lunch, then stop at a boutique Eleana took me to and buy an outfit that makes you feel incredible before the kids and Mimi are done with the Elf and Safety School."

Andrea rose, flashing a smile. "Hell, yes!" Besides cooking, spending time with her bestie and shopping were the best things to brighten her mood. She'd have some girl time, get something that would make her feel fantastic, and maybe catch the eye of a certain Scot.

* * *

Arriving at Laoch Brewery in the countryside North of Glasgow, Andrea drank in the crisp-white buildings with blue accents flanked by brick towers and giant evergreens. The design was modern and rustic at the same time. As she strolled beside Brie and Bryce, she quickly surveyed her surroundings. She caught sight of Hugh already holding court with visitors and whisky connoisseurs. He wore a slate-gray kilt, secured with a black leather sporran, fitted dark sweater, and shiny black boots. He looked down right sexy, and she felt a tangle of excitement whip up in her belly. She threw her shoulders back, adjusted her bra, allowing her ladies to take the stage in the dark-teal, floral wrap dress, and sauntered toward him.

Ring-ring. Her phone shrilled.

"Shit. Not now." She paused and dug into her purse. *Dan–Loan Agent.* "Shit." She'd have to call him back.

"Everything, okay?" Brie asked.

"Yup. I'm going to go say *hi* to Hugh." Tucking her phone away, she approached Hugh.

Yet, he didn't lift his head or meet her come-hither gaze. He was too busy flashing a wide wolf-like smile at a posse of young women. But that didn't deter her. She had him in her sights. She snaked through the crowd and placed a hand on his arm, thrusting her ample chest into his vision.

A grin spread across his face. "Andrea, ye made it."

"I did," she purred.

He signed a few more autographs, including bosomed T-shirts imprinted with the whisky distillery's logo, grinned when people took pictures, and then flashed a smile when a representative joined them. "Thank ye!"

"Ladies and gentleman, Laoch—"

"One more, Hugh!" someone interrupted.

Giddy screams mingled with the throaty cries of females saying his name in the air.

Holy cow. Get a grip! Andrea rolled her eyes, then scanned the crowd of women peppered with a dozen or so men of various ages. Before Brie dated Bryce, Andrea was a dedicated Bryce Fraser fan—a Brycer. But she wasn't anywhere near crazy-fan status.

"How can I say, no?" Hugh threw back his thick curtain of hair. "Remember to check out the *Fear-cogaidh* selection. For the fierce warrior in all of ye."

"And what do you recommend for the lady who will follow the warrior anywhere?" A bold, raven-haired woman pressed closer to Hugh and whispered in his ear.

Slowly, his lips curved, and his eyes flashed like liquid gold. "Aye, that'll do."

Andrea puffed out her chest.

"If you'll follow me"—a representative directed with a sweeping hand, spare gray hair, and cobalt shirt and tie—"I'll take you to your Laoch tour guide who'll discuss how we craft our fine Scotch Whisky."

"Are ye ready?" Hugh leaned closer.

Anticipation danced in her veins. "I am." As she strolled beside Hugh, brushing against him, she faltered when she spied Rory leaning against the approaching *Exit* sign, arms crossed. He wore a cowl-neck, lined wool sweater, a green-and-red kilt, fastened with a thick, brown leather belt, and wool socks tucked into rough boots. She'd forgotten he was coming, but she greeted him with a quick smile before following Hugh and the guide through the door. Yet, as she advanced into the distillery, she couldn't help but glance back.

Rory spoke to Bryce and Brie, grinning and chatting comfortably.

A sting of annoyance curled around Andrea's happy mood. Rory looked rough and cozy, but he didn't look out of place. He fit in with the dark interiors and polished wood accents. When she caught him staring back, she swiveled and collided with the doorframe. "Ouch," she muttered, then rubbed her arm and followed Hugh.

As she listened to the guide discuss the history of whisky, she was distracted by Hugh. His hand dropped low, caressing her butt, and she forgot all about the whisky-making process and imagined their own process tangled in the sheets. His large hand circled, and she leaned into his touch. Five minutes later, the contact drove her crazy.

When they embarked to the next room, Hugh strode toward the large, copper stills, joining the guide.

The stills shot high into the rafters of the building with pipes funneling in and out like giant, golden octopus' arms, while the main containers resembled potion pots. She hoped one would give her a little luck tonight.

Clink-clink.

Andrea glanced up.

The ambassador arranged sample glasses. "We don't rush the whisky, just like the tasting. Fine whisky takes time." He poured two-finger samples. "Remember to swirl the whisky gently, observing the color and viscosity. Now, breathe in the notes."

Andrea grasped a glass and knocked the whisky back.

The ambassador lifted a brow. "Aye, 'tis fine to drink, but when ye take your time, ye get to appreciate the subtelties." He poured her another and waited. "What do ye smell?"

Ready for a challenge, she rolled her shoulders and sniffed. Sweet and spicy notes with a little citrus filled her nostrils. "Orange peel?"

"Aye, right ye are."

"She's a ringer," Hugh boasted.

She winked, then brought the whisky to her lips.

"Now, take a small sip and slowly roll the spirit on your tongue." The ambassador demonstrated.

Sliding her tongue along the rim, she savored the flavor

and caught Rory holding the glass between his bear claw, then knock the drink back. Her lips twitched. He wasn't any better at following the rules than she was. She snorted.

He looked over.

She toasted him with her empty glass.

A slow smirk tugged up his auburn beard.

I wonder what it would be like to kiss Rory? Would he take his time and savor every moment? Or would he—

"*Sgurr Uaran!*" Hugh roared.

Pivoting, she felt her mouth flop open.

Hugh sliced an arm through the air as if he held a sword, then circled and spun, hair flying and roared again.

Whoa. I need some of that.

"Thank ye, Hugh. This is what we call the warrior line —*fear-cogaidh*—a result of our partnership." The guide lifted the whisky glass. *"Slàinte Mhath!"*

"*Slàinte Mhath!*" She clinked glasses with Brie.

Brie sipped, then pressed a hand to her temple, swaying. "Phew, I'll need some food soon."

Bryce chuckled and tugged her to his side. "I've got ye, lass."

"She's a lightweight, which is why"—Andrea unzipped her purse and retrieved a protein bar—"I always pack these."

A few minutes later, the guide announced the start of their private dinner and motioned for them to follow through a large wooden door.

Yet, Hugh weaved out one opposite.

"I'll be right back." Andrea told Brie and followed close on his heels. She didn't need dinner. She needed a man meal.

Crossing the hallway, Hugh walked into a glass bar and was immediately swarmed by women.

Ring-ring! Andrea's phone shrilled. Muttering, she fished it out and hissed. *Dan–Loan Agent*. She tucked into the quiet corner of the hall and tapped the green button.

"Andrea, how's your vacation?"

"Good. Great, actually." She hiked her purse onto her shoulder, imagining him twirling a pen at his desk with his wide-rimmed black glasses perched on his nose.

"Just remember what I told you. Don't buy anything extravagant."

She hummed. "I'm not, but I do have to tell you something."

"I'm all ears."

Embarrassment snuck up her spine, while she puffed a breath. "I lost my job last week."

A brief pause ensued. "Well, I'm sorry to hear that."

With a brush of her hand, she flicked a curl off her cheekbone. "Thanks."

"And, as sorry as I am to say, with your house closing in a little over three weeks, this won't look good."

"Well, it wasn't planned. What can I do besides apply for jobs and pray an offer comes in quick?"

"Do you have any other sources of income?"

She blew out another breath. "No."

"You're pre-approved from your prior employment status. Plus, the lender will conduct a re-verification in two weeks—five to ten days before closing."

"Shit."

"I'll let the lender know you're working on securing another job, but we could run into some hiccups with the purchase. Regardless of what the bank says, you need to consider if you're comfortable making such an obligation without a current salary."

Her chest deflated. "I understand." After ending the call, she pressed her head back against the glass. What could she do? She'd made a commitment to purchase the house, and hell, a commitment to TechCo—and look where that left her. She'd found the modern townhouse after three months of searching. The house wasn't on the beach, but she could walk. And most importantly, it would be *hers*.

"Here's *tae* us!" Hugh yelled.

Twisting, she watched as he wrapped an arm around one woman and the other around another like the distillery's Cassanova. Perhaps he was more similar to his character than Andrea realized. But she didn't need a hero. She didn't need to be rescued or worshipped. What she needed was a distraction from her mess of a life. Squaring her shoulders, she set her course, weaving her way between fans and pressed her tits toward his face. "Want to see if there are any private tasting rooms?"

He grinned slowly like a cat.

"That's my cue," a deep voice said from behind.

Andrea startled and turned, meeting Rory's steel gaze under thick, full brows—a look that made her pulse jump. She hadn't realized he was so close.

Rory brushed by, shoulder skimming hers and strode toward the exit.

She opened her mouth.

"Another!" Hugh yelled.

"Yeah!" Fans cheered.

Andrea glanced back at the actor. He made some sort of toast, but with his whisky-haze, his accent was even thicker. When she pivoted, she saw Rory disappear under the archway. She was surprised to find the pinch of regret that followed. He was a nice guy. A *good* guy. And sexy and mysterious if she were honest. But she had the chance to fulfill her fantasy with Hugh. Wasn't that what she wanted?

* * *

In the corner of the bar under hazy lighting, Andrea kissed Hugh, matching heat to heat. Hugh's hands splayed under her sweater, rubbed her breasts, and groped her backside, while his tongue shoved down her throat. He was aggressive, *really* aggressive, but she pushed herself into the kiss. When his long hair slid across her face, she brushed it off. But what had once been locks to make Fabio envious were now slimy, sweaty tendrils. A chunk of Hugh's hair fell between them, and she got hair in her mouth. She twisted, trying to rid her mouth of the follicles, while keeping up with Hugh.

"This isn't a hotel," someone murmured.

Andrea pulled away with swollen lips and throbbing lady parts.

"I'll ca' a car." Hugh stumbled toward the door.

As she watched him teeter, sending that once-gorgeous hair flowing, she wondered if his commander would even rise to the occasion with that much whisky in his system. Still, she was game to find out.

Ten minutes later, she tapped her nails on the shiny bar. Where had the Herculean Highlander gone?

"Andrea!" Brie called.

She swiveled to find Brie rushing through the opposite door. "Hey! Sorry to skip out, but have you seen Hugh?"

"He just left." Brie tucked a wavy curl behind an ear.

Andrea lifted a brow. "Left?"

"He was calling a car outside and was mobbed by fans. In his drunken state, he couldn't ward them off"—she scrunched her face—"in a professional manner."

Disappointment filled her. "Well, shit."

"Bryce put him in a cab... Hugh's on his way home."

With a huff, she tugged her purse onto a shoulder. "I guess Operation Land the Herculean Scottish Highlander failed." Her lady downstairs was not pleased.

With a laugh, Brie wrapped an arm around her shoulders. "How about we go finish dinner—it's really good. Then, maybe we can have a girls' night at the rockin' rodeo for cowboy *ceilidh*?"

"A rodeo in Glasgow?"

"Yep!" She skipped. "A friend took me there. It's so fun."

"Let's do it." An hour later, Andrea pushed open a door with a neon cowgirl and looping lasso. Country music played, fluorescent-and-warm pink lights flashed, and laughter floated. Excitement twirled inside like the dancers on the floor. "Okay, you weren't kidding." Grasping Brie's hand, she powered forward. "Come on!" She tugged her into the line dance, kicked her feet, spun, and made up her own routine.

Brie laughed and scooted on her boots. "I haven't done this since college!"

"I haven't done this in forever either, but look—we're good." She pointed to a mirror, reflecting their dancing figures.

Brie giggled.

Andrea kicked and scooted around revelers.

A young twenty-something danced to her own rhythm, while another held a solo cup in the air.

As she twirled, she felt her skirt flutter around her legs in wild abandon. She forgot about Hugh, about the loan agent, and her joblessness and danced. Grasping Brie's hands, she swung and turned, laughing and dancing. She needed this— her best friend and their awesome sisterhood. She didn't need a man. Feeling pulled between Hugh and Rory was annoying and confusing! Throwing her hands in the air, she danced all her cares and worries away.

* * *

Although the clock in his forge told him the time was near eleven p.m., Rory needed to pound something. He unlocked the door and tossed on the lights, highlighting equipment and tools with a fierce potency. Leaving the door ajar, he welcomed the cool air and fired up the forge. The inferno roared like the anger within. He shoved on gloves, snatched steel tongs and a thick, cylinder of metal, then placed it inside the blazing heat.

Hugh.

Andrea.

Two words that left a foul taste in his mouth. He'd felt something, and he'd saw the same recognition in her eyes the night before, as well as when he'd held her gaze at the bar. But the lass was stubborn and Hugh, greedy. She couldn't see what was truly in front of her. He rotated the metal, watching as the fire altered the color and chemical makeup of the steel from a slightly red-gray hue to bold-red. He blew a rough breath out and felt his pulse grow steadier. He could always return to the forge. Gripping the tongs, he rotated the metal once more, then stomped toward the power hammer and turned the giant machine on. Immediately, a loud thundering echoed. Flipping on the switch, he pounded metal. He didn't need some American lass who wasn't interested.

Chapter Seven

Seeing a silver SUV pull into the courtyard under partially cloudy skies Monday morning, Andrea released the ivory drape in the living room and smoothed her red jacket. She waved to the kids, then pulled Brie aside. "Are you sure you can't come?"

"No. I'm volunteering in Noah's class this morning. I'm the marshmallow, hot cocoa lady. Have a great time!" She tugged her in for a quick squeeze.

"Thanks!"

Opening the front door, she felt like the cold air smacked her in the face. "Fu—shew"—she caught herself. *Kids.* "It's cold."

Bryce chuckled. "Nah. 'Tis not even snowing yet."

With a final wave to Brie and the kids, she strolled into the courtyard. Andrea thanked the driver who opened the silver SUV door and settled into the buttery leather seat opposite Bryce. Waters, drinks, and snacks shined in the rare patches of sunlight. "Wow, is this how you normally travel? I've got to change up my routine."

He grinned. "Aye, 'tis helpful, so I can review my lines before I arrive on set."

Andrea nodded. Perhaps she should think about transitioning to television. Even actors needed HR. Why not search for jobs in the L.A. television industry? She'd pivot from tech. Maybe that would be the fresh start she needed? She made a mental note to search when she returned.

Twenty minutes later, they exited the motorway, driving a few minutes down a side road, and arrived at *Swords of Scotland* studios. Andrea leaned forward, taking in the giant structure before her—the large jutting tower in rich forest green, the cream-and-white paneling, and the very magnitude of the space. "Holy cow." The studio spanned at least three football fields...American football fields. She'd seen some of the behind-the-scenes footage and knew *Swords* had expert set designers, but was the set really as incredible as she pictured? She rubbed her hands together and exited the car, following Bryce toward a single door on the building's side.

The door opened.

She flopped her mouth open. Unlike Castle Roderick with its strong stone face, lofty towers, and impressive architecture she'd seen nine months ago while vacationing with Brie, this set was made in the twenty-first century. But if she didn't know better, she just passed through time into the late eighteenth century. A town was constructed on the east end with various structures including an inn, mercantile shop, and more, while the side of a castle and interior were fashioned opposite with wide stone, intricate wooden work, floor-to-ceiling tapestries, and glistening swords on display. Actors and extras mingled in full, period costumes and earthy kilts holding takeout coffee cups. On the far side, a vast wall of evergreens looked like the forest woodland. This was *incredible*. This was handmade Scottish fantasy. "Holy shit. It's like Universal Studios in the eighteenth century."

Bryce chuckled. "Aye. Swords Studios is what we call it."

"Bryce. I see you've brought yer guest," a chirpy voice greeted with a heavy burr.

Swiveling, Andrea spied Bonnie Graham with a choppy bob, matching bangs, an ear piece, wide smile, and arm extended with a wrist band. The other held a clipboard. "Hi there. We've met before. Last spring actually."

"Have we now?" Bonnie assessed her with a quick once-over. "Well, welcome back, lass."

"Thank you!"

Bonnie slipped on a neon-yellow wrist band. "There, now. You'll be free to walk around as ye please." She tapped long fingers spotted with freckles on Andrea's wrist and flashed a smile. "Bryce will be heading to makeup. Would ye like to visit the makeup trailer, or shall I take ye around?"

She nodded. "I would." *And wouldn't any sane girly girl who loves makeup?* Excitement zipped through her as she strode beside Bryce to a room with bright, overhead lights, floor-to-ceiling mirrors and chairs, and a colorful array of makeup, wigs, prosthetics, and more.

A curvy woman with fire-engine red curls, matching red lips, and a vibrant muti-colored sweater over red leggings stood beside a makeup chair.

"Moira Kelly, makeup-queen, meet Andrea Accardi, Brie's best friend visiting from L.A."

"*Och*. 'Tis a pleasure to meet any friend of Bryce and Brielle's."

"And you. Red's my signature color, as well."

"Did ye hear that, Bryce?" She held a hand to her heart. "We're best friends already."

Grinning, Andrea settled into a makeup chair and watched the careful application of television makeup, including weathering lines added to Bryce's eyes and between his brows to make him look a few years older. The cosmetics didn't matter though; the details only made him look more distinguished. As she watched the makeup magic, she kept her eye out for another television star.

A few hours later, she sat snugly in a provided set chair with headphones listening to the live scene being filmed forty feet away in an old, dark tavern. The vast, interior set was a constant wave of people like the ebb and flow of the ocean. One minute, a cacophony, and another minute, silence.

"Action!" the director shouted.

Andrea edged her seat.

Bryce and another highlander strode into the tavern, bold-blue and forest-green kilts flapping behind like they were ready for a battle.

Then, she did a double take.

A third highlander appeared out of nowhere opposite Bryce, strong-holding a man with an arm like a giant widow maker and threw him against the wall.

Andrea leaned forward. She'd know Hugh Macrae anywhere.

Towering over him, the man's attempts to rise were quickly thwarted by the tall warrior.

Bryce approached the man slowly, unsheathing his glistening sword, then pointed the weapon at his throat. "Where's the gold, Duncan?"

"Alexander," the man's voice rang with a hint of surprise and reverence.

Watching, she licked her lips and inhaled.

"And cut!" someone yelled.

With a *whoosh,* she released her breath and relaxed into the chair. "Wow." Andrea grasped the bottled water beside her and sipped, while keeping her gaze trained on the actors. They pushed each other good-naturedly, joking and laughing. To be so in character, so on, and then *poof*—with a quick switch, they're back to normal people seemed incredible. How did they do it? Practice? Skill? Natural talent? As she readied for the next take, she saw Hugh toss his head back, sending those brown locks flying like a stallion. Heat fired down below. *He's hot. So hot.* She could forgive his drunken ignorance less than forty-eight hours ago *if* he made it up to her.

Hearing the director announce filming would resume, she glued her gaze to the scene once more. Yet, as they retaped the scene repeatedly, she tapped her nails on her thigh, then adjusted and readjusted in her chair. Sure, plenty of eye candy was strutting about, but between constantly sitting and repetitive scene taping, she grew restless. Plus, she didn't see much difference in each take, other than someone fumbling a line, laughing, or cursing. But then again, she didn't work in the television industry.

She stretched, then rose and meandered across the studio to see what else she could uncover. She strolled through various sets, taking her time filling her fangirl heart—gazing at actors she'd seen on television having a simple conversation beside a dark wooden structure with *Mason* embossed in the front or at the local wares shop with eighteenth century goods for sale. She paused to examine hand-woven baskets used for carrying herbs, flowers, as well as potatoes, and wooden bowls for cooking. She always enjoyed shopping for new kitchen tools and knives, but she rarely purchased them—her L.A. apartment was a one bedroom, after all. But here, she marveled at the kitchen gadgets, including a well-used rolling pin and some sort of silver gauge. She'd loved to see a scene where *Swords* replicated a feast preparation. She continued on, strolling farther until she stumbled upon an area with horseshoes and a few shining swords displayed. She thought of Rory. If she ran into him, she wondered if he'd greet her back? Glancing around, she spied a sign pointing toward the catering building when a *clank-clank* sounded behind. She turned.

A giant man with a larger-than-life axe in one hand and a pile of swords on his shoulder strode a few long strides behind. He wore a leather apron smeared with black marks tucked over thick pecs and a taut stomach, a muddy, blue tartan kilt, and worn, brown boots, while dirt and soot covered his face.

Andrea stopped in her tracks, and her jaw dropped. "Rory?"

He lifted his head. Surprise etched across his face; yet, his features quickly hardened. He didn't say a word.

Sweeping her gaze from him to the giant weapons, she flashed a smile. "That's a huge ax."

"'Tis." He lifted the weapon easily.

Andrea watched his bicep bunch and veins crisscross up his forearm like a map to a muscular destination. "Did you make it?"

He glanced at the giant weapon and then back with a steely gaze. "Aye."

She hoped she hadn't bruised his ego too bad when she'd chased after Hugh. Rory *was* an interesting man with his own sex appeal. *And seeing him walk toward you like a bad-ass warrior warmed your blood, you dolt.* She noted the way his hair had lengthened and fanned around his ears and down toward his collar. Extensions? "Do you always come to work in costume? I did a double take."

"No." He shifted. "I stepped in as an extra today."

Andrea pushed curls off her shoulder. "So, you're an actor, as well? Aren't you full of surprises?"

He shook his head. "I'm no actor, but I'm happy to oblige if a blacksmith is needed."

A woman with a blonde ponytail and fanny pack jogged over, headpiece secured like a headband. "Rory, we'll be calling for stunt swords shortly."

"Aye. I'll be there in a moment with me team."

"Well, it was nice to see you. And, uh good luck with...um,

that." She flung a hand toward the giant brain smasher. "I'm off to catering. See ya later."

With a nod, he clomped in the opposite direction, holding the axe and sword bundle as if they were seamless appendages.

People greeted him as he passed, and she heard his deep brogue rumbling in reply. Watching him walk away all brawny and Highland-warriored-out, sent a little zip of something in her gut. Curiosity, perhaps? Rory was full of surprises. What the heck was a stunt sword? Did he make those, too? Hugh had turned her head—heck, who wouldn't be caught off guard by one of television's most sexy bad boys? But Andrea couldn't deny the pull toward Rory. When her stomach grumbled, she glanced once more at Rory and, with a huff, set off for a snack. She couldn't wait to discover what kind of delicacies caterers served for famous television cast members and staff. Fancy seafood, mouthwatering steak, tiny bites, or something simpler?

Entering catering, she spotted Eleana in a robins-blue dress with curled hair piled atop her head, showing off a long neck, selecting a few pieces of vegetables and cheese from a buffet. "Hey, Eleana."

Glancing up, Eleana's features softened, and a smile spread across her lips. "Andrea, it's a pleasure to see you."

"You, too. I bugged Bryce to bring me."

She laughed softly. "Well, we're pleased to have you."

"I didn't see you on any of the sets today." Andrea snagged a plate.

"I just finished hair and makeup. I don't start shooting until this afternoon, so I thought I'd take advantage of the catering before I do."

"Nothing wrong with that." Hugh strode in and glanced between them.

Interest buzzed within when he settled his gaze on hers.

"Andrea."

"Hey, Hugh. You were fantastic out there"—she leaned closer—"and Saturday night could have been, as well."

He grinned, though his whisky eyes danced mischievously.

She flashed him a bright smile back.

Leaning around her, he brushed her breast with his upper arm and scooped a handful of mixed nuts from the snack platter, tossing them into his wide palm, then directed his attention toward Eleana. "Did ye want to run through lines?"

"Once I've eaten." Eleana lifted her nose and turned, selecting a small helping of salad.

A crackle bristled in the air between the two. Annoyance yes, but something else. Andrea couldn't put her finger on it. Perhaps, it was Eleana's magnetism. She *was* gorgeous, though her beauty was welcoming.

"Hugh!" Someone shouted from the corner of the dining area.

With a smirk, he stomped toward a table where some of the crew lingered. A moment later, boisterous laughter erupted.

"What is it between you two?" Andrea asked.

Eleana lifted a perfectly penciled brow. "Hugh and I?"

Andrea nodded.

"To be frank, I can't stand the man. He shamelessly flirts, though he knows I'm engaged, and parades around town like he's a gift to women. I can't stand men like him." She pursed her lips. "But we have to work together, so I do my utmost to be civil."

The side door opened, flooding fresh light into the catering room. Two cast members arrived who looked to be in their early twenties—a petite blonde with a center part, big, round eyes, and wide smile alongside a tall, lanky man with a straight nose and brown hair that waved to his collar. George and Lettie, she knew. Cast members that had joined the season before and were always photographed together on and off camera.

"Now, those two"—Eleana inclined her head—"give the impression they're an item, but they're truly best friends."

Andrea eyed them. The twosome laughed and chatted as if they were the only occupants in the room—happy and full of life. A little sting jabbed at her chest; yet, she pushed the feeling aside.

Eleana bid farewell a moment later.

Seeing Hugh follow close like a puppy, Andrea harrumphed. "Well, I suppose there's nothing to do except taste this delectable food."

"Please do!" a woman said with a full-bodied American accent touched with a twang. She approached Andrea with a vibrant bowl of salad dotted with raspberries. Her strawberry-blonde hair swung in a ponytail, while short, choppy bangs and jingling earrings matched her jovial personality. "Let me know what you think."

Andrea turned. "Texas?"

She smiled wide. "Dallas."

"Is this your spread?"

"It is." She held out a hand. "Sarah Murray. My husband, Finn, and I run the catering."

Andrea shook her hand. "Impressive! Andrea Accardi. BFF to Brie and huge fan of her fiancé."

"Oh! Brie has told me so much about you. Welcome."

"Thank you." She gazed at the variety of food—an array of crudites, finger food, cheese, fruit, soup, and salads across three long tables. "How'd you get into catering?"

"We fell into it, really." She exchanged serving tongs. "I participated in a study abroad program and, while working at a hotel as a waitress for events to help pay for lodging, met Finn as one of the kitchen hands putting himself through culinary school."

A man appeared with a shaved head and apron, holding a pan containing a giant roast. "It was love at first bite."

Andrea snorted.

"Oh! This is my husband, Finn." She gestured. "I always wanted to go to culinary school, but my parents were against it. Luckily, the business degree came in handy for our start-up, and I picked up a few cooking classes here and there."

Andrea knew the feeling. She'd gone to college to make something of herself and partly to please her unpleasable mother who demanded the best. But somewhere along the way, she grew to enjoy the challenge, the corporate accolades and edge, but look where that left her. At least, she had Scotland. *For now.* "I love cooking, too." Andrea watched Finn slide the roast onto a cutting board, which made her wonder if he'd be carving himself during service. "Italian and Mexican food are my specialty."

"*Och.* Sounds wonderful. Do ye cook for a living then?" Finn asked.

"No, no. Just…a hobby. It's really for my sanity."

"Don't let her pull one over on ye," a familiar voice said. Andrea turned, lips curling.

Bryce approached with his movie hair tied back and a coy grin. "She made homemade pizza last week and then a lamb roast that nearly made me weep."

Twirls of glee filled her. "Thank you."

"Oh, aye?" Finn slung the empty pan under his arm. "And I thought we were your favorite chefs." Winking at Andrea, he continued roasting Bryce.

"Come off it, man. Ye know yer vital members of the *Swords* family. We'd be staggering around with peanut butter and jelly sandwiches if we hadn't found ye. You keep us well fed and ready to work. We couldn't do this job without ye."

Finn wiped a fake tear from his eye. "That was beautiful, truly. Remember that when we're discussing our contract next season and a wee raise." He clapped a hand atop Bryce's broad shoulder and passed through the double doors.

Once Bryce filled a plate with a few pieces of roast meat, pickled vegetables, and a flaky samosa, he bobbed his head toward Sarah. "Thank ye as always." Turning, he waved toward the door. "We'll be resuming shooting in twenty."

"Sounds great!" She gave him two-thumbs up as he exited, then pivoted, admiring the rich and varied platters. "So, Sarah, what's your specialty?"

"We've a blend of good Scottish food with some Tex-Mex and Indian influences."

She inhaled notes of garlic, wine, and cumin. "Well, it smells amazing."

"Thank you so much! Please help yourself. And if you're looking for any recommendations, I suggest the double potato samosas and the spicy shrimp skewers."

Watching Sarah disappear into the kitchen, Andrea added a golden samosa, a shrimp skewer, and a spoonful of kale salad to her plate. She bit into the steaming samosa and felt her lips curl as the flaky pastry and creamy center melted into her mouth. "Mmm like a Scottish pie married a samosa. Perfect." With a sigh, she took another bite of the hand-held fried goodness, filling her stomach and feeding her soul. If she was sexless and job-less, at least she was well fed.

Laughter emanated from the dining tables. Crew members talked and ate together like family.

She gazed at them for a few minutes, and a memory from her last day at TechCo rolled in. Valerie looking smug with the CEO across the meeting table after Andrea demanded to know who they promoted.

The CEO grinning at Valerie.

Andrea whipping her head from the CEO to her assistant shell-shocked. "But I trained her!"

Valerie laughing softly when Andrea stomped out.

The whole episode left a sourness in her mouth. *Andrea Accardi. Apartmentless. Jobless.* But she needed a break from the corporate headache. She hadn't realized how much. Not until she'd arrived in this beautiful, albeit freezing country, hugged her best friend, explored, and began cooking again had she realized how much she'd been working. But that's what a holiday was for—to forget all your responsibilities and worries —to explore, taste, and adventure, wasn't it? She popped the rest of the samosa into her mouth. *Easier said than done.*

"Andrea," a cheerful voice called.

She swiveled.

Standing at the kitchen entry, Sarah waved to her with a bright smile. "Would you like to come back and see what else we're cooking up?"

"Love to!" Andrea wiped her hands on the napkin and popped up. When she stepped through the white double doors, she noted the shining stainless steel and copper pots hanging from hooks on the ceiling above a prep station, while the back of the space held three workspaces where kitchen staff were busily attending to the impending meal. And what's more, spicy, savory, aromatic, and fried aromas wafted toward her. She inhaled deeply, closing her eyes. "I've died and gone to foodie heaven."

Finn chuckled from the stove, then dipped a silver spoon into a steaming pot and lifted it to her for a taste.

She grasped the spoon and closed her eyes, enjoying the rich, meaty bite of fall-apart beef. "Steak stew with thyme and red wine, but something else."

"Aye. Spot on," Finn noted. "Scottish Beef Stew with a wee bit of currant jelly."

"Yum." She placed the spoon in the closest sink. "I make my own version with a splash of aged balsamic vinegar."

He nodded, then stirred the stew with a great, big wooden spoon.

"What's your inspiration for the daily menu?"

"We vet the menu with the producers of the show, but other than a few favorites like quick grab sandwiches and small bites, they've given us artistic license," Sarah noted.

Andrea gazed at the cook stations with pots steaming and preparation stations where kitchen staff chopped vegetables and prepped food. Her fingers tingled. She itched to jump in. "Everything looks fantastic. How long have you been catering for *Swords*?"

"*Och*. Near four years now. They brought us on first as a food truck—that's how we got our start—to cater some of their remote locations"

"Yup!" Sarah piped in. "Limited overhead and perfect for a traveling duo."

"And then when the second season went into production, we got the call. Now, on the off season, we also cater weddings and other events."

"That's so cool."

Finn quickly moved from station to station.

Andrea knew she had to leave soon. They were getting ready for service. Though she would've stood there, planted in place and watching the captivating alchemy before her for as long as she could, she also didn't want to overstay her welcome. Plus, she should go watch the rest of the episode shoot. Straightening, she held a hand out. "Thank you so much for showing me your kitchen."

Sarah smiled and shook her hand vigorously. "Of course! Oh! One second." She jogged to the corner of the kitchen and returned a moment later with a business card. "If y'all would like to come back and observe, just let me know."

Andrea tucked the business card safely in her back pocket. She hoped they were as genuine as they seemed, because she'd hightail it back in a heartbeat.

Chapter Eight

Rory scanned the lengthy table with bundles of steel swords requiring cleaning. The time was near seven p.m., and though the sun had already laid to rest for some time, vibrant lights of the armory kept him focused and alert. Of course, the private shower in his mate's trailer had helped, as well. He didn't know how Bryce wore that dirt and grime on his face and person daily. He gave Bryce credit and respect, and he was happy to step in when needed, but his place was here or his forge.

Grasping the handle of Bryce's large claymore, he allowed his mind to wander to earlier when he'd happened upon Andrea and how her eyes widened, then lit with pleasure upon seeing him in costume. He was no actor, nor did he have any plans to add 'extra' to his CV. He was content with who he was and the direction he'd chosen. Still, he felt pride swell his chest when she'd commented on the weapons in hand. His craft was as much a part of him as the land was his home, and also something that had altered the course of his family life, as well.

Tightening his grip on the handle, he could still hear Da's voice.

"Ye'd abandon your family?" Da had asked four winters back, gutting him.

"No. I'm pursuing a new trade in Glasgow, not moving across the world." Though little did Rory know he'd travel to England, Prague, America, and Asia after signing the contract.

"If the life of an ironworker isn't good enough for ye and all I've passed down wasted, then leave."

Guilt and anger tangled within Rory, and he felt his control slipping.

His younger brother, Collin, stepped in. "Keep the *heid*."

But no matter what he said, he couldn't alter Da's opinion of him or his chosen trade. They hadn't spoken since. He envied his younger brother and sisters who had the freedom to choose what they wanted with their lives. As the firstborn son, Rory knew Da assumed he'd take over what he'd begun. Yet, Rory found something that not only built off his family craft, but also could make his own. He was grateful Collin had a keen interest in the family forge and his artistic talent allowed him to add decorative ironwork to the Cameron's architectural offerings.

When a *clang* sounded from across the room, he shook his head and set to work, finding peace in the mundane tasks, while his team cleaned, shined, and antiqued aluminum stunt swords and gun replicas. He took pleasure in polishing the swords he'd crafted. With soft cloth and a cleaning solution, he wiped the blade clean of syrupy red movie makeup, dirt, and grime, then with a microfiber cloth at the base of the blade, oiled. Lastly, he applied metal polish and smoothed a cloth down the blade until the metal shone.

"Rory." Bryce entered. "See yer all cleaned up and ready for the ball."

Rotating, Rory chuckled. "Aye, thank ye."

"Anytime, mate. I see ye have my sword." He stood in costume—belted Mackenzie tartan secured with a brooch at the shoulder over a linen shirt; yet, his buckled leather belt displayed empty scabbards where his sword and dirk normally rested.

"I'll have it polished and ready for ye for the next shoot."

"Appreciate that." He pivoted and greeted the other workers. "I just sent Andrea home with my driver. Looks like another long night."

He nodded.

"Did ye see her today?"

"Aye."

Bryce elbowed him. "So, ye taking her out then?"

He continued to polish, allowing the routine to steady him. "No, she's no' interested. She seems to have her eye on Hugh—that's clear enough."

"Well, she asked me about yer time with *Swords* and yer skill before she left. Seems to me she's interested. She's just a wee bit insecure around men she fancies, I reckon."

With a cock of his head, he invited Bryce to continue.

"Brie told me her mother did a number on Andrea after the divorce. Her mother is one of those women whom ye can never please and has married quite a few times since. Andrea has never had a steady man in her life, so Brie's told me, but she's loyal to the bone and stayed with Brie through thick and thin the last couple of years."

Rory swiped the microfiber down the length of the blade once again. He could admit he still liked her even with her poor choices as of late.

"That's all I've to say on the subject." He cleared his throat. "I've come to ask ye a favor."

Rory straightened and set the sword down. "What did ye have in mind?"

"I wanted to show you some pictures of the groomsmen attire for the wedding celebration."

Scrubbing a hand over his beard, he glanced at Bryce. "I'll be fine wearin' whatever ye choose."

Reaching into his sporran, Bryce retrieved his mobile and scrolled through pictures. "'Tis not that. Brie has told me what she favors, and I aim to make my wife happy, plus the fine blue argyle will look fetching with the Fraser hunting tartan. It holds special significance to us both."

"That'd be grand." While Bryce went on discussing the celebration plans, Rory thought about his own plans. He wanted a wedding, a lass in a bonnie white dress, and a pedestrian life. But unlike the luck he'd had with his trade, he was struggling to even land himself a date. Perhaps, he'd better prepare himself to ask Andrea out again. "So, what is it yer needing?"

Bryce tilted his head. "Would ye make *Sgian Dubhs* for the wedding to go with our attire?"

A surge of pride warmed his gut and tugged at the corners of his lips. "It would be my pleasure."

"Brilliant! If ye could include the Fraser crest on mine, ye can use artistic license with the rest of the design and with yours, Ian, and Hugh's."

"Aye."

Observing Bryce stride out the door, he thought about his mate's upcoming celebration and the vows they'd repeat that had tied Bryce, Brie, and their families together for a lifetime. He needed to put a fire under his own arse. He was thirty-two and not getting any younger. Sliding the claymore into its protective sheath, Rory wondered what Andrea was so afraid of. Even more, he wondered what she'd say if he asked her out once more.

Chapter Nine

ANDREA TOURED THE GLASGOW NECROPOLIS WITH an umbrella and red wellies the following morning. She didn't mind that Brie was volunteering at the kids' school again; she was content meandering the Victorian-era cemetery on her own with a little help from an app. Besides, Brie was a scaredy-cat when it came to ghosts and cemeteries. So, Andrea explored independently—something she was used to as an only child—and enjoyed the solitude amongst the dripping rain and standing stones. Although upon close inspection, she was surprised to find that not all the gravestones included names, while others, as well as statues, varied from a light, cement color to close to charcoal with age, starkly contrasting the vibrant mossy-green lawns surrounding them.

When she arrived at a large headstone with a male name, she pursed her lips at the forename. "Another Hugh," she muttered. She was done with Hugh Macrae. After a mediocre welcome to the set and unanswered texts last night, she decided she didn't need to waste any more of her precious vacation on a man, even if he was gorgeous. "Time to switch gears and peruse the larder." With an inhale of damp, earthy air, she strolled deeper into the Necropolis. She'd applied for a few more jobs that morning and responded to a recruiter who'd messaged her. Perhaps luck was on her side.

When the rain thickened, she drove to the mall and filled a few hours shopping, lunching, and having her toes lacquered with bold, ruby-red polish. A few hours later, she tapped the steering wheel and sang happily along to a local band, laden with purchases. When she pulled into the driveway, she was surprised to find an older SUV parked out front.

Kids raced around the yard—two of which she knew and loved—and two she'd met briefly a few months ago. She stepped out of the vehicle and strolled over to the side yard where the new playset was in full use by Bryce's niece—a vibrant, red-haired little girl with springy curls who climbed up a ladder and tore across the bridge after Phoebe—and another young boy with wavy, jet-black hair who looked out a porthole with Noah. A smile tugged up her cheeks. Turning, she caught sight of Brie with an arm wrapped around her sister-in-law, peering down at something she held with awe. Andrea's lips tilted, and a tug of jealousy pulled. She pushed the covetousness away and strode toward them. "Hey..."

Brie rotated with a radiant smile. "Oh! You're back. How was shopping?"

"Great..."

Rose Fitzgibbons turned, long dark hair cascading over one shoulder and a bundle in her arms.

Andrea finally saw what had captured Brie's interest: a baby. The little girl's plump cheeks were rosy from the cool air, accentuating reddish-blonde brows below a lavender-and-pink woolen beanie.

"I'm sorry. Where are my manners?" Brie fluttered her hands around her. "Do you remember Rose? My sister-in-law?"

Andrea felt her chest tighten once again. "Yes...it's nice to see you again."

"Aye, and ye." Rose grinned, balancing the baby.

Get it together. She's not stealing your best friend. They're related by marriage. But somehow, that didn't quell the feeling in her chest. "And congratulations. How old is your baby?"

She gazed fondly at the tiny girl. "Little Isla is nearing two months now."

As if on cue, the baby fluttered her eyes open.

Blue-black eyes stared at Andrea.

"Oh," Brie cooed. "She's awake. Can I hold her before you feed her, Rose?"

"Of course." Rose transferred the baby to Brie's arms.

Andrea watched as Brie's face scrunched up with a huge smile, while peering at the baby.

"Hi, sweet pea. Aren't you just the most beautiful thing? How was your nap?"

The baby responded by batting her golden eyelashes and wiggling.

"Oh, you probably need a change." She turned. "I'll be right back."

"Thank ye," Rose replied.

Andrea shifted in her boots. Her happy mood was dashed just like her brightly covered toenails under the heavy, winter boots. "So, do you guys live nearby?"

"About forty or so minutes north of here. The children are on Christmas holiday, so we came for a visit." With a hand over her brow, she gazed where the kids were busy running around the playset.

"I see. Well, that's great."

She smiled, small pink apples forming on her cheeks. "Do ye have children of your own?"

"Oh, God no."

"*Och*. Well, there's plenty of time for that."

Andrea balked. After regaining her composure, she cleared her throat. "If you'll excuse me, I need to grab a few things from the car."

"Of course."

She strode away. *Children? I barely know you, and you're asking if I have children?* She was single and jobless. Children were the last thing on her mind. Plus, children needed parents and commitment, and she was definitely *not* getting married. She trudged to Brie's car and grabbed the full bags, then marched into the guest house. Hanging new dresses and organizing unwrapped purchases, she focused on her closet when laughter filtered through the window. She pivoted and peered down.

Brie lifted the baby and spun her around, while Rose chased the children and then tickled Phoebe.

With a harrumph, she stalked to the tiny kitchen. Since Brie moved to Scotland two months ago, Andrea made frequent calls, but she hadn't visited. Her job occupied her time. But best friends like she and Brie—sisters—they called each other, couldn't be separated by distance, could they? With a huff, she swung into the main house and was greeted by fried, buttery aromas. In an instant, her surliness improved. "Oh, my God."

Rose chuckled. "Aye, a meat pie tends to have that effect on me as well. When I was pregnant, poor Ian had to get takeaway a few times a month."

Andrea glanced at a lanky, tall man with a head full of strawberry blonde hair that looked like he was in need of a trim. "Hey, Ian. Thanks for bringing pies."

"Pleasure." He bobbed his head. "There's plenty in the kitchen. Help yourself."

Andrea nodded and snagged a pie. She didn't want to talk about babies.

Later, after waving good-bye to the Fitzgibbons, she dried dishes beside Brie. "You and Rose seem close."

Brie's face lit up. "We are. Isn't she wonderful?"

"She is." Andrea swallowed. She had work friends and acquaintances, but only one best friend. Before meeting Brie, Andrea kept people at a distance—those she loved always left anyway. And she was happy, or, at least thought she was until Brie opened her office door and filled a part of her life she didn't know was missing.

Brie continued adding plates to the dishwasher, humming happily.

But Andrea couldn't quell the sting in her chest. "Brie, have I messed up our friendship?"

She straightened. "What?"

"You know"—Andrea twirled the towel around her hand to help the words spill out—"I haven't been able to visit."

"No, you didn't mess up our friendship. It's changed. Just like us. I found the man of my dreams and moved to Scotland, and you—"

She quirked a brow. "Got fired?"

"No, that's not what I was going to say. You live in L.A. I live here, and that was my choice, but even a vast ocean couldn't separate us."

"Swear?"

"Cross my heart." She crisscrossed a finger across her chest, then reached a hand out and touched Andrea's shoulder, gazing unwaveringly with those green eyes. "We might not see one another as often, but you're still my person."

Bobbing her head, Andrea felt a weight release in her chest.

Brie straightened, and her eyes shone. "Oh! I forgot to tell you. We're coming to L.A. in March for the kids to spend their spring break with Ryan."

"March is so far away."

Brie paused, eyes glossing. "I'm sorry, Andrea."

Andrea waved the Snowman Christmas towel in the air. "Don't start that." She slung an arm around Brie and embraced her, inhaling her flowery scent. She had nothing to worry about. Brie was still her best friend, and they were here, together, now. With one last squeeze, she released her.

"I've been meaning to ask. How's everything going with the house?"

Andrea puffed a breath. "Going. I need to find another job or income source, quick."

Brie tilted her head. "Can I loan you some money?"

"God, no, Brie." She leaned on the counter. "I'll figure it out."

With a bump of a shoulder with Andrea's, she peered at her. "All right. Remember, I'm here if you need me."

Andrea bumped back. "Thanks."

Brie tossed the dish towel into the sink. "Okay, we need a change of scenery. How about we spend the day together tomorrow? Tea and an expedition? It's my last kid-free day until school releases them for winter break."

A smile tugged at her cheeks. "I'm in. Girl day, plus scones? Let's do it." Joy filled her chest; yet, she couldn't deny the way her gaze caught a wedding photo, hanging above the fireplace in the living room across from the kitchen. Just a few months ago, this was a bachelor's pad, albeit of good taste, but now, the home was a blend of Bryce, Brie, and the children. She wondered where she'd be in a few months.

Chapter Ten

AFTER AN EARLY TEA, ANDREA AND BRIE ARRIVED AT the parking area for Bothwell Castle where dense green trees outlined a grassy turnout. Brie's new novel took place in Medieval Scotland, and the castle played a role in her book for historical accuracy. Andrea was excited for Brie's writing adventure, even though she wasn't sure where or when her own professional adventure would begin again. She'd stayed up until two a.m., talking to a couple of recruiters about positions. One was a contract, interim position for a VP of HR in another county, but she'd have to drive three hours or take the train, and another was for a director-level position—a step below her previous position. *Damn layoff screwed everything up*. For now, she'd get lost in history and forget about her own issues.

As she strolled down the dampened dirt road flanked by vibrant grass, she spied the castle, resting atop a high, steep bank—a fortress if she ever saw one with a large tower on the east and a broken one on the west—no doubt from a history of sieges. Stacks of stone-on-stone pitched toward the dark, gray sky—ruddy and reddish-brown at the base, then darker toward the top from weathering. Surrounded by caramel-and-sage-green trees on two sides and a dense woodland on the other, the castle seemed undisturbed, save for a few wooden staircases and park benches for tourists. "Crazy." She flew her gaze up the grand structure. "Imagine how many people had to carry stones to build this sucker?"

Brie grinned. "Right? It's incredible. It was initially constructed in the late 1200s and then was added on to for centuries."

They wandered around the castle, stretching their legs and breathing in the damp air. A storm was coming; Andrea felt the chill on her cheeks, but even if sprinkles fell, she didn't care—she was spending one-on-one time with Brie.

"Just imagine how many people have literally set foot on the same ground we are on right now." Brie swung a hand around. "People walked up this pathway toward the grand castle for hundreds of years in tunics on foot or on horseback. Brave warriors with swords at their hips stationed at different posts, protecting the castle, while others sparred and trained."

Listening to Brie paint a visual, Andrea imagined the sword-clad warriors in their kilts, and her mind drifted to Rory trudging toward her the other day, kilt flapping, with an axe in one hand and a bundle of swords in the other. She could imagine him living during this time—all serious and focused. He wasn't as warm as he was during their first meeting, or second, or third, but could she blame him? Hugh had turned her head, and she'd made out with him, twice. She might have been a little rude—er, let's face it—more than rude to Rory, but she didn't owe him anything, right? Ugh. She imagined the quiet man had more class than Hugh. But she didn't need to chase after a man. That was Gloria's MO not hers. She glanced back at the formidable structure and heard Brie talking about medieval Scottish dress.

"Women in long, tunic-style dresses in jewel tones, well for the upper class, and earth tones for commoners, warriors in *leine croich* preparing for war, coming and going—"

"Wait, you forgot about the sexy kilts," Andrea interrupted.

Brie swiveled. "No, I didn't. They didn't wear kilts back then."

She stilled Brie with a hand on the arm. "What? You're kidding? And you're writing a book written in that century? I thought you dug Bryce's kilt. Well, and every *Swords* fan ever."

"I did. I do." Brie laughed. "I like it very, very much, and I could just imagine him wearing his infamous Mackenzie kilt on set right now. But I don't need to write about it when I can see him in it myself. Happy?"

Andrea smiled. "Very. And very jealous."

Brie looped an arm through the crook of Andrea's. Continuing acting as tour guide, she pointed at one crumbling tower and the next, discussing what happened in the thirteenth and fourteenth centuries.

Her best friend had been arms deep in research for her new book, and Andrea was impressed. Even though Brie had only moved here a few months ago, she seemed at home. A tug of unease crept through Andrea—the same that had skittered through her the previous afternoon. She knew Brie would do her best to make a happy life with Bryce and the kids, but a part of her wanted Brie to make L.A. her home base again.

When Brie pointed toward a dark gape in the structure, she stepped closer. "Imagine that was where the drawbridge stood, keeping invaders out. Did you know that this once was occupied by a Scottish nobleman who was loyal to England during the Wars of Scottish Independence?"

Andrea gaped. "A traitor?"

"Well, kind of. He actually changed sides."

She wiggled her brows. "Juicy."

Brie kept walking forward, drawing Andrea along.

Arched windows looked out toward the grass, while tops of the castle crumbled and appeared like an unfinished block fort she'd seen Noah constructing just that morning.

"So, during this time some clans were loyal to Scotland and others, the crown. But after this pivotal battle, the Battle of Bannockburn—"

Andrea tilted her head. "The battle is named after Scottish Bannocks?"

Her steps faltered. "What?"

"You know"—Andrea formed a circle with her hands—"the oat-based bread they feature in *Swords* all the time."

"I didn't even put two and two together." She shook her head, while a smile crept up her cheeks. "I have no idea why it's named that!"

"Just think, they could've run out of bows and arrows and propelled rock-hard bannocks at the oncoming enemy." Andrea stepped aside and put her hands on either side of her mouth. "Launch the bannocks, lads!"

Brie snorted. "Original, but highly improbable."

Andrea rubbed her stomach. "With all this talk about food, I'm ready for a snack."

With a shake of her honey-brown hair, Brie trudged forward, pulling Andrea along. "Come on." They passed under a giant, leafless tree, and Brie directed Andrea's gaze to the far corner. "Anyway, back to the battle. It's traditionally regarded as the culmination of the Scottish Wars of Independence, even though Scottish independence wouldn't be officially recognized until some years later. After that battle, a number of Englishman, including noblemen loyal to Edward II, fled to Bothwell Castle for safety. But guess what? The Scottish nobleman changed sides. The English were imprisoned and the castle turned over to the Scots, which in turn helped secure Robert the Bruce's territory and influence. For his good deed, the Bruce granted him another castle."

"A castle as a thank-you." Andrea sighed. She thought back to the last thank-you from her boss—the CEO from TechCo. He hadn't given her a castle or a dream just a severance check and the door, while her former employee got a promotion. No, 'thank-you' for her! "Geez, must be nice. But then again, what's her face stabbed me in the back and got my job."

"Oh." Brie's features pinched, and she gripped Andrea's arm. "I didn't mean to...I mean, my intention wasn't to remind you of...of that."

Andrea waved a hand. "It's fine. I'm still sour, that's all."

Brie hugged her. "They didn't deserve you."

"Nope. And I'm not giving them any more thought today."

"Good."

They pushed forward, walking the gardens. Ten minutes later, Andrea gazed at the arched peaks and vastness. She could envision archers lining the towers and smoke pluming from fiery cauldrons, but what exactly was inside? Perhaps men and women who supported the grand castle bustled in hallways and slaved over stoves or giant fires, feeding an army. That must've been a feat in itself. "I bet there was a great hall where all the warriors and people gathered to eat."

Brie bobbed her head. "Yes! Like the great hall in *Swords*."

Andrea could envision that—a long table filled with silver or wooden cups, rich food on giant platters where filthy, bloody warriors assembled for a meal after a battle, ready to be healed by good food. Closing her eyes, she breathed in notes of grass, earth, and pine and imagined rich roasts, peeled vegetables, thick bread, and more. Then, she imagined a warrior. He was dirty, bloody, and reeking of God-knows-what. She cringed. No deodorant in Medieval Scotland. *Pee-ew*! Thank God for small advances. She opened her eyes. "So, what did they eat back then?"

Brie's eyes shone. "Wild game, thick stews, root vegetables, homemade bread, fresh and dried fruit, and definitely in a castle, rich pastry. Did you know they used to call stale bread trenchers?"

Titling her head, Andrea leaned closer. "Why?"

"They'd use the thick pieces like bowls to soak up the soups or stews." Brie gestured scooping one hand into a hand-formed bowl.

Andrea imagined crusty, thick, and porous brown bread dipped in split pea soup. "Stews..." She thought about bubbly stews boiling over a warm fire with rich aromas filling the air. She'd imagine they'd have been simple, but the cooks could've gathered wild garlic and other herbs, harvesting food from the land and cooking with what was in season, rather than what arrived in shipments globally. The work would've been difficult at times for sure, but fantastic nonetheless. When clouds shrouded the structure and wind whipped hair in her face, she glanced up. "We're gonna get drenched."

"Yep." Brie looked at her watch. "It's time to pick up the kiddos anyway."

Andrea nodded.

"Let's take one last look. All the pictures I've seen don't come close to standing here. Plus, there's something about being near a castle. All the history. All the stories. It's inspiring."

Andrea gazed at her best friend. She could see the wheels turning in her brain. Brie was right; she was inspired. A new idea sprang to mind, bursting and blooming as she imagined herself cooking a few thousand years ago over a fiery caldron. And then she thought back to her visit to the set of *Swords* and Finn and Sarah Murray. The friendly caterers invited her to return to set anytime. Glancing once more at the castle, she made up her mind. She was going back to immerse herself in something she liked—seeing how the kitchen ran and being a tiny fly...er, woman on the wall. Maybe they'd let her chop something or stir a magical sauce, or be the taster. She could get behind that—she'd even bring a dozen clean spoons.

* * *

Back at the Frasers, Andrea perused the deep ivory cupboards and French door-style refrigerator, while Mimi and Brie created Christmas crafts with the kids in the living room. She wanted to visit the Murrays, but she didn't want to arrive empty-handed. She thought of gifts on the way home, but she was stumped. What the heck could she bring chefs? Swinging the doors shut, she pressed her head against the stainless steel. She loved hosting meals and even previously invited some of her colleagues to her apartment to dine. But whenever she cooked, she never really ate until the last guest left. Sure, she had a few bites and wine, but she was busy hosting. "What if I made them a little antipasto to eat in between service?"

"What's that?" Brie strolled into the kitchen.

"I rarely eat when I'm cooking."

Brie cocked her head, then opened a drawer and pulled out a pair of scissors. "Okay...?"

"I'm cooking the Murrays something as a thank you."

Brie smiled brightly. "You're bringing food to their kitchen?"

Andrea popped a hand on her hip. "Sure, why not?"

"I think that's a great idea!"

Snatching a notepad, Andrea considered a few options: crostini or panini—something Finn and Sarah could grab and go. With a huff, she scratched those ideas out. She couldn't bring something so easy to chefs, especially chefs catering her favorite show. Plus, the bread would either get too stiff or soggy in transit, and she couldn't serve either to chefs. Pursing her lips, she glanced at the island where two boxes of lasagna noodles rested on the counter beside bright-red cherry tomatoes. "That's it! A meal in a bite."

"Such as?" Brie asked.

Andrea tapped the pen to her lips. A pasta that would hold up. A pasta that made people happy and could be reheated easily, but also was a work of art. "Lasagna cups! I'll make some with winter squash, creamy spinach, and cheese and also traditional with ground beef and Italian sausage." She scribbled down ingredients. Luckily, she'd planned to make lasagna later that week and had all the ingredients, and Brie always stocked up on vegetables. "I might even add a little antipasto skewer—something light with vegetables and maybe tortellini or something."

Brie nodded. "Yum. Can I help?"

"Sure, once I get organized. Plus"—she leveled her gaze— "I have to make my sauce."

"Are you planning on dropping the food off today?"

"Yeah, why?"

Brie glanced at her watch. "It's already 3:15 p.m., and you have to let Bryce know you're coming. Otherwise, they won't allow you through."

She scrunched her nose. "But I was just there the day before yesterday."

"Show business." Brie scrunched her nose, then threw her hands up. "You know what? I'll call Bonnie and text Bryce. You just focus on the food."

Forty-five minutes later, Andrea sliced al dente lasagna noodles carefully and layered one sheet at a time, allowing the ruffled sides to curl along the edges of the pan, while her red sauce boiled. The process was tedious. Why did she decide to do this? And why two variations, plus a skewer? She huffed. Because she needed a frickin' win right now.

* * *

Andrea paused in front of a sign set aglow by her car lights with a variety of arrows left and right. Immediately, she knew she should've waited until the following day, instead of making a delivery in the dark. Staring at the directional sign, she scrutinized the colorful arrows and columns noting destinations: *Visitors, Main Car Park, Yellow Car Park, Studio, Production Office*, and *Deliveries*.

Two days ago, the driver dropped her and Bryce off at the studio.

Today, she was technically a visitor. She recalled the swell of fans and press by the visitor entry. After pondering for a few minutes, she stepped on the pedal and turned toward Deliveries. She followed the sign and was amazed how much the entrance for commoners differed from that of stars. "Well, duh. Bryce would get the royal treatment. He is Bryce Fraser AKA Alexander James Mackenzie—badass highlander and Scottish King of Television," she said aloud. "And who am I? Andrea Accardi. HR Failure and Foodie. Make way, here I come!"

When she turned the corner, she flashed a bright smile at a man with a clipboard, beanie, and black parka. Though this man was young—most definitely a few years younger than her based on the few creases around his eyes and probably freezing his you-know-what off.

His quick, dark-brown eyes snapped to hers. "Can I help ye?"

"Andrea Accardi. I'm here to see the Murrays."

Watching him check the list, she noticed colorful tattoos of vivid, almost lime-green, red, black, and blue spiral around his wrist.

He lifted his head, and a steely stare followed. "You're no' on the list."

Her stomach sank. The wonderful sharp notes of marinara, salty tang of sausage, and creamy cheese wafted toward her, giving her strength. She straightened. "Look, I'm not some deranged fan. I'm a personal friend of Bryce Fraser and the Murrays—the caterers. I brought something for them as a thank-you."

The man's gaze hardened. "What have ye brought?"

"Lasagna."

His brows jammed together; yet, the smallest flicker of a smile twitched at his lips. "Lasagna?"

"Well, Lasagna Cups."

He folded his thick arms across his chest. "Ye mean to tell me ye've come to set with food?"

"That's exactly what I'm telling you." She shoved the gear stick into Park and reached under the foil to extract a lasagna cup, which was still hot and filled with thick, chunky sausage and topped with golden cheese and flecked with herbs. "See?"

The security guard's nostrils flared with an inhale. "Ye may have a wee—"

A woman's voice carried over the speaker, cutting his sentence short.

Andrea instantly recognized that chirpy voice. "Bonnie! Bonnie, it's Andrea," she yelled. "Andrea Accardi! I'm stuck at the gate."

The guard sharpened his gaze again, sending arrows of warning.

"Look, I know her, okay? Tell her it's Andrea—"

Pivoting, he spoke in unintelligible words. When he swiveled back, his eyes crinkled at the corners. "Aye, she says to let ye in."

Andrea fist pumped the steering wheel, setting off a beep. "Yes!"

The guard chuckled.

"And for you, good sir." Andrea handed him a lasagna cup.

He held the cup in his large hand. "Smells good."

"You bet your ass it does."

With a glance her way, he jabbed a thumb directing her through the gates.

She squealed with delight. As she pulled through, she glanced in the rearview mirror and caught him taking a bite. She smiled with satisfaction. Now, she hoped the Murrays would be impressed, as well.

Chapter Eleven

LIVELY FLUTES AND PEPPY DRUMS MINGLED IN THE air when she walked through the entry to catering. The background music matched her own thudding heart, pounding with exertion from marching across the parking lot to the interior, lugging her giant purse and bags of food. She could create food and a workout—lasagna muscle-ups. Being late in the evening, the dining area was void of occupants and only a few snack platters remained with seasonal fruit, colorful crudités, and an array of cheese and crackers atop dark linens. Even though she feared she was too late, she knew *Swords* would be shooting until close to midnight. The Murrays must be busy in the kitchen, cooking with their staff for a late meal. Squaring her shoulders, she prepared to walk through the kitchen's double doors.

The swift *creak* of a door sounded opposite.

She turned.

Rory stood planted, dressed in snug jeans, dark boots, and a cobalt sweater. His hair was tucked under a gray cap.

Adjusting the bags in her hands, she flashed him a smile. "Hey, Rory."

He strode forward, ambling on those big tree trunks. "What have ye there?"

A faint scent of burnt metal and pine wafted toward her, and she inhaled. *Why did that mixture smell so good*?

He arched a brow.

She shifted the bags. "Something for the Murrays. I was just about to see if they were in the kitchen."

He dipped his head. "Aye, they would be."

"Are you going to see them, too?"

"No. Sarah'd have my hide if I stepped foot in her pristine kitchen after working with metals."

Andrea smiled.

Grinning back, Rory's beard curled around his full cheeks, while his gray eyes shone in the overhead lights.

A skittering of something she didn't recognize zipped through her veins, and she realized she wanted to continue talking to him—the quiet man with the full cheeks and intoxicating man scent. "Are you—"

The door swung and knocked into Andrea.

"Whoa!" She flew forward, holding onto the food bundle for dear life.

Rory's large, thick hands shot out, gripping her forearms.

"Well, hello!" Sarah greeted cheerfully with a high ponytail and Christmas sweater. "Sorry about that. I'm not used to having visitors waiting outside my kitchen."

Rory dropped his hands and stuffed them into his front pockets.

Andrea straightened, even as her heart pounded. "Um. Thank you." She flicked her hair and adjusted the bags. "It's my fault. But I wanted to bring you something as a thank-you for welcoming me into your kitchen."

Sarah's face glowed. "You brought me something?"

"Yes, for you and Finn." Andrea handed her the bag.

Sarah accepted the bag. "Food? You brought us food?" She

sniffed. "It smells delicious. May I?" She placed the bag on the banquet table adjacent.

"Absolutely."

Removing the tray of vegetarian skewers with pops of color from cherry-and-golden tomatoes, roasted mushrooms, black olives, green basil, and cheese drizzled with balsamic reduction, Sarah squealed. "These are so vibrant!" After nibbling one, she hummed. "What a nice, refreshing bite."

Andrea's heart pumped with excitement. "Exactly. A little antipasto skewer and also"—she reached into the bag for the second surprise—"I know when I'm cooking, I forget to eat until I serve."

"We do the same, though I make sure to keep Finn hydrated. The man forgets everything except the magic of the menu he's creating. It's a wonderful trait, but I have to take care that he doesn't pass out!" She laughed and then glanced at Rory. "I imagine you get the same way when you're crafting, Rory?"

He nodded and then roamed his gaze from Sarah to Andrea.

Steel-gray eyes pinned her, and tingles tangled in her stomach. Andrea glanced at Sarah and the way she chewed her food with a small smile that blossomed her cheeks.

"And, what are?" Sarah began, lifting the foil covering. Her mouth formed an *O*. "Are those mini lasagnas?"

Andrea grinned. "They are."

"Oh, they're so cute! And I bet they're as delicious as they are pretty." She carefully picked the vegetarian squash and spinach cup up along with a napkin and then took a small bite. "Mmm, just wonderful."

Giddiness danced within Andrea. A *real* cook liked her food.

"You came at the perfect time. We're prepping for a late tea. You're welcome to join the chaos. Are you staying?"

Her insides frolicked like cherry tomatoes tossed in a hot pan. "I'd love to. Let me just shoot Brie a quick text."

ANDREA

Sarah invited me to help out with catering tonight! Don't wait up.

"Rory?" Sarah asked. "Was there something I can get you?"

Glancing up, Andrea noted how Rory eyed the empty table and then glanced at Sarah. *He's hungry. And, I have bags full of food. But does he like Italian?*

He cleared his throat. "I'll come back later."

Sarah pointed a finger. "No, you will not. A man doesn't seek a kitchen without a growling stomach, and I don't recall seeing you at lunch."

"No."

With a cluck, she turned to Andrea. "Would you mind if I shared one of my lovely lasagnas and a couple skewers with Rory?"

"Not at all." Andrea gestured with a hand.

She popped one on a plate along with two skewers, then flew through the doors. A moment later, she returned with a full plate brimming with aromatic, yeasty bread, beans and rice, assorted vegetables, and Andrea's lasagna and skewers. "Here you are."

A grin tugged at his beard, and his eyes lit with warmth. "Thank ye."

"Anything for my favorite swordsmith. Enjoy!"

Andrea watched him amble to an empty table and sit. A small tug pulled at her gut. She felt the urge to sit with him; yet, she wanted to follow Sarah into the kitchen. With one last glance, she glided through the kitchen doors with Sarah chirping that they had a special visitor, while salty, savory aromas filled her nostrils.

"Andrea, 'tis good to see ye. Would love to chat, lass, but we're about to get a late service started." Finn flipped shrimp in the air, then back into the sizzling pan, while steam fanned around him and reddened his face.

She showed him her hands. "I'm here to help."

"And she brought us some wonderful quick bites, including these cute, little lasagnas." Sarah held up the food.

"Oh, aye?" He turned to the large steel island and did a quick chiffonade of herbs, then tossed them into the pan. "Thank ye. I can't wait to try them."

Andrea beamed.

"I gave one to Rory."

He shot a hand to his heart. "*Och*. And here I thought ye only had eyes for me."

"He was hungry." She lifted to her toes and pressed a quick kiss on his ruddy face. Turning, she swiveled toward Andrea.

"How can I help?" Andrea asked.

Reaching into a drawer below, Sarah retrieved an apron with stars across the front and held it out, then showed her to the wash bin. She introduced Andrea to a few of the other kitchen assistants busily working.

"No way." She spied a kitchen assistant pressing blue corn tortillas. "Taco night?"

"That's right! Got to bring some Tex Mex to the menu! Tonight, we're having Scottish Salmon, as well as shrimp and potato tacos with herb and radish salad, creamy dressing and a spicy tomato salsa, smoky-chipotle beans, and Mexican red rice with peas and carrots."

"Yum."

"We also have traditional creamy Cullen Skink soup, a seasonal kale salad with sweet potatoes, beets, quinoa, and crunchy chickpeas paired with a spicy chipotle vinaigrette, and a few other staples, which is no small feat. Ready?"

Rubbing her hands together, she smiled wide. "Absolutely."

Sarah tasked her with pulling together the salad.

Andrea scraped the warm, roasted root vegetables off the pan and tossed them in the savory chipotle dressing, then added the kale, other vegetables, and crunchy chickpeas, saving a few for the topping. Inside, the kitchen was warm and fragrant. Her hair curled up around her neck beneath her ponytail, and she felt sweat beading her forehead, but she didn't care. Being in the center of the catering production brought her back to when she, as a teen, used to sneak into the kitchen when her mom had parties—her secret retreat. Yet, here and now, she was a part of the catering chaos and loving every second. When she re-entered the dining area, she found Rory polishing off the last of his food, head down and focused on the plate before him. She appreciated a man who could appreciate a meal. "If you stay for a few more minutes, you're bound to get seconds."

He pushed away from the table. "I need to head back. Thank Sarah and Finn for me." As he approached, he side-stepped and set the plate on a clearing tray. "The lasagna was fantastic."

Pride swelled and burst inside. "Glad you liked it. Lasagna is one of my all-time favorites. Comfort food, you know?"

He nodded, but he didn't stir. He stared with intense, gray eyes.

"Was there something else?"

Clearing his throat, he scrubbed a hand over his beard. "I'd like to take ye out sometime. Let someone else take care of the preparing."

"Oh," she began, feeling a little tug toward him.

"Rory, after seconds, are you?" Sarah sang.

"No, thank ye." He tilted his head.

Andrea's nerves skittered, and her heart thumped. She

glanced at the kitchen door, then at Rory. What the heck was happening? And why was he looking all serious? Something swirled low in her gut. "Thank you, but I'm not looking to get...attached right now."

He stared with unwavering gray eyes, then with a quick nod, he pivoted and strode out.

"Strapping man, huh?" Sarah asked.

Andrea heaved a breath. "For some women." But damn it, she looked back at his disappearing figure, including the muscular bubble butt packed into snug jeans. *Cute butt.*

"You should go for it," Sarah caroled.

"I'm not looking for anything more than casual, you know? No entanglements. And he seems like the serious type."

Sarah placed a hand on Andrea's arm. "Oh, I do. I understand that very well." Her lips curled into a slow smile. "I told myself I wouldn't fall for Finn, too, and then he cooked for me."

With a harrumph, Andrea waltzed back through the double doors ready to focus on something other than a Scotsman.

* * *

Just grand. Lugging costume swords, Rory marched to set through wide tunnel-like hallways, decorated with scenes of previous *Swords* episodes and cast. He wished he'd been able to pound a few real, steel swords. He'd taken a chance again, and Andrea had declined. As he shoved a shoulder into the entry door, he walked into the indoor-outdoor highlands set with the historical foundation of the Mackenzie home marked with a wooden frame in between rich earth and tall evergreens and paused.

Bryce stood beside Eleana knee-deep in a scene, working

shovels into the soil to prepare for a new home for the Mackenzies.

Pausing, he absorbed the moment, the joint effort of man and woman—television husband and wife. True, 'twas a show, but the storyline was one of family and, more importantly, duty. He'd done his duty to his family and to the show, and now, he sought what was missing: a lass. Perhaps he should let Moira set him up with her niece, after all. She was single and available. The meat of it was, Andrea seemed interested. He wasn't an *eejit* or puffing himself up. He could see the way her bonnie eyes appreciated him and the bundle of weapons he carried the other day and her pretty smile when she realized he stood a few feet away, looking for scraps. But perhaps, she didn't want more than what Hugh could offer—a night. Muttering, he dropped the swords with a *thud*.

"Rory!" Eleana snapped. "You scared the daylights out of me."

"Sorry." He grasped the bundle and rotated the weapons quietly.

"Cut!" the director called in a black cap and wide-rimmed glasses.

Bryce meandered over in a linen shirt rolled up to the elbows and a green-and-blue kilt. "Been a day."

Straightening, he scrubbed a hand over his beard. "And night." They had at least five more hours. Rory would stay until filming was through, even if his mood had soured.

"We'll be fishing in a few weeks. Ye looking forward to catching some ladies?"

He glanced out of the corner of his eye. "The fish variety?"

Bryce chuckled. "The graylings always put up a good fight. But *och*, that feelin' when ye reel them in 'tis like ye caught the magical lady of the stream herself."

With a bob of his head, he glanced at Eleana getting makeup touched up opposite. "Sorry to disturb."

"*Oft*, yer fine. We've been messing up lines plenty on our own. Eleana even swore a time or two."

He grinned and said his farewells. Back at the armory, he heaved a breath. His team had gone home for the day, and he appreciated the quiet. After being turned down again, he needed a plan. He thought of Moira's insistence to meet her niece, so, he'd set a time to speak with her and ask. Then, he'd call and arrange a date followed by...an outing. But damn, he was rusty with women.

Andrea was the perfect example of his blatant neglect of his own dating life. *Should've asked her out the first time, instead of allowing Hugh to get his hands on her.* He was spending too much time at the forge just like his ma had said. At least, the forge didn't burn him time and time again. He knew what to expect. He knew how to form the metal. Sure, he took liberties now and again, making a sword to order or for his own pleasure, but the essence was the same and something he could depend on. Women were entirely different.

Chapter Twelve

Rain fell in thick watery sheets, adding dampness to the already chilly morning, but Andrea couldn't stop smiling. After cooking with the Murrays, she was inspired to create something of her own. She visited the grocery store and bought whatever struck her fancy, returning to the Frasers with an armload of cloth bags bulging with ingredients. She made seared scallops with brown butter paired with fettuccini and a winter salad with currants, as well as steaks paired with twice-baked potatoes and Brussel sprouts topped with bacon and a balsamic glaze, and lastly, a cottage pie per Bryce's request. But she wasn't done yet.

A day later, a large twelve-by-thirty-inch box awaited her. Eyeing the giant box, she grasped the kitchen shears and sliced through the clear tape like a kid on Christmas morning. A gleaming, silver pasta maker and a wide array of attachments nestled between foam.

"Auntie A opened presents early!" Noah stood in the alcove of the kitchen with eyes wide.

"Nope. I bought this beauty for me." She flashed a smile. "I couldn't wait for Santa."

Slipping off his backpack, he approached, thick sandy brows drawn together. "What is it?"

"A pasta maker."

"Really?"

"Yup. And now, it's time for some double zero flour and pasta making." But as she looked at the lever and pieces, she wondered how they'd fit together. "Well, after I figure out the instructions. Easy peasy, right?"

He stared at all the gadgets, shrugged, then ran outside.

Bling-bling. Bling-bling.

"Shit!" She swiveled, searching for her phone, and clicked the reminder. *4 p.m.: Recruiter Call.* Nibbling her lip, she glanced at her gadgets. Pasta would have to wait.

Fifteen minutes later, her phone shrilled.

"Is now a good time?" Stan, the recruiter, asked with a subtle Southern accent.

"Yes. It's great." She drummed her nails on the cool, granite countertop.

"Wonderful. Thank you for making the time. What interests you about Synergy?"

Corporate talk. I know how to do this. "I've worked in the tech industry for close to ten years, and I appreciate Synergy's drive to..." *Shit. Think.* "Drive to propel their technologies into the future. I know with my tenured leadership I can help Synergy grow by optimizing their employees' success through initiatives, rewards, and more."

"I noticed you were a VP previously."

She pursed her lips. "I was, but I see a lot of the same responsibilities listed that I did as a VP."

"So, you're comfortable taking a different title?"

"Yes." She poked a finger into her temple. She was selling herself for a job she didn't want, for a house that possibly wouldn't be hers. She was a fake.

"And what's your reason for leaving your current employment?"

"I was laid off."

"I see." He asked her a few more questions, including compensation, then noted he'd be sending an invitation for an interview with the VP of HR.

"Great. I appreciate your time." She disconnected and smacked the phone on her forehead. "Ugh. Is this what you really want?"

The people-less kitchen didn't answer.

She wanted a house. At thirty, she'd earned the right to purchase some real estate within walking distance from her favorite spot in Palisades Park. But this rat race of trying to secure any job instead of the right job was wearing on her. A *ping* informed her the recruiter scheduled the interview. Tapping into her email, she clicked the invitation and scoffed. "Wednesday! That's too late, guys. I need an interview sooner, so you can offer me a job, and I can get my house!" She replied, asking if they could accommodate her sooner, then swiped a curl off her head and plopped onto the floor once again.

Tucking her legs, she snatched the pasta maker instructions. The excitement had worn off like the littered mess following Christmas morning. But damned if she'd let her issues ruin the rest of her afternoon. She huffed a breath and did what any sensible twenty-first century woman would do—she searched the Internet for how-to videos. After scrolling a few minutes, she watched a peppy young woman demonstrate how the pasta maker worked. She was ready to make homemade lasagna, ravioli, and other pastas. Who knew that was possible? Sure, she'd made pasta once or twice at cooking classes, as well as giant penne without an attachment before with a skewer, but she'd always secretly wanted a pasta maker like the pros. Her L.A. apartment was tiny, and she didn't have an island. But Brie did.

A short while later, she admired long, buttery-yellow sheets coming from the pasta maker like the most beautiful ribbon she'd ever seen. Suddenly, the pasta moved sideways off the track and pinched the ribbon. She huffed. "Come on. You can do this."

Ping!

Glancing at her phone, she groaned. "Shit. Loan agent."

DAN - LOAN AGENT

How's the job search going?

She chewed the inside of her cheek, then wiped her flour-covered hands on a kitchen towel.

ANDREA

I have an interview scheduled and a few other leads. I'm confident.

DAN - LOAN AGENT

Good. The bank needs a signed contract for something permanent by next week.

ANDREA

I'm on it.

A thumbs-up emoji popped up in response.

She blew out a breath. Setting her phone aside, she removed the stuck pasta, folded it once again, and passed it back through the pasta maker, cranking the handle. Stress eased with each inch of pasta that pumped out, and she squealed with glee. In nearly two hours, she had semolina flour all over the island and four different pastas, including ricotta, spinach, and cheese ravioli prepared. She served dinner family style in the dining room to Brie, Mimi, and the kids. After, her stomach was happy, her feet were tired, and she smelled like food. She felt wonderful.

A few hours later, she selected a merlot to celebrate further, while Brie bathed the kids.

Ding! Her text chimed.

She glanced at her phone. *Hugh.* She smirked and grasped the device. Cooking had kept her happy and busy, but she could use a little extra celebration with some male company.

HUGH
What're ye drinking?

ANDREA
Whatever you're pouring.

HUGH
Whisky 'n coffee. On set.

She harrumphed. Well, that wouldn't work.

ANDREA
How about a sexy picture?

A moment later, an image appeared. Hugh's dark eyes stared from above a black travel coffee mug, while his almost-black mane was highlighted by a glow behind him, making him look like a dark demi-god. Lust speared her in the gut, and she licked her lips.

ANDREA
I can play this game.

She eyed the opened wine bottle. Maybe she could have a little fun? Make him think about what they could do when he was off set... Uncorking the red wine, she rotated the camera to face her and pressed the video button. With one arm, she lifted the wine bottle, while the other held fast to her cell, filming. She opened her mouth and drizzled wine, but only a few drops fell out. She tilted the bottle a bit more. The wine splashed out like a plum waterfall, instantly filling her nose and mouth simultaneously. *Cough! Cough! Cough!* She sputtered. "Oh my god," she heaved. Her nostrils burned, and she imagined she looked like a soggy grape.

"Are ye all right, lass?" Bryce said from behind.

She pivoted.

He ventured into the kitchen and took one look at her and bit back a grin.

Trying to breathe through wine-filled nostrils, she whipped a finger at him. "Don't you dare!"

He tucked his tongue in his cheek. "Did the bottle explode, then?"

"No." She wiped her face and chest. "I was making a video for...Hugh."

His smile grew, and a chuckle chided out and then, rolling laughter.

She tossed the cork at him. "Butthead."

With hands up, he retreated, laughing. "I'll go see where Brie and the weans are."

Trying to salvage the video, Andrea cut and cropped until only the first section was left. Not perfect, but it'd have to do.

HUGH

Thrapple dry, is it?

Heck yes, her thrapple was dry. Chewing her bottom lip, she considered what to text next.

HUGH

A drink soon?

ANDREA

Absolutely! When?

She danced in place. And then she waited. And waited. She showered off the wine, played with her niece and nephew, and ate a giant bowl of chocolate ice cream, but she didn't receive additional texts from Hugh. When she'd settled into bed that night, she snapped on the television in the guest house. Hugh's face appeared on her saved shows list. "Actors!" She smashed the off button.

* * *

Saturday, Andrea spooned her last batch of homemade pasta into a rectangular, stainless steel warming tray with olive oil, then popped a bright-red tomato into her mouth. The fall sunlight streamed through the wide kitchen windows, while salty and savory smells permeated from all around. Near thirty-five people—little girls and their parents—meandered in the yard with pint-sized princesses following a pasta dinner. Andrea had probably made enough food for twice that amount, but she couldn't run out, especially during a party— and a four-year old birthday party for her niece at that.

She'd cooked all morning, though she made her red sauce the day before to allow the flavors to brighten, and now what was left of her prepared sauces and proteins were warming in dishes along the giant island. What else was a horny woman supposed to do when she was left without sexual fulfillment? She fed her appetite another way. For Phoebe's birthday, she'd volunteered to be in charge of the food, while Brie and Mimi took care of decorations and desserts.

Brie made Rapunzel paintbrushes with homemade rice-crispy squares dipped in colorful frosting and lavender-and-pink-swirl cupcakes, while Mimi painted beautiful signs, magical rainbows, and a castle mural. They divided and conquered, and Andrea couldn't stop smiling. Watching Phoebe twirl a bubble wand with her little friends wearing a flower crown and princess gown paired with high-tops bedaz-zled with butterfly wings, Andrea felt like she was part of something bigger like when she prepped with the Murrays. Grasping a kitchen towel, she wiped down the island, then strode outside.

"Oh!" Brie gasped her hand. "He made it and Rory, too."

Glancing over her shoulder, she spied Bryce and Rory ambling toward them—both in ball caps and flannels. They could be mistaken as brothers with the beard Bryce was currently sporting. She was glad they'd arrived, since Brie was nervous Bryce might miss the party due to filming. Though one highlander was missing. She peered around, looking for Hugh, but apparently, the three Scottish amigos were down to two.

A squeal shrilled in the air, and Phoebe raced toward them, flinging her arms around Bryce. "Hi!" Then, she repeated the gesture, hugging Rory. "Hi! Hi! It's my birthday."

Rory squatted to her level and passed her a taupe bag. "Happy birthday, lass."

"Thank you!" Grasping the ribbon handle, she tossed white tissue paper like fluffy clouds all around her. She pulled out a semi-circle with some sort of string and a few colorful, wooden sticks topped with colored balls.

A bow and arrow?

"Look, Mommy!" Phoebe lifted her new toy. "I'm a warrior princess."

"You are! Thank you so much, Rory."

Rocketing back to Rory, Phoebe threw both arms around his legs, and then the next moment, she slung the bow over her shoulder and raced toward the castle.

A grin tugged wide across Rory's face. Sweeping his gaze around the yard, he met Andrea's.

A flurry of something swirled in her stomach. Andrea found herself pinned by his unwavering stare. "Oof!" Someone knocked into her, and she stumbled.

A full-figured woman steadied her with an arm. "Ye all right?"

"Sure, I'm fine." Regaining her composure, she shook her head and strode toward the house, weaving around parents making small talk, huddled by heat warmers, while kids ran around post-sugar high, though she could still feel Rory's penetrating gaze like heat pumping from a bustling kitchen. Once inside, she gripped the faucet lever. "What is wrong with me? And why does that man make me so...so nervous?" She exhaled and cranked the water on, allowing the cool stream to calm her.

A moment later, she assessed the buffet along the long island. She noted the pasta bar was a success. The meaty marinara was nearly dry, pesto had begun to darken slightly with oxidation to a swampy coloring, alfredo sauce still filled a quarter full, grilled chicken and steak had a few pounds left over, while the shrimp were nowhere to be found—and she'd grilled up five dozen—salad was still springy in the cold, and some breadsticks happily filled jars in their curly disarray. She plucked a breadstick from the glass container and bit into it with a satisfying *crunch*.

"What a spread," Bryce commented.

She spun. Bryce and Rory stood shoulder-to-shoulder at the kitchen entry. She swallowed. "Hungry?" she croaked.

"Starved," Bryce said.

Rory nodded twice.

That damn nod. Striding forward, she felt a little zip of something skirting along her veins. *What's wrong with me? I don't want to date him.* Clearing her throat, she flashed a smile. "You got back earlier than expected. Weren't you on location somewhere super-secret, today?"

"We were." Bryce sighed. "Hugh didn't show up."

Andrea tilted her head. "What happened?"

His blue eyes grew icy and jaw clenched. "I imagine whisky got the better of him."

Rory's full lips flattened into a thin line.

"Sorry." She shook her head, wondering what exactly was going on with the mysterious actor. Picking up a couple plates, she handed one to each of them. "I'm sure there's a good explanation for why he didn't show up, but I'm glad you made it. And obviously, Phoebe is too."

"Aye, plus 'twas bloody miserable in the highlands today."

Rory didn't add a word.

"Well"—she flashed a smile—"you're here now. Let's get you fed." She mixed the salad, scooped vegetables, meats, and bundles of pasta, then plucked a small piece of focaccia for Bryce—the man was always watching his carbs. Meanwhile, she filled Rory's plate with a large chunk of focaccia and noticed a hint of an uptick of his upper lip. She admired his appetite. "Here you go." Glancing up, she caught Rory staring. His eyes were like liquid smoke, drawing her in, and her pulse did a little *jump-jump*.

With another dip of his head, he grasped the plate, grazing her fingers with his, and strolled past her on those big ole tree trunk legs with Bryce.

Those notes of metal and man filled her nostrils, and damnit, her fingers tingled where his touched. Andrea wondered if she'd made a mistake. She could be seeing Rory and rolling around the sheets with him. He *had* asked her out...twice. But the quiet man was giving her the silent treatment. *Well, duh, I turned him down.* She shouldn't care, and she definitely shouldn't be annoyed, but she was. That bugged her the most.

* * *

The last place Rory wanted to be was in the same vicinity as Andrea. But wee Phoebe deserved her gift, and he wasn't about to disappoint her. Tugging a chair out, he seated himself beside Bryce at a table decorated with pink-and-white flowers, gold crowns, and pink castles.

A few parents pivoted from their conversations and greeted them.

"Afternoon." He bobbed his head.

"Thank ye so much for coming. Phoebe has been excited for this party for months." Bryce began and conversed with his guests.

Rory, on the other hand, stared at his plate. He didn't have much free time, especially with the holiday season, and he planned to enjoy himself. Spearing some steak and pasta, he lifted the fork and chewed. The meal was good, grand even. He'd never considered other pastas besides bolognaise previously, but the cream sauce was rich and satisfying after a long day's work. When a warm laugh carried across the yard and met his ears, he glanced.

Andrea's head fell back, guffawing with parents of one of the lassies.

He watched her talk with lively hand gestures, even as annoyance crept in. He could admit his pride was wounded. He had a lot to offer a woman—a nice home, stable career, and solid income. Sure, he worked a number of hours, but that was seasonal, and a good woman, the right woman, could admire his hard work. He was also good-natured, though he needed to work on talking more regularly with others—not holed up in his forge. Shaking his head, he focused on his food; yet, he no longer had an appetite. He pushed the food aside and crossed his arms over his chest.

Chapter Thirteen

THE FOLLOWING EVENING, ANDREA AND MIMI played with the kids in the yard, while Brie went on a special errand. Secret Christmas shopping, Andrea imagined. She was happy to give Brie a break. Just like she needed a recharge, so did her best friend. Perhaps later, she could steal Brie away for another night on the town—have a few drinks away from the kids, dance with some sexy Scots with hilarious pickup lines, and have some girl time.

Grinning, she chased Phoebe around the yellow-brown yard, until she huffed and puffed like a dragon, then drew hopscotch squares across the cool concrete. When the clouds darkened and rain began to fall, they retreated inside for board games, hot cocoa, and dinner preparation.

An hour later, Andrea swirled a spatula over mashed potatoes.

Brie entered the kitchen with an armful of shopping bags paired with a gigantic smile.

"So, how were the errands?"

"Fantastic!" She smiled brightly. "Oh, Bryce will be home early tonight, too."

"Great!"

Lifting her nose, she inhaled. "What are you making?"

"Shepherd's pie with dark gravy."

"Yum." Pivoting, she exited the kitchen.

Forty minutes later, the six of them sat around the dining room table, finishing the shepherd's pie with cheesy, garlic bread.

"Thank ye for dinner, Andrea. Ye've outdone yourself again." Bryce settled in his chair.

"You have!" Brie pointed a finger. "I'm cooking tomorrow and giving you a break."

"I can cook, as well. Perhaps some bread bowls with clam chowder?" Mimi asked.

Waving her napkin, she shook her head. "I have to do *something*."

Brie glanced at Bryce with a smile that lit her green eyes, then looked at Andrea.

"What?" Andrea asked.

"Tell her!" Brie's eyes shone.

"What?" she repeated. "Do I have food on my face?"

With a giggle, Brie shook her head.

Bryce leaned forward on his elbows. "I have a proposition for ye."

She lifted a brow.

"*Swords* is heading to an undisclosed location for a half-day shoot to make up for yesterday, and we need a caterer. There will be fewer actors and crew—fifty in total. Ye can create your own menu as long as it has selections for vegetarians and vegans, and you'll spend a day in the highlands, paid." He retrieved an envelope from his pocket and handed it to Andrea.

Opening the envelope, she gulped, then gasped at the five-figure check. "Holy shhh." Her eyes widened, and she glanced at Bryce. "Are you serious?"

"Aye. The Murrays can't add the makeup day to their busy holiday schedule. I thought since you've been inspired in the kitchen, ye might consider it."

"That's wonderful! You'd do a fabulous job," Mimi added.

"What's Auntie A doing?" Phoebe turned with shining cheeks smeared with butter and herbs.

Mimi filled the children in.

Andrea's head spun like a tornado of pasta in a pot. "Cater meals for *Swords of Scotland's* actors and crew..." she murmured. "How many meals?"

"Lunch, plus snack, right?" Brie asked, then giggled. "Boy, I sound like a mom."

"Ye do, love, and you're brilliant at it." He tugged her close, pressing his lips to her forehead. Then, he turned back to Andrea. "Just plan lunch. That's what the Murrays would do."

"Okay." She thought back to a week and a half ago when she cooked with her heart and soul and the delighted dinner guests. And then a week ago, when she joined the Murrays' kitchen, and yesterday leading the charge in the kitchen for Phoebe's birthday party. Cooking felt good. *So* damn good. She glanced at Brie and Bryce who were staring with big, shining eyes. She could cook. And, she *could* save her house. She toasted them with her wine glass. "Lunch, it is! When?"

"Thursday."

She sloshed the wine over her hand. "This Thursday?"

"Aye."

"It's Sunday!" She wiped the wine up vigorously. "That's less than five days from now!"

"I have faith in ye."

"Well, I'll need to figure out what to bring up there and how. Maybe rent an easy-up? Wait, it's Scotland in the middle of winter. Duh. A fifth wheel? Or, maybe a food truck?"

Bryce nodded. "Catering will be separated about four

hundred meters from the filming location. They'll have tents on location for breaks and such that the crew will set up."

Brie grasped her hand. "And I can be your assistant that day!"

"You bet!" Mimi agreed. "The kids and I will have our own adventure."

"But where do I, how do I?" Andrea sputtered.

"Call Sarah Murray. She said she's happy to answer any questions and help ye where she can."

"Sure, I'll call Sarah. Okay." Andrea swallowed thickly. What did she just agree to?

* * *

Andrea paced the kitchen. She'd scrubbed the pots clean, even though Mimi offered to help, and now, the stone and stainless-steel appliances sparkled below the recessed lighting. But she was up shit's creek—catering's creek. Sure, she had a check and an invoice for catering that she emailed to the loan agent as an additional source of income, but she actually had to cook for fifty people. What would she make? She pressed her forehead into a palm. *Think*. Italian sandwiches, soups, and maybe a cold pasta salad? "Uh, these are actors!" Plus, they weren't filming at Swords Studios; they'd be shooting in freezing weather, possibly snow.

She opened the pantry and began selecting diced tomatoes, tomato puree, an onion, garlic, dried herbs, and red chili flakes. She did her best thinking while cooking. And red sauce was her thinking sauce. While the onions caramelized, she grabbed a can opener and pierced the tooth into the can. The crank didn't budge. A slew of cuss words followed as she strong-armed the can and opener. She'd had an all-out-war with can openers over the years, which included slicing a palm in a semi-circle after a battle with a steak knife trying to open a twelve ounce can. She set the opener down and dropped her head back, gazing at the ceiling. Inhaling and exhaling, she reassessed. She needed to chill out. This was an opportunity that could save her house—save *her*. She grasped the can opener once more, piercing the can with the small knife. The gear turned. She added the canned tomatoes and herbs to the sauce, then stirred to combine. Once the sauce simmered, she picked up a pad of paper and jotted down notes.

Catering List
Kick-Ass Food
Drinks
Cutlery, napkins, plates, bowls
Linens?
Warmers?

If she rented a food truck, she could prepare some of the food early, then finish cooking on site. But...that depended on what she was making. She drummed her fingers on the cool countertop. What she was making would be dependent on her set up. She searched truck and trailer rentals and called to make reservations, but most of the fifth wheels were not meant for commercial food use and those that were, were spoken for during the busy Christmas season. Plus, she didn't know the exact mileage. She hadn't been informed exactly where she'd be cooking and serving people, although she knew she'd be in the highlands.

'Near Inverness,' Bryce had said.

She rolled her eyes. She couldn't blame Bryce for being stingy with information. *Swords* fans were a passionate bunch. But boy oh boy she wished she knew, so she could paint a full picture and have the information needed to ask for a pricing guestimate.

Tapping a finger on her phone, she thought of her next

step. Immediately, a sweet Texan's face appeared in her mind. She retrieved Sarah Murray's card.

After a few rings, Sarah's cheerful voice came on the line. "Are you ecstatic?"

She blew a breath out. "That's one way to put it."

"This is such a great opportunity." She chirped. "You'll do wonderfully!"

"Thanks. And about that...I have a few questions. Do you have a couple minutes to chat?"

"Sure do. Shoot."

Andrea explained the terms of the lunch catering and her concerns. "Do you know of any good food truck rentals?"

"Hmm. There are a few, though they might be low on supply with the local Christmas markets."

Andrea harrumphed and rested a hip on the counter. "That's what I've found, as well."

"I tell you what. In the spirit of American camaraderie, we'll loan you our extra truck. All you need is to get it serviced before you go, get a sign to cover our logo, and temporary vehicle insurance."

"Are you sure?"

"Of course!"

Relief settled over Andrea. Step one: check. "Thank you so much."

"Also, you'll need a restaurant space to cook in—I'll send you a few recommendations. And think about what you'll serve the food in, how you'll dispose of it, and something to get your name out there," Sarah added.

Andrea hummed. "But I don't even live here. And I only have four days!"

"Even so, you'll need something with your logo or name."

Once she thanked Sarah and said good-bye, Andrea considered a name for her pop-up catering business. "Andrea's Appetizing ...Appetizing Andrea? Hmmm...Double A Catering?" She glanced at her full breasts. "Definitely not double A." She drummed her nails on the counter.

Ping. 1 New email. Glancing over, Andrea tapped open the email and immediately snarled.

Andrea, your RSVP is waiting.

Gloria had called earlier while she was playing with the kids, reminding Andrea about her not-so-little party. Andrea repeated that she was in Scotland through the New Year, but that didn't satisfy Gloria. She noted she could fly home and bring Hugh. Oh, yeah, and apparently, she wasn't trying hard enough to snag the sexy highlander. But she didn't need Hugh Macrae in her life. She didn't *need* a man.

"Of course, you don't need a man; you want the attachment to show that you're doing better than the average housewife," Gloria had said.

Andrea clicked the link set up by Gloria's assistant because her mother did not create electronic invitations. A bold black-and-gold invitation with a shimmery circle around *Gala* announced Gloria's Glamourous Christmas Gala with live entertainment, dinner, and more.

"Even her party has a name." Flipping her phone over, she closed her eyes. "Food by me. Catering by Andrea. Crafted Catering by Andrea." She sunk her hands into her hair, tangling in the curls. "Oh my God. Why is this so hard?" Eyeing the pasta on the counter, she considered. "Italian... Andrea's American Italian? Ugh, but I'm just a hobby cook, not a chef. *La Cuoca*, like *Nonna* used to say." She straightened. "That's it! *La Cuoca* Andrea!" Now, all she needed was to craft a menu. At eight p.m., Andrea sneered at the unimpressive zucchini pappardelle she'd learned to make at her cooking class the other day with an etching of green skin on the exterior and ivory center. "Fucking zucchini." Part of the zucchini 'noodle' was thick and the center was thin. Definitely *not* her best work.

"It looks great!" Brie tugged a stool out and sat.

Andrea grabbed another zucchini and slid the peeler down the length, taking her time, peeling one zoodle at a time. Ugh, preparing pappardelle was laborious. Did she really want to make enough for twenty-five paleo people? "Why can't everyone just eat pasta? Pasta for some, vegetarian for others, and paleo for the picky. Instead of these vegetable pasta knock-offs? I mean I'm all for vegetables, but shit, this is a pain in the ass."

Without a word, Brie rose from the stool and picked up a fork. She twirled a bundle of cooked zucchini pappardelle, then dipped the tiny bundle into the spicy garlic tomato sauce, popped the forkful in her mouth, and hummed. "Yum. It's so good."

"It's a bitch to make." She wove her fingers through a tight curl. "Ugh. I need to change gears."

Brie shook her head. "I don't think so."

"I do. There are too many variables with these special noodles, plus actors have costumes on, right?"

Brie titled her head. "Right."

"Well, I'm sure the last thing Eleana Evans needs on her eighteenth-century reproduction is pappardelle slurp marks."

Brie nodded. "I see where you're going."

"What about soup? I can make a hearty vegetable soup like minestrone with meatballs and short pasta. Keep the meatballs and pasta separate, make a garlic sauce or spicy marinara, so I can meet the needs of a variety of diets. Oh, and whip up a few batches of fresh focaccia to finish it all off."

"That sounds great!"

She pushed the zucchini aside and rubbed her hands together. *Time for take two.*

While Brie and Bryce took the children to the Christmas

market the following morning, Andrea diced onion, garlic, and a variety of colorful vegetables—squash, carrots, celery, etc., then retrieved cannellini beans and began her soup recipe. She'd made Minestrone soup hundreds of times, but this would be served to movie stars. So, she found a few five-star-rated recipes online and printed them, then handwrote a new recipe with a few local vegetables and the star ingredient—a parmesan rind for extra flavor. *Merry, Merry Minestrone Soup!* Once combined with stock, she set the heat to medium and let the flavors marry. When she perused the fridge, she noted pork sausage and ground venison stared back. *Hmm venison meatballs? Venison was more Scottish, right?* Remembering a scene in *Swords* when Alexander and Hamish were on the run from the redcoats after days of no food and hunger for company, and a large buck came into view, she considered. They tracked and hunted the deer, gave thanks, then skinned and cooked it, replenishing their strength. Her gut told her to pair the two meats—the rich venison combined with the fat and flavor of the pork.

But her gut also told her she'd get that CHRO position a few weeks ago. She glanced at her phone. She couldn't call Bryce. She wanted to impress him when he returned, so that left three Scottish people. She'd already called Sarah about the food truck, and she wanted to appear as if she knew what the heck she was doing. Rory had a hardy appetite, but would he answer? She blew a breath. Probably not. And that left a sourness in her stomach. Then, there was Hugh. He might not even reply... *What the hell.* Grasping her phone, she texted.

ANDREA

How do you feel about venison meatballs?

While she waited for a reply, Andrea caramelized onions and garlic, then mixed herbs and added both to the ground venison and pork sausage with breadcrumbs. Next, she added a flax egg for Phoebe in place of a real egg, but she'd use real eggs when she made her meatballs at the restaurant space. Finally, she measured and splashed balsamic to balance the flavors of the meats. Then, she grabbed a medium-sized ice cream scoop, dampened her hands, and scooped and rolled meatballs.

Her phone chimed ten minutes later as she popped meatballs into the oven.

HUGH
Rather strongly.

ANDREA
You'll have to try mine sometime.

HUGH
Ye'll have to try mine, as well.

ANDREA
Oh, really?

She snapped a picture with her phone and sent it along with a one-word question.

ANDREA
Jealous?

HUGH
A Scot has no reason to be jealous.

Grasping the Christmas tree oven mitt, Andrea fanned herself. "Damn." She was all hot and bothered just from a few text messages. But was he just a flirt, or did he actually want to date her? He'd proven he was a horrible texter before, and she'd waited on him more than once...

Ding! The oven timer sounded.

"Okay, enough man thoughts. Back to your kick-ass

meal." With a shake of her hair, she grasped the mitts and retrieved the golden meatballs that she'd finish in the soup. "Hearty soup needs hardy bread." She learned how to make focaccia last week. She couldn't believe how simple it was! She thought baking was out of reach and here she was a pizza, pasta, and bread maker now. She made a duo: three-cheese laced with pesto and sundried tomato, and classic rosemary and garlic.

That night, Andrea served Bryce and family the trial meal alongside giant meatballs.

After finishing a large bowl, a side of meatballs, and a piece of focaccia, Bryce leaned back and rubbed a hand across his stomach. "I'm impressed. And now I can tell ye where you'll be serving this fantastic food."

She arched a brow.

"In the Cairngorms."

Her jaw dropped. "Isn't that a national park?"

"Aye, 'tis. And with the bone-chilling, damp winter weather and limited daylight, we have our work cut out for us. It's going to be an epic finale, but yer braw feast will warm our bellies and keep the crew going."

Andrea bobbed her head as nerves tangled in her stomach. Cooking amongst friends in a warm kitchen was one thing, but cooking in a food truck, in the middle of winter in a national frickin' forest was something else entirely.

Chapter Fourteen

UNDER THE BRIGHT BEAM OF THE PORCH LIGHT, Andrea waited for the food truck's delivery with her third cup of coffee in the dark. Glancing at her watch, she wondered what the Scottish food coach would look like. The last time she'd seen the coach as Finn called it, the truck still had the Murrays' branding on the rectangular length. But Brie had told her not to worry about the logo—she'd take care of it. And honestly, between the visits to the grocery store, preparations at the rented restaurant space, and more, two days had flown by.

A peppy *beep-beep* sounded, and a flash of headlights shot through the pitch-black morning. The once blue, green, and dash of red paint was now black, white, and red with a watercolor tomato, wooden spoon, and garlic bunch beside *La Cuoca Andrea*. Her jaw dropped. She didn't know how Brie pulled it off, but the result was beyond Andrea's wildest imagination. She set the coffee cup on the step and jogged toward the truck.

Once parked, Brie jumped out of the driver's seat in a

festive green-and-ivory flannel, green coat, and ivory beanie. "Ta da!"

"Oh, my God!" She cupped her face with her hands. "This is amazing."

Brie smiled broadly. "Yay! I knew you'd love it."

"Did you paint the logo?"

"I did. And I even purchased"—she pulled her hands from behind her, showcasing a couple tomato-red aprons with *La Cuoca Andrea* in swirly script on the front—"these!"

Gripping Brie's hand and an apron, she jumped up and down. "Ah! These are fucking awesome."

"I want to support you. Like you've supported me."

With a tug, she embraced Brie. "Thank you. You're the best friend a girl could ever ask for."

"Back at ya, bestie."

Fifteen minutes later with the food truck packed, supplies stored, waterproof jackets and boots, and checklists triple checked, Andrea cranked the engine over. She noted the thick clumps of clouds filling the dark skies like a smoky plume outside the window. "Hopefully, the weather holds. I don't feel like driving up snow-slicked mountains with this big ole truck."

"We'll be fine. They packed snow chains, remember?" Brie plugged in her phone.

Andrea gripped the steering wheel. She remembered, but she didn't want to use them. An entire cast and crew were depending on them for a meal.

"And according to the map, we'll be there at eight sharp. Four hours before service starts." Brie tapped the phone.

"Let's do this!" Andrea turned onto the lane, ready for a catering adventure in the highlands. She drove through Glasgow, past the city and industry where streetlights lit their path, and soon, they were on the winding highway. Outlines of rolling hills filled her view, tinged light and dark brown from the recent frost like the marbling of a steak. As they drove higher and higher, she stared at snow-capped mountains reaching toward puffs of gray-and-white clouds. The storm was coming. She prayed it would hold until they finished and were well on their way home.

Two hours later, the *Cairngorms National Park* sign appeared with an osprey holding a fish in its talons. A familiar man with an orange safety vest, thick, black parka, and tattoos climbing up his neck stopped them with a raised glove.

Andrea rolled her window down. A blast of cold, damp air hit her in the face.

"Name?"

"Angus! It's Brie!" Brie leaned, waving vigorously.

"Brie?" His face softened. "What are ye doing in there, lass?"

"This is my best friend, Andrea. She's the caterer today, and I'm helping out."

His green eyes warmed. "Well, why didn't ye say so?"

Andrea snorted. "You mean you can't see the big ass truck with a giant tomato all over it?"

He glanced back.

"Remember me? Ms. Lasagna?" His stone-like expression returned; yet, there was a hint of humor in those dark eyes.

"Come on through. Ye'll head up about two hundred meters where there's a flat, temporary carpark. Bryce and the rest of the cast are up about three hundred meters to the west."

Giving him a thumbs-up, Andrea drove into the snowy oblivion, searching for the carpark. Sure enough, a makeshift parking lot with a handful of cars and trucks emerged with a few easy ups and forty feet or so of four-walled, white tents, no doubt where the crew would be dining out of the cold. She swung the van around and backed the truck into the thick forest. "Fucking beautiful."

They unloaded the truck and then quickly threw linens and utensil containers on pre-set tables in the tents, while wind tossed Andrea's curls around her face. Tucking them under a beanie, she heard a shout echo across the ravine. She glanced toward the route marked for cast members where the soft morning rays highlighted the snow-covered path. "Can we sneak a quick peek at filming?"

Brie grinned. "I wouldn't mind seeing Bryce. Let's do it."

She strode quickly up the path, boots crunching on the frozen grass. A fluffy rabbit skittered across the road, while birds chirped and flittered from snow covered tree-to-tree. As they rounded a bend, she spotted a half dozen temporary tents, as well as lawn chairs and gear.

Crew members milled around and busied with tasks—snaking cords, trudging through snow with tartan fabric, and more.

"There they are." Brie pointed up the mountain.

At the top, a tall, highland warrior, with long, brown hair whipping in the wind—Hugh Macrae aka Hamish—shouted at a woman she recognized as Eleana aka Lady Charlotte a few inches from him.

Lady Charlotte lifted her chin and tossed intelligible words back.

Two cameramen in black with crazy, large cameras and equipment attached to their hips and shoulders filmed closely.

With a hand above her brow, Andrea watched.

Lady Charlotte's wool dress fanned around her, tangling and merging with Hamish's kilt like a dance; yet, no words escaped either's lips. They stood fiercely looking at each other until a cry tore through Lady Charlotte, and she crumpled.

Hamish caught her in his arms, kneeling beside her in the frosty snow. His hand fisted on her dark blue cape as she bowed her head and shook.

A twinge settled in Andrea's chest. But she pushed it aside.

This was a television show. A scene. Fiction. But damn, they were good.

Gaelic cut through the air.

On the opposite mountain, Bryce stood as Alexander James Mackenzie. His red beard and hair were flecked with snow, and his blue-and-green Mackenzie kilt and jacket were weathered, dark, dirty, and torn.

Charlotte's head snapped up. "Alexander!"

Alexander lumbered across the frosty landscape.

Charlotte trudged through the snow, dragging her hem in the white slush.

Andrea's heart pounded.

Picking up speed, Alexander nearly leapt over the snow.

Charlotte reached for him.

Alexander grasped her hand, and their lips and bodies merged—dark hair swirling with rich red—a flash of color in the brilliant, white oblivion.

"CUT!" the producer hollered twenty feet from them.

The actors separated.

"Wow, I wonder what that scene has to do with the plot," Brie commented.

"Yeah." Andrea glanced once more as Hugh stared across the scene where Eleana stood with a makeup artist touching up her lips and cheeks. Perhaps, he was still in character—his character was secretly in love with Lady Charlotte. But maybe there was more to Eleana and Hugh. With one last glance, she turned on her booted heel. "We better start cooking."

They walked side by side a hundred feet with Brie remarking about the beauty of the land beside them.

A golden eagle soared across the gray sky that darkened by the minute. Still, she found her mind wandering back to Hugh and Eleana clutched in a fierce embrace. She was attracted to Hugh, but some crazy cosmic connection didn't exist between them. Not like Brie and Bryce. Hugh had texted her the last couple nights, and she was pleased as punch to have a little sexy exchange, especially when thoughts of Rory drifted in and out of her mind. *Ugh*. She couldn't think about Rory, even though she wondered where he and his swords were hiding. A tangle in the sheets with Hugh was all she wanted. She flicked her head, tossing curls, but couldn't dislodge the envy that had wedged in her chest from the scene she'd just witnessed. "How do you do it, Brie?"

Brie inclined her head. "What?"

Flinging an arm out, Andrea gestured behind. "Eleana and Bryce. They play a couple with a passionate connection, and their scenes seem so real. Don't you get jealous?"

"Oh." She sighed. "Well, I trust him and Eleana, but more than that, I know his heart. And his heart's home is with mine."

"You never worry? Even after all that happened with Ryan?"

"I'm human, so, of course, there is always that tiny doubt sneaking into my mind every now and again. But what Bryce and I have is so different than what I had with Ryan. From the moment he crashed into me, I felt a tug within, and he, him, like a recognition of one soul to another, and everything changed."

Andrea trudged forward. She'd never felt anything like that with someone. She hadn't allowed herself to. She had a career or *had* a career, but she never let anyone get that close. When she heard the unmistakable clank of swords echo in the distance, she thought of Rory and the way he held her hand in the kitchen the first day they met. A little buzz fluttered around her stomach. She shook her head, tossing the memory aside. Serious stuff was for serious relationship people. Not her.

* * *

Dancing in place, Andrea created a slight rumble in the truck like a California quake, swaying silver pots and swinging red kitchen towels on hooks. "I've got to pee."

Brie blinked. "Oh, we should've thought of that! Why don't you walk back to set? There are portables. I'll hold down the fort."

Andrea scrunched her nose. "Nah, that would take too long, and we've got to get lunch going." With a glance outside the front window, she noted the thick forest that lay behind. "I'm peeing in a bush."

Snorting, Brie shook her head and continued grating parmesan cheese.

Andrea traipsed through knee-high ferns and ivy beneath a canopy of evergreens speckled with fresh snow. As woodsy, sweet, and earthy notes filled her nostrils, she found a space to relieve herself. With a quick look both ways, she went about her business. Between the extra-large coffee she guzzled and nerves, a pee break was inevitable. She was cooking for fifty people. *FIFTY!*

Crunch-crunch.

She froze with her pants down. *Shit. Here I am squatting, and I'm about to get devoured by a bear!* She pulled her pants up, trying to stay low.

Foliage rustled.

She widened her eyes, and her heart pounded a million beats. If this was the universe telling her to pack her amateur cooking gear, food, and go, message received!

A white-and-brown muzzle poked through the foliage with a shiny, black nose.

She held her breath.

Swish-swish! Crunch-crunch.

The muzzle pushed through the dense green followed by dark-brown eyes with a fluff of inky lashes, soft, fuzzy ears and a short pair of light-brown antlers.

"A reindeer?" Andrea released a breath, backing up slowly, unsure if it was friendly or a foe. "Good reindeer..."

The reindeer pawed forward one step, then two.

With antlers, the animal was a few inches taller than her. Andrea's pulse skittered.

A foot from her, the reindeer flicked its nose in the air, then nuzzled her hand gently.

"Friendly, are you?" She rotated her hand, feeling the soft fur. Though incredible, when a few more reindeer walked into view with varied lengths of antlers, Andrea's heart palpated faster and faster. "Holy cow." With a nervous glance at the furry creatures, she backed away slowly, then jogged out of the woods, weaving between evergreens, and dashed toward catering. "Holy shit, Brie!" She gasped for breath at the entry. "There're reindeer up here!"

"What?" She paused with a wooden spoon in hand.

Andrea flicked her hands above her head. "Reindeer! I was sitting there doing my business and Comet appeared out of nowhere."

Brie's brows knitted. "Are you all right?"

"Yeah, thought I was bear chow. Great way to start catering." She strode past and scrubbed her hands in the sink, while she scoured her gaze over the counters. Ingredients rested on cutting boards, pots on burners, and a full catered lunch awaited her. Her heart hammered once again.

Setting the wooden spoon down, Brie wiped her palms on a towel. "I remember Rory telling the kids and me about the reindeer before, since we'll be visiting the Reindeer Center at Christmas. Reindeer used to be native to Scotland, you know, but they went extinct a number of centuries ago."

"Oh really? Thanks for letting me in on that little secret." She stripped off her jacket, yanked a drawer open, and snatched an apron.

"It's not a secret. What's wrong with you?"

Andrea unfolded an apron, noting the knot in the middle. "Ugh!" She tossed the apron on the counter. "I'm freaking out here."

"Why?"

She threw her hands up. "We have to have all this food ready for fifty people in three-ish hours. What the hell was I thinking? I'm not a professional caterer."

"You're not, but you're a damn good imposter." Brie grinned.

Andrea yanked her beret off and puffed a breath. "Thanks."

Reaching a hand out, Brie rested hers on Andrea's forearm. "They won't all show up at once. There's an hour window for lunch."

She blew a curl out of her left eye. "Yeah, I remember."

"Andrea"—Brie's voice softened—"you've been rolling meatballs since four a.m., prepared focaccia all afternoon yesterday, prepped tons of vegetables, and your hair is still curled perfectly. You've got this."

"You're right. My hair does look amazing." She lifted a hand to her curls.

Brie smacked her with a cooking mitten, hitting Andrea square in the chest. "Glad you finally agree."

"Hey! That's friend abuse." She grabbed the mitten and tossed it back.

Brie caught the mitten, then wrapped an arm around Andrea. "Seriously, you've got this. You cooked dinner for almost ten of us without batting a beautiful eye and then prepared close to forty guests' worth of meals for Phoebe's party. You can do this."

"You're right. That was fun."

"And this is, too. We're on another adventure in the beautiful highlands." Brie circled a hand toward the snow-capped Cairngorms beyond. "Cooking—you're favorite thing, and I'm right here beside you one hundred percent."

"You're right. I'm done freaking out. I can do this"

Brie gripped Andrea's shoulders. "You *can* do this."

"I can do this." Andrea grasped the red apron, untied the knot, then slid it over her head. "Once you're done sautéing the onions and garlic, add the stock and pre-packaged herb seasoning blend I made. There are three—one for each of the three batches."

"Got it."

She pushed her sleeves up. "Time to kick some catering ass."

Three hours later, Andrea busily ladled soup, served meatballs, and snugged focaccia into to-go containers for the set crew.

Brie relayed orders, popped on lids, and added cutlery and napkins to bags. "Hey, you," Brie greeted. "How's it going out there today?"

"Fine, though there's a nip in the air that says a storm's coming soon enough."

Andrea's ears pricked up. She knew that rumbling Scottish brogue.

"That's what I hear! We've got some good food to warm your stomach," Brie sang. "What can I get you?"

"Em, soup with meatballs, a side of meatball and sauce, and em...the rosemary bread."

"You got it." Brie scrolled the order, then pivoted and bumped firmly into Andrea.

"I've got it," Andrea told her. She smiled at Rory.

He nodded and pivoted toward a crew member.

A tinge of guilt pinched Andrea's chest. Hugh had that undeniable charm and sex factor, but there was something about Rory. She filled an extra-large soup cup, added a pile of mini meatballs, then selected a second container and set a giant meatball in the center, smothering it with marinara. Lastly, she added a large chunk of garlic-rosemary bread and looked out.

Rory stood with his back to her, speaking to a woman with a long, blonde braid.

Hopping down from the truck, she strode the few steps toward him. "Rory."

He turned. A flicker of surprise filled those steel-gray eyes below a charcoal beanie.

She handed him his order. "Stay warm out there, okay?"

With a nod, he grasped the bag, brushing her fingers.

A zip of something shot up her arm and twirled in her gut. "Thank ye." He turned.

With a purse of her lips, Andrea hiked back to the truck. Upon re-entering, she muttered, "Well, I guess I deserve that."

Brie pivoted. "What?"

"Rory hates me."

"He doesn't."

"Does, too." Andrea harrumphed and focused on not burning meatballs. But when she glanced outside once again, she found Rory staring right back. That little twirl in her belly spun like a spoon in a sauce pot.

Chapter Fifteen

"INVERNESS?" ANDREA TOWELED THE LAST SLOTTED spoon dry.

"I've wanted to visit since we vacationed in Scotland last spring"—Brie shook her hair loose and smiled—"so when in the highlands with a hunky husband and an offer from Mimi to watch the kids tonight, we seize date night."

"Hell, yeah." She tossed the spoon into the drawer. "I think I'll see about my own, too." When she caught a hint of smoke from the food truck's oven, she thought of Rory. Those eyes. Those broad shoulders. That scent. The...what was she thinking? She couldn't call Rory. He wasn't interested anymore...right? He seemed chummy enough with the blonde earlier. She twirled a finger in a curl and snagged it on a knot. Roughly extracting her forefinger, she huffed. But *Hugh*. The Herculean Highlander was single. So, was she. He didn't seem to want any kind of attachment. Well, perfect. Neither did she. *But what about the food truck*? She swiped her gaze over the now-sparkling, stainless steel interior. Where could she park it? The Murrays had entrusted her with their extra truck, and she couldn't just leave it anywhere. With a sigh, she snatched her phone. First things first.

ANDREA

How about dinner and a nightcap in
Inverness tonight?

The wind whipped up, shaking the truck and sprinkling tiny raindrops. Although the clouds parted earlier with a brief hint of golden sun, the clouds now fused with an ominous steel shade. She wanted nothing more than to be cozied up with a hot Scot. Andrea checked her phone once more, then, because she needed to do something with her damn hands, touched up her makeup and hair again in the mini-mirror, before topping her semi-flattened curls with the red beret.

A dark-tinted, black four-by-four crunched down the road and stopped in front of them.

The door opened.

Andrea's pulse pounded.

A black boot and jeaned leg stepped out, followed by a tall red-haired Scotsman.

She puffed an annoyed breath.

"If you're not the most beautiful sight I've seen all day." Bryce strode over with eyes only for Brie. He enveloped Brie in his arms and lifted her off her feet for an applause-worthy kiss. When he finally set Brie down, he tucked her close.

"Where's your kilt?" she asked.

He cocked his head. "Me kilt?"

"I thought you could leave it on for...later." She blushed.

Andrea snorted. "Right here."

"Don't ye worry. I have my own surprises." He pressed a kiss to her forehead and turned. "Are ye heading out, as well?"

Wind weaved and danced through the snowy pines and birches, making natural music and rising goose bumps on her arms. She tugged her jacket closer. "I'm waiting on Hugh. You know, see if he wants to show me the sights, as well."

Bryce shifted. "Em, are ye sure? Hugh left over an hour ago."

A pit formed in her stomach. "Oh, that's fine. He must've not gotten my texts."

"Aye, he might not have reception."

Brie leveled her green eyes at Andrea. "Do you want to join us for dinner?"

"Nope. I'll find my own fun. You two enjoy!" With farewells, Andrea swung behind the wheel of the truck and shook her head. "Idiot. You're an idiot." She'd allowed herself to listen to her mother's annoying chirp in her ear. *Land the highlander.* But she'd severely underestimated Hugh's interest. They'd had one amazing make-out session and then gone out what once, kind of? She blew out an annoyed breath. Luckily, she hadn't slept with him. Now, she could give him the stink eye, knowing she hadn't given him the satisfaction of seeing her naked.

On her return to Glasgow, Andrea sang to a pop song on the radio. She'd served food to Hollywood and Scottish A-listers and crew. They'd smiled and thanked her, and a few even returned for seconds and asked for her card. She couldn't have received a better compliment. She would put men out of her mind and enjoy the rest of her vacation. Who needed a man anyway?

Clu-clunk, clu-clunk. Clu-clunk, clu-clunk.

"What the?" Andrea muttered.

Clu-clunk, clu-clunk.

She rubbed the truck's dash. "You're okay. You're, oh... shit." As the speedometer tacked down, she gripped the steering wheel and veered the truck to the side of the road. The box rumbled for another few seconds and then coughed. A whirring sound followed, and the van stalled. "No. No, no, no.

Come on." She turned the key in the ignition, but the engine didn't catch. Not even a few lights glowed on the dash. She dropped her head onto the steering wheel.

BEEP!

"Shit!" Andrea lifted her head. "Damn horn. Stupid food truck. Ugh!"

A car whizzed past, shaking the truck. Andrea glared at the disappearing taillights. The wind ruffled tree tops outside her window, and sprinkles dotted her windshield. "Perfect. Just perfect." She waited a few more minutes and tried to start the truck once more. But nothing happened. "Shit." She dialed Brie. After four rings, her happy voicemail chirped. She texted.

ANDREA

Help! This fucking food truck broke down!

After waiting impatiently for ten minutes, she scrolled through her phone. A chill penetrated the cabin. She grabbed her scarf from the passenger side and wrapped the cashmere around her neck and head, then rubbed her hands together and popped her gloves back on. The sun had already dipped below the mountains, even though it was only mid-afternoon, and darkness closed around her with specks of white snow. *Thanks, Scotland.* She continued scrolling but couldn't find Bryce's contact. She rubbed a gloved hand over her forehead. "Why don't I have his number?" She decided on a Hail Mary and called Hugh. The call went straight to voicemail. She smashed the end button before his annoying voicemail finished. Only one other Scottish number remained. Andrea sucked up her pride and dialed.

Chapter Sixteen

RORY MANEUVERED HIS TRUCK, DESCENDING DOWN the mountain pass between thick evergreens dusted with snow, while he kept a firm eye on the road for a food truck with a massive tomato. Andrea called near forty minutes prior, and with the turn in weather, loss of daylight, and drop in temperatures, he needed to find her quickly. Rounding a bend, he spied the white-and-black truck off to the side of the road, wheels already covered in a few inches of snow and pulled to a stop. Relief flooded him when he saw a hand wave behind the snowy windshield. The woman was nothing like he'd ever experienced. Vivacious one moment and expressing interest, then slamming the brakes the next. She was unattainable and damn irritating. But here he was responding to her call. He couldnae allow harm to come to her, even if he was sore. Swinging out of the cab, he trudged toward the truck, crunching in the snow-laden dirt. And then, he saw her. His lips twitched, and he stifled a laugh. Andrea sat in the cab with a scarf wrapped around her neck, ears, and tied above her head like a Christmas gift.

She flung open the door. "I thought I was going to be a

femsicle!" Her nose and cheeks were red with cold, but her eyes were bright and shiny.

He tilted his head.

"A female popsicle. I'm too young to be a frozen femsicle!" She yelled, and then her eyes widened, and she lifted a hand above her head. "Shit."

Rory cleared his throat. "Are ye all right?"

"Yes." She huffed as she untied the scarf and wrapped the material a few more times around her neck. "Thanks for coming." Snow began cascading in thicker flecks like little bits of torment, and she scrunched her face.

They stood awkwardly for a minute. Not a single car drove past.

Andrea jabbed a thumb toward the truck. "Well, it coughed and hacked, then passed out."

He lifted a brow. "May I?"

Stepping aside, she swiped a hand. "Go for it."

Rory climbed inside, fitting his large frame into the seat. His knees pressed into the steering wheel, and his arms rounded until he reached under to adjust the seat. With the door open, he turned the key. Nothing happened. No lights. No noise. Not a bloody damn thing. He tried once more, and when not a flicker of sound emerged from the truck, he glanced at her. "It might be the battery. I'm not sure a jump will get ye all the way back to Glasgow safely, though."

"Shit!" She kicked the snow-laden dirt.

Rory swung out of the cab and ambled toward his truck, while Andrea followed, teeth chattering. He had a plan. Propping the door open, he removed his navy-and-slate-gray flannel and extended the jacket to Andrea.

With a tilt of her head, she lifted a coffee-toned brow.

"Take it. Yer shivering."

She swiftly nodded and lifted an arm as he helped her into the heavy jacket. She closed her eyes and inhaled.

With a grin, he tugged on a waterproof jacket, then retrieved his phone. After dialing the local towing and recovery in Glasgow, he relayed the condition of the truck and their whereabouts to Rupert. "Aye, put it on my tab."

Rupert verified the information.

"What's he saying?" Andrea whispered, brushing against him. "His accent is so thick; I can't understand anything!"

Rory slid his gaze toward her, then returned his focus to the phone and a spot in the distance. Andrea's scent—something warm and spicy with a hint of metal from his own jacket—was intoxicating. Even though he knew she was covered with layer upon layer, his mind strayed to the ample curves that lay underneath. Rupert's thick voice drew him back into focus. He cleared his throat. "Under the bonnet. Appreciate it." Ending the call, he angled toward Andrea. "The tow will be here in a couple of hours."

"A couple of hours!" she shrieked. "I'll freeze to death! What am I supposed to do now?"

"Ye can wait here, or you can ride with me. I can drop ye by the Frasers after I switch vehicles at me shop."

Andrea blew a bouncy curl off her forehead. "I don't think I have much choice."

He nodded, watching her.

"Is it safe to leave the vehicle?" She swiveled toward the borrowed truck now covered with a dusting of snow. "I purchased the vehicle insurance, but I'm not sure that covers a curious thief who could break in and steal the contents. And I *really* like the Murrays."

"Should be." He walked toward the food truck, then opened the door once again. He retrieved her purse and charger before handing the items over. "Do ye have everything ye need?"

As she slipped the purse strap over her shoulder and shoved the charger into the center pocket, she glanced at the truck. "I need to get a few things." She clomped toward the back door, swung it open, and squeezed through sideways with the load of jackets on her.

Rory tucked his hands in the front pockets of his jeans, wondering what he'd gotten himself into. Although annoyance flashed through him when he saw her name burst across his phone, he couldnae just ignore her. He could be gruff and quiet, but he wasn't an arse who'd leave a woman in peril, especially one that drove him mad—body and mind. Plus, he imagined leaving behind what she'd worked so hard to achieve a few hours ago would be just as difficult as watching his own thieved work vanish before his very eyes.

A moment later, Andrea hopped down and waved two large-stemmed, heavy-duty, wooden spoons. "You can never have too many of these bad boys."

He snorted. "Spoons? That's what yer after?"

Andrea flicked her head, sending curls flying and smiled. "That's right."

Her smile speared him in the gut, and he found himself grinning in turn. He was every bit in trouble of allowing this woman to push her way back into his good spirits.

Chapter Seventeen

AFTER LOCKING THE TRUCK AND STOWING THE KEYS under some part of the engine, Andrea climbed into Rory's truck and was now on her way back to Glasgow. The truck was meticulously clean, save for a large canteen in the center and a thick, bound map on the dash that crinkled at the page ends. She peeked at Rory from the corner of her eyes. Although she'd seen a crack in his stony exterior previously, she was back to hanging with the quiet man.

He drove, focused on the road ahead.

The silence was partly her fault. She stopped whatever had kindled between the two of them. But she couldn't deny that Rory and his scent—one of burnt metal and woody resin mingled with pine—affected her. The scent was one of strength and confidence and a man connected to his environment and trade. He smelled good. *Too* good. He'd even caught her inhaling after she put on his cozy, warm coat. *Damn.* She fished for something to say. "I didn't know you drove one of these."

He checked his mirrors. "Only when I need to bring me swords."

"Oh, really? Do you travel a lot?"

"No."

Andrea rolled her eyes and gazed out the window at the towering mountains whose tips were encased in a mound of cream. Now that she was safely out of danger, she found the picturesque landscape beautiful. She'd forgotten how calming this country could be.

They rode in silence for a solid fifteen minutes. Well, silence save for the *squeak* of the old box truck and *clink-clang* of whatever he stored in the back. If she didn't know he was a swordsmith, she'd think he was an ax murderer. All those sharp, mysterious sounds coming from the truck and an unmarked, white van screamed horror movie. When a *squeak* indicated Rory shifted beside her, Andrea glanced over.

He stared at the road ahead, dark, ruddy lashes framing those intense, gray eyes.

Rory had rescued her. She called, and he came. They weren't best friends, they weren't lovers, or family, but he came. His actions said something about the man beside her. And she had one item left to settle.

He continued staring straight ahead.

She chewed her cheek. She could cut the tension with a damn butcher's knife. And she knew it was her fault. The unsaid was stuck between them like a wedgie. She just had to pick it. But did she want to? She gazed at Rory's profile, noting the long nose, swell of cheek, and full, tidy beard out of the corner of her eye. "How long have you had the beard?"

He downshifted when they began to descend. "Near three years."

"I always wonder what guys are hiding under them."

Turning his head briefly, he cocked an eyebrow, while a grin teased at his lips. "'Tis not a kilt."

The crack in his exterior spurred her on. "I know, but is it hiding a butt chin, a tough come-punch-me-chin, a weak or square jaw, tiny lips, or no neck? There's so much mystery in a beard."

His lips twitched. "Sounds like ye've put a great deal of thought into it."

"I have, though I've never dated anyone with a beard." Andrea caught her lower lip between her teeth. *Shit*. She changed the subject. "So, would you ever shave it?"

"No."

"Why?"

"Because I like it."

She considered. "It suits you, but I'm still wondering."

He slid her a glance across the seat.

"And, I owe you an apology."

Rory's brows jammed together, and he turned his attention to the road. "Don't worry about it."

"No." She reached out and touched his thick thigh with her fingertips.

Angling his head, he glanced where her hand rested, then captured her gaze.

"You were sweet, and I was, well let's just say I haven't been myself, okay?"

He nodded.

God. She wished he'd say something. Maybe she should stop feeling bad. Apparently, he hadn't lost sleep over it.

He pulled to a stop behind a blue car with stickers across the bumper and turned with focused steel eyes. "I can take a hint, though I was taken aback when ye called."

"Yeah, um, thank you again. I couldn't get ahold of Brie and H"—Andrea bit her lip, catching herself—"Anyway, thank you. I really appreciate it." She shifted, glancing out the window and away from his penetrating gaze. If she wasn't interested, why were little zips buzzing around her stomach?

Chapter Eighteen

RORY PULLED TO A STOP OUTSIDE A BLACK, IRON gate with wooden accents and a beautiful cross-hatch pattern flanked by grassland now covered with a speckling of snow and a perimeter of trees on either side. Rory hauled himself out of the cab and hiked up to the gate.

A clinking sound carried toward Andrea as he opened the gate wide. From the passenger seat, she glimpsed a white farmhouse with stone detail near fifty feet ahead, while a large, steel-gray garage was set off near a cluster of trees with rolling hills in the distance. His home reminded her of a fortress—the surrounding fields, lines of evergreen, and remoteness of its location—keeping the world at bay. Much like the man who owned it.

When Rory re-entered the truck, he slid the gearshift into drive and continued up the dirt road.

A sliver of light cut through the gray veil of clouds, and a line of cerulean blue was visible. *A lake?*

When he pulled to a stop in front of the house, he turned briefly. "I need to unload a few things before heading to the Frasers."

"Sure." She squirmed in her seat. "Can I use your restroom?" He eyed her in that pensive, assessing way of his for a moment.

"I'll unlock the house." He swung open the cab door.

A brisk swoosh of cool, damp air flooded the toasty warm cabin and whipped her hair in a zillion directions. Now, she really had to pee.

A fluff of golden-yellow flew by the front of the truck and placed large paws on Rory.

"Evenin' to ye, Maggie." He rubbed her head, then hunkered down and scrubbed a hand from head to toe, talking to her in his deep brogue until she rolled over onto her back.

Hell, I need some of that.

When Rory rose, he angled toward the house.

Maggie jumped up, tail wagging, wiggled her way to Andrea, and pushed her nose against her palm.

"Hello to you, too!" She petted her soft head, while her lips curled. She always wanted a dog, but Gloria wasn't fond of animals. Glancing up, she noted Rory strode down the gravel path.

With a *woof*, Maggie gave Andrea a quick lick, then trotted after him.

While her boots crunched in the rocky pebbles, she noted the sturdy, well-crafted, low fence that hugged the yard and garden inset. A few friendly pink-and-white flowers peeked out beside...wait, what? She stopped, peering closer over the edge of the fence where stringy, bottle-green tops of carrots and wide-leafed something with tiny white clumps of flowers grew. She didn't think bird crap did that. Apparently, he was the kind of man who grew flowers and vegetables and also happened to chisel swords out of rock-hard steel. *Interesting.* The jingle of Rory's key had her glancing up and wondering what other little surprises she'd discover about the quiet man.

When he swung the front door open, he pivoted and

scanned the interior of his home. "The toilet is down the hall to the right."

"Thanks."

Yet, Rory didn't move. He settled that hard gaze on Andrea for a moment, then flipped his collar to shield against the chill and ducked back into the night with Maggie on his heels.

Sighing, she stepped into Rory's home. Creamy walls accented by dark, wooden shelves and furniture greeted her, while gray stone accented the fireplace. A Christmas tree stood in the corner, perfuming the air with subtle notes of pine. The evergreen was bare; yet, fresh and vibrantly green with the base tucked into a sack and container, as if he'd dug it himself. A few portraits of mountains and swords decorated the walls, while select picture frames graced a wooden mantle. She stepped closer, eyeing pictures—Bryce and Rory holding fish on lines with broad smiles, pictures of Rory with the cast and crew of *Swords*, and a family photo tucked behind. She glanced around, and when she didn't see Rory, she lifted the family photo. Rory stood beside a more stout, older man she considered to be his dad and another man with a light beard, but with younger eyes. Two women with lighter shades of red and blonde hair squeezed beside him and a full-figured woman who was the shortest of the bunch.

When coarse sounds from outside met her ears, she put the picture back and moseyed to the bathroom. She used the restroom, combed her hair, and added a smear of lipstick. No need to look like a ruffian. After tidying up, she plopped onto the couch and checked social media. Comments, shares, and retweets numbered in the thousands, and her mouth flopped open. "Holy shit." She perused food pictures she'd snapped and others cast and crew had posted and tagged her in. Much to her surprise, one included Bryce taking a bite out of a giant meatball. She smiled. Brie had snapped up a good one.

Excited fans commented left and right, asking what it was like to meet Bryce Fraser, while others asked for teasers.

Andrea snorted. "In your dreams." What she hadn't expected were asks about her website and a link to her catering page. She was speechless and that rarely happened. But what had she expected? She'd anticipated she'd gain something... some confirmation or validation that her cooking was more than a side hobby, hadn't she? That she wasn't a complete mess of a person at thirty. And people wanted to know where they could eat her food. "Hot damn," she uttered. But she hadn't planned anything past today. How could she when her brother-in-law asked her to cater a special episode a few days prior? She only had time to focus on the catering event, not the big picture.

In her previous career, she looked at the whole picture—at her entire organization's hiring strategy, business planning, and more. But now, she could have a future with food, and she salivated at the thought. She'd enjoyed the fast pace, the tight, warm quarters, working to produce great tasting food, and warming bellies. And she loved working with Brie. Of course, she couldn't be a regular assistant; Andrea would have to hire someone, but she loved the teamwork. She'd have to do some thinking.

Still, a bitchy, nagging voice lingered with second-guesses. Could she really succeed at a catering career? She didn't have any credentials or formal training, save for a few package classes she purchased for a steal here and there. The L.A. food scene was cutthroat. And what about her house? Exhaling, she continued scrolling, but she paused when she noticed a picture from the Brycers Fan Club of a man with long hair kissing a woman in a bar. She swiped to the next picture, and her heart sunk at the shit-eating-grin of Hugh Macrae. They weren't dating; yet, he could've at least had the courtesy to tell her he wasn't interested. She puffed an annoyed breath. "No 'sorry,

I'm just not into you,' or 'let's be friends.' No, they just ghost you." She threw her phone across the couch. The device landed with a *thud* on the opposite end as she let her head fall back into the buttery leather cushion.

Scrape, scratch, scrape! Maggie swung around a corner and trotted over, planting herself firmly against her legs.

"Hey, girl." Andrea rubbed her head and smoothed her soft ears, then trailed a hand down Maggie's golden coat, feeling the tension ease.

Bang-boom!

Bounding up, Maggie straightened and, with a bark, tore toward the front door.

Andrea glanced outside. "Great, you better not be stuck under something heavy." She marched out the door and toward the box truck. The black metal door was rolled up. Yet, no Rory. She swiveled and searched for the quiet man. Fifty or so feet away, the large garage doors were open wide, beckoning her. She trudged through pebbles and snow, then flew her gaze around the space, large presses, huge machines, things Andrea had no idea what in the heck they were, and a wall of weapons —broadswords, axes, and more. Still, peering around and up the lofty ceilings to the concrete floor, she didn't see him. *Shit. Oh, shit. Please don't be dead. You might be quiet, but don't be that damn quiet!* She bent low, looking for icky signs of blood, but the floor was swept clean and the garage quiet.

Clang! A door banged open from the rear.

Rory ambled in with a large, rectangular box propped on one of his mighty shoulders.

"Jesus." She pressed a hand to her chest. "I thought something happened to you."

"Delivery," he replied simply, muscles bunching.

Andrea's mouth watered. How could a man holding a box look so sexy? Seeing him cock a brow, she quickly pivoted and scanned the area. "So, this is your shop?"

"Aye. I built it a few years ago."

"You built...this?"

"With help from a local contractor."

"Impressive." She didn't know any men who used their hands. She worked with white-collared, smooth-handed-and-talking men with agendas always on their minds. But Rory was neither of those. He set the box down, giving her an ample view of his beefy butt and then methodically put away tools. Flying her gaze around, she spied a drawing on the wall and strolled over to get a closer look. Strong pencil strokes on graph paper brought fierce swords, delicate handle detail, and designs to life. *Interesting*. She rotated.

With a grunt, Rory hauled a large press up from the box. His muscular forearms wrapped around it with his thick middle holding tight.

He looked like one of those strong men she'd seen Bryce watching on television who lifted big-ass rocks of all things. Apparently, lifting rocks was a tradition in Scotland. She could just imagine men sitting around in the old days, elbowing one another with coaxing grins and a deep brogue, 'I bet I could pick up that rock.' *Such a man thing.* But glancing back at Rory, she admired the bulging muscles, thick chest, broad back, and thighs like frickin' Christmas hams, and pictured him lifting one with ease. The thought stirred something within...perhaps there was something to this rock lifting, after all.

Rory twisted.

Those intense, gray eyes focused on her like a steel vise. She smiled brightly. "I bet you don't even need to go to the gym with all this heavy lifting, huh?"

A grin tugged at his beard. "I've no' stepped into a gym in some time." He set the box down.

God, his single sentence answers were obnoxious.

"Are ye hungry?"

Her head whipped up. "I can eat. Just point me to the stove and I can—"

He shook his head. "No. 'Tis me home. I'll put something together for the two of us."

With a mumble of "thanks," Andrea followed him to the house. A moment later, she heard the *squeak* of a cabinet, followed by a *clank* of a board, and something unwrapping from the small adjoining kitchen. She tugged her boots off and propped her wool-socked feet atop the dark-stained coffee table with metal accents. But just as she was getting comfortable, something gleamed from the corner of the living room: an ornate sword with a meticulously-carved handle and long silver knife beside a few other pieces.

She rose and peered closer. The handle was smooth and glossy like mahogany, while the sterling silver at the top was inlaid with another material. In the center of the handle, a crest of five arrows in red and gold, and along the blade, an inscription in old-fashioned lettering, showing detail, skill, and precision all wrapped into a lethal, exquisite sword. But the man who crafted the weapon was so unassuming. She glanced at his wide, broad back as he hunkered over a small, wooden cutting board, peeling potatoes. "Yours, I assume?"

Lifting his head, he met her gaze. "Aye." He set down the peeler and ambled around the tidy kitchen. "The other two are from the eighteenth century. I collect a few, as well."

"Really?" She leaned in, admiring the craftsmanship. She'd seen his moving van and witnessed him sharpening a blade or two on set, but she hadn't realized what a craftsman Rory was. "You'd never know yours is a reproduction. It's really well done." When she shifted to touch the knife, she realized Rory stood less than an arm's length from her. Awareness hummed through her body.

"Thank ye."

She peered closer. "What does the inscription mean?"

"*Aonaibh Ri Chéile*," he said in Gaelic. "Let us unite. The Cameron motto."

"You're an artist."

The corners of his lips twitched into a slow smile. "Like ye with food."

She waved away his compliment. "I'm just a cook."

With a shake of his head, he stepped a rough boot forward, gray eyes skimming her face.

Her pulse quickened.

"When ye put yer heart and soul into something, it shows. And that's what you've done with yer cooking. I've been fortunate to eat a few of yer meals, and now, so has the cast and crew of *Swords*. 'Tis something to be proud of."

"Thank you. It was an experience, let me tell you." She turned to focus on the sword display on the wall, rather than the hammering within. "Can I hold one?"

With one hand, he lifted the huge sword by the beautifully detailed handle and extended it, handle out. "Have at it, lass."

She grasped the handle above his hand, gripping the soft leather. The sword was larger than she thought, and she narrowly wrapped her hands around it.

"Careful, now." Rory glided his hand down the knife blade.

As the full weight of the sword swelled between her hands, she felt her arm strength wither like she held an anvil. The sword's tip immediately pitched toward the ground. She grasped the handle tighter, putting her weight into preventing the sword from crashing embarrassingly. "Wow, this is as heavy as it looks."

"Aye, 'tis."

"I imagine this is a warrior's sword?" She eyed the hefty sword. "A man's, right?"

He nodded.

She huffed a breath. "A woman could've easily handled

this sword as well as any man with some training." She lifted the sword with a grunt until she pointed the weapon at a seventy-five-degree angle toward Rory in challenge.

Lifting a large hand, he tipped the sword down by the width of the blade. "'Tis possible, but not likely. If ye were a lass in the eighteenth century, ye'd have a *sgian-dubh* tucked under yer stocking for protection." He gestured toward the smaller knife on the wall.

Andrea gazed at the miniature, sharp blade, while trying to hold onto the damned heavy beast in her hand. Hugh held a similar sword in *Swords* and that boiled her blood. She whipped her gaze at Rory. "It looks lethal enough, but why did they always give women the small blades? Oh, right, chauvinism in the eighteenth century, of course."

He studied her, gray eyes darkening in the shadows of the night. He moved in slow, gaze set on hers until she bumped into the wall. Rory's large hand encircled the sword handle, rough fingers brushing over hers and forearm grazing her breast as he dislodged the sword from her grasp.

"Oh." She laughed and smiled. But Rory wasn't smiling, and he had an edge of danger as he easily hung the sword and moved closer, never taking his gaze off her until he pressed firmly against her torso to torso, hip to hip. He set one hand on the wall opposite her hip and the other beside her head, trapping her. Heat radiated off him and that sharp metal and woodsy scent of his snuck up her nostrils. She licked her lips and stared at his full ones.

"When yer this close, it doesna matter how big yer sword is."

Andrea's mouth watered, and every part of her fired, including the part pressed against his bulge. This close, she was thinking about another sword entirely.

He stepped back. "Tea?"

Andrea expelled a breath and pressed a hand to the wall.

She would not swoon, but hot damn. She'd underestimated him. The quiet man was Mr. Sexy. Her underwear held the proof.

* * *

"So, how'd you get into the swords and stuff?" Andrea sliced off a chunk of sausage. She sat across from him in a solid, brown dining chair with a loaf of artisan bread centered between them, cut in thick slices, and the glow of the dining and living room lights around them.

"My *da* was a blacksmith, retired now. I grew up working in the forge with him and my younger brother pounding horseshoes, fashioning gates, etc." His knife paused on the plate. "My younger brother runs the forge outside Inverness now."

"Oh, you have a brother?"

He nodded. "Younger by a few years. I have two sisters, as well."

"Are they into"—she gestured with her fork—"smith and art, too?"

"Caitlyn's still in college. Luna's a dreamer with her head in the clouds. She'd rather be out wandering in nature studying the flora and fauna than behind a fiery forge."

With a tip of her head, she fanned her fork through the air. "So, she's an environmentalist?"

"Botanist turned highland ranger."

Stunned, she stilled her fork. "A ranger? Like a park ranger?"

"Yes."

"Hmm" was all Andrea could utter. She wondered if his sisters had Rory's steel-gray eyes or something different? When the thought came, she brushed it off. She wasn't looking for anything serious and that included meeting Rory's family. She shifted her attention to him, instead. "And what about you?

Have you ever thought about bringing your swords and skills to Hollywood?"

He settled back and crossed his arms. "I've been to Los Angeles, but my place is here."

"Really? I mean it's beautiful, but don't you want to see other places?"

"Ye can travel all around the world, but nothing calls ye back like yer home. Scotland calls me like the ancient traditions of swordsmith and the whispering wind, telling stories of clans through the mountains and glens."

As tingles tangled in her stomach, Andrea licked her lips. *Were all Scotsmen poets?* "But what happens when *Swords* ends?'

"I imagine there'll be another show. *Swords* has brought more television and film traffic to Scotland, and tradesman like myself are grateful. But I also have my own side business."

She lifted a brow. "Really?"

"Aye, I sell my swords and other pieces around the world. Some to collectors, others to fans, re-enactors, and museums."

"People actually buy these?" She glanced at the wall of swords. "They are pretty cool."

He nodded again. "Aye, many. I've a slew of orders, including custom orders, to get through before Christmas."

"That's great. I guess I could imagine your sword," she began, then caught herself.

His eyes shone like freshly polished silver. "And ye? Will ye be catering more in the future?"

Remembering the complimentary staff and crew, Andrea grinned. "I hope so. I thought Bryce was out of his mind when he asked me to cater, but it was incredible. Unbelievable. Blew my expectations out of the water and made me feel proud of myself for the first time in a long time."

Nodding, he grasped his beer. "'Twas an opportunity for ye to start something new. Possibly a blossoming career?"

"I don't know. Catering one event doesn't necessarily mean...but I"—her mind started spinning with images of food, while delicious smells invaded her memories. Could she? Shaking her head, she pivoted. "Speaking of food, was that a vegetable garden out front?"

He ran a hand over his beard. "Aye."

"A swordsmith who grows his own vegetables."

The corner of his right lip tipped up.

The Swords of Scotland theme song began playing from her phone with long notes of the aching ballad.

Rory quirked a brow. "Is that...?"

She pushed away from the table. "It's my phone. Brie's calling." She excused herself and walked to the hearth.

"I'm so sorry I missed your calls! My phone died," Brie said. "I plugged it back into the car once I noticed. Are you okay? Where are you?"

"I'm okay." She glanced at Rory, who watched her quietly. "I'm with Rory."

"Rory? What? How?"

"He picked me up when the truck broke down."

"Oh, thank goodness!" She heaved a breath. "Something could've happened!"

While listening to Brie, Andrea peered at Rory. He continued watching her in an unnerving, focused manner that made her stomach flutter.

"We can leave right now," Brie said.

She pivoted toward the wall of swords, shaking her head. "What? No."

"Bryce is beside himself that we weren't there to help you. I am, too."

"Don't you dare! I'm good."

"Are you sure?"

"Positive. Go have fun with Bryce!"

An exhale carried through the phone. "Okay, see you tomorrow."

When she disconnected, Andrea remembered she needed to let Sarah know the tow truck would be bringing their food truck back to their yard. She sent a quick text of apology and then thanks. Turning, she heard the distinct chime of an email notification. Tapping into the app, she stilled her hand.

Andrea,
Hope Scotland's treating you well. While you were able to secure additional income, unfortunately, the income as you noted is not for consistent employment. Your income is no longer sufficient to meet the lender's mortgage requirements. The bank has denied your application. Call me after the New Year. We'll discuss reapplying for a smaller loan after you've secured your new job.
Dan

In an instant, her foodie high was squashed like a busted mashed potato tower, running gooey gravy over her dreams. She was homeless. She'd have to call her landlord and beg for an extension on her lease.

Bling!

HUGH

Hey

She saw red. He might be a beloved actor, but not by her. She trudged to the table.

"Everything all right?" Rory asked.

"Just dandy."

He nodded; yet, he didn't prod further. Instead, he ate quietly beside her, glancing up every so often with a questioning look in those gray eyes.

She hated being the recipient of pity like the looks staff gave her when she was young and asked where her mother was as party preparations were under way or during galas when Andrea would retreat to the kitchen to play tic-tac-toe on the chalkboard with the cook and then, watch them create meals, while warmth filled the kitchen and fire flamed on burners. Gloria only wanted what was shiny. But Rory had a way of looking deeper. She couldn't stand his assessing gaze.

* * *

Something was amiss. Andrea had gone from talking comfortably to brooding. She gripped the sponge like a vice and washed dishes with vigor, her gaze fixed on the wall behind the high-back sink, while Rory dried. She didn't say another word, nor did he, but they washed dishes amiably in silence. There's something to be said about working alongside someone. No words were needed, just the task at hand. When his fingers grazed hers as he lifted a plate, he glanced over, meeting those big, bonnie brown eyes. Light from above fired her dark eyes with sparks of red like scorched metal.

Setting the plate in the rack, she shifted so that her curves brushed his, and her hand slid over his arm.

His blood roused under her touch and body fired with awareness. "Andrea..."

"Yes?" She traced a finger up his arm and swirled his bicep. While her gaze stayed on his, she placed her mouth firmly against his.

The spark that he'd tempered, ignited. A groan escaped his lips. Feeling her tongue dance seductively with his, he was ablaze. Hell, he couldn't think. He tasted her—hints of spice along with Andrea's own rich flavor. He told himself to take things slow, but this woman gripped him like a raging fire, and he was aflame, burning with her.

When she eased back a moment later, arms still encircling his neck, she glanced up with swollen lips and heaving bosom. "Do you want me?"

Need tangled and balled in his gut. "Aye, I do."

"Then take me."

Yet, those eyes that held desire also pinched with sorrow. With regret, he eased back and lifted a hand to hers knotted at his neck. "Not like this."

Andrea threw her arms up and pushed at his chest. "Then take me home."

He was so surprised, he almost stumbled. Of course, he was a man and had needs, but under that layer of anger, Rory saw the light sheen over those molten, dark eyes. "Andrea." He placed an arm on either side of her, trapping her between him and the sink.

She whipped her head up. "What?"

"I'm no' sure what happened in the last twenty minutes, but I can wager something's wrong. What is it?"

She glanced away, eyes glossing further. "Nothing."

"I'd be a fool not to want ye, but not like this."

"Why?"

"You're upset."

She lifted her chin, challenging him. "I am not."

Rory clasped her chin gently between his fingers. "Ye are, and if and when I've a mind to take ye to bed, I want to do it right." A tremble passed through her, and he noted the gloss over her brown eyes.

A second later, she flicked her head out of his hands and pressed her lips together. "Whatever. You're just someone who doesn't want a quick fuck." She pushed his chest once, twice, but he didn't budge. "What the hell's wrong with you? Let me go!"

His body tensed.

"Let me go!"

Lifting his hands, Rory stepped back.

Andrea stomped past and tore through the house, gathering her things.

With a whine, Maggie pranced around with the sudden clamor.

Rory swore under his breath. He'd felt the air shift between them a few hours prior, and he'd learned who Andrea really was—strong, caring, and talented—similar to when he'd strolled into the kitchen the first time he'd seen her cooking. Then, something happened. He wasn't sure what the catalyst was, but apparently, something disturbed her, and he couldn't help. Not the way he wanted to. He imagined it had something to do with the event—though to him, catering had gone smoothly based on comments and observations from cast and crew.

She reminded him of himself a handful of years back when he stood on the precipice of change, knowing he was good as a smith, but being drawn to the art of swords. Temper followed him until he seized his desire. But he couldn't help her. All she wanted was a one-night-stand. And he wanted a relationship. He didn't see a way forward. He strode through the kitchen, grasped a jacket, and seized the truck keys. They rode to the Frasers in silence with the darkness of the night filling the cab of his truck and not a star visible above the gray-black cloak.

Chapter Nineteen

THE HAZE WAS THICK LIKE COBWEBS WHEN ANDREA rolled over the following morning. She pressed the heel of a hand to her forehead, which blistered from the red wine she'd finished off last night. She should be celebrating. She'd successfully catered an event for over fifty people with prospects of a career, if she had the guts to do it. But then the bank and Hugh went and put a major damper on her spirits, and her temper got the better of her. *Ugh, then there was Rory.* She exhaled loudly. The quiet man had come to her rescue, and she took her frustration out on him when all he'd ever been was kind.

But that was her problem, wasn't it? She never dated the nice guy. She went for the unavailable guy or the outrageously attractive hunk like Hugh who only cared about himself, so she wouldn't get attached. *Just fun.* That's what she'd always said. And she'd tried to put Hugh behind her and get under Rory, but that went about as good as hell in a handbasket. If they'd had sex, things would've been fine. She'd get that itch scratched and be done with men for a while. But then Rory looked at her with those steel eyes laced with concern, demolishing her last barriers. Why the hell did he have to look at her like that? His sympathy twisted inside her. She needed a lover, not a concerned friend.

When her phone buzzed annoyingly like a whole frickin' hive was swarming, she groaned. Andrea pressed the device to her ear. "Hello?"

"Andrea? Are you still in bed at this hour?" Gloria's voice echoed in her ear.

Shit.

"Yeah, sleeping in. I'm on vacation, you know."

"Hmm."

Andrea rolled her eyes as Gloria didn't utter another word, allowing her annoying as hell judgey, non-word answer to linger.

Gloria cleared her throat. "I saw some pictures you posted on social media. What are you doing serving people? Just because that company didn't recognize how valuable you are doesn't mean you join the help. If you need money, ask. And go back to L.A. already. I'm sure your father could pull a few strings. He always had that talent and has plenty of connections still."

Pursing her lips, Andrea flicked a piece of lint off her pajamas. "I don't need money or Dad. And I didn't join the goddamn help, Mother. I catered an event. People loved my food. And those pictures? Those pictures were from the set of *Swords of Scotland*, a television show with a global audience."

"I'm aware of the show. Your best friend has to rub it in that she landed the lead actor. Well, she found herself her own little fairytale, didn't she? But she got something right—marry well, and you don't have to worry about anything anymore."

"Brie's—" Andrea began, but stopped. She didn't need to tell Gloria that Brie earned her own money and just sold her first book—a memoir—to a big five publisher.

"I know she's your best friend, but really, she needs to

introduce you to some of Bryce's people. Make some connections."

"She has," Andrea replied between gritted teeth. "Bryce's co-stars have even dined with us at the house and enjoyed my cooking."

"Well, that's wonderful. Just don't convince yourself you're a Michelin star chef. People are happy to tell you they like something when it's free."

Andrea bristled. She felt like she'd been slapped. "Seriously? Can't you be happy for me? I succeeded at something I like. Something I wasn't even sure I could pull off, but I did. Sure, it was a one-time thing, but I—"

"No need to get upset," Gloria interrupted. "Enjoy your time in the kitchen. Just don't forget what you should be doing. And, sweetheart, it's past ten there. Get dressed and put your face on."

"Ugh!" Andrea smashed her phone into the pillow and roared. Fucking fantastic. She needed to screen her phone calls. Pushing herself out of bed, she grabbed a few aspirins and downed a glass of water. But a nagging little gnat whirred in her mind. She'd successfully catered a small, one-day shoot, but what made her good enough to cater full-time? To begin a new career? She wrenched the mini-fridge open. A single piece of pizza and yogurt stared back. She could go to the main house, but she didn't think her already jack-hammering brain could withstand the squeals of her niece and nephew right now. She seized the cold pizza and devoured it on the way back to bed. Yet, the salty bite didn't calm the gnat circling her head mercilessly. She snatched her phone and searched, *how to start a restaurant business*. Way too many articles popped up, so she took her time perusing. She would need time, money, and skill. Then she searched, *L.A. Food Trucks*. Zillions of pictures of food trucks flooded the screen. What could she offer L.A. that they hadn't tasted?

But then a thought popped into her mind. A crazy thought. *What about Scotland?* She searched, *how to start a food business in Scotland.* Multiple links and sites popped up, including *Starting a New Food Business.* She clicked the link with her fingertip and scrolled. "Start a new business from home," she read and then huffed. "Well, I don't have a home." She was like a ship caught between two shores with no final destination. She grumbled and kept reading.

"Registering is free and easy," she read aloud. But she needed a Scottish address. Glancing out the window at the green surrounding Brie and Bryce's beautiful home and the towering buildings in the distance, she wondered if she could live in the guest house until she figured things out. Brie did say she could stay and even told her to come early... but that didn't mean she could stay forever. Plus, what was she—a loafer at thirty? *Great, Andrea. Just great.* She couldn't mooch off Brie's kindness. She wouldn't do it. So, she'd have to dip into her savings and possibly cash out a bit of her 401K for a deposit on an apartment. *Er, flat.* That sounded so much more sophisticated than the American version. She could apply for a work visa, but...she needed a job first. She threw her hands in the air. What the hell was she thinking? Perhaps Gloria was right. She flipped her phone over and settled back into her pillow. Cooking for the stars and for Brie and family was incredible, but running a successful food business seemed as elusive as catching a shooting star.

Boom-boom and *boom-boom.*

She glanced through the sheer curtain eager to talk to Brie.

Mimi opened the blue SUV driver's door, readying to take the kids on an adventure.

Brie is still in Inverness having a romantic overnight getaway with her husband, and I'm sulking in my bed. Alone. Andrea pulled the covers over her head.

* * *

As the sun sank beneath the tree line, Andrea heard a car pull in the driveway.

Bryce's familiar SUV circled and parked.

After a pause, Bryce strode around the car, opened the door, then yanked Brie into his arms, pressing a firm kiss to her lips. When he stepped back, he gave Brie a look that told Andrea he'd be back for more as soon as possible.

Andrea's chest twinged. *Shit*. She needed some of that. Seeing Bryce drive away, Andrea quickly tugged on a coat and boots. She flew outside, catching Brie glide toward the house. "You're back!"

Pivoting, Brie set down her bag and threw her arms around Andrea. "Hey! How are you?"

She muffled a response between the hug.

When Brie stepped back, she smiled. "I talked to Mimi on the way back. They're at the zoo."

"Great." Andrea tried to keep her cool.

"You should see what we found for her in Inverness." She dropped down and retrieved two shiny green and lavender bowls. One had various-sized holes punched around the edges. "It's a hand-thrown watercolor bowl and brush caddy!"

"She'll love it." Andrea attempted to sound enthusiastic as Brie opened the front door. "How do you feel about bacon mac and cheese tonight?"

Brie swiveled. "Uh-oh. What's wrong?"

She waved a hand in front of her. "Nothing."

"Come on. It's me. I know your comfort food. You did amazing yesterday. I even opened up my socials earlier and saw all the shares and comments from staff and Bryce."

Kicking her boots off, she moseyed into the family room and plopped on the sofa. "Oh, yeah. Incredible right?"

"It is! You could open your own catering business."

Andrea shrugged. "I don't know."

"What are you talking about?" Brie seized Andrea's shoulders with her hands. "You could leave HR and do something you love. Come on, Andrea, get excited!"

"I am...or at least, I was."

Brie pointed a finger. "Spill."

She leaned her head into the cushion. "I lost the house."

"Andrea..."

"And Gloria called."

Brie leaned forward. "Whatever she said, forget it, okay? Her opinion doesn't matter."

Swallowing thick, bitter self-doubt, she turned. "L.A. is flooded with foodies and restaurants and food trucks. Would I really have a chance in hell? One experience doesn't equate to a long-term paycheck, Brie."

"That's true, but you could do it on the side for a while and see what happens."

Andrea shrugged. "Yesterday, I was all jazzed about it, but now"—she blew a breath—"I don't know."

"Well, you have a few weeks to think about it." After a brief pause, Brie squeezed her hand. "And I'm so sorry to hear about your house."

She exhaled. "Me, too."

"I thought the catering gig would help."

She bobbed her head. *Me, too.* "There's something else."

"What?"

"Rory."

She tilted her head, while her brows formed a *V*. "Did something happen?"

"Yeah." Andrea exhaled. "He rescued me from the road, fed me, and I planted a kiss on him, then propositioned him for sex, and insulted him when he declined."

Brie's eyes widened. "Andrea!"

She threw her hands in the air. "It wasn't all my

fault. We were having a good conversation, and by the way, who knew Rory, aka the quiet man, had this sexy side?"

With a tip of a lip, Brie grinned.

Andrea fanned the air again. "But that's beside the point. I saw this post with Hugh kissing some woman outside of a bar last night, and then I received that email from the loan agent about the house, and the cherry topper—a one-word text from Hugh right after."

She nudged her shoulder. "I'm sorry."

"It's not even like we were dating or anything, but ugh! Why do I even care?" She huffed. "Seriously, Brie, why?"

She gazed with soft, kind green eyes the color of moss. "You know why. Even if you can't admit it to yourself. Your parents ran you through the wringer. It's no wonder you're scared to get involved."

Straightening, Andrea felt the sting of tears. "That's low, Brie."

"You've told me yourself what happened when you were younger"—she rested a hand on Andrea's—"and I've picked you up after S.S. *Gloria* plowed through your life over and over."

Covering her face with her hands, she groaned. "I'm a damaged thirty-year-old!"

"You're human." Brie rubbed a hand on her back, circling slowly. "The right guy's out there."

She heaved a breath of frustration and swiped hair out of her eyes. "I don't need a man."

"You don't."

"But I need sex!" She threw her head back, then exhaled and faced forward once again. "Sex would make things easier, you know? Clear my head and have some fun, then get my life back together."

Brie chuckled.

"I shouldn't even be worried about Rory, right? He's an adult. He can handle it." She slid her gaze toward Brie.

She studied Andrea. "He can."

"But I'm the asshole."

Brie pitched a brow. "Well, I wouldn't put it that way, but he's a friend of ours and a good guy. I'm sure he'd appreciate an olive branch."

With a huff, Andrea shoved her hands through her mass of curls. "What am I even doing? I'm leaving in a few weeks anyway."

Brie's eyes danced. "I remember having a similar conversation about Bryce not so long ago."

"That was different."

She tilted her head, green eyes shining. "Was it?"

"Yes." She rose, then threw her hands up once again. "Damnit, I don't know. I'm not looking to get involved."

Brie stood. "You don't have to date him, Andrea."

"I know."

"Why don't you let things simmer for a bit before you reach out?"

Andrea exhaled. But beneath the anger and frustration, she could admit that something inside her churned. And it had everything to do with the quiet man.

Chapter Twenty

Wrapped in a thick robe, feet cozy in fuzzy boots, and holding an extra full mug of steaming coffee, Andrea stepped outside the guest house into the cool morning.

Happy squeals from Noah and Phoebe, racing on scooters, swooped through the air.

"We're on Christmas holiday!" Phoebe sang.

"Vacation." Noah swiped a leg out, spinning.

Phoebe scrunched her face. "No. Mrs. McLaren said we were going on holiday."

"No!"

Andrea grinned. "It's the same thing. They just call vacation *holiday* here, so enjoy it, kiddos." She glanced up at the sky, which was growing darker by the minute. "Plus, it looks like it's going to rain, again."

The kids raced around the side of the yard.

Brie appeared with a large cup of coffee, pale skin, and smudge of smoky rings under her eyes.

Concern prickled. "You feeling okay, Brie?"

She sat gingerly on a wicker chair. "Feeling a bit off this morning. I didn't sleep well. Bryce came home after eleven o'clock last night—late production meeting discussing the last scenes for the final episode—so I talked with him a while before bed. I was already tired and shouldn't have waited up, but I missed him."

With a pat on Brie's shoulder, Andrea sat, then cupped a hand in hers.

"And then I had this really weird dream"—she wiped a hand over her forehead—"I can't remember it now."

She squeezed Brie's hand. "Go rest. I'll play with the kids."

"I'm fine, really. Just needed to eat something and have an extra cup of coffee." She raised her mug.

The kids parked their scooters in front of them.

"Well, cheers then." Andrea touched the rim of her mug to Brie's. "So, what's on the schedule for today?"

"Christmas presents!" Phoebe jumped up and down, flinging her golden-brown pigtails like pom-poms.

"It's not Christmas yet," Brie replied.

Andrea smirked. "How about we go shopping for Bryce and Mimi and then we can go ice skating at Elfingrove?"

"Can we get something, too?" Noah skated over.

"Of course! It's Christmastime."

Brie elbowed Andrea.

"See, you're feeling better already!" She flashed a smile.

Noah thrust his hands in the air. "Yes!"

And maybe while she shopped, Andrea would figure out what the heck she'd do about Rory. She'd opened her text app and closed it a half-dozen times the night before, staring at his name. But she didn't know what to say. Texting *I'm sorry* seemed lame. He'd kept her from turning into a femsicle, and she'd thrown herself at him, then stormed out hotheaded. She could only imagine what he thought of her now. She wished she could press rewind, but she didn't know how.

After shopping, lunch, and more shopping, the kids whined, even with a new doll and truck.

The droves of people and long shopping excursion were wearing on them. But they weren't alone. Andrea was ready to bust out of the mall and open the amazing merlot she'd snagged. She loved her niece and nephew, but she was tapping out. "Brie, let's call it. Okay?"

Brie's eyes widened. "But I still haven't found something for Bryce. It's our first Christmas together, and I can't find the perfect present."

Andrea almost quipped that all Brie needed to do was wrap herself up in a frickin' bow on the bed, and Bryce would be pleased as punch or er, as Scotch? But she didn't because her best friend was frazzled and a bit pale. She paused and touched Brie's shoulder. "Christmas is more than a week away. You have plenty of time. Let's head back to the house."

"What about ice skating?" Noah whined.

Brie blew out a breath. "You're right. We promised we'd go ice skating."

At Kelvingrove Art Gallery, sparkling lights and festive garlands decorated a giant, clear tent in front of the historical structure. The shining lights transformed the baroque-style architecture with cone-topped towers into a fantastical, colorful, fairytale castle, while festive Christmas music brought warmth and cheer.

Once their ice skates were tied, Noah and Phoebe walked toward the rink's edge, eyes big and round with wonder and enchantment.

"It's the ice rinks of all ice rinks, huh? Like Rockefeller Center meets Fantasy on Ice." Andrea gazed at the domed rink and Christmas décor with a golden-lit Christmas tree in the center and strands of snow-white lights cascading and mingling with sparkling disco balls. A moment later, she pushed away from the short, safety wall and glided across the ice, glove-in-glove with Noah. Gloria had enrolled her in ice skating for a year when she was younger, but Andrea was in no way a pro and found herself flinging her opposite arm out for balance. "See? Easy peasy."

Noah flashed a wide-mouthed grin. "I can do it." He released her gloved hand and gripped the wall.

"Wait for us!" Phoebe squealed. Her pink, fuzzy gloved fingers held tight to Brie's.

Andrea smiled.

Noah held a knuckled death grip on the wall and swooshed his feet back and forth in choppy movements. Slowly, the tension in his body eased, and he glided bit by bit. A smile curled at his lips. "I've got it!"

"You do!" Andrea gathered her own footing, then swung her arms, while simultaneously sliding her skates forward to propel herself like the Lady of the Ice. Growing confident, she turned and felt resistance. "Ah, toe pick!" She fell beside Noah who tumbled on top of her.

"Are you guys, okay?" Brie glided over.

Giggling, Andrea rose to a sitting position. "Fine. I've got plenty of padding." She smacked her ass and shook it sideways at Brie.

With a laugh, Brie continued slowly with Phoebe.

A girl flew past Andrea, spinning into an axel a few feet away.

"Watch out!"

Brie swiveled, and her eyes widened as the ice skater flew near her and Phoebe. She tucked Phoebe in front of her protectively.

The ice skater landed a breath away from Brie, swinging a leg out horizontally and then dropped to the ground in a spin, missing Brie and Phoebe by an inch.

Brie helped Phoebe to the wall beside Noah. "Mommy needs a minute, okay, honey?"

As Andrea watched Phoebe and Noah inch down the rink wall, she noticed a man skating faster and faster like he was Mr. Smooth Skates.

Suddenly, his arms flailed out, and he lunged forward off balance. He flapped his arms like a flightless bird and wobbled his legs and skates. Yet, he didn't slow down. Mr. Smooth Skates propelled toward Brie.

"Brie!"

He slammed into Brie's back.

She flew forward, landing on her hands and stomach, her golden-brown hair a cloud against the white ice. With a cry, she collapsed.

"Mommy!" Phoebe screamed.

Seizing one of Noah's and Phoebe's hands, Andrea skated over, while fear raced up her chest.

The man who slammed into Brie extended an arm. "I'm so sorry." He wobbled to standing.

Andrea crouched down. "Brie, are you okay?"

Brie pushed herself up a few inches, only to clutch her stomach and crumple once more. "Oh, my God!"

"Mom!" Noah cried.

"Brie. Take a moment." Andrea tried to sound calm, but her pulse raced. Brie's skin had paled like a ghost, and her breath came out in raspy spasms. Then, she glanced down. Bright-crimson blood stained the inside seam of Brie's snowflake leggings. Panic leapt into her throat.

Staff members appeared in parkas, pushing through skaters who congregated.

Andrea whipped around. "Call an ambulance!" She didn't know how much time passed between holding Phoebe and Noah, and talking to Brie when the medics arrived with a stretcher, but she felt helpless.

Phoebe stood with thumb in her mouth and tears glossing her face, while Noah was frozen.

She embraced them tighter.

"Call Bryce, Andrea... Call...." Brie fainted.

"Get her to the hospital, now!" Andrea shouted. As lights flashed, she skated toward the lockers with Noah and Phoebe and rummaged through Brie's purse. She plucked her phone out and punched in Brie's password—*FRASER*—and pulled up Bryce's name. She called twice with no answer. She texted. Nothing. "Shit, he must be filming." With trembling hands, she searched Brie's phone for Eleana Evans, but the line went straight to voicemail. Andrea held the phone to her thundering chest, watching the disappearing clover-green-and-yellow-striped paramedic jackets. With a shake of her head, she glanced at the phone, then up once more until the jeweled colors disappeared. Who could she call?

She looked around erratically. Feeling Noah's small hand squeeze hers, she exhaled. She needed to calm down. Brie needed her. The kids needed her. She called Mimi and left as calm a message as she could muster. She was still in Inverness, and Andrea didn't need her panicking. *Think. Think. Think!* And then, all at once, she knew. She dropped Brie's phone into her bag and snatched up her own. She dialed.

He answered on the third ring.

"Rory—it's Brie. She's hurt. Please, can you—" Before she finished her sentence, a string of Gaelic words ran across her ear. "What?"

"What happened?" His rough breath coursed through the phone.

She quickly summarized what occurred. "Can you—"

"I'll tell him."

When she hung up, Andrea tossed Brie's purse over her shoulder, tucked Phoebe's and Noah's hands in each of hers, and jogged to the car. She pulled out of the carpark and was nearly blinded by headlights from oncoming traffic. "Shit!"

She swerved and squealed, narrowly missing a head-on collision with a big-ass truck. "Come on, Andrea! Left side. Left side." Once she righted herself on the correct route, she glanced back.

Noah cried quietly.

Phoebe rested with her head against the plush, purple car seat, thumb in her mouth.

They were safe. And so was Brie. Nothing would happen to her best friend. Nothing. Brie was strong. The strongest woman she'd ever known. But as the vibrant lights of the ambulance flashed into view and the crisscrossed yellow-red pattern on the coach's back blinked into her sight, she couldn't deny the sinking feeling in her stomach. She swallowed hard and pushed the feeling aside. Brie would be all right. *Brie will be all right, damnit.* She stomped on the gas and kept a steady eye on the ebb and flow of traffic.

At the emergency room counter, she gave her name and information, while holding Phoebe in her arms and Noah close to her hip. Overly bright fluorescent lights illuminated the room around her.

"Patient?" a woman with clear glasses and tamed ponytail asked.

"Brielle. We're here to see Brielle Hunter-Fraser," Andrea said.

"Are you family?"

"Yes." She lifted her chin. Brie was her best friend and closer than any family she'd ever known.

"Room 19A." She handed them visitor badges.

Andrea thanked her, hiked Phoebe higher on her hip, squeezed Noah's hand, and power-walked through the white corridor. The smell of cleaning disinfectant accosted her nostrils. A slew of nurses moved to and fro between rooms, while she scanned the glass sliding doors for 19A. Spotting the room number, she picked up the pace and pushed the door open. Her heart slammed into her throat at the sight of Brie pale and chalky with her honey-brown hair cascading across the white pillow, while a doctor leaned over. Nausea rose, and she swallowed to keep the vomit from coming up. Why hadn't she noticed? She'd seen the paleness in Brie's pallor that morning. Why didn't she tell her to stay home?

"Are ye expecting? Is there any chance ye could be pregnant?" The doctor's bald head shined in the blinding white lights.

"No."

"Are ye on any kind of contraceptive?"

"Yes," she said slowly. "I take them regularly." Then, her eyes grew wide. "When we moved, I missed taking one of my birth control pills on the flight and then getting settled with the time difference, I... You don't think—"

"We'll need to run a few tests before we can make a determination." The doctor turned to the nurse and requested a plethora of tests and bloodwork, then returned his attention to Brie. "Have ye experienced this pain before?"

She pressed her eyes closed. "No."

"All right." He slid on baby-blue, plastic gloves. "I'm going to palpate yer stomach to see if there are any abnormalities or tenderness."

Brie bobbed her head.

When the doctor placed his hands on her abdomen, he pressed down with his fingertips and moved his hands around in a circular motion.

Brie cried out.

"Ultra sound," he instructed.

The nurse rolled over the machine, lifted the ultrasound wand, and squeezed jelly on it, then handed him the tool.

Lifting her sweater, he circled the wand over her abdomen.

"There"—he pointed to the screen—"yer pregnant. About eight to ten weeks, and yer having a miscarriage."

"I—I'm pregnant?" Brie gasped. Her hands covered her mouth as tears sprung from her eyes and body shook. "Oh, God. Our child."

Andrea sucked in a breath at the same time Noah released her hand.

His small gaze was set on his mother as he walked forward. "Where's the baby?" He looked at Brie's covered stomach.

The doctor glanced from Brie to Noah. "It would be best to take the children to the waiting room until we've finished examining her."

Bobbing her head, Andrea hiked Phoebe higher on her hip. She couldn't get a word past the thickness in her throat. Sadness blanketed her, and tears stung, then fell.

"No. Mommy!" Phoebe kicked.

Andrea quickly put her down.

"I don't want to leave Mommy!" Phoebe ran to Brie.

"It's okay, baby." Tears cascaded down Brie's face. She held onto her children.

"Mommy's hurt," she cried.

Noah began crying, too. "I'm staying with Mom."

"Mommy's...going to be fine. The doctor needs to give her a checkup, okay?" Andrea tried her best to sound normal, though all she could see was her best friend looking lifeless and lost in the starchy, white bed. She wanted to stay by her side, but she knew she needed to be Auntie A right now.

"No." Noah gripped Brie tighter.

Unclasping a tearful Phoebe, Andrea drew her into her arms and rubbed Noah's back. "It's okay, buddy."

"Go with Auntie A," Brie whispered.

Noah looked from Brie to Andrea with wide eyes.

"It's all right." Andrea extended a hand. But as she crept through the automatic doors, she gave herself a silent pep talk, while gently squeezing Noah's and Phoebe's hands supportively. A loud commotion carried down the hallway accentuated by deep brogues. The waiting room was in a frenzy with people talking over one another, phones out, and a loud, male voice booming over it all. Bryce demanded answers from the receptionist still dressed as Alexander James Mackenzie and looking as fierce as she'd ever seen him in his role, kilt flapping, movie blood and makeup on, and Rory beside him. The two men seemed to take up the entire corridor.

"Gentleman, we can't have all these people," a voice rose an octave from the waiting room.

Security ambled in from the exterior dressed in their white-and-blue uniforms.

Bryce and Rory towered.

Weaving through the chair-lined aisles, Andrea drew closer. "Bryce!"

He turned with eyes wild and moved through the people like a holy storm.

As they approached, Noah released her hand and sprinted toward Bryce, flinging himself onto him.

Phoebe followed, running into an awaiting open arm as Bryce crouched.

Onlookers snapped pictures with their phones obtrusively, while other awaiting patients held phones on their laps filming discreetly.

Andrea took two steps forward to use her body to block a portion of the camera views and nearly slammed into Rory who had taken two, giant strides forward, as well. He stood beside her—a tandem barrier. Even as her eyes were damp with recent tears, she glared at the onlookers, imagining invisible beams flying from her eyes, destroying each and every damn phone.

A security guard approached with a soft belly roll flopping over his dull, black belt.

She leveled her gaze, which wasn't difficult since he only topped her five-foot-five by an inch, and pointed. "Do you have a private room? These kids have been through enough without the world catching it on camera."

"Aye." Bryce lifted Phoebe and Noah into his arms.

"If ye'll follow me." The security guard directed them through the patient entrance and then to a door at the end of the hallway, which opened into a small waiting room.

A handful of dull, charcoal chairs lined two walls, while a small, yellow wooden table and low-level television comprised the rest of the space.

"How is she?" Bryce's blue eyes searched hers for answers.

Andrea batted back tears. "She's okay."

Bowing his head, he released a heavy breath.

"You should go. She needs you."

"I'm going, too." Noah looked Bryce square in the eyes.

Nodding, he knelt to set the children down.

They clung even tighter with Phoebe's head pressed against Bryce's large arm, golden-brown hair spilling over the blue Mackenzie tartan, and Noah clutching both hands around Bryce's neck.

"'Tis all right. Yer mother will be fine," he said with red-rimmed eyes. "I'll make sure of it, but ye need to stay with yer aunt for now."

"But she's...my mom." Noah pushed away from Bryce. "She needs me."

"Noah—"

"You're not my dad." His eyes brimmed with fear and anger. "You can't tell me what to do."

Andrea's body tensed as a memory floated into her mind when she told one of her mom's husbands the same thing. She remembered the anger, the resentment, and the discomfort when a new man came into her life, but none of them compared to Bryce. He was the stepdad she wished she had.

Even still, Noah was bound to have feelings, plenty of feelings, and he was hurting.

With a nod, Bryce grasped Noah's shoulder. "I'm not, but I love yer mother fiercely and ye."

A tear rolled down Noah's cheek, and he swiped it away with the back of his hand.

"And I know 'tis difficult to understand, but I'm here for ye. Yer mother isn't going anywhere but home, and soon, ye have my word. I'll bring her myself once the doctor's say 'tis all right."

Noah bobbed his head. He clenched his fists together, released, and tightened them and released again. With a cry, he threw his arms around Bryce.

After a long hug, they separated. "I'll see to yer mother. But she needs ye to help take care of yer sister. Can ye do that?"

Noah bobbed his head once again, shuffling those sandy blond locks.

After watching Bryce stride out, Andrea glanced at Rory. He stood in the center of the waiting room with a thick brown-and-caramel flannel and marked, tan pants, sturdy as an oak tree. His gaze caught hers and held, and she felt relief flood her. She'd never known a man who could convey so much without uttering a sound. But his presence said, *I'm here. You're okay.* She didn't even realize she needed him—the support—until she spotted him alongside Bryce. Did she think he'd just drop Bryce off and leave? He wouldn't. He wasn't that kind of guy. He was...dependable. And kind. And real. And here she was, staring like a dingbat with her eyes sore from crying. She opened her mouth and closed it, then opened it again. She tried to think of something more substantial than a simple *thank-you*, but the emotion of the afternoon wore on her. "Thank you for coming," she said and meant it.

He nodded.

"I know I don't deserve your kindness after how I acted, and I—"

"Leave it for now, lass," he whispered.

Cracking her already crumbling exterior, she bobbed her head.

Noticing Noah sniffling, Rory knelt on his haunches, so he was only a head taller than Noah and rested a large hand on his small shoulder. "Chin up, lad."

Noah pressed his face into Rory's wide chest.

Rory wrapped a strong arm around him.

Holding Phoebe, something within Andrea shifted as she watched the quiet, hard-working swordsmith with Noah. Her hard exterior softened like a bottom round roast cooked low and slow for hours.

Phoebe tugged Andrea's scarf tail. "I want Mommy."

She hoisted her higher on her hip. "I know, sweetie, but Mommy's seeing the doctor right now for her owie. How about we head home?"

As an answer, she pressed her face into Andrea's curls and stuck her thumb in her mouth once again.

"I'll see ye safely." Rory rose, then gripped Noah's shoulder once more. "Stay here while I locate a discreet exit." Opening the door, he scanned the hall before walking out. A few minutes later, he re-entered. "The press has gathered outside. They know Bryce and the family are here. We've been told we can exit out the back. Security will accompany us."

"The press is here?" Anger pumped in Andrea's veins. She couldn't believe people would be so selfish—to post pictures in a hospital of all things. Her friend was fighting loss, grief, and pain, and all these jerks could think about was splashing pictures of Bryce Fraser in costume in the E.R. and wondering why he was there. *Hashtag annoying! Why the heck do you think, assholes? He's here for a reason. They*—her mind paused. Not even two weeks out of a job she'd done for near six years, and she'd already forgotten her skills at analyzing people.

"Do ye have Brielle's keys?" Rory inquired.

She fished them out of her purse and dropped them into his awaiting hand. "We valeted. But won't the press be watching for us to come out the other end?"

He grinned. "*Dinna fash*. I've a plan."

Chapter Twenty-One

"Pure dead brilliant." Bryce stared at Rory with an uptick of a lip. "But are ye sure, mate?"

Rory shrugged in the center of the spare waiting room with fluorescent lights and the quiet murmur of a television playing in the background. "Do ye have a better idea?"

"No." Bryce rocked back on his heels. His eyes were weary, red-rimmed from emotion, but also alert.

Rory clapped a hand on his shoulder and squeezed.

Bryce bowed his head and breathed.

Standing beside his mate, Rory held on until Bryce exhaled and stepped back. He'd lost a wee bairn before the child even had a chance to see the world, and Rory couldn't even fathom the pain and loss he was going through. He might not be a father, but he could be a friend and a good one at that. He'd take care of the rest of the family, while Bryce stayed with his love.

"How fast do ye think they'll catch on?" Bryce asked.

"A moment or two, but that's all Andrea and the weans will need." His mind was on Andrea and the children and their safety. He didn't care if he made a fool of himself in the process.

Bryce dragged him in for a bear hug. "Thank ye."

"Come on now, off wit' it." Rory exchanged clothes with Bryce—trading sweet, syrupy-smelling-movie-blood-and God-knows-what-else-crusted-costume—for his familiar flannel and jeans. Christ, being a star was not as glamorous as people made it out to be.

"Ye need a hand wit' the kilt?"

He steeled his eyes.

With a chuckle, Bryce raised his hands, then buttoned the flannel.

A few minutes later, Rory adjusted the leather belt over the Mackenzie tartan and stuffed his feet into Bryce's boots with a wee squeeze. His toes pinched at the tips, but he could bear it for Andrea and the children. Finally, he swung the jacket around, sliding one arm through and then the other into coarse material. The jacket pulled and constricted him like a bloody tight-jacket. "*Och!*"

Bryce tugged the jacket off. "Leave it, mate."

They settled on his hat for a play at distraction and Bryce's sunglasses, which would conceal some of Rory's features. The press would think Bryce had removed his wig and a few costume items while visiting Brie, and Rory would allow them to believe it. Thankfully, Bryce had grown a beard this season, and Moira, bless her, tinged it a wee redder for the role. Otherwise, their plan would have failed before it even began.

Knock-knock.

Rory opened the door.

"Ready?" The security guard stood outside the private waiting room.

He was a small man with a gut, but when he puffed his chest, Rory thought he knew how to do his job.

Another guard, tall as he was thin, stood beside him.

With a brief nod, he slid Bryce's sunglasses on. "Aye." He followed the security guards toward the main entrance and, with his heart pounding like a tenor drum, dipped his head slightly to evade a close inspection and walked through the automatic doors.

Instantly, the press swelled and cameras flashed.

Raising a hand above a brow, he acted as though he was covering his face.

An arm shot in front of him with a recorder. "Bryce! What happened?"

"Sources tell us your fiancée was rushed to the hospital. Can you comment on what happened?" another paparazzo asked.

"Mr. Fraser, can you give us any sneak peeks of what's to come in *Swords of Scotland*?"

"Bryce! Fans need to know what's going on!"

"What happened?"

"Can ye comment?"

Rory ignored the questions and weaved through the maze-like press, steadily and swiftly. Hearing the security guard's radio go off with the secret code relaying Andrea and the children had gotten out safely, he relaxed. They'd escaped. He grinned and removed his sunglasses.

"Wait. He's not Bryce Fraser!" a paparazzo yelled.

"Where's Bryce?" another asked.

"Who are ye?" a tall, blonde narrowed her gaze.

"Are you Bryce's stunt double?" another questioned.

With a grin, Rory trudged forward.

"Bryce must be making a run for it!" Another press member dashed in the opposite direction.

Rory kept walking as the press dispersed, dashing toward the E.R. and main hospital entrance, in case Bryce was sneaking out an alternate exit. But they wouldn't find him. He was snug in the room beside his beloved's bedside. Although

Rory didn't have the fire for acting, he couldn't suppress the triumphant feeling swelling inside. He'd successfully outwitted the press for a solid two minutes. And now, Andrea and the weans were safely on their way home.

When he climbed into his truck a few minutes later, he couldn't stop the smug grin tugging at his lips. He retrieved his phone from Bryce's sporran and felt his smile grow.

ANDREA

You're amazing! I owe you.

His chest expanded. He wouldn't mind having a lass indebted to him, especially one who made his blood scorch with hunger. Even after everything that had happened between the two of them, he felt that energy—that flint spark —at the hospital. He wasn't ready to give up on her yet; he knew from experience that good things often took time.

* * *

Andrea slept in Noah's bed with Phoebe curled beside her, and Noah sprawled on the opposite side. The bed was small, and her sleeping space was even smaller, but she couldn't say, *no*. Not when Noah's glistening eyes held back tears. He was trying so hard to be strong. With her here, he didn't have to. Being a few years younger, Phoebe didn't understand the gravity of what happened; yet, she understood her mother was staying at the hospital. That's all it took for her to have a tearful bedtime. Snuggling close, Andrea inhaled the calming lavender bath essence lingering on Phoebe's hair. When she shifted, she felt Noah's hand flex, then relax on her collarbone. Slowly, she, too, drifted.

Sometime later, a soft light shined through the doorway. A warrior's silhouette appeared and grew with the shadows until the giant arched over the walls.

Andrea blinked once, twice. *Am I dreaming?*

The warrior remained.

She rubbed her eyes until she realized the figure wasn't a figment of her imagination, but Bryce. He wore Rory's flannel rolled up at the forearms, jeans, and his wig loose past his shoulders like she'd seen earlier. Yet, Bryce stood like a man who'd been to battle and back. "They're all right," she whispered.

He nodded slowly, then let his head bow.

She stared at her best friend's strong husband, and realization hit. She'd held him in this unbreakable light. He was Alexander James Mackenzie—the fictional warrior of all warriors—and Television King of Scotland, but he was also Bryce Fraser, Brie's husband. And he was hurting.

Crossing to the bed, he knelt beside the bunk. "They're keeping her overnight," he whispered. Reaching a large hand across the bed, he swept golden strands out of Noah's eyes and let his hand rest on his forehead for a moment before repeating the gesture with Phoebe, brushing her hair across the pillow. "I saw her up to her room, but I was told to go home. She was asleep when I took my leave."

"She needs to rest."

He nodded.

"Just like you."

"Aye."

She tugged the blanket that slipped from Noah's chest. "I'll stay with them."

"Thank ye." He rose.

Andrea watched him walk out of the room like a man who'd fought a war and returned broken. A piece of him was missing, and she understood because a piece of her was also. She closed her eyes and prayed for Brie, Bryce, and the children. Lastly, she said a prayer of thanks for Rory.

Chapter Twenty-Two

CLICKS AND CLACKS, AND GEARS AND CHIMES sounded in the interior of the modern Glasgow Science Center. Noah ran from a hand-cranked Edison bulb to a spinning wheel, then turned gigantic gears, while Phoebe built a soaring tower of foam blocks. Next, they ran to the rainbow musical floor keyboard and danced a duet.

Andrea's phone chimed in her pocket. As she retrieved the device, she felt her stomach dance like the whirlpool in front of her. *Rory.*

RORY

How are ye?

She laughed. The man had a way with words. She didn't know what she did to deserve his help and trust, but she was determined to make it up to him.

ANDREA

Okay. Hanging with the kids at the Glasgow Science Center. Great idea. Thanks!

RORY
Brilliant.

Her lips curled. The Science Center was his idea. One he'd suggested earlier after he checked in with another *how are you?* She told him she didn't know how she'd keep the kids from being upset at home. She and Mimi—who'd arrived around midnight—distracted them for a bit with outside play and then a salt-and-watercolor art project. But when Mimi left to the hospital at nine a.m., Andrea noticed the unrest in the kids' eyes. *Take them to the GSC*, he'd texted. So, of course, she searched the attraction online, admired the modern-designed, crescent-shaped structure with prismed windows and shiny, titanium buildings, then clicked to view activities for kids. Throngs of colorful pictures with children exploring, building, running, and smiling filled her view, and she quickly bought tickets. But when she clicked back on the page, she was surprised to find the search of Glasgow adventures and GSC unveiled a few surprising pictures and headlines. A sturdy man in a kilt with the tag *Bryce Fraser's Twin?* was front and center. After a double-take, Andrea realized it wasn't Bryce, but Rory who stood with his hand up, walking through the throng of press. Other pictures showed Rory with a hat and sunglasses and another, hatless and grinning like a triumphant athlete. The old bait and switch had worked.

Other headlines weren't as fascinating. *Fraser Family Troubles* and *Bryce Fraser Fiancée Dying?*

She'd punched the window closed and flipped her phone over on Noah's nightstand.

A rolling giggle snapped Andrea out of her thoughts and back to the present.

Phoebe danced in a splash of lights before a white screen, watching her colorful shadow bounce around like Peter Pan.

RORY

And Brie?

Andrea sighed. Although they were having a good time at the Science Center, she felt her heart ache for Brie every time she passed a family or saw a squealing baby.

ANDREA

She's being released at 1. It'll be good to have her home.

RORY

I can imagine. Off to set. Take care.

ANDREA

You, too.

Brie's release was a good thing, but Andrea also knew she had a long road of recovery ahead—mind, body and soul. And she'd be by her side the whole time. Nearly fifteen years ago, she'd witnessed Gloria miscarry. She still remembered the crimson blood on the stark-white tile, her mother's anger, and her own desperation to help. She was sent to her father's—a solo trip on an airplane with a stewardess checking on her, while Gloria recovered. When she returned a week later, she found Gloria to be even more distant and self-absorbed. Gloria had requested a hysterectomy after the miscarriage, but Andrea had always wondered what it would've been like to have a biological brother or sister. Sure, she had her half-sister, Gia, but she was eight years younger. They were barely acquaintances, lived on polar opposite sides of the states, and somehow, linked by blood. Brie was her soul sister. And she ached for her.

* * *

Entering the house later that afternoon, Andrea held a protective hand on Phoebe's back as she slept on her shoulder —still passed out from the day and car ride. The spare afternoon sun cast shadows over the living area.

Noah ran from room to room, looking for his mom.

"Let's be quiet, buddy. Mom might be sleeping."

He tiptoed up the stairs.

Andrea followed, then stripped Phoebe's shoes and tucked her into her own bed. After, she padded down the carpet-lined landing to the master bedroom. The moment she stepped inside, she froze.

Brie lay in the center of the large bed with Noah curled beside her, hair spread out on the ivory pillow, face makeup free and nearly as pale as the pillowcase.

Beside the bed, Bryce sat on a sturdy, wooden chair with a hand clasping Brie's lightly, and on his lap, a stack of unread lines curled at the ends.

The faint smell of medicine lingered in the air. Stepping backward, Andrea retreated. *Creak-creak.*

Bryce lifted his head.

The few lines on his forehead seemed deeper, the smudge under his eyes, darker, and sadness etched his features. So much was written on the man's face like last night.

"Andrea, come in," he said quietly.

She padded closer.

Brie opened her eyes. Red with fatigue and puffy from crying, her eyes exuded pain.

Andrea ached, too. Inching closer, she stopped at the edge of the bed and willed herself to sound upbeat. "Hi, sleeping beauty."

But Brie didn't smile.

Bryce brought Brie's hand to his lips. "I wish I could take your pain, *mo ghràdh.*"

A tear slipped down her cheek.

"Don't cry, Mommy," Noah's sweet voice said.

Heaving a burdened breath, she leaned her head toward Noah, while his small arm wrapped across her.

"Do ye need anything?"

She shook her head gently.

Bryce rose and motioned for Andrea to sit.

The last time she'd seen her, Brie had been bloody, shattered, and heartbroken. Though she might not see the damage, Andrea knew Brie was still shattered. She sat with her and squeezed her hand softly. After a few minutes, she noticed Bryce pacing. She rose and drew him to the corner. "She's going to be all right, right?"

"Aye, the doctor said it'll be a few weeks of healing, but she can conceive again, if that's what she wants."

Andrea twitched. "If she wants? I thought you guys have been talking about it."

He inhaled into his broad chest and released a heavy sigh. "I *dinnae ken* if I can bear to see her in pain again with something we've created."

Shaking her head, Andrea searched for words. "These things...happen." *Great, very eloquent.* "But she wants to add to her family, to your family. You'll need to talk more when she's feeling better."

He dragged a hand through his hair and shifted, glancing at Brie.

"Is there something else?"

"Aye. I rearranged scheduling for today to finish the night shoot. I *dinnae ken* what to do. Brie needs me, but I'm contractually bound by the show. I'd give the whole bloody thing up for her." His voice rose an octave.

"She knows that."

"Bryce," Brie's soft voice carried across the room. "Finish your shoot."

He strode to her side, knelt, and fitted her hand in his once more. "Are ye sure?"

She nodded weakly. "I need to rest."

He cupped her face with his large hands and brought his forehead to hers, while tracing a hand down her hair. "I'll be here before sunrise and by yer side before ye stir."

Lifting an arm slowly, Brie wrapped it around Bryce's side with Noah still cuddled in the curve of the other. They held onto one another.

Andrea watched the intimate moment from the corner of the room—all their love and fear tangled together as they held onto the moment of love and onto the hope that they would be whole once again. She never believed in true love—the kind between two people—the inseparable kind. She believed in the love between friends, but she'd convinced herself that love with another—with a man—didn't exist. Gloria showed her that time and time again. But how could she deny what was in front of her? Something that was so blindingly raw and real?

Chapter Twenty-Three

RORY WANTED TO CALL, TEXT, OR SOMETHING. BUT he'd already done that. He didn't want to seem desperate or push Andrea, but hell, something burned and fired when their gazes fixed a few nights ago—not just the emotions of the night. He wanted to see what that kindling would lead to and give what fired between them another chance. He could be stubborn, as well—his refusal to visit his parents and mend the relationship between he and Da was a prime example—but he also could be patient. She'd be taking care of Brie and the children with Bryce finishing the last scenes tonight, though he knew his mate wanted to be anywhere but there a few hours prior.

Of course, Rory was concerned for Brie; she was like another sister to him. He prayed she'd recover soon. But he couldn't shake the look Andrea had given him—a softening in her exterior—a vulnerable gaze that told him she was glad he'd come. With a scratch of his beard, he exhaled and returned to his trade. The glare of the overhead lights in the armory kept him awake and attentive, even as his own body roared for rest. But this was the final night shoot. If they had to film straight through morning, they would. They'd done it before.

Pulling out the polish, he seized a towel and shined stunt swords. They might be model replicas made of resistant polypropylene plastic, but he'd ensure fans wouldn't know the difference.

"Ah, Rory. There ye are." Moira walked in, red hair standing on end.

He straightened and smiled warmly. "Evenin' Moira. What can I do ye for?"

"My niece, Colleen, will be in town for the Christmas season. She's eager to meet ye."

Sheathing the sword, he held onto the basket-shaped guard. He'd forgotten to call Colleen. "Thank ye. Em"—he cleared his throat—"I've recently...started pursuing a lass."

"Oh, aye?"

He nodded.

"Well, I'm glad to hear it, but if anything changes, my Colleen's a real sweetheart. Bonnie, too."

Bleep! The radio on his workstation beeped. "Security to location four. Medical technician to location four. Moira Kelly to location four," a thick brogue carried across their radios.

Moira whirled. "What the devil?" She nabbed the radio and fired questions.

Meanwhile, Rory snatched the stunt swords and swung out of the armory. When he neared the set, he spotted a battle scene between two men—one with fire-red hair and another, the color of night. Curses flew, while grunts merged with the *clang* and scrapes of metal on metal. But that was what was so damn confusing—no sword fights were in the script today. Rory was privy to every scene where his swords made an entrance, how they would be used to ensure the safety of both cast and crew, and what they needed to look like. The traditional eighteenth-century steel Claymore replicas were supposed to be used for closeups this evening, not sword fighting. What the bloody hell happened?

Security circled, seeking the best opportunity to separate the fighting warriors, who, together with their costumes, were a sight.

Bryce's face was red with anger, nostrils flared, and chest heaved as he went after Hugh. His curly mane whipped along with his kilt in a fan-like motion as he spun and struck.

In defense, Hugh swung his sword up, blocking the blade.

Trudging forward, Rory dropped the sword bundle and stood on the outskirts of the fight. Swords glistened in the overhead lights and *clanked* again and again.

"What's gotten into ye?" Hugh hollered at Bryce as the applied dirt and grime mingled with fresh sweat on his face and neck. Deflecting another blow, Hugh blocked, then scraped his sword in a circle around Bryce's until both blades were pointed toward the ground.

Rory exhaled. They'd be done.

A mighty roar escaped Bryce, and he thrust a shoulder into Hugh, knocking him a good meter before attacking once again.

Hugh jumped up and swung, blocking Bryce's advances, and in doing so, nicked Bryce on the forearm. Instantly, blood oozed. "Enough!" Hugh yelled.

Bryce lifted the sword again.

Rory knew this wasn't the normal actions of his mate, but of a man warring inside. He couldn't help Bryce with Brie or their wean in heaven, but he could save his friend from injuring himself further. With adrenaline pounding in his ears, Rory grabbed a spare sword and waited for his chance. He weaved between the guards and swung the sword high, blocking Bryce, then with an elbow, knocked the sword out of his hands. He couldn't have his best mate injured, especially with his own bloody swords. "That's enough heavy ragin', mate."

Security removed the swords quickly and blocked Hugh.

Bryce fell to the earth, head bowed and shaking, while blood streamed from the slice on his forearm down to his fingertips and onto the dirt. The air infused with an iron tinge.

With a shake of his head, Rory looked upon Hugh, who heaved heavily, standing tall, arms across his chest, and thick brows knitted. "What the hell'd ye do?"

"He's wired to the moon! I was poking him a wee bit to help him relax as he was lookin' *peely-wally* and told him not to take it out on his *boaby*."

"Did ye, *aye*?" What an *eejit*. But perhaps Hugh didn't know what had happened.

Hugh's chest puffed. "I wasna about to let him skewer me. We had a square go."

"It was my fault." Bryce swiped a hand over his mass of red curls. "No one else's."

Rory clamped a hand on Bryce's shoulder.

"I'm gutted about Brie and the babe. And when Hugh—"

"'Tis fine," Rory interrupted, glancing at Hugh. "He had it coming."

With an exhale, Bryce bowed his head.

Marching toward them, Moira started in on Bryce like a mother hen, hands on hips, hair flying. "And what the devil do ye think yer doing? Fighting like animals?"

Bryce snapped up to attention.

"Now, ye've gone and hurt yerself and made a mess of the scene."

"'Tis just a scratch," Bryce growled.

"Just a scratch, ye say? Well, then why is there real blood over the movie blood I so meticulously applied a few hours prior?"

When Bryce opened his mouth to speak, he was quickly silenced by Moira.

"Let the lads have a look at ye."

Rory stood aside, so the technicians could clean and bandage Bryce, but damned if he'd allow him to suffer alone. He stayed firmly planted an arm's length away.

After an incident report was completed, apologies were made, breaks were had, and makeup reapplied, they resumed shooting.

Rory watched the final scene, again and again, until the director got the material he needed, then gathered the swords and returned to the armory. Once the door was closed, he slumped back against it. Women drove men mad with worry and everything else.

Chapter Twenty-Four

NEAR MIDDAY, ANDREA KNOCKED ON THE MASTER bath's door, but no answer followed. She pushed open the ivory door and found Brie lying with her head against the bathtub headrest, staring at the wall, eyes glazed. Brie's pallor didn't differ much from the surrounding white tile. "Lunch is almost ready," Andrea whispered. "Chicken tortilla soup—your favorite. I even added some potatoes and a splash of cream."

She nodded slightly.

Heaviness filled Andrea's chest. Her best friend was drowning inside, and she didn't know how to rescue her. She walked inside and sat beside her. "I made it more Scottish. Hope you don't mind." Plus, she knew potatoes with a little bit of skin would add more iron, which Brie needed right now.

Brie didn't utter a sound.

Her cheeks appeared more hollow than normal, and the paleness of her skin subdued her natural blush-and-cream hue. She looked fragile, but she was still there—silent and still. Determined to brighten her day, Andrea scooched closer. "Mimi's making her famous Christmas sugar cookies. Did you know she said she'd copy the recipe for me? I had to remind her that I don't mess with sweets or bake, save for pizza. Well, and focaccia."

Brie sat motionless.

Refusing to be discouraged, she continued telling her about Noah and Phoebe and how they'd made the vegan sugar cookie dough with Mimi and, while sitting atop the island, ate more dough than there were cookies. "They even found your stash of vintage cookie cutters and happily cut out a myriad of shapes and animals!"

Brie nodded, while her right hand rested along the arm of the tub.

Setting her hand atop Brie's, she squeezed gently. "We're here for you, Brie—me, the kids, Bryce, and Mimi. We're all here."

A tear tumbled down her cheek like a watery snowball, and a guttural sound tore out. "But what about the baby?" She cried. "We...didn't even know if the baby was a boy or girl. I didn't get to follow the fruit and vegetable growth chart and celebrate every obstacle, miracle, and tiny milestone. I didn't even..." She hiccupped. "I didn't even know the baby was here...inside me." She fanned her hands over her bare stomach. "What kind of mother am I?"

"An incredible one. A strong one. A sacrificing-you-want-to-give-them-the-best-life one. A mother I would've loved to have and admire daily."

Tears continued to cascade down Brie's face like a delicate glaze over porcelain.

Leaning forward, Andrea settled her forehead a few inches from Brie's. "You will be a mother again. I know it."

Brie bit her lip and then threw a drenched arm around Andrea, sending droplets of water around like a sprinkler.

Andrea tugged her closer, allowing her best friend's salty tears to streak down her own cheeks and the warm bath water soak her blouse. "I know it," she repeated. "Like I know the ingredients to red sauce like the back of my hand."

Brie let out a tearful, single laugh.

She'd never heard a better sound.

* * *

A day later, Andrea towel-dried a pot, keeping her gaze fixed across the kitchen where Brie rested on the forest-green couch in the living room.

Brie lifted a spoonful of rich, tomato-carrot bisque to her lips. And then another.

Andrea exhaled. Brie was eating. The day before, she only ate a few, spare bites. *But there's something about a favorite meal. It comforts and wraps around like a hug.* Food healed. She understood this, and so did Mimi, who hummed as she stirred a rich, bubbly mixture of chocolate cream in a medium sauce pan.

"That looks like a lot of cream for one pie."

She winked. "I always make two."

With a grin, Andrea glanced at her phone, resting on the counter. The quiet man had been silent since yesterday, and she'd been thinking about him.

Mimi splashed vanilla into the decadent chocolate, perfuming the air with caramel notes.

Inhaling, she watched Mimi stir the rich mixture once more, then pour the chocolate cream into two, golden pie shells. Andrea lifted her phone and snapped a picture of the decadent duo and sent the image along with a text to Rory.

ANDREA

> Mimi's making chocolate cream pie, and I
> have a warm pot of tomato-carrot bisque
> on the stove.

She stared at the message, then added a few more words, erased, nibbled her lip, and finally sent the last sentence.

ANDREA

We'd love to thank you for all you did.

Noah strolled past her with a wooden spoon covered in chocolate pudding. Fudgy smears crisscrossed his cheeks and smudged his chin.

"Hey, and just where do you think you're going with my spoon?"

His eyes flashed a challenge and then he took off around the corner.

"I'm going to catch you!" Andrea sprinted after him, then slowed when she neared Brie. "This looks like a much better idea." She plopped down, noticing an old romcom with Meg Ryan and Tom Hanks.

"It is." She smiled softly. "Thank you."

Andrea squeezed Brie's hand and held on.

An hour later, her text chimed. *Rory.* Rising, she read the text.

RORY

Sounds grand, but I've a few more pieces to finish before the night is through.

"And what's brought your beautiful smile out?" Mimi handed Brie a hot cup of tea.

"I'm not..."—She walked into the kitchen with searing cheeks.

Mimi strolled in behind her. "And blushing, as well?"

"What?" Brie asked from the living room. "Andrea's blushing? Are you sure it's not from the stove?"

"Nope," Mimi sang.

Andrea shrugged. "It's nothing."

With a shake of her head, Mimi aimed her you-better-break-the-news-to-me look.

Throwing her hands up, Andrea huffed. "Fine. It's Rory. We've been...texting for a few days."

Mimi slid on the rainbow bangles she'd removed for baking back onto her wrists. "That looks like more than a text."

"Well, since you're so nosy, I invited him to join us for soup earlier, but he must've been asleep—having been on the night shoot and all. Now, he has a few rush pieces to finish before the holidays."

"Hmm." With a sizeable measuring cup, Mimi scooped sugar, then dumped the tiny crystals straight into the mixer. "If the mountain won't come to you, then you have to go to the mountain."

Andrea raised a brow. "What?"

"Go see Rory, Andrea!" Brie squeaked coarsely from the other room.

Andrea jolted. "I will," she yelled back and turned to Mimi, lowering her voice to a normal range. "I wanted to thank him for helping us the other night, and well, rescuing me before."

"What did you have in mind?" Mimi asked.

"Cook for him."

"That's a great idea. Nothing pleases men more than food."

Andrea snorted. "Food and sex."

Mimi fumbled the spatula, splattering swirls of sweet whipped cream around her. "Yes...you're right. So, you'll be having both then?"

Andrea laughed out loud. Tossing her hair, she pivoted toward Brie. "Mimi is asking if I plan to have sex with him."

Brie grinned in response.

"What's sex?" Noah walked in with Phoebe on his heels.

Andrea slid her gaze toward Mimi.

Mimi simply bit her lip to keep herself from laughing and cranked on the mixer.

"It's uh...well, it's....something adults do."

"Is it fun?" Phoebe piped in.

Oh, my fucking god. Andrea glanced around the corner at Brie who was concealing her smile with two hands. "Sometimes?"

Noah gave an exaggerated eye roll, flopping a blond wave over his forehead. "Come on, Phoebe. Let's play."

Andrea picked up her phone and texted Rory.

ANDREA

How about I bring dinner to you?

RORY

I can't say no to that, but working late.
Tomorrow? 8?

ANDREA

8, it is. 😌

Chapter Twenty-Five

EXACTLY TWENTY-FOUR HOURS LATER, ANDREA pulled up to Rory's property and grinned at the open iron gate. *A good omen.* The SUV's headlights shined on the snow-flecked drive, and she drove forward. Now, she wouldn't have to scale the fence with dinner. And she'd made a kick-ass dinner. The rich, meaty and savory short rib perfumed the car like the interior of an oven. She imagined she smelled like eau-de-ragu—Scottish beef short rib slow-simmered in red wine with crushed tomatoes, caramelized onions, roasted garlic, diced celery, chopped carrot, and a mixture of fresh and dried herbs—and she didn't care one bit.

She'd dipped a bit of her favorite, spicy perfume in all the best crevices, but that would just enhance the dinner aroma. She wanted to present herself in the best manner possible. She *had* thrown herself at him, then cussed him out. And, he *had* rescued her and helped her out, twice. This was a makeup dinner, but shit, she needed a good scratch, and she imagined the quiet man had a few tricks up his sleeve. When she threw the gearshift into Park, she smiled as Maggie jogged over with her fluff of golden fur flying in the wind.

She stopped beside the door, tail wagging.

Andrea swung the door wide. "Hey, girl." She climbed out and scratched Maggie's head and back, looking around for Rory. "Where is he?"

"Woof!" Maggie jogged toward the forge.

Andrea rose and trudged through the frozen rock road.

Inside, Rory sat on a stool hunched over a grinding tool of some sort with safety glasses on, holding a piece of metal in his gloved hands. With expert skill, he rotated the metal back and forth, grinding, and turning, grinding and turning. At one with his work, his focus never wavered as the piece began to take on a diamond shape. When he shifted and leaned back, he spotted her.

She lifted a hand.

He turned off the machine, removed his safety glasses, and rose.

Maggie immediately trotted over to him.

"I didn't want to disturb you."

He nodded. "Appreciate that. This piece is near two hours in the making." He opened his palm, revealing the dark, diamond-shaped metal.

"Really?" She advanced. "Is it the top of a handle?"

"'Tis." He set the metal aside and stared, gray eyes softening.

"Your work is so fascinating. I always thought smiths just made horseshoes. I didn't realize people actually made swords."

"You sound like my *da*," he said quietly.

She arched a brow.

With a shake of his head, he lifted his hat and slid a hand under his auburn hair. "Long day."

"It's all right." She twisted her hands together. Why was she so nervous? She should've carried the crock pot in, then her hands would be busy, but she couldn't afford to trip on one of these big-ass machine legs. She wouldn't dare waste an ounce of that glorious sauce.

Rory fixed his gaze on hers from under thick lashes and turned over the piece in his hand. "Would ye like to see what I'm working on?"

"I would."

He set the piece on a metal dish beside a grinder and ducked under a large, black cabinet. A moment later, he rose with a second pair of neon-orange rimmed glasses. "For safety."

Grasping the glasses, she stretched the strap over her hair and set them on the bridge of her nose. They slid down a few inches. "Oh." She reached a hand to fiddle with the strap and connected with Rory's. Tingles tangled down her arm.

"Allow me."

Stripping off a second glove, he lifted a giant hand to the frame, cupping her cheekbone.

Warmth spread across her cheeks, while burnt metal and his own musk filled her nostrils as he secured the glasses in place. He stared at her—serious and soft at the same time—and her pulse quickened. Stepping back, she pressed a hand to the glasses, even though they now fit perfectly. "Thank you."

With a brief nod, he turned and walked toward a smoky cross between a cave and pizza oven.

She skirted behind, passing a large blackish-brown anvil scuffed with marks on the side, giant metal machines, and then paused before the fiery pit.

He grabbed a lengthy pair of tongs. "This here's the forge. I've fired a piece of steel to make it more malleable, but it'll also give me a more pure, hard metal."

"This might sound stupid, but isn't metal already hard?"

When he grinned, his cheeks brushed up against the safety glasses, giving him a bit of a chipmunk look. "'Tis but this makes it even stronger and pliable, so I can shape it into a sword." He flipped a switch on the machine next to the forge, which brought a giant hammer barreling down.

Smash! Smash! Smash!

She jolted. The steel sledge looked like it could punch through the earth. As the hammer continued its pounding rhythm, the sheer force rattled her teeth.

Motioning for her to step back, Rory gazed at the machine.

Andrea gladly obeyed. She didn't want to get near that contraption.

Grasping tongs, Rory reached into the oven and pulled out a bright-red cylinder of steel near nine inches long. He immediately set the metal on the giant hammer. The large hammer smashed the fiery steel once, twice, and again and again as he expertly rotated and adjusted the rectangular piece, then folded and stamped the steel again.

She couldn't believe that he could actually fold metal like silly dough. No wonder he wore those thick gloves and glasses. Watching him hold that hot metal, so poised and controlled, Andrea felt a rush of heat course through her body to her toes.

Slowly, the steel lengthened into a rectangular shape that would represent a sword. After a few minutes, Rory retrieved a large-handled hammer from out of thin air with one hand. With the other, he grasped tongs and set the rectangular-shaped piece on the anvil. He flicked the switch off the machine, then dropped the hammer down, pounding the scorching piece. Tiny, metal fragments flew off.

She pressed her safety glasses up the bridge of her nose.

"I need to finish roughing out this blade before I call it a day," he said loudly over the roar of his efforts.

"How long will it take?"

"About half an hour, maybe a wee bit longer." He glanced up. "I'm sorry, I'm running behind."

She studied her watch, noting it was after eight now. "No

biggie! If you don't mind, I can put water on for the pasta and the sauce into the oven."

With a nod, he continued hammering. Beads of sweat formed on Rory's forehead, and his powerful forearm muscles bunched with each drop of the hammer, while his thick veins bulged.

Her lady-area fired and mouth watered. Who knew sword smithery could be so sexy? She wiped the drool from her mouth. With one last, long look at Rory's profile, she wobbled out of the shop. And she could admit, her heart rapped in her chest like that damn, giant hammer.

Chapter Twenty-Six

Rory strode into his kitchen with a day's worth of healthy sweat and stink and paused at the entry. Andrea sang at the stove, swaying those wonderful hips to a local tune, while stirring something in a great pot, which no doubt was the reason his home was filled with a fantastic, meaty aroma.

Maggie happily sat a foot away, tail wagging.

The sight warmed his blood. "Smells good."

She turned and smiled.

Damned if that didn't give him a jolt to the gut.

"You're done! How does it look?"

"'Tis coming along fine." He noted she'd dressed the kitchen table with two settings including silver, glasses, napkins, and a small vase filled with rust-and-rose-colored blooms. She'd taken the time. Good news, since he planned to wear her down gently.

"Awesome-sauce. And this sauce is even more awesome." With a flick of her wrist, she dumped a wee bit of salt into her palm, then sprinkled the seasoning into a second pot, causing steam to swirl around her like a smoky haze. "It'll knock your socks off. Short rib ragu slow-cooked for four mouthwatering hours in veggies, herbs, and wine."

She looked like a sorceress, working her cauldrons. And, she looked as good as the food smelled. "Sounds grand, but first I, em"—he glanced at his marked trousers and soot covering his arms and chest—"I'm in need of a shower, if ye don't mind."

Flicking her gaze up and down his body, she purred, her smile spreading. "Not at all. Water's boiling. I'll drop the pasta in once you come out."

"Then, I'll make quick work of it." He ambled down the hall and closed his bedroom door, wrenching his clothes off. Having a woman cook a meal in his kitchen wasn't an usual occurrence. And damned if he'd keep her waiting.

Within ten minutes, Rory dressed, tugging on a light-gray jumper and stone-colored jeans. Ripples of nerves coursed through him as he combed the hair away from his temples and, lastly, tamed his beard. When Andrea texted him the day before inviting him to dinner, he declined, not only because he was behind on an order, but because if she truly wanted him, the choice to come would need to be her own. Then, she'd offered to bring a meal. He couldn't reply fast enough. Now, he strolled to the main area and paused in the archway of the kitchen.

She stood at the counter, chopping fresh herbs.

Christ, she was a picture. He wondered if she knew how natural she looked in the kitchen and how confident. Instead of the apprehension he felt the first time she'd entered his home, here and now, pleasure spread within and expanded across his chest.

When she glanced up and met his gaze, she smiled.

Pushing away from the archway, he strolled over. "Did I keep ye?"

She shook her head. "No, go ahead and sit. I'll pop in the

pasta. It cooks quickly. It's fresh. I mean, I made it a few hours ago. But you know, fresh earlier?"

His lips curved. She was nervous—that was plain to see, which told him she liked him, as well. And knowing that reinforced his frame of mind—he was keen to show her courtesy.

Andrea dropped pasta into the awaiting pot and stirred. "I brought some beer and wine. I didn't know what you preferred with a meal, but Bryce mentioned this was your favorite." She turned toward the fridge and removed a dark beer with a blue-and-gold label.

"Aye, thank ye." He opened the bottle with a quick grip of a hand and lifted the beer to his lips. The cool, crisp brew refreshed him.

Stirring the pasta once more, Andrea glanced at Rory.

He watched her over the top of his beer. She'd kissed him once. *Och.* Thrown herself at him, and he'd halted the action from going any farther. Though she was pissed as punch then, he wouldn't have changed his actions. He wanted more than one night together.

With a quick flick of her wrist, she lifted the pot lid and spooned thick noodles into the ragu. Slowly, she stirred the noodles, coating each strand with the wine-colored sauce.

Inhaling, he felt his stomach rumble. "Do ye need a hand?"

"Sure, can you grab those big, white bowls? I found them in your cupboard and thought they'd work well. Hope you don't mind."

"No." He set his beer down and grasped the bowls, then held them out.

She scooped pasta and twirled the thick noodles into a pretty pile atop the dishes, then added thick chunks of roast, slices of fresh parmesan, and a sprinkling of herbs.

He inhaled the salty cheese and fresh, clean herbs that mingled with the rich roast. "That's grand." Placing the bowls at each setting, Rory rotated and drew Andrea's chair out.

Her eyes widened.

Gesturing, he waited for her to sit, then pushed her chair in slowly. After they settled at the table, he lifted his beer. "To a fantastic meal and chef. *Slàinte mhath*."

Flashing a bright smile, she touched her wine glass to his beer. "*Slàinte mhath*."

After forking a spoonful of pasta, he groaned in delight at the first rich and meaty mouthful. "Incredible."

Her brown eyes shone as she twirled a large forkful and tried the dish herself. "Mmm."

"What did I do to deserve such a feast?"

She lifted her gaze. "You rescued me and brought Bryce to Brie when I couldn't get through to him."

With a nod, he speared a thick hunk of roast and took a bite.

"And dinner is also an apology. I'm sorry for the other night after I catered the shoot—the way I acted…"

He set his fork down, giving her his full attention. He welcomed the opportunity to understand what happened and peel back those tightly-wrapped layers.

"You went out of your way to help me."

"Aye, I did."

"And I was a bitch." She flicked her fork.

His lips twitched. "Something was on your mind that was plain to see."

She turned her fork and twirled pasta, not allowing her gaze to stray. "There was."

He waited for her to continue.

She threw her hands in the air. "Fine. I'll just come out and say it, okay? That night, I found out I lost my house that was pending with a bank. I'm a risk, since I was laid off a few days before this trip. Did I tell you that? Well, I was. It was a hell of a shock to my ego. Then, there was Hugh, who, by the way, didn't answer the phone when I was stuck in the Cairngorms. I had a crush on him, but apparently, he wasn't interested. I discovered a picture on social media, documenting him kissing some girl. We weren't really dating, at all. I mean, we went out once and that was a group outing that you—"

"He's an *eejit*."

She laughed, quick and sharp. "You sound like Bryce."

"Aye, well Bryce and I are in agreement."

"Anyway. When you showed up, you made me realize that maybe I went after the wrong guy."

His chest puffed, and he felt the corners of lips curl and shift his beard. "Is that so?"

"Look, don't get all full of yourself, okay?"

He grinned and dipped his fork into the pasta, eating quietly with Andrea while their spoken words settled and sparkled around them. As the minutes passed, he glanced up between bites and found her smiling right back.

When she finished, she pushed to standing, then picked up his empty bowl and hers before turning toward the sink. "Anyway—"

Her soft form collided into his chest. His body throbbed and thundered with wanting. Watching her eyes round, Rory brushed his lips across hers.

Chapter Twenty-Seven

ANDREA'S HANDS WERE TRAPPED HOLDING THE bowls between them, while Rory's full lips melted into hers. His scratchy and soft beard skimmed her cheeks and chin, sending electricity over her skin, while his hand pressed into the base of her spine. She felt herself letting go as he slid his tongue over her lip and deepened the kiss. She tasted the rich wine from the meal and Rory. Just Rory. And for once, she was speechless.

He drew back. "Ye were saying?"

"Uh...I..." He'd wiped her mind clean. With a shake of her head, she looked up. "I'm not looking for anything serious." She stared at his full lips, while curls of lust tangled in her stomach and that wonderful smoky scent of his with a hint of pine filled her senses.

"I like ye, Andrea. We can see where this goes, if you let it." He extracted the bowls from her hands, then strolled toward the sink.

Blinking, she gawked. "Wait, you can't just kiss me like that and then walk away with the dishes!"

"Why don't ye relax on the sofa? You cooked. I'll clean."
He turned the water on and began washing.

Throwing her hands up, she trudged to the couch. The quiet man was back. He drove her crazy. Perhaps she should just leave, but lust still pulsed in her veins. She slid her gaze over to Rory once more, scanning his profile. Two could play this game.

With a crack of thunder, rain poured down outside, drumming on the roof.

"Well, looks like I won't be driving back anytime soon," she drawled out.

He bobbed his head, shuffling that rich, burnt-red hair and continued washing dishes.

Watching him wash achingly slow, Andrea's own need throbbed. She shot lasers at his broad back with her eyes. *Hello, horny woman over here!*

Rory grasped a towel from the dowel and turned. "Do ye play chess?"

"What?"

"Chess." He rotated back to the dishes. "There's a box under the coffee table. Pull it out, will ye?"

Andrea could think of a lot more things to pull out than a flipping chessboard. She flicked her gaze over his beefy butt, wide back, and thick shoulders.

With a yip, Maggie pranced around the kitchen.

Rory folded the dish towel. "She needs to go out."

Andrea rolled her eyes. Didn't he want to get laid? She stooped down to wrench the box out from under the table and paused at the smooth chess container with metal detail. No doubt, Rory had made the set himself. She set the box gently on the table and drew the latch open. While setting up the board, she heard the front door close.

Rory reappeared in the entry. Beads of water dripped from his nose and off his hair and beard, sparkling on his shoulders like tiny stars in the soft entry light. While he shrugged out of his coat, he glanced up and caught her staring.

Her lips curled in response.

Stooping down, he kept his gaze on hers, removing one boot, then two. When he rose, his chest heaved.

She watched his ribs rise and fall like that big-ass hammer, and her own passion, which had simmered since she heard the door slam, now stirred, and her body hummed with anticipation.

As he strode forward, he crossed and sat opposite her. He adjusted the chessboard and cleared his throat, even as a muscle in his neck twitched.

She leaned, pressing her breasts a few inches closer, never taking her gaze off him.

"I'm trying to take this slow," he muttered.

"Don't." Swirling a socked foot up his trousered leg, she felt his leg go slack.

He growled low and rumbly, and his head shot up.

She wet her lips and enjoyed the way his gaze flicked to the movement.

Clearing his throat, he reached for a pawn.

But Andrea slid her foot higher, pressing against his thigh, then snaked toward his groin. When her toes found the large swell against his fly, she flashed a smile. "Checkmate."

His eyes normally the color of slate gray, darkened into liquid smoke. "Christ, Andrea. I'm trying to show ye a care, but yer driving me mad."

Grinning, she fingered the edge of her sweater and, in one swift motion, lifted it up and over her head. She pushed her full breasts toward him over the edge of the table and, with the raw look of delight in those dark eyes, fisted her hand in his hair and pulled his mouth down on hers. Chess pieces scattered under them like dominoes. Andrea drew away briefly and tugged her teeth along Rory's beard, drawing a groan from him once again.

He pushed away from the table, knocking the kitchen chair down, igniting a bark from Maggie.

"And where are you going?" Andrea purred.

"To get ye." Rory grabbed her and tossed her over his shoulder. "Enough of the games, woman."

Andrea slid her hands into his jeans' pockets and squeezed his butt. "Firm."

He strode into the bedroom and kicked the door closed.

But Andrea wasn't laughing now. And all she could see was Rory. He lifted her off him like she weighed nothing—a feat since she knew she'd gained a few extra pounds since arriving in Scotland—and set her in the center of his bed. He followed her, saying nothing and so much with those smoldering, smoky eyes focused on her, and hands that fisted her curves like he was starving to touch her. She kissed him, tangling her tongue with his in quick, sharp swipes, drawing him deeper and deeper.

When Rory's large fingers skimmed the underside of her breasts, then slid around and unsnapped her bra, he pulled away a moment and stared. "Yer so bonnie."

"You're not so bad yourself." She slid her hands up his muscular back.

He chuckled, then cupped her breasts with his hands and circled and teased.

Dropping her head back, she moaned. *Rough hands. Oh, my God!* While his incredible hands roamed down her back, she reached down and unbuttoned his jeans, but when she attempted to tug his pants down, they failed to slide because a certain something stood at attention. "Well, hello." She slid her hand up and down the large bulge, drawing a guttural growl from Rory as he moved his hands down her back to grip her butt once, twice, three times. But her urgency for him grew. She tugged his black briefs down.

He yanked her leggings and panties off in one fell swoop. "I've a need for ye." Reaching over to the nightstand, he retrieved a condom.

She arched under him, grinding her sex against his and glided her hand down until she found him. "Show me."

He grunted. "God, woman."

"Hurry."

He slipped the condom on and drove into her.

Pleasure pulsed through her as they moved in rhythmic, quick slaps, urgently, and greedily. She wrapped her legs around him, drawing him deeper and deeper until that amazing throbbing within exploded inside her. Rory consumed her, filled her, and they finished in a heap together.

When he'd regained his breath sometime later, he sighed. "I'd meant to take my time with ye."

She flicked a hand down his thick pectoral peeking out from his half-opened flannel. He hadn't even fully undressed. "I didn't give you much of a choice."

"Aye, ye didn't." He pressed his lips to hers, then rolled beside her.

He was a picture with his jeans tangled around his ankles and flannel half on. A laugh bubbled up, then another until a full belly laugh escaped.

"*Och*. And what's so funny?"

She swatted the flannel. "You."

He glanced down. Realizing he hadn't finished undressing, he threw off his flannel, then swiftly kicked off his pants. Next, he stalked into the adjacent bathroom, returning a moment later, climbing back into bed. "Ye were keen to get me in bed."

Leaning forward, she nipped his broad shoulder peppered with freckles. "I was. And I'm very happy we did it."

"Did it, ye say?" He pressed a kiss to her jaw, sweeping to her lips, then joined her on the opposite pillow.

"Yes. I've been wanting to see what's under all those layers of control."

He raised a brow.

"I wasn't disappointed."

His cheeks filled with a wide grin. "Good."

She lay beside him with an arm over her head, satiated and deliciously relaxed. When she heard his breathing slow, she glanced over.

Rory slept quietly.

With a shake of her head, she tugged the covers up, then tossed his flannel on and tiptoed to the bathroom. Noticing a bottle of cologne on the counter, she lifted the amber-colored bottle and sniffed. Soft pine and woody notes filled her nostrils. She sighed. After she used the bathroom and freshened up, she crept out of the room.

Maggie shoved her soft muzzle into her hands.

"Well, hey, girl." She laughed. "There's no need to be jealous." Crouching, she ruffled Maggie's fir.

Maggie simply fell to the floor, belly exposed.

With a snort, Andrea rubbed her belly and then strode toward the kitchen in search of some chocolate. But after opening a few cabinets, she didn't find any candy. Alcohol, yes, including a nice twenty-year-old whisky. But she felt like something decadent. Nothing like sex and dessert. Opening the freezer, she found chocolate ice cream. She did a happy dance and grabbed it. "Rich chocolate ice cream with dark chocolate flakes? Fuck, yeah." She opened a cabinet with a *squeak* and grabbed a bowl, then fished for a spoon in the silverware drawer.

"What're ye doing?" Rory barked from across the room.

Andrea jumped. "Shit! You scared me."

He'd tugged on a pair of jeans, but he looked nothing like

the man she'd seen a moment ago—lazily asleep after hot sex. He had an edge about him with those steel eyes and brows drawn.

She lifted the ice cream tub. "Want some?"

"Yer sneaking around getting ice cream?" His shoulders settled and face relaxed.

She dug a spoon into the ice cream. "I wasn't sneaking."

Ambling toward her, he pressed a kiss to the soft spot below her jaw. "I heard something and saw ye weren't beside me..."

She arched a brow.

He shook his head. "Never mind."

Andrea scooped a whopping spoonful of chocolate into her bowl and then another. She popped the lid back on the ice cream, then turned. "There's something you should know about me."

He tilted his head.

"I don't share ice cream."

With a chuckle, he nodded. "Fair enough."

When she lifted a small spoonful to her lips, she sighed at the rich, creamy and smooth chocolate.

He tugged her toward him and kissed her. "Delicious."

She giggled and pushed him aside. "Jerk," she teased, leaning into him anyway, enjoying the taste of Rory and chocolate.

When they separated, she licked the spoon with her tongue, dragging along the chocolate-coated end. Rory's breathing grew heavy, and those eyes darkened like the smoky haze before a firing blaze.

He set the ice cream on the counter, then pressed her snuggly against the freezer.

The combination of the heat radiating in her netherlands and the cool of the freezer sparked something inside her.

Toying with the buttons of the flannel, Rory popped the

first open, then slid his calloused fingers down the flannel until he found her.

She threw her head back as he lifted and pressed her on the countertop, dipping his head toward her hot center. The air grew thick around her as wonderful licks of pleasure twirled within her and grew. Who knew what a beard and mustache could do downstairs? The friction between his beard and tongue intensified, consuming her. She gripped his shoulders and cried out.

When he was done, he drew her close and nuzzled her neck before lifting her and the chocolate up. "I'll take my dessert in the bedroom."

She laughed and held tight to her bowl. "I'm not sharing!"

After a steaming shower, she stood beside Rory in a clean flannel and green-plaid pajama pants, eyeing his dark-blue brush nestled in a plain white, utility-style cup. She would've loved to stroll around naked, but Scotland was fucking cold. "Do you have an extra toothbrush?"

"Aye." He reached around her, sliding a bunched, muscled arm across her shoulder, and opened the second drawer of a three-drawer utilitarian-style dresser. A two-pack of toothbrushes and extra toothpaste nestled next to floss packs in an orderly manner. He opened a packet and handed her a red-and-white brush.

"Thanks." While brushing, she observed the man and his bathroom. Rory was a planner and thought about the next time he needed something. She wondered if he'd have gallons of water and an emergency kit in his garage, too. Flicking a glance his way, she caught a quick grin before he toweled dry and handed her another fresh towel. But what did that mean? That he was always looking ahead? Looking forward? She too often ran out of paper towels and shampoo before she remembered to go to the store. She wondered if he'd planned to be with her. *Well, hell, Andrea, you wanted the sexy, serious man, too. And you planned dinner...* She plunked the brush down, pushing aside thoughts. Just because they'd had sex and dinner didn't mean they were planning to be...in a relationship. She was still trying out the menu.

* * *

When sunlight snuck through the unadorned window the following morning, she dressed in his room and gathered her cooking supplies, while he slept. As she finished tidying up the kitchen, she saw Maggie jump up and race toward Rory's room.

He appeared in the doorway, jeans tugged on and a flannel draped across his shoulders, unbuttoned.

Flutters filled her ribcage. "Oh, I didn't want to wake you. I need to check on Brie."

He nodded, shuffling those sleepy auburn waves.

All she could think was he smoldered—sexy, beefy, and manly.

He strolled toward her. "I had a grand time."

Her flutters vanished. "Me, too."

"I'd like to take ye on a date."

She tipped her head, swaying two-day curls. "A date?"

"Yes." He reached up and tugged a curl.

"You have my number."

With a chuckle, he reached an arm out and grabbed her wrist, yanking her to him.

Firm lips on hers, he kissed her until her body went limp like a noodle. "And then there's the way you do that." She stepped back on not-so-steady legs. What had she gotten herself into?

* * *

Twenty minutes later, Andrea strode into the Fraser kitchen. Golden rays from the winter sun streamed through the wide windows, highlighting Brie's hair with caramel ribbons and shining the marble tile beside an array of colorful vegetables. "You're up and about!" Joy danced within, and she flung her arms around Brie.

"Hi," she whispered.

When she released her, she stuck her nose in the air, immediately inhaling the pungent aroma. "Chili?"

Brie nodded. "I need to move, but I'm going slow, so I thought this slow-cooker meal would be a good start." She picked up a spoon and walked toward a steaming pot.

"How are you feeling?"

"A bit better." She lifted the lid and stirred.

Andrea slid onto a barstool. "Good." Yet, she kept an eye on Brie. Her color had improved—delicate pink cascaded across her cheeks, but she still moved slowly.

Brie swiveled and turned her full attention toward her. "So, how was your night?"

Peering around her, Andrea noted the kids relaxed in front of the television in the living room, watching a Christmas movie. Andrea flicked her head, sending curls flying off her shoulder. "As someone who underestimated the quiet man, let me just say, 'wow.'"

"Oh." Brie leaned closer. "Oh, really?"

"Yeah. He has this way of looking at you that's so serious and unnerving; yet, at the same time, he's so attentive. I imagined he'd be a good lover—just look at the way he takes his time with those swords. And, he was...very...detail-oriented," she dropped her voice an octave eliciting a giggle from Brie. "And that beard, a foreplay tool like I've never known. He didn't disappoint."

"That's great."

"It was." She leaned her elbows on the counter and swiped

a carrot, then bit into the sweet vegetable with a satisfying *crunch*.

"When are you going to see him again?"

"That's kind of the problem."

Brie tilted her head. "Why?"

"He wants to go on a date." Andrea exhaled and set the carrot down, scrunching her nose. "Like a date-date."

"I know that tone. What's up?"

"You know me. I'm not the relationship type. Plus, I'm only here through New Year's. I want casual, but now, I have to go out with him, don't I?"

"Why not? You had no problem pushing me to date Bryce earlier this year, if my memory serves." Brie wiggled her brows.

"What was that?" Bryce asked from the other room.

"Andrea likes Rory."

Andrea smacked Brie playfully on the shoulder.

"What?" She smiled coyly and sat gingerly on a stool with a pad.

"Oh, aye?" Bryce appeared in the arched doorway. "I'll tell the lad to watch out or else we'll have two Americans on our hands."

Andrea glared in his direction. She didn't want him to tell Rory a thing.

With an arm against the arch, he leaned forward. "So, is it the knives that turn ye on or the mighty fine beard?"

"Bryce." Brie half-laughed, clamping a hand over her wide grin.

"'Tis the beard that does it for me, to tell ye the truth."

Rising, she strolled toward the entry. "Glad to see you two are having a good time talking about my relationship affairs."

"Andrea, we're just teasing! Come back."

"I'm going to the market." She paused. "Anyone want anything?"

"Chocolate," Brie replied. "And a big ole baguette."

"Sure." Before she left, she popped into the living room, said good morning to her niece and nephew, and hugged them tight. Striding back out, she glanced at Brie and Bryce embracing in the kitchen. *Darn, perfect couple.* She swung out the door and marched toward Brie's car. But as she sat behind the wheel, she stared at herself in the review mirror. She wasn't annoyed at her friends or their near-perfect-marriage. She was annoyed at herself. She'd just returned from a sexy night with a man who respected and satisfied her in *all* areas, and now, she was second-guessing him, again. What was wrong with her?

Chapter Twenty-Eight

Two days later, Rory drove toward the bright lights of the city and switched on the windshield wipers. A gentle drizzle covered the glass, while a bouquet of red roses rested on the dash. Forty-eight hours had passed since he'd seen Andrea, and when he'd called to ask her on a date the following morn, she'd been hesitant and replied with a text that she needed to spend more time with Brie. So, he did what any man would do when faced with a squirrely lass—he bided his time. Luckily, she'd texted a few hours earlier, stating she needed to get out of the house. He was more than happy to indulge her.

When his phone chimed, notifying him of a message and then another, he glanced over, then refocused on the road. His truck wasn't built like those fancy new ones with the automated touch screens and such, and he was glad. He liked the peace his old truck afforded him. Ten minutes later, his phone rang. He craned his head, wondering if Andrea was cancelling. Upon seeing the name flash across the screen, he grinned and pressed the speaker at a stoplight.

"Are ye stuck under the power hammer?" Rory's younger brother, Collin, asked in greeting.

Rory chuckled. "No. I'm on my way to pick up a lass."

"Oh, aye? Ye should bring her to meet Ma at Christmas."

He cleared his throat. He had to take their budding relationship slow. He couldn't chance bringing her home with Da's sour attitude.

"'Tis due time you came home, Rory. Ma's chirping about how long it's been since she's seen yer gob, and it wouldn't hurt to remind yer only niece that she has an uncle, either."

With a shake of his head, Rory grasped the steering wheel tighter, even as guilt weighed on his mind.

"Hannah's coming home from university for Christmas, and I'm sure Luna will make an appearance after she clambers off the mountain. Ye don't have to come for Da."

Rory gritted his teeth. He'd scarcely spoken to his father in three years.

"Come for Father Christmas and to see yer beloved brother, sisters, ma, and wee niece."

Scrubbing a hand over his beard, he considered. Family was important and, of course, Da was a pain in the arse, but his family deserved better. "I've a horde of orders to get through before I can visit."

"Bring your items. I'll help ye. It'll be like old times again —you on the anvil, me telling stories, and working the fine details."

"Ah, brother, but ye just make decorative steel now."

"*Och*, don't break me heart."

Rory laughed loud and warm.

"Yer done with shooting for the year, are ye not?"

"Aye, I'm working on something else right now." He glanced at the red roses, reminding him of the red beret and sweater he'd seen Andrea wearing the first time he'd met her.

"Oh, aye? Broadening your horizons, are ye?"

"Working on a lass."

"The ones that make ye work are the ones who're worth yer time."

With a curl of his lips, he agreed and said his farewells. Twenty minutes later, he punched the familiar code into Bryce's keypad. The gate opened. 'Twas time to court Andrea and indulge her foodie nature.

* * *

The glow of Christmas lights sparkled above them in colorful array, while festive music danced in the air and delicious savory aromas wafted toward them at the Christmas Market. Now that the rain had stopped, Rory strolled beside Andrea. Between the pop-up shops, food trucks, and sitting areas, he imagined they'd stay fairly dry. He'd taken Andrea to a different Christmas market from the one she'd visited with Brie and the kids, not wanting to bring up negative memories from the previous week. Stopping in front of a chip shop, he inclined his head. "Ready to try some local flavor?"

She flashed him a bright-red smile that matched her beret. "Am I ever."

"Order what ye like."

With a tilt of her head, she hummed. "How is this going to work? Are we sharing?"

"If ye like. There're many shops, so if ye want to try them all, I'm happy to oblige ye."

Andrea wiggled a brow. "I do. Good thing this is a stroll and dine, or I'd be filling out my pants even more."

With a flick of his gaze up and down her body, he leaned forward, lips curling. "Ye have nothing to worry about from where I'm standing."

Grinning, she ordered loaded chips with brisket and barbeque sauce. "I'm paying."

"'Tis my treat."

She leveled her dark-brown eyes. "This is the twenty-first century, Rory."

"Aye." He retrieved his wallet and withdrew fifteen pounds.

She threw up her hands. "Fine. Thank you."

With a nod, Rory paid the barista, while keeping an eye on Andrea. "I'll steal a few chips."

"So now, you're a chip-stealer?"

"Might be."

She rolled her eyes, but a smile tugged at the corners of her full mouth. "I guess I can spare a few."

Chuckling, he accepted the chip order and extended the basket toward Andrea, breathing in the salty, smoky aroma mingled with Andrea's spice. He enjoyed their banter, and even more, he enjoyed being with her. He felt himself relaxing, strolling and chatting more than usual, talking and commenting about the varied fare and local favorites, drawn out of his shell by the fiery woman beside him. He just hoped he wouldn't get burned, again.

* * *

Andrea tried to decline going out with Rory to keep what was between them light and non-relationship-y, but she had to admit, something about Rory attracted her. Besides, why couldn't she go on a few dates and have some fun? She didn't need to jump in the deep end; she just wanted to do a few laps, especially since he knocked her wool socks off a few nights prior. Glancing at Rory comfortably dressed in packed jeans, a snug wool sweater, and workman boots reaching for a thick chip, she grinned.

"What? Have I sauce on me face?"

"Nope." Popping a fry into her mouth, she closed her

eyes, enjoying the salty, tangy, and crunchy goodness and the not-so-silent-man's company. Next, they shared a bratwurst bursting with spices and sauerkraut, decadent crepes, spicy kabobs, Mediterranean wraps, and more. She was in foodie heaven.

An hour and a half later, she thought she'd burst like an overstuffed pasta shell. She exhaled loudly. "I don't think I can eat one more thing."

Rory slowed, stopping at a booth with cheerful red-and-white decorations strung between strands of festive lights. "There's one last treat ye've got to try—a local favorite."

She placed a hand on a full hip. "Okay, I'm listening."

He jabbed a thumb toward a fry shop. "A deep-fried candy bar."

She laughed quick and sharp. "You're joking?"

"*Och*. I'd never joke about something so decadent."

After ordering a deep-fried candy bar and two coffees, she sat beside him at a tiny table for two with wooden chairs. She stared at the rectangular, corn flake-colored, crispy chocolate bar surrounded by fried air bubbles and crinkled her nose. Their final course didn't look appetizing. In fact, the candy bar looked like poop—fried poop. The treat could use some powdered sugar or chocolate drizzle like Brie was always doing to cookies and cupcakes to make them more appealing.

"Ready?" Rory asked with a deep rolling *r*.

"Yup." She cut the bar in half and, scrutinizing the chocolaty caramel center, picked up a piece. "Here goes nothing." Biting into the bar, she immediately tasted fried tempura-like batter with melted chocolate. "*Mmm*. Damn. It's not much to look at, but you're right. It's delicious."

Rory chuckled. "Glad yer enjoying it."

"Have any more foodie secrets?" She wiped her lips.

He leaned forward, dipping his head. "One," he whispered. "But then, I'd have to kill ye."

She burst out laughing. Joy spread through her chest and filled her cheeks as she giggled and Rory joined in—her laughter marrying with his deep vibrato. After a few moments, she sighed and trailed her fingertips over his hand, wrist, and forearm, pausing where the tip of his sword tattoo peeked out from pushed up sleeves. Tracing it further, she inclined her head. "Tell me something."

He nodded, while his gaze flicked to her hand and then back up.

"You spend all that time in your forge by yourself."

He peered over his coffee. "When I'm not on set."

"Don't you ever get bored?"

He kicked up a brow. "Are ye bored in the kitchen?"

With a snort, she bobbed her head, shuffling curls, then dipped a finger into the chocolate. "Touché, but you know, sometimes, I like having someone to bounce ideas off of." She licked the chocolate off, watching his gray-eyed gaze follow and Adam's apple bob.

Clearing his throat, he pushed aside the dessert. "I see yer point. My brother is a smith and makes fine architectural and decorative ironwork and such in Inverness, but he's not a swordsmith. I do send him pictures, though." He swigged from the coffee cup. "I also converse with a historian I'm connected with and Bryce, at times. Even Hugh's been known to visit to test certain combat swords."

She gaped. "To test swords? What do you mean?"

"We have a square go."

She arched a brow.

He leaned forward. "We spar."

Her eyes widened. "With real swords?"

"Aye. Though they're blunted on the end—part of the combat rules. Still, as a competitor, ye can get seriously injured, even lose a finger"—he held up a hand with a deep gash across the knuckle—"or end up in the hospital."

"Seriously?"

"Yes. But 'tis a grand time when I get to knock Hugh on his arse."

She laughed. "I'd love to see that! Is it legal, though?"

"We have metal gear—iron mail and padding. Hugh, myself, and a few of my mates are members of a Historical Sword Club, but not Bryce. He's worried about his *Swords* contract."

"Like full on knights-of-the-round-table shit?"

"Aye. We're on break currently, but tournaments will resume in late spring."

Her heart thudded in her chest. *A real-life highlander with a sword.* "That's hot."

Grinning, he set a beefcake arm on the table. "I also have a pell—a solid wood pole—used to strike with the sword to see how it arches and carries."

"So, you play with your swords?"

His smile spread, rounding his cheeks. "I do."

"I want to try it." She stroked his muscular forearm, tracing the sword. "Tonight."

* * *

Although rain pounded when they pulled up to Rory's house, the forge was dry and lit. Andrea followed him inside and strolled to the far end where swords were mounted on the wall on wooden supports, and others were secured in some sort of a multi-drawer cabinet with combination locks. But she realized, she didn't see anything that said *Rory's Forge*. He was so unassuming. An idea came to mind for Christmas. She loved giving presents and even more, presents between friends. Noticing Rory unlock cabinets, she felt anticipation dance inside. She remembered how heavy the claymore was. Would he give her a similar weapon now?

He moved methodically, retrieving two sets of gloves, jackets, and a few other items, then set them on a steel table. "Let's get ye outfitted properly."

"Will I look like one of those Knights of the Round Table?"

Chuckling, he shook his head. "No. We'll put on some sparring equipment. The gear I wear weighs near forty kilos."

Her mouth flopped open. "Holy shit."

"Ye can never be too careful."

She rubbed her hands together. "All right. I'm game." Excitement bubbled within her like a rolling, boiling pot of pasta water. She was ready to jump in and transform into a kick-ass medieval warrior. Seeing Rory lift the jacket, she slid her arms into one quilted sleeve at a time. With their seven-inch size difference, Andrea's arms swam in the jacket. "Um, big guy, short girl."

Grinning, he picked up a belt, then snugged the leather around her body.

She felt his warm breath on her neck as he cinched the belt, making her extra toasty in all the warm places.

With a flick of a firm finger on the belt, he tugged her close and planted a smart kiss on her mouth. He backed her toward the cabinet and captured her lips once more, while his hands roamed over the jacket. A moment later, he stepped back.

"Hey." Andrea licked her lips, then tugged down the jacket. "None of that. I'm going to be a frickin' warrior princess."

He grinned. Next, he helped her into thick, leather gloves that stretched over her wrists and onto her forearms and then popped a soft leather helmet onto her head with protective steel bars across the front.

She could see everything, which was surprising. She swung her arms around, while Rory tugged on a pair of gloves and a similar jacket. She cocked a brow. "Aren't you putting armor on?"

A smirk tugged at one side of his beard. "I'll be fine."

She rolled her eyes. "I could hurt you."

The smirk widened.

Fury boiled in her veins, and she flung a hand out. "Give me the damn sword."

"Widen your stance and bend your knees a wee bit," he instructed.

She followed his directions, ready to kick some ass.

With a swift nod, he swiveled, selecting a short sword. "'Tis a stunt sword." He handed her a short, rubbery sword.

"I want that one." She pointed to the massive sword on the table.

"Aye, ye'll have it after some practice."

"Fine."

Rory showed her how to step and swing, lift and turn, and step and strike. After five or ten minutes of practice, he unsheathed another sword—a shiny claymore.

"Holy shit."

He passed the sword, basket handle facing her. "Can ye hold it with one hand?"

"Yes." She squared her shoulders and told herself to channel the Amphipolis princess. Grasping the handle with one hand, she held the sword tightly. Yet, as he released the full weight, the heavy mass fell on her, and her arm shook. Fire burned within, and she squeezed the leather holder. "Now, what do I do?"

"Lift the sword and swing it like we went over. The weight will help ye with the movement, but hold firm, keeping the tip from hitting the ground."

With determination, she gripped the sword even tighter and swung it not so prettily right at him. "Ah!"

Chapter Twenty-Nine

RORY SIDESTEPPED AS ANDREA SWUNG THE SWORD and hit the ground with a *clang*.

Her lips turned down into a pout. "Shit."

"'Tis all right. Ye won't damage it by a few hits to the cement. The tips blunted slightly for contemporary combat anyway."

As she readjusted, she heaved a breath and righted the sword, holding it up high, while her cheeks flushed. She pointed the sword once again.

Pride swelled his chest. He was impressed by her spirit. "Slash the sword toward my shoulder."

Stepping forward, she heaved the sword once again with eyes shining. "It's too heavy."

"Slash my arm."

"Hiii-ya!" She swung.

Rory countered, swinging his sword to meet hers and stopped above her shoulder, ending pressed into her bosom, heat to heat.

"You cheated!"

He smiled wide. "*Och*. Never."

Her eyes fired, turning them into deep dark chocolate, while her chest heaved. He wished he could kiss her, draw her in, and taste that fire, but she was already gripping the sword, readying. He stepped back. "Again, but"—he reached into another drawer and pulled out a poly plastic *sgian dubh*—"use this."

She stuck out her tongue. "Not the tiny knife again."

"*Sgian dubhs* are lethal."

Her lips curled. "Oh, really?" She gazed at the three-to-four-inch blade. "Do I swing it the same?"

"No. When I raise me arm, ye go under to gut me in the stomach or from behind and pierce me lungs. When yer opponent canna breath, he canna fight."

She lunged forward.

The poly plastic pressed into Rory's quilted side.

"Got ya."

"Aye, ye did," he replied proudly.

She backed up, then with knees bent, took her position. "Again." She advanced with rosy cheeks and struck.

Deflecting, he gripped her around the waist, so she was facing him. His heart thundered, and his blood thickened with lust, while her bosom swelled and heaved with the effort against him.

Her lips parted and irises darkened. "Do you want me?"

"Aye." He hoisted her onto the metal table, then untied the fasteners on the helmet as she tossed her gloves. The helmet *crashed* onto the ground. He uncinched the jacket and pushed it aside, reaching under the thick sweater to smooth a hand up her silky back. Watching her head tip back, he kissed a trail down her cheek, jawline, and finally her neck, where a hint of spice and salt lingered on her skin, then toyed with the top of her pants.

She wrestled with his thick belt, then tugged his pants down.

"Christ. Would be easier with a kilt."

She wiggled her brows. "I'd like to see that." She shivered.

He drew back. "Are ye cold?"

"No."

Titling his head, he scanned his gaze over her. "Sure?"

"Yes." She tugged him forward and kissed him, tangling her tongue with his.

She drew him deeper into the blaze, until his control edged. She made him want, desire, and claim. With a growl, he picked her up with one arm, wrenched her pants down with the other, then set her lovely bare ass on the steel table.

"Fuck, that's cold." She shuddered. Pressing closer, she tugged his boxers down. "Now. Inside me. Now."

"Aye." With a shred of control left, he grabbed his wallet, retrieved a condom, and after fastening, slid into her slick center. Like the wee sparring they just did, they arched and moved, giving and taking, driving one another higher and higher until the grand release. She clung to him after— gorgeous curves wrapped around, warm breath whispering along his neck, and heaving heartbeat rapping against his. He'd meant to romance her tonight, but this woman did something to him he couldn't explain. She was a fiery flame, and he a moth.

Chapter Thirty

The following morning, Andrea walked into the main house and found Brie and her family in the kitchen. The partially cloudy sky created a half-moon of silvery light, covering Brie and Bryce with a soft halo.

Brie blinked over glossy eyes, bottom lip trembling.

"All will be well, *mo ghraidh*," Bryce crooned and leaned his forehead against Brie's, smoothing a hand through her hair, stopping at her chin to caress a cheek.

"What's going on?" Andrea set the keys on the counter.

Brie turned. "I have a...checkup today. To check..." She sniffled.

Walking forward, Andrea reached a hand out to Brie's shoulder. "It's okay. I understand."

The kids stared from the child-sized table, a few bites of pancakes left on their plates. Questions peppered in their eyes.

Andrea flashed a smile. "Come on, kids. Let's go play hide-and-seek in your castle fortress."

"Can we, Mom?" Noah rose from his green chair. "Will you be okay?"

She grasped his face between her hands and kissed him on the cheek. "I'll be fine. Have fun."

"Yay!" Phoebe jumped up, then ran to Brie and gave her a kiss. "Kisses always make the doctor's better."

"They do." Brie smiled.

After bundling them into coats, hats, and gloves, Andrea threw on her own, popped on her beret, and followed them into the yard. Stepping into the brisk morning, she stared at the few, fluffy, white clouds peppered between large sky-blue lakes. *It's a day for exploring.* The kids needed to get out of the house. She retrieved her phone and searched *things to do* in Glasgow during Christmas. Lots of options appeared, including visiting Santa and his reindeer, but she knew Brie and Bryce were planning on a surprise visit to see Santa and real reindeer in the Cairngorms on Christmas. *Scratch that idea.* Hearing the kids giggle, while they hid, she continued perusing, then paused when she came across a fairy trail. "A fairy expedition," she whispered. Just something Brie would take the kids to that would light up their imaginations and get them outside to use all that boundless energy.

"Auntie A, come find us!" Phoebe squealed.

She climbed the wooden ladder, hands gripping the wooden rungs with the vibrant scent of cedar all around, and crossed the bridge. She searched high and low and in each nook and cranny.

Phoebe tucked under a table above the lookout with her golden-brown hair concealing her like a curtain.

"Found you!"

"Eee!" With a giggle, Phoebe jumped up. "Let's go find Noah."

Hand-in-hand, she and Phoebe searched for Noah until they discovered him in the top tower. "Got you!" Andrea tickled him.

Noah giggled. "Come on, Phoebe. Let's hide again!"

Andrea took that moment to call Rory. "I need to get the kids out of the house and let Brie and Bryce deal with everything."

"Oh, aye. What've ye got up yer sleeve?"

"I found this cute little fairy trail in the woods. Thinking that's just what the kids need. Have you heard of it? Is it any good?"

"Can't say I have, but I can spare a few hours if ye'd like company."

Andrea paused, humming in response. She flicked a finger over a fissure in the red-toned wood where tiny, dark cracks vined up like a fault line. After incredible sex in the forge, she'd taken a slippery, sexy shower with Rory, then made out on the couch. But with the fire crackling romantic embers of gold and ginger around them and soft music playing in the background of Rory's living room, she felt panic course through her and asked him to drive her home—using Brie as her excuse. She liked him. He was a great lover and talked just enough to drive her crazy. But she couldn't cuddle and be cozy together. She *couldn't* fall for him. "Don't you have work to do?"

"It'll keep for a few hours. I've been at it since before dawn."

With one last glance at the natural fracture, she agreed. She hoped she wouldn't regret her decision.

* * *

Driving down the designated road between lush, green trees to the fairy trail, Andrea spied a rugby club sign. Brief panic enveloped her, thinking that she'd made the wrong turn, but as she pulled over, another car passed with a toe-headed little girl waving a wand out the window. "If in doubt, follow the fairy." She continued and parked by the playground where a building boasted a hand-painted wall with a plum-purple arrow pointing to the fairy trail. And there was Rory, standing beside his truck, arms crossed, wearing a forest-green beanie, navy-blue sweater, and dark winter vest. *Warning, sexy lumberjack in the fairy forest.*

"I see Rory!" Noah unbuckled, then shot out and launched himself into Rory's arms.

Rory chuckled. "Hello, lad."

With Phoebe's small hand in hers, she strolled forward. "Are you sure you have time to spare?"

Nodding, he smiled. "Aye. Phoebe, are ye ready to find the wee fairies?"

"Yes!" She jumped.

While the kids dashed ahead, Rory grasped her hand in his and strolled forward.

Andrea glanced at their entwined hands—his large, blunt-fingered and fair with a few freckles, and her golden-toned woven between like two-toned pasta. She'd never been one for hand-holding, but something about Rory's strong, firm grip made her feel at ease. She didn't let go.

With a gentle squeeze of a hand, Rory inclined his head. "How's Brie?"

"She's visiting the doctor today. She seems to be improving, but she's still having some rough moments. Healing will take time." Although Brie seemed better before leaving the house, sadness still etched around her eyes. Bryce was also quieter; yet, he hadn't left her side, save for the final day of work.

Rory nodded and continued forward, gaze fixed on the children.

She walked through the welcome area where ivy twined and curled over walkways and sharp, pungent grass filled her senses. As she walked toward a canopy of pines beside Rory, she inhaled the scents of Christmas along with damp earth that'd already stuck to her boots. "This is so cute! And I'm glad we put our boots on." She wiggled her feet in her new, Christmas-red Wellies she'd purchased last week.

"Aye. I've never heard of this particular trail, but Scotland has many hidden gems."

"Any others I should add to my list?"

He considered, scrubbing his free hand through his beard. "Loch Ness is as lovely as it is mysterious, and if yer lucky"— he leaned with a twinkle in his eye—"you'll even spot Nessie."

Andrea snorted. "The Loch Ness monster? Are you for real?"

His brows shot up. "Ye dinnae poke at one of our most famous legends."

Eyeing him, Andrea grinned. Rory was full of surprises.

When Phoebe yelled for them to come see the fairy house she found, she skipped around the front of a tall pine tree as they approached. "Look! A door." She knelt and pointed to a tiny, four-inch wooden door carved at the base of the tree. "Come out, fairy. Come out!"

Dropping to his haunches, Rory placed a finger on his lips. "Shh, ye don't want to scare the wee fairies with yer boisterous hollers now, do ye?"

"It doesn't even open. It's not real." Noah looked at the tree with a scowl.

Phoebe stomped a rain boot. "It is real!"

"He's just being silly." Andrea knelt beside Phoebe. "Everyone knows you need fairy magic to open the door or"— she paused and watched their eyes round—"an appetizing treat."

Phoebe's eyes widened.

"Candy?" Noah asked.

"Fairies are creatures of the forest. I'm sure they'd love some candy, but they like wild fruits and natural plants harvested, too. Such as"—she flew her gaze around and spotted a buttercup-orange cap with curled edges—"this mushroom." She walked over and plucked the chanterelle. "How about we make them a fairy stew?"

With a squeal, Phoebe skipped to a pile of leaves, while Noah found bark shaped like a bowl.

Rory rested his back against a tree opposite with a grin playing on his lips.

Andrea, meanwhile, searched for other ingredients and came upon a few small rose bushes with bright-red rose hips that looked like holly berries. She plucked a few off and added the hips to the colorful stew, then gestured to Phoebe and Noah. "Well, if that's not the most appetizing fairy stew!"

"It looks dewicious!" Phoebe said.

"It's cool," Noah added.

Whispering unintelligible words, Phoebe brought the bowl carefully down with Noah hovering his sure hands next to hers and placed the stew beside the door.

"Perfect. Now, we wait and watch."

A few minutes later, the sun peeked through the clouds and shined through the evergreens, alighting dancing orbs along the forest floor. The orbs zipped like lightning bugs.

"I saw a faiwy!" Phoebe said.

"Me, too," Noah yelled.

"They're excited for their meal. Let's say 'hi' and then go look for some more," Andrea told them.

Phoebe skipped around, following light orbs and waving *hello*.

Noah whipped his head around.

"Ye've a gift with the children." Rory leaned toward her.

She flashed a smile. "Well, I'm Auntie A, that's my job. I never thought I'd be an Auntie, but Brie and the kids have added a whole new level of fun to my life."

With a nod, he lifted a branch to let her pass. "Ye'll be a fine mother one day."

Andrea froze. How did they go from talking about her niece and nephew to having kids? She pressed down the bubbling annoyance. "A mother? So, all's a woman's good for is popping out children?"

"No." His steel eyes watched her.

Running a hand through her curls, she exhaled. She'd never even considered kids. Work, yes. Fun, definitely. But kids? That was a whole 'nother enchilada. Kids involved care and two people—maybe even marriage—something she definitely didn't want, especially coming from parents who valued themselves more than their child. What the heck did she have to offer kids anyway other than fun aunt status? When she glanced up, she saw pops of magenta-and-red jackets weave around a bend—Noah and Phoebe—and alarm streaked through her. She strode forward. "I'm going to catch up with the kids." Power-walking, she put some space between Rory and his ideas.

* * *

Rory watched Andrea dash ahead. She didn't want a family? He'd thought it natural she did, especially the way she carried on with the children. Of course, she'd never mentioned children, but a woman with all her care and maternal instincts was bound to want them. Her remarks and body language perplexed him. *She didn't want a family?* They'd never talked about anything so serious. But they were getting along, and the topic was bound to come up.

With a shake of his head, he glanced at Andrea's disappearing figure. He wanted a family. A grand one with weans running around and family dinners. And by what he'd gathered about Andrea, she did, too. He wondered what she was so afraid of.

Chapter Thirty-One

PASTA EQUALED HAPPINESS. THAT'S WHAT ANDREA always believed. Plus, nothing helped relieve frustration like rolling out some homemade dough. She'd had fun at the fairy trail earlier, then Rory put his own ideas in her head of who she should be and what she should do. She was a grown-ass woman. She knew what she wanted, didn't she? She lugged the flour bag across the counter. Why did she go and get involved? The serious, quiet man obviously had more on his mind than fun. And she did *not*. Though she did order him a custom Christmas present...that didn't mean anything, right? He needed the sign for his shop. With a huff, she dipped a large measuring cup into the flour.

Noah hoisted himself up beside her. "What're we making?"

"Ravioli and caprese salad."

He poked a finger in the flour, making a dimple. "I love raviolis. What're we going to do first?"

She twisted. "Are your hands clean?"

He grinned mischievously and held his hands up. "Just washed them."

With a nod, she adjusted the few ingredients. "Well, the flour is already in, so now we need to add a little salt, aquafaba since this is egg-free for your sister, and water." They added the wet ingredients to the dry and mixed.

"Now, we'll knead the dough until smooth, then we'll let it rest in the fridge for thirty minutes or so while we make the mushroom filling."

Making a gagging sound, he scrunched his face. "I don't like mushrooms."

She snorted. "Well, I do. We're making sausage and spinach ones, too." Though she knew Noah had eaten the mushroom filling before, she figured what he didn't know wouldn't hurt him. She moved the liquid measure toward him. "Okay, buddy. Let's measure half a cup of aquafaba."

He measured carefully with his lip tucked between his teeth.

Seeing Noah so focused and caring, Andrea felt warmth flood her insides. He was such an incredible kid. She ruffled his hair. "Great job, kiddo." Next, she showed him how to mix the dough, then turned the mixture onto a lightly floured board and asked him to knead.

He scooped the floury crumbs with his little hands and turned and rolled, combining the dough until a loose clump took shape.

With her hands atop his, Andrea guided his small hands, helping shape the sunny pasta ball. Once done, she wrapped the ball in plastic and stuck it in the fridge to rest.

"Mom's writing today." He swirled a finger over the flour-dusted counter.

Nodding, she collected measuring cups and spoons. Brie had told Andrea the news after returning from the doctor's—that she could have more children. Although full recovery—mind, body, and soul—would take time, Andrea knew this was joyous news. She smiled. "She is."

He glanced up. "I think she's feeling better."

"I think so, too, buddy." She bumped a shoulder with his. "Let's let her write for a bit and whip up the fillings."

He flashed a huge grin. "We better hurry before Phoebe wakes from her nap."

"It's okay. She can help."

"But I like making pasta, especially when it's just you and me. I'm your sous chef, right?"

She hugged him tight. "You betcha, big guy." Amongst the warm flour aroma in the air, she caught his little boy scent of soap and dirt. Her heart soared with love. Maybe having kids wouldn't be so bad, especially if they were anything like Noah and Phoebe. But she wasn't marriage material...and kids needed a mom and dad. She thought about Rory—how she'd left him staring quizzically following a quick good-bye at the fairy trail. She was bound to screw up whatever they were doing if she hadn't already. With a shake of her head, she focused on Noah and the meal.

Half an hour later, Andrea stirred balsamic vinegar in a small saucepan, while Noah finished sealing the ravioli, and the sun dipped lower in the patchy sky.

"Yuck! What's that smell?" Noah covered his nose with his arm.

"Balsamic reduction, boy-o. Once that vinegar boils off, we'll have sweet, luscious balsamic glaze."

Knock-knock.

She frowned. "Do you think Bryce locked himself out?" He'd gone to the gym a few hours prior to work out his feelings, she imagined. But he had an access code.

Noah giggled, then jumped off the stool. "I'll check!"

Mimi glided through the foyer. "Oh, it's Rory."

Andrea froze.

The sound of the large, wooden door opening cut across the quiet space.

"Hello, Rory! How are you?" Mimi's warm voice greeted.

"Well, thank ye, and ye?" his deep rumble returned.

"Great! I fell in love with Inverness, and the artists were so talented. I can't thank you enough for telling me about your hometown."

"Yer welcome," he said and then with a grunt added, "*Och*, hello, lad."

Noah spoke a mile a minute, telling him about ravioli making.

Andrea's chest thundered.

"I'm sure you're here to see our Andrea," Mimi said.

What was he going to say? No, I'm here to see Bryce. If he was here to see her, why? To tell her, *Let's not do this anymore? or let's break up? But how can he break up with me if we were never really together?* Her pulse picked up and started skittering like droplets of water across a scorching pan. Hearing footsteps approach, she grabbed a cup and transferred the balsamic reduction to cool, then rinsed the saucepan. If her hands were busy, she couldn't overthink everything.

Rory entered the kitchen, filling the entire space with his big burliness.

She glanced at him—at his calm demeanor, cozy flannel, and reddish beard where his plump lips nestled in between, then back at the sink.

Clearing his throat, he strolled farther, boots scuffing on the wooden floor. "Ye left yer gloves atop the car."

She turned off the faucet and snatched a kitchen towel. "Oh, thanks."

He reached into his pocket and retrieved her red gloves. Yet, he didn't proceed forward.

Twisting the towel in her hands, she retreated to the stove and grabbed her water glass. Why was her throat so damn dry? She took a sip, and fire-hot balsamic reduction scorched her tongue and teeth. She raced to the sink and spit out the reduction, then stuck her face under the tap to cool her fuming mouth. "Oh, m—"

"Are ye all right?" he asked from behind.

She felt heat radiate from him, even though she had the cool water on full blast. *Too close. He's too close.* She bobbed her head and, identifying the correct glass, pivoted and cooled her mouth down with two, giant gulps. She twisted around and found Rory staring intently, brows pinched. "I'm fine. Fine."

He nodded.

A moment passed.

Then two.

Then tree.

She threw her hands in the air. "Look, I'm sorry about snapping at you earlier, okay? I'm not girlfriend material."

He kicked up an auburn brow.

"I'm not."

"All right."

She continued staring. "Isn't that what you want?"

He tucked a hand into a front pocket. "We don't need to put a title on it."

"No?"

Ambling two steps forward, he stopped a foot away. "It seems that we enjoy one another's company, *aye*?"

She eyed him. "Sure."

"Let's leave it at that for now."

"For now?"

He nodded, steadfast gaze on hers.

She shrugged. Maybe she was making too much out of nothing. "I don't like when someone makes assumptions about me."

"I'll take care to remember that."

She stuck a hand out. "Friends?"

He grasped hers in his bear claw. "Friends."

But damnit, little zings shot up her arm to her belly when he touched her. What was she going to do about him?

* * *

Rory stayed. He hadn't intended to, but Mimi wouldn't let him get away, looping an arm through his and steering him toward the artistry work she'd done in Inverness, while Andrea prepared dinner and Brie played with the wee ones. He needed to return to his forge to fill orders and think through a few things, though he'd done plenty of thinking after returning home following the fairy adventure. He liked Andrea. And he knew she had feelings for him, but damned the woman was stubborn. He'd have to wear her down slowly and allow her to take the next step, instead of two steps back.

Bustling sounded in the hallway, and the Fitzgibbon crew along with Bryce's mother strolled in, bringing the volume up three notches.

"'Rory! 'Tis good to see ye." Ma Fraser enveloped him in a hug, pressing her gray curls into his chest.

Instantly, he thought back to his own ma who, though a foot shorter than he, loved a grand hug. "And ye."

"Now, where are my other grandchildren?" She ambled away.

"Rory," Ian greeted with his tidy beard and hair in disarray. "Ye off for holiday, as well?"

"I have a few pieces left to finish for Christmas orders." He glanced at his watch. "I should head back."

"*Tsk*." Rose clucked with a babe in her arms. "Ye'll be doin' no such thing until ye've eaten. I'll lend a hand in the kitchen. There'll be plenty." And with that, she stalked away.

Ian chuckled beside him.

Rory scrubbed a hand over his beard. "Does anyone say *no* to yer wife?"

"No." He elbowed him good naturedly. "A drink?"

With one last glance toward the kitchen, he watched Andrea laugh with Brie and Rose. "Aye." Perhaps staying wasn't a bad idea after all. He ate beside Andrea at the long dining table with Bryce at the head next to Brie, while Ma Fraser sat at the other end with her brood of grandchildren. He couldn't stop grinning. He hadn't had a family dinner in some time, and he enjoyed the laughter and warmth, children's antics, and Andrea at his side.

"Rory, how's your mother?" Ma Fraser asked.

He nodded. "Well."

"Oh, aye? How'd ye know unless ye've spoken to her as of late?" She leaned forward, dark-eyed gaze focused.

Grimacing, he lifted a forkful of ravioli stuffed with rich sausage and herbs and took a large bite. He'd forgotten that mothers talk. And his and Bryce's became thick as thieves as soon as they'd met a few years ago.

"I spoke with her yesterday, and she told me ye haven't been home for Christmas in years. Now, do ye want to break yer mother's heart and send her to the grave early?"

He swallowed, feeling the guilty, half-chewed pasta lump in his throat. Grabbing a glass, he drank, but he found all gazes on him. He cleared his throat. "I've been busy getting my business up and running. The show won't be around indefinitely to pay my bills."

She bobbed her head. "I can see what yer saying, but be a good son and visit yer ma. I hear yer sisters are in town, as well."

"Aye."

"Rory's afraid Collin will show him up on those sword skills," Bryce shot out.

That drew a grin, and he could feel the mood lightening. "*Och*, a crafter's got nothing to be afraid of. I've my own specialty." But thinking back to Collin's call the other day and the conversation now, he considered making a wee visit. He knew how to handle Da, even if it did tend to bring out the worst in him. "I'm considering visiting for Christmas."

Ma Fraser nodded. "That's grand. Give yer family my best."

"We'll be up there as well," Brie noted. "We have a winter cottage near the Cairngorms, and we're visiting the reindeer after we open presents, right, kids?"

"Yes!"

"It'll be fun petting old Comet and giving him treats after those long Christmas runs, huh?" Andrea winked.

Rory swiveled. He wasn't aware Andrea would be in the highlands, as well. Perhaps he could convince her to go with him to his folks' place, but damned if he knew how. She was as skittish as a housefly.

After dinner, he moseyed into the family room for drinks and hot cocoa. Seasonal swags of greenery decorated the fireplace, while a giant tree with colorful decorations stood tall, front and center, and pictures of the children with Santa Claus throughout the years, decorated side tables.

"Why the hesitance when Ma Fraser asked about visiting your family?" Andrea sidled close with a tartan mug. "Is it your dad?"

He exhaled. "Aye. We don't see eye-to-eye."

She bobbed her head, shuffling dark curls. "I get that, but you should go. I visited my dad a few years ago. I yelled, he calmy answered me, I yelled some more, he explained, and we hugged. The conversation helped put away a lot of the anger I had growing up."

He turned. She'd shared something personal. A first step. "Oh?"

"Yup. You should go." She sipped the *swally* topped with cream, then turned with a quick smile. "You know what? I can go with you."

Angling his head, he opened his mouth to confirm.

She swooshed a hand rapidly in front of her. "*Not* to meet your parents—that's definitely not my thing, but I'll stay in the car, and you can tell them your travel buddy is sick. It'll give you an out. *Hi, bye, etc*. I'll be your bonnie-getaway driver."

He chuckled.

"But if things go well and you want to stay, just give me the signal, and I'll head back to the cottage with Brie, Bryce, and the kids.

"Genuinely?"

She toasted her mug. "As serious as spaghetti."

He smiled smugly.

"Besides, you've saved my ass more times than I can count. I figure I owe you." She elbowed him gently and settled a round hip against him.

Placing a hand on her waist, he welcomed her presence here and now, and at Christmas. Still, he hoped the trip wouldn't backfire.

Chapter Thirty-Two

Brie stared with wide eyes in the near-spotless kitchen later that evening. "You're meeting Rory's family?"

"No." Andrea set down the dry serving dish. "I'm going *with* him. I'm his escape goat—his bonnie-getaway girl. You know, so he can leave early. Get out of uncomfortable family dinners. Lord knows I have more experience than I care to share."

Brie's lips tugged into a smile. "Well, then it'll be a party in the Cairngorms for Christmas! After dinner, you two can head to our holiday house in the mountains. It's near the ski resort, perfect for Boxing Day. The place has five rooms plus a master, so you'll have your own to share with Rory. It'll be great."

"Thank you for that and, shit, for everything, this will be the best Christmas ever!" She slung an arm around Brie and hugged her tight. Since meeting Brie, she'd experienced those special Christmases that she'd only even seen on television, though, she secretly watched them, admiring the freshly deco-rated Christmas trees, families stringing popcorn by the fire, homemade hot cocoa, thoughtful gifts, and more. Perhaps this would be a Christmas to remember.

* * *

The following day, after an early Christmas Eve dinner with the Frasers, Andrea thought of Rory. He'd told her he had to finish one last order before the holidays. She could appreciate a man who worked hard. Hell, she used to. Now, she was a lady of leisure...at least for ten more days. She'd steadfastly ignored social messages and emails about potential employment—she needed a break after the loss of her house and lackluster interviews for positions she didn't even want. Her out-of-office message was set on her personal email and social media accounts because that's what she was—out of office.

Her text chimed. A smile spread when she noticed the sender was Sarah Murray.

SARAH
Merry, merry Christmas Eve!

ANDREA
Thanks! You, too. What did you whip up?

A picture of two golden pies flashed on the screen beside a colorful vegetable salad followed by a message.

SARAH
Steak and stilton pies. It's just the two of us this year. Tomorrow, we'll be catering and roasting turkeys with haggis stuffing, a giant ham, traditional sides, and desserts at a personal event, so there's still prep to be done.

ANDREA
Wow! That sounds incredible.

SARAH

If you're up for it, we'd love an extra hand in
the kitchen.

Andrea's chest danced like little Christmas elves preparing
a feast. But she'd already promised Brie, Bryce, and the kids
she'd go to the Cairngorms. And then there was Rory. She
could apologize and come back early to help the Murrays...
Hearing squeals of glee, Andrea glanced out the front window
and saw a soft flutter of snow. She couldn't forget how Rory
saved her when she was about to be a femsicle. She couldn't
cancel.

ANDREA

Would love to, but I have plans with Brie
and the family in the highlands.

SARAH

Sounds amazing. Y'all enjoy!

Still, Andrea wondered what she'd miss. Back home, she
never said *no* to extra work. But here...she was in Scotland, on
holiday, and enjoying herself and the company of a very sexy
man. So, why did she feel like she was letting herself down?

Chapter Thirty-Three

CONTROLLED CHAOS ENSUED WITH SQUEALS OF delight, flying wrapping paper, laughter, and love on Christmas morning. Andrea had exchanged gifts and ate a cozy meal complete with Mimi's tofu scramble with crispy potatoes, sweet bell peppers, and sauteed spinach topped with sharp Scottish cheddar alongside leftover Christmas pie. Also served were Scotch sandwiches in an airy roll with Lorne sausage—simple, tasty food that was salty, airy, and meaty.

Brie and Mimi had both joined forces, telling her she wouldn't be cooking on Christmas morning, since she'd cooked with Rose the night before.

Andrea was grateful, though she didn't mind cooking. She'd even prepared an extra rosemary focaccia bread last night that was currently baking in the oven for Rory's family—cooking centered her. With a sigh, she watched the kids build blocks with Mimi and Brie as she spooned a heavenly bite of overnight *cranachan* Brie made for Christmas Eve—Scotch-soaked oats with cream and raspberries—into her mouth. She'd enjoy this delicious dessert and Christmas merriment for a little longer before heading to the highlands to see Santa and his reindeer.

Ding! The peppy timer dinged.

She opened the oven door and inhaled the bright rosemary and salty notes, then set the bubbly focaccia to cool and tidied the kitchen. Next, she changed into a cute outfit complete with a new candy-apple-red hat and matching wool scarf Brie gifted her. As she was touching up her hair with the curling iron, she heard Rory's deep voice rumbling downstairs. She switched off the iron and jogged to meet him. "Merry Christmas!"

He grinned in a festive red-and-black flannel. "Merry Christmas to ye, Andrea." He pressed a kiss to her lips.

The kiss was light and soft, and she wondered what the heck was going on with her chest. The pounding beneath her ribcage was a new level of joy she hadn't experienced. Separating, she rubbed her breastbone and told herself the cause was Christmas, which was slowly becoming her favorite holiday.

Rory presented gifts for the children—a rocking horse for Phoebe and a hand-crafted shield for Noah—to excited squeals of mirth. Then, he glanced at Andrea, a smile tugging his beard.

"Who's that for?" Phoebe pointed to a lengthy present leaning against the wall.

"Andrea."

She titled her head. "For me?"

He passed the package wrapped with simple white-and-red wrapping and twine. "Merry Christmas, lass."

With glee, she tore the wrapping off. *A.A.* was carved on the base of a shiny, red-leather roll case. She glanced at him, while her lips curled.

He gestured for her to open the case.

Intrigued, she unbuckled the clasps. The case rolled open, displaying an assortment of new chef knives, as well as scissors and a galley knife. She widened her eyes. "You bought me knives?"

He watched her with a slight furrow between his brows. "Since I've never made cutlery knifes, I wanted to buy you the right ones. If you don't—"

"No. This is the best gift! My few knives are in storage, and I've been taking cooking classes where they loan you knives, but now, I get to bring my own." She beamed and wrapped him in a hug, breathing in his warm, smoky scent. "Thank you!" Once she stepped back, she crossed to the tall Christmas tree and grasped a large, rectangular box. "This is for you."

With a grin, he peeled the paper, uncovering a metal sign with a man holding a hammer in one hand and a sword in the other above an anvil. Below, *Cameron Swords* was cut in square lettering along with *Forged by Hand*.

Twisting her hands together, Andrea watched his wide-eyed assessment. "I noticed you didn't have a sign in your forge. When Brie helped me get everything together for my catering event for *Swords*, she told me that you have to market yourself."

A smile tugged at his lips.

"I know you have your website, but I took some artistic license with the local artisan and combined your motto and name."

"'Tis brilliant." His smile grew and extended to his cheeks. He turned toward her with shining silvery eyes. "Thank ye."

"You're welcome." She kissed him, but that feeling swirled inside her again. She knew the present would be a hit, but something was happening she wasn't prepared for. She couldn't put her finger on it. At the same time, she felt both happy and like she would vomit at any moment.

* * *

After visiting adorable reindeer in the snowy Cairngorms where shiny tinsel and festive decorations adorned paddocks in a quaint Christmas village, meeting Santa—and yes, she sat on his lap—and flopping into the fluffy snow with her niece and nephew to make snow angels, she and Rory arrived at the Cameron home in the mid-afternoon. The cloudy sky washed the green-brown hills with a speckling of white, like cream atop a big bowl of mint-and-chocolate ice cream. Mature trees lined the perimeter, while a bungalow-style, green-and-white house stood at the end. Opposite the house, a shed of some sort was closed; yet, a few pipes and metal pieces rested outside. Like art? Metal art? Or was that just her eyes playing tricks?

Rory exhaled and shoved the gearshift into Park.

Swiveling, she eyed him. "Ready?"

"Aye, 'tis been some time since I've returned home."

"I get it. But you'll be fine. It's like pulling off a bandage."

He scrubbed a hand through his beard.

Rolling her shoulders, she relaxed into the buttery leather. "Text me if you need saving, and I'll make up an elaborate excuse."

Clearing his throat, he turned. "'Tis barely one degree Celsius. Ye'll not want to stay in the truck. It's best if ye come inside."

She gawked. "And meet your family?" Invisible alarm bells sounded in her ears.

"Aye." He wrenched the truck door open. "It'll only grow colder by the hour and more snow's set to ensue."

"Rory! That's not what I signed up for." She tugged her coat close and stared at his backside.

He pivoted. "Ye'll be fine."

With a hiss, she waved a hand. "I should've looked up the weather before volunteering to be your bonnie-getaway girl."

He grinned wide. "Aye, 'tis known to snow in Inverness."

"Rory, I'm serious. I'm not the meet-the-parents type." With nerves zipping through her, she glanced at the frosty windows shiny from the cold and saw her own breath fogging the glass. She twisted the plastic covering over the focaccia in her hands. The cold was already closing in as was the early evening. Glancing back at Rory's childhood home, she noted the warm, yellow glow of lights.

"Ye'll be fine," he repeated.

"Shit." She gripped the focaccia, along with the Christmas cookie tin from Brie, tight. If they asked her personal questions, then she'd eat a cookie. If she had a mouthful of cookie, she couldn't speak, could she? With an albeit terrible plan, she strode forward with Rory, boots crunching in the snowy path.

He walked into the house without a word.

Andrea glanced at Rory and the hard line of his lips. She wondered what exactly had transpired between he and his father, but based on Rory's appearance, she'd find out soon. She stomped her boots, hung up her coat, and removed her hat. Wood paneling and accents were everywhere including wood-and-glass paneled doors that opened to a family room. Following Rory, she swallowed her nerves and lifted her chin.

"Rory! 'Tis wonderful to see ye." A round, older woman with soft, white curls approached with arms open wide and an apron tied around a white-knit Christmas sweater.

Rory wrapped her in a hug, one arm snugging the sturdy woman to his chest.

When they parted, the woman flashed a full smile at Andrea. "*Och*! And who have we here?"

"Andrea." She jutted a hand out. "I brought homemade focaccia...and Brie Fraser sent some Christmas cookies from her and the kids."

She beamed, showing deep dimples. "Thank ye and welcome to our home. I'm Ailes. Ye may call me that or Ma."

Andrea sputtered, then shoved the cookie tin and bread at

Ailes. What had she gotten herself into? Now, this woman wanted her to call her *ma*? She wouldn't be her mother-in-law. Of course, she called Ma Fraser that because she was Bryce's mom, but Ailes was Rory's mom. That was an entirely different enchilada. She followed Rory inside, blowing a breath out.

An older man with thick, gray hair and a scraggly beard who she assumed was Alistair Cameron sat in a recliner when they walked into the main living area where plaid garlands strung across the wide front window and mis-matched Christmas décor perched on side tables. A wiry younger man with red hair a shade lighter than Rory's sat on the carpet beside a petite blonde woman playing with a toddler girl with butter-yellow curls building a puzzle. Another young twenty-something girl with strawberry-blonde hair that waved to her shoulders and puffed sleeves perched on an old tan couch, scrolling on her phone. But wasn't there one more sister? She could've sworn Rory had two sisters.

"Ye made it!" The young man grinned and rose. Clamping a hand on Rory's shoulder, he beamed showing a deep dimple. "And ye brought a lass. Well, this is something. Rory's never brought a girl home. I'm Collin."

Andrea tried to laugh, but her pulse raced. "Andrea."

"And an American, too," the young girl said from the couch. "I've got an American flat mate in London."

Andrea nodded. How the heck did she end up here?

"That's Hannah." Collin gestured to the young girl. "And this is my beautiful wife, Lauren, and wee Maisie."

Just keep smiling. Just keep smiling... Andrea flashed a smile. Rory's brother was a younger version of him with a firm chin that showed a slight darkening from a five o'clock shadow.

Rising, Lauren smiled politely and wrapped Andrea in a hug. "Pleasure."

"You, too," Andrea heard herself say. *See, this isn't awkward*. Yet, her pulse continued to hammer.

The man in the chair rose, and everyone's gaze went to him as he ambled over. "So, ye've returned. Realize that yer family's worth something in all those bright, bonnie lights, have ye?"

Clearing his throat, Rory stood stoic a few feet from his father. "*Nollaig Chridheil*, Da."

Andrea narrowed her gaze at the old man, while her blood boiled. How could Rory greet him? The old man had just insulted him. Of course, no one wanted to be caught in the middle of a family feud on Christmas, but *hell*, she couldn't let him get away with that, could she? She fisted her hands.

"*Och*, would ye look at the time? Dinner's almost ready," Ailes announced. "Why don't we check the roast?"

Andrea followed the women into the kitchen—her safe haven. Once they passed through a swinging door, she was blasted with toasty heat and savory aromas. "Oh, thank God."

"We'll let the men remember their manners, whilst we ready dinner. Andrea, did ye make this loaf, then?" Ailes glanced up, holding the focaccia.

"I did. Just pop it in the oven for seven-to-ten minutes, and it'll be warm and ready to eat."

"Lovely. Thank ye." She turned to adjust the oven, then rose. "Now, how long have you and Rory been seeing one another?"

The shrill of a timer saved Andrea from answering.

"That'd be the ham."

Andrea swallowed and glanced at Ailes' retreating backside.

During the meal, she focused on the food and answered questions about her travels to help stave the mood, but Rory was back to being quiet. And for some reason, that didn't bode well. She conversed easily with Collin who kept the mood light, spinning yarns and tales. He was easy to get along with. Their dad, on the other hand, ate quietly like a perturbed portobello in the corner.

After dinner, Andrea excused herself to use the bathroom. She stood in a small room with a tiny pedestal sink. *Why pedestal sinks when so many options existed?* With a huff, she sat on the throne and breathed. "You used to deal with people all day long. People who complained about the weirdest shit, people who had real issues, and people who needed you." She grumbled. "But this is personal..." She combed her fingers through her curls.

Ring! Ring! Her phone shrilled.

Andrea retrieved the device from her pocket and stared at the name. *Gloria.* She sent the call to voice mail. "Just who I need to talk to right now." Exhaling, she stared at herself in the mirror, but the white walls seemed to press in. She slipped out of the bathroom and muttered a quick apology that she forgot something in the truck, then slid on her boots and jacket and power-walked out the front door as fast as her booted heals could carry her ass. As soon as she stepped onto the porch landing, she was hit by the frosty breeze with speckles of snow. Sucking in the crisp air, she tugged her collar up and breathed. After a minute, she fished out her phone and dialed Brie. At the sound of her bestie's voice, Andrea shimmied in place. "Brie. Thank God, you picked up!"

"Everything okay?"

Andrea shook her head vehemently. "What am I doing? I'm at Rory's parents' house. His dad is a complete jerk, and Rory isn't saying anything! Oh, and also, his brother, sister-in-law, sister, and mom are totally sizing me up."

"You—"

"I couldn't stay in the frickin' truck because I'd be a popsicle, Brie!" she interrupted. "Why the heck did I agree to come?"

"Because you care for him."

"Send a car. Send a helicopter. Send something. I'm putting out an S.O.S. Shit-oh-shit! What have I gotten myself into? I'm not a relationship person. You know that, right? So, why did I tell Rory I'd be his bonnie-getaway girl?"

Brie's soft laughter filtered through the phone.

"It's not funny, Brie. His whole family is here."

Slosh-slosh. Something moved in the grass nearby.

She glanced around her. If another reindeer appeared out of nowhere, she might just jump on him and fly to the North Pole. At least there'd be presents and elves. Elves weren't intimidating, right?

Instead, a woman with a short crop of blonde hair stood at the edge of the woods, highlighted by the glow of a single flood light. "Fightin' again, are they?" The woman questioned with a beautiful, rich lilt.

Watching her near, Andrea realized that she wasn't more than twenty-five. She had a doe-eyed look with dark eyes, a petite pixie nose, and compact build. She looked like a fairy. "Uh, yeah."

"Can't blame ye for wanting some fresh air. The stars beckon out here."

"Sure." Andrea glanced at the few twinkling stars between brooding clouds, then back as the woman walked past and into the house. "Maybe that's Rory's sister, Luna? The nature girl or something."

"What?" Brie asked.

"Oh, nothing."

"I'm sure you can schedule a car, if you really want to leave."

"I do." Andrea refocused on the conversation. "I really, really do."

Muffled shouts carried through the door.

Craning her head, she leaned toward the door, trying to

hear. The deep voice was Rory's and the other she couldn't quite pinpoint.

"Andrea? You there?"

"Something's going on. I'll call you back." She flung the door open and marched inside.

Chapter Thirty-Four

"What's a movie business goin' to give ye? Lookin' for the bright lights, rather than what's important—respectable work and family."

"Da," Rory warned from the edge of a red-plaid chair, gripping the armrest and staring at Da from across the living room. The Cameron Forge. His father had continued the business over thirty years ago following his own da's legacy. It was his life's work and done to his satisfaction. That is, until Rory ventured into a new direction.

"Da, leave off it," Collin muttered, then leaned toward Lauren. "Why don't ye take Maisie into the other room?"

"I'll come with," Hannah muttered and rose.

Luna strode into the living area. "Seems I've arrived in the nick of time. Happy Christmas." She hugged Ma and grasped Maisie's hand, smiling at Rory.

Sighing, Rory rose. "Happy Christmas, Luna."

"Let's go color," she told Masie and exited the room.

"What happens when the show ends? Ye'll be left high and dry and crawling back here. I guarantee it," Da fired.

Rory scowled, but he couldn't get away from Da's steely

gaze. His eyes were as gray as his father's—the only thing they shared at the moment. Da had his opinion, and Rory, his. He might have been cut from the same cloth, but Da only wanted things his way. And Rory couldn't. He was his own man and had his own craft—a damn successful one at that.

"When ye work as long as I have in the trade, ye earn a reputation. What have ye earned?"

"Alistair," Ma hissed.

Clenching his fists, Rory saw red. Nothing he ever did would be enough for Da unless it was done his way. He was ready to finally—

"Rory's an incredible swordsmith," Andrea said.

He swiveled.

She stood in the archway between the entry and living room with white flecks of snow topping her cap and dusting her curls. "World-renowned actually, if you'd take the time to ask." She walked toward him. "Museums have his swords displayed, collectors request unique, hand-crafted specimens, and I know for a fact that *Swords of Scotland* couldn't depict the timeframe fully without his historically accurate Scottish broadswords, *sgian dubhs*, and all the other incredible pieces he and his team create."

Coming to a stop beside Rory, she looped her fingers in his.

Rory gripped them in turn.

His father's brows drew together, then he opened his mouth and closed it.

Collin smiled broadly.

"And another thing, Rory's told me about your family forge. Where else would he have gotten such exquisite training to even try tackling the art of swords without having a solid foundation?"

Glancing at Andrea, Rory's heart seared with gratitude. She was playing both sides, and she was damn good.

She turned her bonnie frame toward him. "Rory, I think some fresh air would do us some good."

He nodded and, with her hand tucked in his, said a quick good-bye, and strode outside into the crisp, evening air. Back in the truck, he drove toward River Ness, seeking the lull of the water to calm the pounding in his mind. "Thank ye," he said quietly a few minutes later. "I dinnae mean for ye to get involved in Da and my…disagreements."

"Disagreements? You guys were shouting loud enough for the entire neighborhood to hear, that is, if you had one."

He cocked a brow.

She shook her head. "You're both being stubborn idiots."

"Careful, now."

Andrea jabbed a finger toward him. "Do you know what it is to have a family who cares about you? Who loves you?"

Pressing his lips in a thin line, he waited for her to finish.

"Not everyone can say their family cares, even if they have an odd way of showing it."

"Weren't ye just defending me?"

She pitched a brow. "Yes, but that doesn't mean you weren't being an ass, as well."

He turned onto the familiar road and pulled to a stop in the wee car park. "Now, wait—"

"No. You need to hear this. From an outsider in, under that rough exterior, your da misses you. Do you ever call him or your mom or visit your family?"

Rory thought, but he couldn't remember the last time he rang him or Ma. He spoke to his brother a few days ago—though his brother had been the one to ring. "That's not the point. He can'na accept me for who I am. Ye heard him."

"I did," she agreed. "Perhaps that's the only way he knows how to get you to talk to him. To get your hide up. I don't think he really wants you to run the family forge, seems like Collin's doing a good job, when really all he needs is his son."

Grumbling, he exited the truck. He inhaled the frosty air and gazed at the rolling river, flanked by snowy banks, and the way the streetlights cast shadows on turns and coves and flooded the banks brightly. He'd butted heads with Da for near ten years now. Da only looked at the past—what once was—instead of what Rory had created. They'd grown up so tight, not even he could've known the direction he'd taken. Making his own way was what he needed. But he could only choose that road because his family, including Da, paved the way—placing tools in his hand, guiding him, and teaching him the trade. Perhaps there was some truth to what Andrea said. Guilt jabbed at his side.

"I know what it's like to be in a family of convenience," Andrea said from behind.

He hadn't even heard her exit the truck.

"My mom called while we were at your parents' house, and I silenced it. Twice. I know I should've answered and said 'Merry Christmas,' but we're not close. Not like yours. You should be grateful for what you have."

Pivoting, he noted the sheen in her eyes. "Tell me about your family, Andrea."

"It's not a family." She expelled a breath. "My parents divorced when I was seven. Dad moved to New York, remarried a year later, had another daughter, and I stayed with Mom when it was convenient. Otherwise, I had a nanny."

He nodded for her to continue.

"I'm Italian-American. I went to Italy after I graduated college when *Nonna* passed, and I felt like an outsider. Sure, the people were friendly, food was incredible, but it wasn't my home—just a beautiful destination. My mom arrived a few days after I did—the gift that kept on giving—and dragged me to parties and such. You have a family...a home. I"—she opened and closed her mouth—"I have nothing."

He shook his head. "Ye have the Frasers."

With a bob of her head, she sniffled and turned.

He touched a hand to her sweater, pausing her progress and lifted the other to her cheek. "And ye have me."

Her brown eyes widened and irises pinpointed. She backed away a step and twisted toward the frosted water.

Did she not believe him? Rory had gotten along with women, and he thought he'd loved one, but something was different about the woman before him. She made him feel something other than he'd felt before, a churning in his soul and a longing he couldn't ignore. He needed her to understand, but he had to bide his time. "Andrea..."

Shaking her head, she glanced back. "What?"

"Let's head to the cabin."

"What about your family? Don't you want to go back?"

He shook his head. What he wanted was her. "Not tonight."

Chapter Thirty-Five

DRIVING UP A SNOW-AND-GRASS-LINED DRIVE, THEY stopped in front of a two-story, lodge-style home with wood siding, large glass windows, and an arched, pitched roof, snug against a backdrop of white-topped evergreens. Yet, when Andrea stepped out of the car, she noticed the absolute quiet. No other cars were parked outside the vacation home, and just one light blazed from the interior. Other than the man beside her, the only other company were the trees and rocks. Anxiousness coursed through her. "Where are Brie, Bryce, and the kids?"

Rory craned his head right and left. "Perhaps still exploring?"

"Maybe." She strode toward the main entrance. Fishing out her phone, she pulled up her notes, then entered the code Brie gave her earlier that morning into the smart lock. "Just in case," she'd said. A gift basket with a variety of local fruit, buttery biscuits, shortbread cookies, and other items greeted them in the foyer. But upon closer inspection, she noticed an envelope topped the basket with their names scribed in a familiar, cursive penmanship. Curious, Andrea plucked the envelope off and read.

> *Merry Christmas to two of our favorite people! You've helped us and held us more times than we can count these last few weeks, and we're indebted. The cottage is our gift to you for the weekend. Enjoy!*
> *With love,*
> *Brie and Bryce*

"Sneaky," Andrea muttered.

Rory strolled in with their bags. "What's that now?"

"They're not coming."

With an arch of a thick brow, he reached out and clasped the note in his right hand.

Stepping further inside, Andrea looked around the exquisite cottage with fresh white walls, beamed ceilings, rich-brown couches, and warm-copper, forest-green, and brick-red accents, including a red hairy coo and a buck painting in the living room, while the opposite held wedding photos of Brie and the children. She knew Brie had the best intentions by giving her a weekend with Rory. *Alone.* Who wouldn't want to stay in a beautiful vacation home with a sexy Scot? Nibbling her lip, she glanced back.

Rory stared in that serious, focused manner.

He wanted more. She could see it in his eyes by the river-side, but she told him before she couldn't be his girlfriend and that her family was a frickin' mess, so why did he want more?

Her phone shrilled.

Grasping the device, she scrunched her nose and tucked it back away. Hearing the ring a second time, she rolled her eyes and answered. Better to get the call over with than be continuously pestered. "Merry Christmas." Andrea strolled into the adjacent kitchen with white cabinets framed by dark, overhead beams. "But I really can't talk right—"

"Sweetheart, I can't wait to see you tonight," Gloria gushed. "The florist is already here, and you should see the house. It's gorgeous!"

Andrea exhaled. "Mom. I'm in Scotland, remember? I declined the invitation."

The front door closed.

"Well, have that movie star buy you a ticket and get on the next flight! You know my parties always last until the next day, and I'd love to see you and meet him."

She puffed a breath, watching Rory amble back to the truck for the rest of her luggage. "I'm not seeing Hugh Macrae."

"Andrea."

"I'm kind of"—she swirled her hand—"seeing someone else now." She continued strolling through the house.

"Oh?"

"He's a swordsmith."

"A"—her mom gasped—"what?"

"Kind of like a blacksmith, but he makes swords that are ornate and magnificent, and heavy as—"

"A blacksmith?" She shrieked. "What will people think? You need to keep up appearances."

"He's actually pretty—"

"No. I won't listen to another word! You're being stubborn and selfish, just like your father."

Andrea leaned her head on the hallway wall. When a sniffle carried across her ear, she braced herself for the next part of the roller-coaster.

"I expect to see you, sweetheart." Gloria wept. "You're my only daughter. You should be here."

"I can't—"

"You can," she said clearly, without a sniffle. "I have to go. The caterers just arrived. I'll see you soon. Kiss-kiss."

Andrea stared at her phone for a milla-second, then pivoted toward the master suite and rocketed the device at a chair in the corner. The phone smacked the cooper-brown cushion and slid into the crack between two forest-green pillows. One thing her mother was right about was she had to get back to L.A. But not today. She wouldn't give her that satisfaction. As she steadied her pounding pulse, she heard Rory moving around the living area, making a fire, she imagined, lugging thick pieces of wood and hunkering down. He was always doing something and thinking about her, in comparison to Gloria, who only thought about herself. She hated the way Gloria dismissed him. Just like his own father had. Rory was valuable and his trade, too. But she wasn't sure she could give him what he wanted.

Glancing at the giant, king bed with a plush, mossy-green comforter and earthy accent pillows, she smoothed a hand down her side. Of course, they'd sleep together. Their attraction hadn't simmered, but she'd have to deal with her thoughts later. Right now, all she wanted was to enjoy this beautiful gift. As she pivoted, something caught her eye. Outside the French doors, a wooden gazebo framed a hot tub and seating area, lit with a string of lights nestled in front of a tree-lined alcove. "Oh, my God." Her jaw dropped. "There's a wooden spa."

Sidling behind her, Rory slid his arms around her waist and settled a cheek against hers.

She relaxed against him, feeling his soft beard on her skin. She had to admit, something about the man calmed her when he wasn't making her overthink everything.

"'Tis probably just wooden side paneling. Care to have a closer look?"

His warm breath caressed her ear. "Definitely. I need to change into a bathing suit."

"*Och*." He unzipped her jacket. "Ye'll manage."

She spun and poked a finger into his thick pectoral. "As much as I'd love to strut around here naked, there might be neighbors. Plus, if someone knows this is the Frasers' vacation hideout, they'd have my *derriére* plastered on the front page."

He chuckled. "Fair enough." Tugging her closer, he roamed his hands down her back to her butt and squeezed.

She smoothed hers over his broad chest, circling his neck. "Who knew the quiet man was full of surprises?"

He tipped his head.

"That was my nickname for you when we first met because you barely said two words."

Rory stared with those molten steel eyes. "Well, ye made me nervous."

She shook her head. "Not me."

"Aye, ye. With yer fast talk and forward nature, but I *couldnae* keep my eyes off ye. I still can't." He brushed his lips across hers.

The tender kiss made her sigh into the calm cloud that was Rory. This man made her want. Separating, she stripped her clothes, then sauntered into the bedroom, tugged on a suit, and pulled on boots. A few minutes later, she dipped her toes into the foaming spa. "It's perfect." She slid into the tub and moaned as the hot, bubbling water surrounded her. "Fucking fabulous."

Rory climbed in and stretched a long arm peppered with auburn hair over one side of the spa and the other around Andrea.

She rubbed a slick foot up his calf and down.

He sucked in a breath. "There won't be much relaxing in here if ye keep that up, lass."

"Oh?" She pushed away from the wall and straddled him.

A groan escaped his lips.

His large, wide palms found her waist as she sat atop his bulge and wiggled her butt against him. Smoothing his hands over her hips, he trailed them down and gripped her ass, kneading it with those amazing large hands. While his hands were busy, he traced his tongue along the outline of her neck, the breadth of her collar bone, and the swell of her full breasts before returning to her mouth.

They made out like a couple of teenagers until the bubbles faded, and she was so turned on, all she could think about was what was under Rory's boxers. "How fast do you think we could make it to the cottage?"

"Fast."

She planted one, more, quick kiss on his full lips and then climbed into the snow. The icy powder shot needles into her feet. "Shit!" She danced in the snow, struggling to pull her boots on as Rory's laughter echoed through the evergreens. She glanced back.

He rose like a cat, gray-eyed gaze laser focused.

She took off toward the house and slid open a French door with Rory on her heels. Kicking off her boots, she turned to find him breathing hard behind her, beard damp from the spa.

Backing her up to the wall, he swiftly picked her up, gripping her butt with his wide hands.

She wrapped her legs around his strong middle and slid her hands up his cool chest and muscular shoulders. She wanted him so bad, her entire body throbbed. But to her surprise, Rory walked her slowly to the bed, then took his time stripping her high-waisted bottoms down achingly slow and kissing her from the arch of her foot to the underside of her breast. He drove her mad. He unclasped her bikini top and massaged her breasts with those calloused, wonderful hands, while pressing his lips to her throat. Delicious pleasure coursed through her, and she grinded against him, desperate for more. "Do you have a condom?"

He nodded, but he continued to attend to her body.

"Hurry," she murmured.

Rory didn't answer. He slid a calloused hand down her body until he found her.

Moving against him, she ached for more. But he continued with slow strokes and tender touches, gazing at her like she was the most precious being in the highlands. Something inside her cracked and shifted...this didn't feel like sex. She felt *more*. But she couldn't...she... She shook her head. "Rory. Don't—" But he took her higher, gave her more, until all she could see, think, and hear was Rory. She gasped. "I need..."

"Aye?"

"You. I need..." She moaned. "You."

A moment later, he was off the bed and back, rolling a condom on and settling smoothly inside her. "I'm here, lass."

When they came together, she felt her entire being sigh like she'd eaten the most amazing meal of her life. What the heck was she going to do now?

* * *

Near nine p.m., Rory relaxed into the soft, white patio cushion with Andrea snugged beside him. The night was quiet save for the delicate snap of pine trees shedding their branches. His breath created cloudy plumes, matching the snowy landscape surrounding the holiday cottage. Tugging the tartan blanket around them, he held fast to the steaming hot toddy. He was surprised how much the cinnamon stick Andrea added enhanced the whisky.

"Are you going to start the fire?" She inclined her head toward the circular fire pit nestled in the snow a few feet away.

"No."

She leveled her dark chocolate gaze. "Rory."

"Andrea." He gestured toward the clear, starry sky made even more vibrant with the lack of cottage lights. "'Tis better for stargazing." He'd been notified by an alert on his phone ten minutes prior. Aurora was likely to occur.

With a sigh, she glanced up and immediately, her eyes widened. "Why are the stars so much bigger here?"

"The storm has moved on, and there are no other houses or streetlights around. Low light pollution helps yer eyes see clearer."

She tilted her head, while her lips curved. "Light pollution? You're surprising, you know that?"

He grinned. "I can say the same for ye."

"I still can't believe we have this entire place to ourselves. It feels like we're the only ones for miles."

"Aye, privacy. Something Bryce is fond of. But I welcome it, here and now, with ye." He pulled her closer, rubbing his cheek along her mass of soft curls and trailed a finger down the length of her gloved hand. A hint of spice and something subtly sweet met his nostrils as he breathed her in. She was comprised of incredible layers. Some, he'd seen when they first met, and some, she recently trusted to show him. But he wanted to discover more. The fall and winter seasons had been busy with *Swords* and his business had grown, but *och*, he was grateful for rest, especially with his lass by his side. He was ready to focus more on his personal life and truly see where this could go. He'd introduced Andrea to his family. A step forward, even if it did take them both by surprise. When he caught a green-and-purple streak weave across the dark sky, he lifted a hand to cup her chin. "Aurora has come to wish us a happy Christmas."

Her eyes widened. "Holy shit. Are those the northern lights?"

"Aye. Ye can spot them in late fall and winter."

"I've never seen them." She leaned farther. "Holy cow. Fucking Aurora. Beautiful."

With a smirk, he watched her bonnie face alight and lips curl as warm-red streaks danced with neon-green and rich-purple, illuminating the sky with a rainbow of colors. They sat together just he and Andrea and Aurora Borealis.

"Your country keeps surprising me."

He grinned.

"In a good way. You keep surprising me, too." She tugged his jacket toward her and pressed a smacking kiss on his lips.

"Good. That was my master plan."

"Oh yeah?"

"Aye."

She laughed and snugged closer.

The way the lights changed and shifted and waved and weaved reminded him of his relationship with Andrea. They'd danced around each other for weeks before coming together. She was beautiful and complex, and he wanted to know every-thing about her. As he watched her gaze at the brilliant sight before him, he felt something inside stir and shift around his heart. Her time in Scotland was drawing to an end in near a week's time. He wanted more.

Chapter Thirty-Six

HOLDING FAST TO THE STEERING WHEEL, RORY braved the snow-laden roads to show Andrea one of the most breathtaking views at the top of the Cairngorms. But the sky had turned gray, and the trees restless. The unsteadiness of the weather reminded him of his lass. He'd tried to ignore the way she escaped his embraces that morning by flashing a smile and shoving food in front of him—incredible food—Eggs Benedict with hollandaise, but he wondered what exactly was going on in that head of hers. Feeling the steering wheel tug to the right from a sharp gust, he gripped the wheel and glanced outside. If the wind kicked up much more, they'd close the runs. He accelerated.

"Are you sure you don't want to go shopping in town, instead?"

He glanced warily at the brooding clouds. "Nah, 'tis a fine time for a ski." Fifteen minutes later, he and Andrea had their skis on and poles in hand with the lift swiftly swinging T-bars toward them.

With brows furrowed, Andrea sneered at the metal T-bar, snug in ski boots and jacket.

He'd kept the conversation on the short drive light, but now watching her face the run head-on, she seemed to forget what was bothering her and shot all her annoyance at the lift, rather than him. He counted his lucky stars. "Problem?"

She huffed. "Lifts and I don't really get along. Why couldn't we have taken the fun thing?"

"The Funicular's convenient, but ye have to be up for a wee bit of adventure now and again."

"Adventure?" She sized up the pole and watched a young-ster somersault off, then another. She stepped back.

He grinned. "The lads are just messin' around. Now, when the T-bar comes near ye—"

Without a word, she grabbed for the fast-moving T.

"Let that one go," he instructed.

She swung around, shooting a dagger-filled gaze. "I thought you said to grab it?"

He lifted an arm. "Look behind ye, grab it with yer right hand, and put it between yer legs. Don't sit on it. It won't support ye. Just stand and relax."

"*Pfft*. Easy for you to say."

Gesturing, he motioned. Another T-bar approached. When he saw her grip the rope, he couldn't curb the nervous-ness filling him.

Andrea strong-armed the bar and tucked it under her bum.

He grinned and followed her. The brisk wind whipped across his face and whiskers, and he noticed the swirl of snowy clouds thicken the higher they rose as if the mountain and the sky were one. Rory realized how much he'd missed being in the highlands. Remembering skiing with Collin and his mates as a young lad, racing down runs, drinking, and more, brought grand memories up once again. When they neared the top of the run, he shouted to Andrea to wait until she was on the flat before letting go.

But she didn't respond. As she reached the precipice, she slung the T-bar away.

His chest tightened.

She rolled backward in slow motion. Her arms flapped with poles like she was a bird tossed in flight.

Squeezing the poles in one hand, Rory prepared to grab her with the other. He knew the T-bar wouldn't hold both of them, so he leaned forward and prayed the lift's momentum would be enough. With an arm out, he grasped Andrea as she fell into him.

A squeak escaped her lips.

"I've got ye." He hung on tight, while trying to relax on the T-bar as they teetered over the edge and onto the straightaway. He quickly tossed the T-bar aside.

Andrea faceplanted.

Another skier came up quickly.

He yanked her up. "Ye all right?"

"Fine." She swished the snow off her face and hair and slipped her boots back into the mounts. "My pride's bruised."

He chuckled. "Ready for a ski?"

"As I'll ever be." Straightening, she glanced down the run and exhaled a heavy breath. "This"—she pointed—"is not *wee*. And I haven't skied in ages."

"Ye'll be fine. It's like riding a bike."

She snorted. "Some bike."

"Aye." So, he had the advantage here. He liked that and enjoyed it even more when she gripped her poles and turned toward the hill, prepared to take off. The woman was a contradiction—tough with nerves of steel one moment, then anxious and soft the next. He was looking forward to peeling back even more layers. When he saw she hadn't moved, he leaned over. "Let's ease into it."

Nodding, she gripped the poles and stared down the run.

"How is it ye haven't skied in years as ye said?"

"I've been working. And other than Christmas with Brie last year, I typically volunteer to work the holidays."

He kicked a brow up. "Why?"

"I was trying to get ahead. Plus, family and holidays sucked." With a flick of her scarf over her long neck, she dug her poles into the snow. "All right, let's do this. I'm going to make this mountain my bitch."

He chuckled.

"Show me your stuff, swordsmith."

"Aye." Yet, with one last glance at Andrea, unrest settled within. He hoped he'd made the right choice to bring her up the mountain.

* * *

Rory glided down the mountain effortlessly leaning to and fro as he cruised in front of Andrea. The big man was good on skis. Hell, what couldn't he do? A pinch of annoyance gripped her insides. Andrea wiggled her butt and tried to mirror him. She'd told him she hadn't skied in years; yet, here she was another moron on the mountain shaking like a leaf. She huffed a breath. She could do it. Hell, she'd conquered more these last few weeks than she ever thought possible. And she was figuring herself out bit by bit.

She loved cooking.

She loved spending time with Brie and the family.

She loved adventuring.

And she...she stared at Rory... Her legs wobbled, and her pulse skittered. Something happened yesterday. She didn't know how or why, but something changed between them, and she felt the shift like the slow simmering of water beneath her whisk this morning as she tried to push her feelings aside and whip up holiday hollandaise. But she was freaking the fuck out. She couldn't fall for Rory, even though

289

she knew her feelings had grown. They were more than friendly. Something she'd desperately tried to avoid. *Then, I whipped up Eggs Benedict after the most incredible sex I've ever had.* But it wasn't just sex. Oh no, she'd woken up spooning. *That's right. Big spoon, little spoon. And it felt good. Too good.* She had to get out of bed, which was why she made incredible, velvety hollandaise sauce and Eggs Benedict to distract her. But even breakfast was surreal—eggs were in the house, along with a fully-stocked fridge and a feast for Christmas dinner last night including sticky Scottish pudding for dessert. The house was empty, except for her and the quiet, serious man. She cooked, so she wouldn't think. She just cooked.

Now, she watched Rory glide down the mountain. She supposed she should follow. Gripping her poles, she propelled forward. The icy wind whipped through her curls and stung her cheeks. With a sashay of her hips, she slid slowly to the right and left. "This isn't so bad. See? I can do this." Relaxing little by little, Andrea set her gaze on the snowy horizon. Soon, she gained speed. And it felt fucking amazing. The brisk air, swirling dark-and-cream-colored sky above like gravy, and the feel of the run beneath her skis made her forget everything else.

A rock jutted up from the snow and kicked up a ski, but she righted herself. "I've got this. I've got this," she repeated. Picking up speed, she stuck her poles into the thick, white velvet and pushed forward. She gained more and more momentum. The course curved and snaked. She leaned to the right. Her left ski skidded and bumped along the uneven section, veering sideways. She righted it. Suddenly, her right ski connected with a snowy bump, knocking her off balance, and she rocketed sideways. "Ah!" She flung her poles wide to steady herself, but she veered off the trail. As she flew through a hole in a waist-high wooden-post fence, she swallowed a scream as fear snaked up her spine.

* * *

The woman drove him mad. But madness wasn't what filled Rory's mind at the moment—unrest did. He'd swiveled his head and noted Andrea wasn't behind him. He slowed and looked around once more. She couldn't have skied past him; she was out of practice and taking it slow. Wasn't she? *Och.* He should've taken her on the beginner slopes to truly see how out of practice she was.

He knelt, tucking the poles under his arms, and sped down the rest of the run. When he spotted the lifts, he prayed she'd just fallen over or was sitting there on her fine behind, taking a break. Taking the lift up, he scanned the snow-white canvas, searching. Once at the top, he tightened his goggles and propelled back toward where he saw Andrea last, winding down the summit to the slope. He slowed, sought, spraying snow, and allowed other skiers to pass, while searching the pearly surface. Where was she? When he spotted a snow patroller, he flagged him. "I lost sight of my girlfriend, Andrea, just up ahead if ye can keep an eye out. She's wearing a red beanie and red, white, and gray winter jacket, most likely resting on her laurels for a break, but I lost sight of her."

He nodded. "Happy to, mate."

Rory skied behind the patroller. A moment later, he caught sight of a hole in the fence at the same time the patroller did. He waved him over, flying through the gap.

Andrea sat in the snow with her skis off, covered with white powder, berating herself.

"Andrea!" He slid to a halt before her, unsnapping his boots and pressing down the panic that had carved its way into his chest.

She crinkled her nose and swiped a hand around. "So, you've found me."

He squatted. "Are ye all right?"

Shifting her legs, she pointed toward her left foot. "My ankle's killing me. I think it's sprained from that damn mountain. I was feeling like I'd gotten the hang of skiing again and started turning and burning, then I pivoted and face-planted."

"Turning and burning? Yer no' the queen of the mountain."

She glared.

Clearing his throat, Rory cast his gaze at the curvature of the mountain behind her. A few more meters, and she'd have really gotten herself in trouble.

The ski patroller padded over to Andrea, bright-red-and-white safety cross centered on his chest, while a helmet was secured to his head with goggles he'd just propped up. He glanced at Andrea.

Responding to the mountain rescuer's questions, she huffed.

Rory tried to hide his smile. He was just so damn happy to see her and those big, brown eyes, even if they were shooting daggers. He thought they'd have a grand time, but he didn't imagine she'd get hurt on his watch.

The patroller radioed to base, noting he'd be assisting a skier down with the sleigh, then removed a red pack and evaluated Andrea.

She craned her neck toward Rory. "Don't diss the baby slopes again."

"Aye." He clenched his jaw.

She leveled her gaze. "Are you all right?"

"Ye near shaved ten years off me life."

She pursed her lips.

Needing to do something with his hands, Rory gathered Andrea's skis and poles, moving them aside, so the patroller could set her foot in the traction boot. Ten minutes later, he helped her walk to the sleigh. Hearing her swear in pain, he gripped her tighter.

After a short ride down the mountain, Andrea rested in the snow chalet with ice on top of her foot and a cup of steaming coffee in hand. She hissed as the patroller set additional ice packs on either side of the splint. Her hair was a wee bit frizzy from the beanie that now rested alongside her, and she had a run of liner across her cheek.

Rory stared, while guilt ground in his gut. "I'm sorry I lost you."

"Lost me?" She flicked an annoyed look his way, brows fused together. "I'm not a puppy. I'm in charge of myself. And stupid me, thought I was the queen of the snow runs and took a turn too rough."

He grimaced.

With a sigh, she placed a hand on his arm. "Rory, it's not your fault."

He nodded. But he couldn't deny the protective instinct to take his lass down the mountain and hold her the rest of the night.

Chapter Thirty-Seven

AT THE COTTAGE, RORY HOVERED. HE WAS LIKE A worried Scottish momma—brooding one minute and fussing the next. He placed a buttery bowl of popcorn and a second cup of black tea beside Andrea—the first, now cold with barely a sip taken, he removed from the whitewashed coffee table. Then, he marched to the hearth, squatted down with those beefcake calves and layered firewood in a crisscross pattern like his life depended on it. But Andrea and he both knew the house had a furnace. "Rory, I'm fine. Go visit a pub or something. No need for both of us to be stuck here with nothing to do."

He swiveled and faced forward, gaze set on hers, eyes darkening like charcoal. "My place is here with ye."

She gulped. Since arriving after the Cameron Christmas disaster, she felt the shift—the change—in their relationship. She wanted to just keep cruising along as planned. Vacation fling. No-strings-sex with a sexy swordsmith. Relation-less. But that look reconfirmed her apprehension that morning. She didn't want all those feelings and mess that came with relationships—the baggage. She'd seen enough in her short life-time. Plus, Rory was a good guy. A *really* good guy. She sighed. *Her guy.* At the thought, she seized the teacup, sloshing a few hot droplets onto her hand, then downed the supposedly soothing brew. Instantly, the hot liquid seared her tongue. She spit the tea back into the cup. "Shit!" She slapped a hand over her mouth only to find Rory kneeling beside her a moment later, pressing a cool glass of water to her lips.

"Drink."

She guzzled because she couldn't not. Her mouth, tongue, and tonsils were scorched. Instantly, the cold water alleviated some of the pain. She held it in her mouth like cool mouth-wash and closed her eyes.

"Ye need to drink it or spit it out."

She winged her eyelids open. She'd forgotten he was standing there. Grabbing the glass from his hand, she spit the water back. "There. Will you relax?"

He tilted his head. "How's the burn?"

"I need to go to the hospital immediately," she said coarsely. "Or maybe you can call the snowmobile ranger again? Now that was the highlight of my day."

Grimacing, he gazed out the dark living room window.

Andrea pushed to sitting. "What's wrong with you? I'm the one laid up."

With a sigh, he rubbed a hand along the outline of his beard. "Aye, I can see that."

"So?"

"I thought I might've lost ye on the mountain. A million thoughts went through my mind when we were looking for ye. And the thought of not seeing ye again…well, it was like a dagger to my heart."

At the mention of his heart, she froze.

"Look, Andrea, I—"

"I'm fine, okay." She tossed her hair over her shoulder and settled back into the couch cushions. "Just forget it." Yet, she felt his stern gaze.

"Andrea."

As the heavy air of seriousness settled, she refocused on the television where Bruce Willis sprinted across the top of a building and changed the channel. "Want to watch a horror flick?"

He kicked a foot onto the coffee table, clothed in a thick, gray-wool sock, and crossed his arms over his broad chest.

Ten minutes later, she thought he'd fallen asleep until a chuckle escaped his lips. She slid her gaze over. He was seriously laughing at a horror flick. Who does that? Well, besides her.

When he caught her staring, he shifted.

She refocused her attention on the screen, watching people running into a cabin.

"Do ye ever think about the future?"

Her heart began rapping uncontrollably in her chest. Even though she knew what he was not so subtly saying, she evaded. "I've started to browse some possible job opportunities in HR. I need to face the fact that I have to return to a real job and L.A. soon, instead of playing chef and vacationer."

With a nod, he rested a hand over one of hers. "I know what it's like to change directions and alter the course of yer employ. But from what I've seen, yer not just playing chef. Ye could begin a new career."

She sighed. She *loved* cooking, but she couldn't change her life just because she'd had a few weeks of fun. "Cooking... cooking is the best, but I can't go back to L.A., change careers, and open my own restaurant. I wouldn't even know what that future would look like."

"And what of our future?" He smoothed his thumb over her hand.

Tingles spread across her fingers. She gulped.

"I know ye said ye were only here until the New Year."

"I am." She tugged her hand free and grabbed the bowl of buttery popcorn. "So, let's make the best out of these next couple of days, okay?"

Rory didn't move.

Continuing to feel Rory's expectant gaze, she pretended to be wrapped up in the movie, leaning in, focused on the screen, but pretending could only go so far. The minutes stretched and pulled like a tight rubber band.

Rory cleared his throat. "What if I wanted to see ye after the New Year?"

She chewed. "Why?"

"What do ye mean, why?" He grasped her shoulders gently, urging her to look at him. "Because I care for ye. Why else would I introduce ye to me family?"

"Well, I didn't ask you to." She selected a few kernels of popcorn. "I was helping you get away." She dragged the last word out for emphasis, then tossed the popcorn into her mouth.

"But ye agreed just the same."

A flicker of annoyance flashed through her. She continued focusing on the screen, crunching one kernel and then the next, but the popcorn didn't disintegrate. Instead, the kernels turned into a lumpy mass. Out of the corner of her eye, she saw him shake his head.

He stood and strode past her.

A moment later, the click of the back door echoed through the interior.

She swallowed thickly, then blew out a breath. "Shit." Glancing out the large, back window, she caught sight of Rory encased in the glow of the porch light, while the forest beyond was barely visible in the blur of snow, save for a faint outline of treetops. He stood tall with shoulders rounded slightly as if his arms were crossed. What was she thinking? Of course, his arms were crossed. He was in his quiet man stance, staring off into the white oblivion probably wondering how he'd plan his way out of his disappointment. She imagined if he'd lived hundreds of years ago, he'd march straight into that snow-soaked forest, cut down timber, and fashion a house with his hands, so he wouldn't have to deal with her. But that wasn't Rory. *He* thought about tomorrow. He planned, calculated, and walked into his next move with the foreknowledge of what he would do next. But for Andrea, during this time in her life, she liked that she didn't have to think of her next move. Was that so bad? Sure, reality was closing in—and soon—but why did he have to force her to face up to it? The New Year hadn't come. The bell hadn't rung, or pipe piped, or whatever. Couldn't she enjoy herself? Enjoy him? Why make everything so serious? That was Gloria's job—date a man, hook him, and marry him before he could back out. Not that Andrea wanted to get married.

Glancing out the window at Rory, she blew a breath out, while a pang of guilt settled in her stomach. She didn't want to upset him, but she also didn't want to lie. When her ankle began to throb, she smoothed a hand down the swollen skin, but pain continued to radiate. She glanced around, looking for the medicine on the coffee table between cups of tea and a winter bouquet with silver-blue thistle, evergreen sprigs, caramel-brown pinecones, and deep-red roses, then across toward the kitchen. The white bottle stood solitarily beneath the rich-brown upper cabinets. Rory had given her the medicine a couple hours ago. Now, she'd either have to ask for his help or pick her sorry butt up and teeter over. With a wince, she rose and grabbed the crutch, huffing and puffing, shuffling to the counter.

Rory burst through the door. "What do ye think yer doing, woman?"

"Getting medicine," she snapped. But when she saw Rory's appearance, she snorted and dropped the pill bottle. Snow peppered Rory's beard and hair, and he looked more like the abominable snowman than a sexy swordsmith. Laughter bubbled up and burst out.

"Have ye gone mad?"

She bent down and in doing so, forgot about the crutch she was balancing and lurched toward the floor. Slapping an arm out, she braced her fall. "Ugh." She flopped onto her back.

In a second, Rory was heaving her up with two hands under her armpits. "Christ Jesus, ye planning on injuring yourself further?"

"Well, you came in looking like a damn abominable snowman!"

"A...what?" He stared, brows fixed, snow still speckling his auburn beard.

"You know—the big, white scary guy with red eyes that goes after Rudolph." She lifted an arm up like a claw. "It fits actually. You're so grumpy."

His eyes fired. "Well maybe if ye had an ounce of compassion I wouldna be stomping around."

"Excuse me?"

"I said I cared for ye. There's no' many women I've cared for. I can count them on me hand and me sisters and mum comprise the majority of them. We have something. 'Tis not just fun and games."

She swallowed the unease bubbling up. "Sure, we have chemistry."

"And ye care for me, don't ye?"

She bobbed her head. She wouldn't lie, but she also couldn't give him words she wasn't sure she had.

With a nod, he stretched a hand out. "I'll help ye back to the couch."

"Actually, I think I'll turn in early. Maybe I can sleep off this"—she gestured—"ankle." *And escape from serious relationship talk.*

Without a word, he wrapped a strong arm around her waist and the other under her legs, and lifted her into his arms.

She gasped. "What are you doing?"

"Carrying ye."

She wasn't a damsel in distress. She was a...who was she kidding? She could barely walk. Resigned, she relaxed into his arms, soft chest, and familiar scent, resting her head in the curve of his shoulder.

He carried her to the bedroom and set her gently on the edge of the bed.

Andrea tugged off her sweater and pulled on a nightshirt, but when she tried to strip off her leggings, pain shot up her foot and ankle. "Oomph." Pressing her lids close, she sat back.

Rory dropped to a knee and rested a warm hand on her thigh. "Let me help."

"Please."

He carefully peeled off her leggings, guiding the fabric down her thighs, knee caps, calves, and around her good ankle first, then the swollen one. Next, he slid pajama pants up her legs.

Goose bumps appeared where he'd touched. She still couldn't believe such big hands could be so gentle. "Thank you."

"Yer welcome."

Lying beside him a few minutes later, she glanced at his profile as he rested—noting the way cinnamon weaved and accentuated his auburn beard, the strong prominent cheekbones above full cheeks, thick brows, and...she paused. His lashes curled slightly on the ends. *Curled lashes.* As she felt a grin form on her lips, she itched to brush a fingertip across those soft lashes. She lifted a hand, then paused and set it back down. Turning, she glanced out the window where not a single star was visible in the inky darkness. Caring for Rory was the scariest and most wondrous of feelings, but how could she give him words if she didn't know how? Plus, she'd always be leaving...it was just a matter of when.

Chapter Thirty-Eight

ARRIVING AT THE FRASERS IN GLASGOW A DAY
later, Rory's truck lights pierced through the thick rain and
highlighted the center pitch of the house like a lighthouse
tower. Andrea gingerly set her foot on the cobblestone
driveway.

Rory appeared, handing her the crutch.

"Thanks." She slid her booty off the seat, while rain pelted
her like angry rounds.

Brie rushed outside with a multi-colored, striped umbrella
like a mama hen. "What happened?"

"I have to toss away any ideas of being a snow bunny."

"What?" Brie half-laughed, half-questioned. She slung an
arm around Andrea, offering to help carry some of her
weight.

Once under the protection of the interior, Andrea sighed.
"I sprained my ankle skiing." She hadn't told Brie before
because she didn't want her to worry. But she also thought
she'd wake up feeling right as rain. Wrong-o.

"I'm so sorry! Let's get you propped up on the couch."

Stepping into the entryway, she shrugged off her jacket,

then slowly kicked a boot off. The other foot was covered by three, thick wool socks—Rory's, of course.

Rory set her bags aside, then stood there, taking up the majority of the doorframe with water dripping from his hair to his brows, off the tip of his nose, and beard.

He'd been so attentive the last few days that she needed some space to breathe. "I'm good, Rory. Go home. I know you need to check on Maggie."

His brows jammed together. "Are ye sure?"

"Definitely. I'll survive. Promise."

He stared at her with that quiet, surveying look, then with a brief nod, turned to Brie. "Thank ye for the vacation. Be sure to extend me thanks to Bryce, as well."

"Oh, you're so welcome!" Brie flashed a full smile and hugged him.

When they separated, Rory turned to Andrea. Leaning in, he kissed her with cool lips still wet from the rain.

"Bye." She watched him venture out into the torrential downpour—a large shadow amongst the darkening night. Then, she turned and ambled over to the couch, sitting gingerly. She lifted a leg with a grimace onto the square cushions, followed by the other, then tucked a pillow under her back.

Brie slid another under her bad ankle. "Are you hurting?"

"No, it's not that bad." She adjusted and breathed deeply.

With hands on hips, Brie lifted a brow. "So, what happened?"

Andrea cocked her head. "I told you—"

"No, why were you so quick to send Rory home?"

"OH." She expelled a breath. "He's been...fluttering around me."

"Well, he loves you."

With a jerk, Andrea winced and adjusted the pillow, while her heart rapped in her chest. "No, he...he cares, obviously, he's Rory. But he doesn't *love* me." She picked up the remote and narrowed her eyes at *The Holiday* playing. Brie loved romcoms, but Andrea was in no mood for mushy romance. She pressed buttons until she found *The Great British Baking Show*.

Brie sat on the edge of the couch. "Did he say that?"

Andrea flicked a piece of lint off her leggings.

Scooting over, Brie nudged. "Hey. It's me. What's going on in there?" She tapped a fingertip gingerly to Andrea's forehead.

"He's afraid I'll poof after the New Year."

"Okay..." Brie continued to stare with those deep green eyes of hers.

Throwing her hands up, Andrea huffed. "Rory wants to continue seeing me after the holiday is over, but there's no happy ending, Brie. It'll end in disaster." She thought of her dad leaving, Gloria snuggling up to a new man, the tears when the new man left, and then pure glee when another man entered Gloria's life the following week. They were all players in this game called love. But it wasn't real. Nothing lasted.

Brie poked her in the arm.

"Hey!" She rubbed the spot. "That's friend abuse."

"You're not injured there." Brie poked her again. "Pay attention. Just because you've convinced yourself you're doomed for relationship disaster like your parents means nothing."

With a sputter, Andrea opened her mouth. "I—"

"Zip. Zilch. *Nada*," Brie interrupted.

Andrea crossed her arms. "Just let me watch delicious delicacies, okay?"

"Nope. Not going to happen. You're my best friend, and you deserve to be happy. You deserve love. Look at Bryce and me."

She pursed her lips. "That's different. You guys are one-in-a-million."

"We're not. And sure, it sounds crazy that you could be in a serious relationship with a man from another country, but what if? What if you work out? What if Rory is your sous chef?"

Andrea winced. "Seriously?"

Brie grinned. "I'm just trying to put it in your terms."

She punched the volume up. "Well, he's no sous chef."

"What is he, then?"

Andrea opened her mouth. She didn't know. He was Rory. "I'm tired. Do you think I can sleep on the couch?"

With a soft shake of her head, Brie stood and draped a Fraser tartan blanket over Andrea. "Sure, just be prepared for the kids to rouse you awake in the morning."

After watching Brie leave the room, Andrea stared at her ugly, eggplant-colored ankle. Was that like her heart? Was she damaged and dark and twisty inside? Gloria glorified every relationship she'd ever had, except Andrea's father. She adored being adored, and being in love, even if she wasn't. She threw *I love you* around like a party favor. And then once she snagged a man, she bathed in the adoration until the shine wore off.

Was that real? Definitely not. Andrea used to laugh at the way Gloria molded herself into what she thought her newest catch wanted and hooked him like a cougar on the prowl. Funny she always married older men, though she had her fun with younger men, too. But Gloria made no apologies. She got what she wanted. Many thought her to be the trophy wife, but she had them fooled. And, love? It wasn't about love. It was about being seen. Men delighted in all the phony attention and dazzled Gloria with jewels, gifts, and more.

But what about Andrea, herself? Her relationships also served a purpose—entertainment, company, or pleasure, but she wasn't callous...was she? No, she definitely wasn't her mother.

Was she?

No.

And what about Rory? Sure, she was having fun, but she told him what she wanted. She was clear that she wasn't girlfriend material. She wasn't playing games. But now, he wanted to be all serious. Why? Why couldn't he leave well enough alone? "Ugh, because he's Ro-ry," she drew out the last syllable. The man didn't do anything on a whim, well, except for a few sexy surprises. Her lips curled at those spectacular memories. Yes, the quiet man had a few surprises up his thick sleeves, but why get all serious? She could imagine him brooding with Maggie's head on his beefy thigh, conditioning leather for a handcrafted piece. She had less than a week left. Did she really want to spend it without him? She had Brie, the kids, and Mimi, and she had the New Year's Eve Gala and *Ceilidh* to look forward to. That should be enough.

Chapter Thirty-Nine

"Ready, Cameron?" Hugh asked the following morning, helmet bent, sword gripped between a mittened, titanium-clad hand.

"Aye, *fear-fiadhaich*." Rory tilted his sword, feeling his armor shift into position like a second skin, and touched swords.

"Fight!"

Rory swirled his sword left, then right as Hugh approached. He swung and connected, mashing metal on metal as it echoed in the quiet, dewy morning. In the wee green glen to the rear of Hugh's farm, horses neighed and puffed with excitement thirty meters or so away; yet, not another soul existed, but he and Hugh.

Slashing, slicing, and slashing, Hugh pushed forward and met him metal fist to fist as their swords entangled like the saltire of Scotland's flag.

The weight of the steel longsword and smell of sweat and metal breathed fire into Rory. With a roar, he drove his elbow and pushed against Hugh's towering frame. Hugh might have him with a few inches and agility of a lean physique, but Rory was strong and the sword, an extension of himself.

Hugh stumbled back; yet, he readied in a moment. The wild man in the black titanium armor advanced once again.

Rory sidestepped, holding his sword at the ready.

Slashing his weapon side to side, Hugh pivoted at the last moment and struck Rory in the gut.

"*Och*!" Rory jerked and then scythed Hugh's upper arm.

Hugh kicked Rory in the upper thigh with a sabaton.

"Ah!" Even with his brigantine, Rory felt the blow radiate deep in his muscle. Swinging his sword, he struck Hugh's middle, sending his sparring partner back a meter.

Inhaling, Hugh readied. *Slash, strike, and slash*!

Rory fought, deflected, and sidestepped. As he battled, his sword tangled, profanity flew, and grunts rumbled. Nothing else existed, save for the fight. He felt the stress of the last few days—the expectations of Da, frustrations surrounding his relationship and the woman he cared for, and his laborious trade—purge with every strike and blow. The fire within him swelled like a blazing ball of power. Through the small grates of his helmet, he saw Hugh straighten and step back, sword high. Rory spun and blocked as Hugh's knee connected with his side. "Argh." Twisting, he backhanded Hugh in the helmet, only to have his sparring mate take the punch and slice down the opposite direction. Rory stumbled.

Hugh attacked, connecting with his right pauldron, then kicked his left leg once again.

Falling to one knee, Rory raised his sword.

Hugh swept a leg under, mashing metal on metal.

Rory tumbled into the damp earth. He relaxed his full weight and that of his armor in the rich dirt. "Thought I had ye."

Hugh laughed loud and clear between deep gulps of air.

Offering a hand, he grasped Rory's and helped haul him up. "An ale?"

"Aye."

Loosening his custom, hand-fitted gear, Rory breathed easier. Though he'd had the gear for over a year, the fit in the waist of his brigantine was a wee bit snugger than he remembered—a result no doubt of being well fed by a certain lass. He sat beside Hugh in the cool air. He couldn't stand the man on a personal level, but he was a *braw* fighter and one of his team's secret weapons. Hugh kept his identity a secret, choosing not to fight under his real name or else they'd have a whole flock of hens panting at the gates.

"Anytime you want to combat, just ring."

"Aye." Rory guzzled the crisp brew.

Hugh swiped a hand through his damp hair. "Who do I have the pleasure of thanking?"

Rory angled his head.

"Was it your father this time or a lass?"

Rory blew a breath. "A lass." He needed to battle—to strike, roar, and fight—since he'd had that frustrating conversation with Andrea. He needed something to convince her to stay and to face her feelings, but after tossing the night prior, he still hadn't figured out how.

"Well, good luck to ye." He lifted the beer. "In my experience, the less ye promise a woman, the less they expect."

Though his hands and body were tired from exertion, Rory felt fire coursing through his veins and soul once again. Grasping a titanium mitten, he smoothed a thumb over the mountainous knuckle plate, remembering sliding gloves onto Andrea's bonnie hands and the way she smiled and her own determination. But her own fire had simmered. She spoke of returning to HR and America, instead of branching out with her culinary craft. He needed to help her find a way to ignite her passion once again. Perhaps then, she'd have an answer for him.

* * *

Arriving at the gated entry of his property later that afternoon, Rory exited his truck and extracted mail from the box. He stared at a card with *Fraser* scrolled on the top left. Tearing into the envelope, he gazed at Bryce and Brie's Christmas photograph and save the date for their celebration, highlighted by a lenticular angle of light from between the trees. Their courtship was a whirlwind—a few months and then their engagement. Yet, he'd never seen his mate so happy. Rory had only known Andrea for close to a month, but he, too, yearned for more.

A welcome bark sounded, and Maggie dashed toward him. Wiggling her length and pushing soft fur against his hand, she whined.

"Hello, girl. I missed ye, too. How 'bout a treat?" He scrubbed a hand from head to tail. Holding the door open, he waited for Maggie to hop inside, then drove the short distance home. Parking, he glanced at his forge. He'd promised himself a holiday, and he wouldn't set foot in the forge until after the New Year. His hands and mind were tired from the long hours. He'd made more swords this year than ever before, and he was proud. As he stared at the structure, he swept his gaze over the sign Andrea designed that hung front and center. The gift was thoughtful—something carefully crafted and designed. She thought about others, about him, even if she wouldn't allow herself to believe how much she cared for him, but what of herself? She believed she had to return to a career she'd chosen because she couldn't picture the next step. Well, he did, but he needed to figure out how to help her see that subsequent stride—that is—after he returned from his annual fishing trip with Bryce.

He studied the forge sign and then glanced at the white-and-brown box truck parked alongside the building. Pivoting, he glanced back at the forge, then angled once again to consider the truck. An idea slowly sprang to mind like setting a candle wick aglow with flame—wee and sparkling at first— then spreading, firing, and dancing in his mind. Fishing out his phone, he typed *Mobile Catering Vans for Sale*. A wide variety of trucks displayed across his screen. A grin formed on his lips. He hoped Andrea would be as keen on the idea as he.

* * *

Knock-knock! Two, sharp knocks rapped on the Fraser front door.

Angling her head, Andrea glanced from the couch toward the entry where the twilight, burnt-orange rays danced along the front window panes. She hadn't yet ambled back to the guest house with her swollen, sore ankle. She'd been parked on the couch since the previous evening. Still, at midafternoon, she wondered who stood on the other side. Brie, Bryce, and the kids were at some secret spot outside of Glasgow sledding, while Mimi was attending a basket weaving class—a gift from Brie and Bryce. She wondered if Rory was at the door. She needed a break from his attentiveness and, frankly, from the question that still stirred and tangled within like a missing ingredient she couldn't remember.

He'd texted her last night, asking how she was doing. And she'd replied with a simple:

ANDREA

I'm good. Just resting.

Knock-knock!

With a harrumph, she rotated and tried to stand, but her ankle smarted. Swearing, she grasped the crutch and hobbled over. When she swung the door open, she found Sarah Murray staring back with a bright smile paired with a gray-and-white cotton-ball, sparkly sweater and in her hands, a basket brimming with baked goods. "Sarah! How—" Her words were arrested by a buttery, baked cinnamon scent wafting toward her. "Oh. My. God. I've died and gone to heaven."

"Heard y'all had a little stumble," Sarah greeted. "Nothing helps you feel better than some freshly baked biscuits." Walking inside, she hugged Andrea and removed the red-checkered Christmas napkin, exposing golden biscuits dusted with shimmering sugar, a bag of thin, oatmeal cookies, a jar of something with a burnt-tangerine hue, and another with a cinnamon-colored butter. "Some cinnamon-honey butter, my famous Oatmeal Lace cookies because cookies just always help, and special turmeric paste."

Andrea inclined her head. "Turmeric paste?"

"Yes! Turmeric is a natural anti-inflammatory. You can spread it on a warm, wet towel and wrap your ankle or add it to warm milk to drink."

Andrea twisted the lid and instantly, warm, rich notes flowed up her nostrils. She eyed the yellow-orange paste. "It smells good enough to eat! What's in it?"

"Turmeric, coconut oil, and water with a pinch of cinnamon."

"Wow. Thank you. I'll try it."

Following her into the living room, Sarah assisted Andrea in settling onto the couch, then strode into the kitchen only to appear a moment later with a cool towel in one hand and two butter knifes, a plate, and napkins in the other. She smeared some of the turmeric paste onto the towel and helped Andrea wrap her ankle.

Warmth spread immediately into her skin—a welcome feeling after the icy foot bath Bryce prepared a few hours prior. She had no idea how he fully immersed himself in a freezing bath every morning. He must be part polar bear like Rory who slept with his bedroom window open, while snow flaked outside. Seeing Sarah halve a biscuit and heap honey-cinnamon butter atop the nooks and crannies, Andrea snorted. "I don't know if I'll get better or fat, but this is great!"

With a grin, Sarah sat beside her.

"Aren't you having any?"

"I'd love to." She selected a biscuit.

After a decadent bite of a buttery biscuit with cinnamon spice and sweet honey, Andrea exhaled. "Brie tells me you're catering the Hogmanay gala."

"We are. It's going to be fantastic. Traditional music with a five-piece band, bagpipes, dancers, a four-course meal, and more."

"How fun! I need to focus on something else besides being an invalid." Andrea wiped her hands. "How many people have RSVPed?"

"Near 100."

She felt her jaw drop. "A hundred? Is the producer's house that large?"

With a lift of a brow, Sarah leaned in. "As large as a Texas estate, minus the cattle in the pasture."

They laughed jovially together.

"Wow. So, what's on the menu?"

Dabbing her mouth with a napkin, Sarah straightened. "We need to be traditional and incorporate haggis along with a few Scottish dishes, but we're also spicing up the menu with a little Texas flare. We have two mains—herb-butter-roasted game hens with crispy skin alongside a roasted trio of spiced potatoes and fresh broccolini, and then individual Scotch beef

Wellingtons with black pudding, smoked bacon, and an herb salad."

Andrea felt her mouth pool, salivating. "Yum."

"For the starters, we're preparing seared scallops paired with chorizo and a pea puree and a salad we haven't ironed down yet, but there's still time. We're also making a trio of canapes, including meatballs two ways, bacon-wrapped-haggis bites with a smoky whisky sauce, and mini tartlets with roasted tomato, smoked cheddar, green chiles, and caramelized onions."

"That sounds delicious." *And a cooking experience.* Andrea wished she could join the Murrays. "Have you tried the onion and mushroom pies here? I had one on my first visit to Edinburgh and oh, my God, so good. That would be amazing as a mini app, too."

"I have! That's part of the inspiration." She flashed a smile. "I still have to decide on how to incorporate salmon. Finn smoked fresh salmon earlier this week, and he's considering an herb salad with a light vinaigrette or a niçoise salad."

"Either sound great. You could even pickle turnips for the niçoise salad, since the Scots love their *neeps.*"

Sarah tapped her lip. "I like it! I'll jot down a note to test a few recipes."

"Oh"—Andrea swished her hands through the air—"what you have is great. Ignore my comments."

"No, you're right. This is Hogmanay. Traditional Scottish food or foods that evoke memories for the New Year. I've added a dash of my own background like these sweet Oatmeal Lace cookies to the dessert menu paired with Scottish coffee, as well." She retrieved the glossy bag filled with thin, caramel-colored oatmeal cookies.

Andrea peeked over. "May I?"

"Of course." She tilted the bag. "I can never resist them, either. I made batches of cookie dough in preparation for New

Year's Eve, though I couldn't help but bake a batch for nostalgia."

Andrea selected a caramel disk and took a bite. The thin cookie melted into her mouth and reminded her of butterscotch candies *Nona* used to carry in her bag mingled with earthy oats. "Yum. These are amazing!"

Sarah smiled, flashing twin dimples. "I was right. These babies definitely deserve to be highlighted." She bit into one and sighed. "*Mmm*. So good!"

"Uh, yeah." Andrea relaxed into the cushions, enjoying talking of food and catering with a friend. Yet, all the talk about food made her itch to get back into the kitchen. Gently wiggling her toes, she exhaled. She still had a couple days of recovery.

"The event is such perfect timing."

Andrea tilted her head. "For?"

"We haven't told y'all yet, but"—she leaned forward—"we just secured a restaurant space."

Andrea cheered. "What? That's great!"

"Thanks. Finn and I are ecstatic. We get the keys on January second." She sighed and rested her head into the cushion as a smile flashed across her face. "Our own official space. Of course, we rent the commercial space for *Swords* and our food truck, but this will be ours. Just ours."

A sudden ping of jealousy filled Andrea's chest cavity—to be able to cook whatever she wanted and shop the local food scene sounded incredible. She wished she could strike out on her own and embark on something different from HR, but cooking was something she did for joy, not for employment.

Sure, she had the one gig in the highlands, but that was a one-time-deal. She wished she could cook one more time before she left. That would bring her out of this funk. She imagined Hogmanay with all the lights and music, and she in the kitchen preparing food with a sassy smile. With an idea in mind, she glanced at Sarah. "Do you need any help with the menu prep for the gala?"

"I'm not sure if you'll be on your feet in four days, but if you are, then we'd love an extra hand or two!" She patted her hand.

"Great." Excited energy zipped up Andrea's veins.

"We're prepping at our rented restaurant space starting around six a.m. on New Year's Eve. Finn is getting all the seafood fresh that morning, while all the other fare will be delivered the day prior. Some of the staff you met on set will be working, as well."

Excitement zipped through Andrea's veins.

"You can come in the morning for a few hours, but then you must skedaddle and show up in a fancy ball gown later."

"You got it!"

"You'll be going with Rory, right?"

Andrea felt her cheeks sear. "Uh, yes."

She pressed her hands together. "See! I told you he was a good one. Did he cook for you after all?"

Andrea thought back to the night after Rory rescued her in the highlands—how he prepared a meal following his own long day—and struck a fire within her. "He did." She cleared her throat. "Are you dressing up to?"

"You bet your ass I will. No one keeps a former Texas Pageant Queen from enjoying a party." She flashed a full-toothed smile. "Once the final dessert goes out, I'll slip into something incredible. Our Scotsmen won't know what hit them."

Andrea stilled the hand that held an Oatmeal Lace cookie. *Our Scotsmen.* She never considered Rory to be hers.

Chapter Forty

THE NEXT DAY, ANDREA AWOKE WITH A DULL THROB in her ankle. Dipping her toes toward the guest house's creamy carpet, she flexed her foot slowly upward. She'd hobbled up the night before, and even though soreness remained, the sharp pain had vanished. *Thank God for small miracles.* She didn't want to be laid up and stuck inside, during the last few days of her vacation. She needed to get back on her feet and fast! Glancing at the guest house side table, she noted the salve from Sarah was almost gone. With a smirk, she dipped a finger into the fragrant cinnamon-and-flame-colored balm. The color reminded her of Rory's beard in the firelight, highlighted with rich-cinnamon and burnt-orange flecks. She glanced at her phone. He hadn't texted her last night. Rory was back to being the quiet man. And for some reason that didn't settle well.

A ping from her professional social network set her phone aglow.

She exhaled. She had to face the inevitable. *Soon.* Rory made her aware of that, too. *But who the hell wants to think of work on vacation? Well, except working in the kitchen with the*

Murrays, but that isn't work. It's fun. Clicking into the app, she noticed a message from one of her previous executives at TechCo.

Andrea,
I see you're out for the holidays. Call me when you can spare a few minutes to discuss an opportunity.
John Gonzalez

Pursing her lips, she wondered what the heck TechCo wanted. She'd rather be jobless than walk into that building again. But when she clicked into John's profile, she was surprised he listed another company as his employer. The start date: December 10th. *Interesting.*

She called and left a message. Next, she scrolled through social media, ignoring the insane number of messages on her account—they were most likely scammers, anyway, or crazy fans—something she'd noticed after the catering pictures were published. She didn't need drama in her life. Instead, she scrolled, perusing photos and comments from when she cooked for the stars.

After a few minutes, she closed the app and opened her photos. She laughed at herself kissing a reindeer a few days ago, sitting on Santa's lap, playing with the kids, and finally, skiing with Rory. Gazing at his bearded smirk, she felt a little tug in her gut. Ugh. She missed him. His slow walk, even slower smile, and slow way he did so many wonderful things. What was her problem, anyway? Why did she have to make things difficult?

Sure, she was headed back to L.A. next week. Rory knew that from the beginning. She didn't need to feel the pressure of keeping the relationship going—she'd talk to him straight. They'd see one another through the New Year, and what the hell, maybe she'd consider seeing him when she visited Brie next. She was an adult. She could be an adult about her relationship. See? She even called this a relationship. She was turning a page!

With her mind sorted, she searched the web for things to do during December in Scotland and clicked a link noting *Things to Do and More!* She stuck out her tongue at the first option: skiing. She continued reading. "Husky Cruise on Lochness? Well, that sounds fun, but with this nearly-healed ankle, f-no." She returned to her go-to. She'd invite Rory to make something with her. Something Scottish and Christmassy? Shit, she hoped he didn't say sweets. That was Brie's territory... Maybe some chipotle shrimp and grilled vegetables with crispy potatoes? He sure liked *tatties*.

She opened the text string.

ANDREA

Dinner?

Setting her phone down, she waited impatiently, smelling sweaters hanging over the edge of the bed and crinkled her nose. She tossed two toward the laundry pile. A couple minutes later, her text dinged.

RORY

Can't tonight.

"Don't tell me you're making more swords," Andrea muttered. "Christmas is over, and the show's not returning for another five weeks." She marched to the washing machine, opened the lid, and shoved clothes inside. "And people called me a workaholic." Slamming the lid, she started the wash, then marched back to her phone.

ANDREA

What about tomorrow?

RORY

Plans as well.

"Plans? What plans?" She huffed.

ANDREA

Look. I'm sorry, okay? I was hurting and cranky.

RORY

Thank ye.

She threw her hands up. "If you're playing hard to get, this isn't funny," she yelled at her phone, then pushed the device across the tiny dining table. But as she huffed with annoyance, a thought crossed her mind. *Maybe he's done. Maybe he wants more than I can give him.* A pit formed deep in her stomach, swirling like bad takeout. *Are we done?*

The squeals of kids outside brought her out of her head. She grabbed a crutch and hobbled out. After hugging the kids and Mimi, she propelled into the kitchen.

"You're walking so much better today!" Brie beamed as she filled a glass of water.

"Thanks. It's feeling a bit better, too, but I'm still grabbing some aspirin." She wrenched open the kitchen cabinet, twisted the bottle, and popped two into her mouth. She crunched the potent, acidic pills, wincing. "How are you doing?"

Brie handed Andrea the water. "Good. Being with the kids has helped." She tilted her head. "Everything all right?"

"Everything is not." Andrea huffed and then gulped water, sloshing drops onto her blouse. She set the glass onto the counter. "Date the swordsmith, she said"—Andrea made air quotes with her hands—"he's nice,' she said. 'Apologize,' she said. Now, I'm here twiddling my thumbs."

"You apologized?" Brie brightened.

"*Psh*. Little good that did. And besides, why am I always apologizing?"

Brie arched a golden-brown brow.

"Seriously, why? I shouldn't apologize for being me. If anything, he should apologize for asking questions he knows I can't answer."

Brie hummed.

"I even asked if he'd like to join us for dinner. He has plans."

"*Hmm*." Brie turned and opened the fridge, selecting a box of bright raspberries.

Andrea cut her gaze toward Brie. "I know that *hmm*. What? Do you know something?"

"In fact, I do." Brie rinsed the rosy fruit. "He and Bryce are going fishing for some ladies—"

Andrea slammed her hands on the counter. "I knew it! Never trust a man."

"Andrea."

"Here I was apologizing." She swirled with anger. "Apologizing! Where's my phone? I'm going to text that son of a—"

With a hand on her arm, Brie stilled her movements. "Andrea."

"What?" she yelled.

"They're going fishing."

"What?"

"Bryce and Rory are going fishing. They left at four a.m. and are on their way to the borders to fish for Graylings— Ladies of the Stream." She bit her cheek, but the smile still pulled at her lips. "I just thought it was such a lovely name."

"You bitch!" Andrea smacked Brie lightly on the arm. Now, she had to wait for Rory. She didn't like it. Not one bit.

Chapter Forty-One

AFTER A NEAR TWO-HOUR DRIVE, RORY ARRIVED IN the Scottish Borders region with Bryce under a dark-gray sky, thick with cobwebs of the night like a wool blanket. The four-by-four's lights cut through the dawn and reflected over partially-snowy plains. Not even near eight a.m. and the sun had still not risen. Ideal for two braw men ready to wrangle a few ladies.

Exiting, he grabbed his gear and trudged down the snow-laden path beside Bryce. Rory breathed in the brisk air laced with rich earth, fresh snow, and boggy water, relishing in the silence save for the crunch of his boots on the path.

Bryce directed him through the thicket of Scots pine and birch, winding through brown brush and straw-like grass until they arrived at a pebbly bank.

"Bonnie spot," Rory said.

Bryce nodded. "One of my favorites."

He set his chair and gear besides Bryce's, then tossed on his vest over a waterproof jacket and waders. He spoke quietly, discussing the best spots, while securing nymphs and weights onto his line. With a long drink of dark coffee, Rory tugged his wool beanie low, hooked the net to his side, and checked his vest.

"Ready to risk your fingers and toes?" Bryce turned with a smirk under a cap and beanie.

Rory's lips curled. "Aye."

"I'll head a wee bit up river," Bryce directed.

Rory nodded. Watching Bryce cover ground swiftly, he wondered what his mate was thinking. Was he thinking about simply catching a Grayling or of his bonnie wife? For himself, Rory valued the quiet the river offered. He observed the course of the water—the current, tucks, turns, and rocks—and searched for a pool. He treaded carefully into the marsh, so as not to disturb the rocks at the bottom or alarm its occupants. He felt the pull and strength of the cobalt river, even with his neoprene waders and gazed downstream. He'd fished since he was a wee lad, especially in the highlands and now and again in Loch Lomond. He knew well that a pool with gravel at the bottom would attract a Grayling.

With the fine trout and salmon season ahead, Rory was keen to get seasoned once again. Maneuvering through the water, he gazed at the habitat before him as aware as the steel beneath his hand when shaping. Awareness was key, especially with the short winter days, demanding six hours of focus and grit. When he spotted the seams in the water where two different flows met, he tipped the rod close to the water's surface, then tilted it backward, slowly at first, then faster past his shoulder until the line tugged. He angled the rod, allowing the line to unfold in the air like a slight ripple in the wind, then tilted his rod tip toward the water. Allowing the fly to sink a moment, he slackened the line, keeping his gaze trained on the surface, watching and waiting, while the nymphing leader ran between his middle and forefinger like a delicate strand of hair.

Hearing a low whistle pierce the air, he glanced upstream

in time to witness Bryce netting a decent-sized fish. *Of course.* Just like his mate had snagged Brie quickly, he'd also caught the first lady of the stream. He was pleased for him. How could he not be? Bryce deserved to settle down. And so, did he. But Rory needed a better way to draw Andrea in, instead of frightening her away. He had a lot to think about these past few days, including about the woman who'd warmed his bed and heart, and frustrated him to no end. He'd been thinking of a plan since Christmas. He knew she cared for him, but she needed convincing for the future.

Well, he had some ideas of his own. After remembering her bonnie face appearing in the catering van's window to announce his order on the remote location for *Swords of Scotland*, he started formulating. Andrea was a career woman—a brilliant one from what he'd heard, though she had countless times mentioned the lack of fulfilment. She was a creator—a cook who dazzled with dishes that fed and brought warmth to the soul. He'd seen the joy in her eyes when she cooked for others. So, he'd taken a chance. After searching for catering trailers and food vans, he settled on one. When he and his mate, Matt, a motor mechanic, viewed the van for themselves, Rory listened to Matt's assurances the van was a sound choice, and he'd help turn it into what he needed. *What Andrea needed.*

A light tug on his forefinger pulled him out of his thoughts, and he struck.

A fin speared out of the water, then a tail flicked, and the fish somersaulted.

The strong pull told him it was a good size, so he set his stance and fought the wee beast. As he reeled the fish in, he thought about Andrea and how she'd like to cook the glistening lady. *A lady for a lady.* With a grin and a grunt, he set to work steering the fish away from snags and then felt the line go slack. "Damn." With his jaw set, he put a few more nymphs on and cast once again.

He let his mind wander back to Andrea's almond-shaped eyes that widened when he asked if they could continue seeing one another after the New Year. She was scared—just like a doe in the headlights. So, he'd slow down again and continue planning for the future.

Until she caught up.

He tugged the line, allowing the thread to glide along the water. Keen patience was essential for fly-fishing, in addition to great vision. He could be patient for Andrea to come around, as well. He knew what he wanted, even if she couldn't see it for herself yet—though the text yesterday was a welcome surprise. His pole bent in his hands followed by a tug and then a greater yank. He'd hooked another! Now was the fight.

The braw grayling pulled with power.

Rory reeled and adjusted, keeping a keen eye on the water level and adjusted his footing as his rod bowed. The glorious lady weaved toward him, flipping and flapping like a bloody dolphin. He lifted his rod and readied with his net. With one fell swoop, he netted and captured the lady. He gazed at the brilliant, shiny dorsal fin, the sheen of its iridescent turquoise-and-silver scales, and the glossy, dark eye staring back. Like the Lady of the Stream, Andrea took her time coming to him. He enjoyed her spirit and fire, and, of course, she was bonnie to look at, but she had something that made him feel alive. He wasn't ready for her to leave.

Bryce waded over. "Saw ye caught a decent-sized lady."

"I did. And, ye? Was she large enough to keep?"

"Nah." He displayed an empty net. "I released her. She was too beautiful to keep for myself." With a grin, he bumped Rory's shoulder.

Rory chuckled. Hiking up the bank, he set the fish into

the bucket, then rinsed the net and relaxed beside Bryce in their outdoor chairs.

"Care for a nip?" Bryce handed Rory a flask.

"Aye." He drew a quick nip, allowing the fiery whisky to warm his belly, then passed it back. Gazing at the rippling current and trees still in the fresh, marshy air, he exhaled.

"Bloody gorgeous," Bryce noted.

"Aye."

"'Tis a grand time when ye can throw a line with your mate in blessed peace."

Rory tilted his head. "A wee loud at home, is it?"

Bryce grinned. "'Tis, but I wouldna change it for the world. Don't get me wrong, it was a swift change—living by myself and then having another three suddenly under the roof with me—but I don't know how I got so lucky. One moment, I'm coming home from press in L.A., and the next, I'm staring into the most beautiful green eyes I've ever seen. 'Tis like strolling into a glen on a clear day with the sun shining."

With a shrimp-shaped nymph in hand, Rory paused. He'd been similarly struck by Andrea peering down from the guest house's window. Then, he thought he'd missed his opportunity. Now, he grinned to himself, thinking that he wanted to actually thank Hugh for being such a goddamn *eejit*.

"Then, there's Noah and Phoebe." Bryce chuckled.

"Ye all seem to have settled in fine."

"*Och*, but we've experienced our share of moving pains with the children missing their friends and school, and Christ, I've learned never to leave a door unlocked."

Sliding a glance toward Bryce, he cocked a brow. "They saw ye taking a piss?"

"Phoebe." Bryce laughed. "Lord and then the questions. How come you have a penis like Noah and I don't?"

With a laugh, Rory shook his head. He thought of his

younger brother, sister-in-law, and wee niece. He'd visited only a short while at Christmas before Da inevitably started in again. But he hadn't said a proper good-bye. He needed to remedy that.

"Even still, me heart has ne'er been so full."

"That's grand, mate. Ye seem happy."

"I am." Bryce looked sideways. "And ye'd know since you've been stopping by regularly." He drew out the last word slowly.

Rory quirked a hand over his beard.

Glancing over a shoulder, Bryce stared at the sights behind them. "Melrose Abbey."

Rory nodded. Being a Scot, he knew the historical significance and the King—Robert the Bruce—whose heart lay buried there.

"Brie's been doing research." Bryce relaxed into his chair. "She's writing a fantasy historical romance and including the Bruce. She's fascinated by the Bruce and Elizabeth's story, as well as their separation during the capture and reunion eight years later. Of course, the book is fictional, but she's including some historical elements."

Rory bobbed his head.

"Andrea's something else, 'tisn't she? Tough as nails and a damn fine cook."

"She is that." He busied himself by putting on his vest and preparing to wade back out.

"But I don't think she's the staying kind."

Rory glanced over. "What do ye mean?"

"She's talking about L.A. one minute, then going to cooking school in Italy the next. I know you. Ye plan."

He glanced back at the abbey. "Let me worry about that." He stared at the outline of the Gothic structure—the gables and tower visible, though he couldn't ignore the churn in his gut. The same churn he'd felt a few days ago in the cabin. He was falling for the lass and planning for more. He hoped he was sure where Andrea's heart rested.

Bryce rose. "Let's land us some more ladies."

Nodding, Rory stood, attached the net once more, and picked up his rod. Yet, the elusive lady in the water was not the one on his mind.

Chapter Forty-Two

THE FOLLOWING EVENING, ANDREA STARED AT AN unfamiliar number flashing across her phone screen and sighed. She hoped the caller was Rory, but the quiet man had yet to resurface.

Bryce, however, called Brie an hour ago, and Brie already had a chicken potpie in the oven.

But what about Rory? Was he on his way back, too, or making a detour? Gazing out the kitchen window where fresh snow sparkled in the inky-black evening, she was brought back to the banks of River Ness and Rory framed by the winter wonderland behind him. Was he thinking of her, too?

Seeing the same number call again with an L.A. area code, she answered.

"I have great news," John Gonzalez said on the other line. "I've joined a start-up, and we want to bring you in as Chief Human Resources Officer."

Andrea slumped onto a kitchen stool and rubbed a hand over her brow. "Wow, you—wow." She knew John would make her an offer. His message hinted, but CHRO? The news was as surprising as the catch in her chest. This is what she wanted—what she wanted over a month ago—and what she should still want. She had a reason to go back to L.A. and continue the career she'd chosen. But why did she feel as though the wind had been knocked out of her?

"I know it's unexpected, but given the circumstances earlier this month, I thought you could use some good news. You'll need to interview, of course, but that's just a formality."

"I'm flattered, really I am," she began. But what? She'd been vacationing and putting off the future, and here it was, literally on a silver frickin' platter.

"Can you come in Monday?"

The *A* apron Brie purchased lay folded a few feet away by the pasta machine. Walking over to the side counter, she traced a finger over the soft fabric and swirly *A*. "I'm actually out of town right now, but I'll be back Wednesday."

"How does Thursday sound? Say, ten a.m.?"

Glancing around the empty kitchen filled with hints of Brie—the muffins in a glass jar and remnants of flour and a rolling pin from potpie making on the counter—and the children—artwork on the fridge and tiny aprons hanging on hooks—Andrea's heart pounded. She didn't want to leave, but her future was calling.

"What do you say?" John asked.

Inhaling the rich, buttery notes of potpie permeating from the oven, she calmed her nerves and straightened. "Sure. Thank you for the opportunity, John."

"Pleasure. Looking forward to seeing you next week."

After disconnecting, she stood and rotated her ankle. The almost-normal feeling combined with the support of the wrapped ankle band gave her confidence. She walked sans crutch in search of her best friend and nearly ran into Mimi removing her coat in the entry. "You're back! How are the basket weaving classes going?"

"Incredible." She beamed with hazel eyes shining in the

interior light. "The method is as old as Scotland itself, but just as true. And the artisans have been so wonderful and welcoming." She held out her wrist, showing off a natural woven bracelet with light brown and mahogany hues below a jewel-toned, quilt-style sweater. "I made this and a small basket." She reached beside the chair and lifted a woven basket.

"It's gorgeous!"

"Isn't it? I can't wait to learn more." Her eyes shone.

"You'll need to buy another suitcase for your flight home."

"Yes...I suppose I'll have to bring a few things back from Scotland." Her eyes misted. "I don't know how I'm going to leave them."

Andrea nodded. These last few weeks had grounded and revived her and brought more joy than she'd had in months. But she couldn't live here. Not forever. She'd miss Brie, Bryce, and the kids so much. And...Rory.

Mimi exhaled. "I've decided I'm going to retire at the end of June."

Andrea's eyes widened. "What?"

"I was planning on doing it in a few years, anyway, but Brie asked if I could move to Scotland and Bryce insisted, as well, and I thought, 'Why not?' My family is here, and I've been talking to some local artisans. They said they'd include me in some painting rotations with outdoor, art classes, so I can apply for a work visa. I'd love to teach a few classes part-time and be with my family."

"Won't you miss your students?"

"I will, but I know my co-workers will be happy to have them." With a smile, she smoothed her sweater. "And you? Are you eager to get back to L.A.?"

She shifted and tucked a wild curl behind her ear. "I am." But even as the words left her lips, she felt them sour like a mouthful of bad milk. What option did she have besides to go home?

* * *

Finding Brie with a book resting on tucked legs and a small piece of fudge in hand a few minutes later, Andrea leaned against the office door frame. "I've got an interview scheduled. John called."

"John?" She popped the last piece of rich chocolate into her mouth. She chewed, then inclined her head. "John Gonzalez from TechCo?"

"The one and only. He was released the same time I was and joined this start-up. They want me to join as CHRO."

"What?" Brie tossed her book and jumped up. "That's great!"

Andrea glanced at her mug and back. "It is. It's great news."

"But what about your cooking?" Brie tilted her head. "And Rory?"

Andrea sighed. "It's been fun. I have a notebook full of recipes, but I'm leaving in a three days. And Rory"—she blew out a breath—"he's great. I'm going to enjoy him and whatever this is for a few more days if he still wants to."

"Are you sure?"

Flashing a smile, she set a hand on Brie's arm. "One hundred percent." When savory smells met Andrea's nostrils, she glanced toward the kitchen once again. "Your potpie's done."

"Oh!" She angled. "I didn't even hear the timer." Brie rushed into the kitchen with Andrea on her heels. Noting the timer on the oven with three minutes left, Brie opened the oven door, wafting buttery, rich potpie aromas. "It is done! Golden and perfect. You have such good cooking intuition."

Andrea shrugged, but she couldn't fight the grin that tugged her lips.

Setting the pie on a cooling rack, Brie pivoted. "Did you invite Rory over?"

"No. I'm surprising him at his place. But first, I need to shave my legs, get out of these sweats, and pick up some groceries. I don't have much time."

Brie wiggled her brows. "Bring some of Mimi's fudge for dessert."

"Great idea." She winked. "Don't wait up."

* * *

When she arrived at the edge of Rory's property, Andrea found the gate closed and locked. Since Brie told her Bryce and Rory hadn't yet arrived at the house, she knew Rory wasn't home. She had to get creative. Luckily, smoke puffed from the neighbor's chimney nearby. She remembered Rory mentioned a certain neighbor would feed Maggie if he was running late on the set of *Swords*. She hoped that this was the one.

A few minutes later, Andrea rang the bell with one hand and held a tin of rich fudge in the other.

An older gentleman with bushy white brows and a beard that reached near his chest opened the door and stared through large-rimmed glasses. "Can I help ye?"

"Hi! I'm Andrea Accardi. I'm seeing Rory next door."

He bobbed his head. "Rory's a fine lad." He extended a hand weathered and peppered with age spots. "Benjamin."

She smiled and shook his hand. "Nice to meet you, Benjamin! He mentioned you feed Maggie when he works late. I was wondering if you had a key and could let me in. You see, I have all this food prepared to surprise him." She gestured toward the car. "I brought some homemade fudge, as well."

His brows rose, and he smacked his lips.

"My best friend's mom made it. It's the best. Just try eating one." She handed him the wrapped chocolate.

With another smack of his lips, he opened the tin and selected a large square. He popped the chocolate into his mouth and hummed, beard bouncing up and down as he chewed. "'Tis great, lass." He ate another and grinned. "Thank ye kindly. Just a moment." He lifted a hand, then disappeared and returned a few seconds later, jangling a wad of keys.

She trudged back to Mimi's rented SUV, careful of her newly healed ankle, and swung behind the wheel. She waited for Benjamin to start his pickup. Following him, she drove to Rory's gated entrance.

After unlocking the gate, Benjamin led her up to the house, then exited his truck and walked up the short path toward Rory's front door.

A tiny hesitation tickled her chest as Benjamin inserted the key into Rory's front door. Would Rory mind that she asked his neighbor to let her in? She wondered briefly, pausing, then pushed the hesitancy away when Maggie let out a couple happy, welcome barks.

Maggie greeted them with tail-wagging.

"Hey, girl. I have something for you, too." Andrea gave her a quick scratch, then one of the rawhide bones she'd selected at the market. With a quick good-bye and thank-you to Benjamin, she flipped on the lights and hauled groceries into the kitchen. Pushing up her sleeves, she got to work. Rory wouldn't know what hit his tastebuds.

Chapter Forty-Three

Rory drove up the rocky drive with snow peppering his windshield, while his headlights cut through the blackness of the night. But instead of a dark house awaiting him, lights shone from the interior. He gripped the wheel tightly. A silver four-by-four parked outside. He threw the gearshift into Park and swung out of his truck, boots crunching on the path as he marched toward his front door with apprehension in his chest and a large wrench in his hand.

Opening the door, he halted. Something cooked under a flame on the stove, music pumped in the air, and his table was set for two. *What the devil?* He tore off his jacket and hung it on a hook, scattering snow.

Andrea swung around the corner in an apron and screamed. "Shit! You scared me." She pressed a hand to her heart.

"What the hell are ye doin' here?" He rubbed his pounding head. The lack of sleep from the second three a.m. wakeup call and cold, exposed elements fishing had taken their full affect.

"Cooking!" She smiled and approached him with a sashay. "And I brought dessert." She shook her tits.

His jaw dropped. She wore nothing save for an apron and ankle boots. Desire sparked as anger flared.

Swinging toward him, she scrunched her nose. "What is that smell?"

"Me."

"Well"—she trailed a finger up his jumper—"this wasn't exactly how I planned tonight, but go ahead and shower and then we can have our fun." She wiggled her brows before turning with her ass hanging out.

"What is this? And how'd ye get inside?"

She dipped a spoon into a deep pot and lifted some rust-colored rice for a taste, then set it in the sink. "*Mmm.* Good." Pivoting, she flashed a smile. "Oh, your neighbor, Benjamin. I told him I had a special surprise, and he was more than happy to oblige and let me in."

He swiped a hand over his forehead. "This is my home. Ye canna just let yourself in."

Her smile faltered, and she stood for a moment, opening and closing her mouth, then cast a hard glare—brown eyes reducing to dark slits.

If looks could kill, Rory'd be skewered. Instant regret welled his growling gut.

"What the hell am I doing?" She wrenched the cutting board off the counter, sending colorful vegetables flying and dumped the remainder into the sink along with the board with a *boom*.

Maggie barked and jumped.

"Down, Maggie," Rory snapped.

Maggie dropped her hindquarters on the floor.

"I'm such an idiot!" She cranked off the fire and tore off the red apron, then snatched an onion and rocketed it toward him.

He swore and ducked. The onion rapped the door behind him. Lifting his head, he narrowly missed being hit with a bright-red bell pepper. "A—"

Andrea wrenched the pot off the stove and slammed it onto the countertop. Then, she stalked naked to the opposite room.

Rubbing the heel of a hand to his temple, Rory tried to suppress the headache. He'd planned to throw something in the microwave, maybe sit in front of the tele. Now, he'd have to smooth things over with Andrea when it wasn't even his fault to start.

She stalked back into the kitchen, tugging on a jacket over scrunched leggings. "I'm such an idiot. This person isn't me. I don't spend an afternoon planning a surprise meal for a man who doesn't give a shit."

He pinched the space between his brows. "That's not—"

"The hell it's not!" She stomped through the kitchen.

"Will ye slow down? I come home after a weekend trip, spent and tired, and I find ye here unexpected."

"Unwelcome, you mean." She breezed past him, only to whirl around once more. "Don't worry. I'm leaving."

He grasped her forearm. "Don't."

"Don't touch me," she hissed.

"I'm not doin' this right. Please wait, Andrea." He released her.

Her gaze continued to pin him with anger, but she paused.

After rifling a hand over his cap, he removed it. "I dated a woman for a while, Jennifer," he said slowly.

She eyed him with dark eyes pinpointed like daggers.

"We had a good thing going for a while." He heaved a breath. "I gave her a set of keys."

"*Pfft*. So, you don't like commitment after all? I'm—"

"No lass," he rasped. "She stole pieces."

Andrea's brows jammed together. "Swords?"

He nodded. "Aye. I thought perhaps I left a piece on set, but then a few more would go missing. I couldnae wrap my head around it."

"How do you steal swords? Those suckers are heavy. You can't just sneak…" Her eyes widened.

"I was working a fortnight at *Swords*—long days and even longer nights. The only reason I discovered her was due to a night shoot being cancelled." He swept his gaze over hers. "Thunderstorms."

Andrea's brows jammed together as she waited for him to continue.

He paced around the kitchen, noting the littered counter-tops. "When I came home, the gates were open, and she and her mates were making away with some of my most expensive pieces, and some, I'd made on contract. 'Twas like I'd just stepped off the television set and back again."

Andrea pressed a hand to her mouth. "I'm so sorry, Rory."

"Yer welcome in me home." He strolled back, pausing an arms-distance away. "I care for ye. But ye have to understand, I have boundaries."

Her lips curled. "That's not what you said at the cabin." She traced a hand down his jumper.

God, this woman.

"But I get it. I'll let you know next time I surprise you naked with dinner."

"Next time, aye?" He leaned in and inhaled her scent—something spicy and sweet mingled with Andrea's own ample flavor and richness from the stove no less. "Don't leave."

She held up a finger. "On one condition."

"Aye."

"Shower." And with that, she turned on a heel.

He caught her wrist in his hand, pausing her movements. "Join me."

Her eyes warmed, while a slow smile bloomed on her full lips.

Gliding his fingers from her wrist to her hand, he led her toward the bedroom. He'd reacted wrong, but she stayed. And he'd do everything in his power to show Andrea she should stay longer.

Chapter Forty-Four

SITTING WITH STEAK FAJITAS, SPANISH RICE, AND kidney beans, Andrea relaxed as did the mood, which had simmered into congeniality since the soapy, sexy shower. Rory smelled better, too. "So, what exactly did you and Bryce do the past few days?" She speared a piece of juicy steak.

"Freeze our bollocks off fly-fishing."

She laughed. "I've never fly-fished in my life. Correction, I've never fished, and based on your smell when you came in, you won't find me fishing." She twirled the fork in the air, then pointed it. "Ever. But I will cook the catch."

With a chuckle, he scooped beans. "Aye, 'tis not for everyone. Yer standing in sub-zero temperatures for long periods of time, waiting on the lady—the Grayling—and then when ye finally hook her, if she doesn't throw the hook, ye have a hard, dogged fight reeling her in. She'll even use her dorsal fin like a kite to try to escape."

"Smart lady."

He nodded as a grin tipped up and widened his cheeks. "That she is. But connecting to nature and standing in the glistening, albeit freezin', water brings welcome peace and calm."

"I can see that. It's like making a homemade sauce for the first time, then stirring the liquid marvel and watching the texture change from this fluid consistency to velvet. All you have to do in the world is focus on that one thing—the rest of the world doesn't matter."

With an incline of his head, he urged her to continue.

"But inevitably, you have to come back to reality. Speaking of which, I have an interview scheduled in L.A. next week."

He jerked, dropping rice from his fork. "Next week?"

"Yep. I had to start thinking about my future, even if working in HR brings back bad memories. I was good at it." She shrugged. "Thanks for the nudge."

With a scruff of a hand over his beard, he cleared his throat.

"And I was thinking you could be my date for the New Year's Gala. You're going right?"

He relaxed into the chair. "I am."

"Great. See, look at me looking at the future." She toasted with her beer. "I don't suppose you'll be wearing a kilt?"

With a soft chuckle, his lips curved. "I've been known to on special occasions."

She leaned forward. "I still remember the one you wore to the brewery."

He quirked a brow.

"Sexy."

He grinned.

"And speaking of sexy, I gave away our dessert to your neighbor, but I don't think you'd mind if we had our own dessert." She unbuttoned her sweater and watched his eyes turn into molten, silvery pools.

"And will ye return to Scotland?" he asked thickly.

Rising, she slipped her sweater off her shoulders. "Oh"—

she stepped toward him and unbuttoned her blouse one button at a time—"I'll be back for spring vacation and the wedding celebration, of course, which I might extend to a short...summer vacation."

Watching her unbutton, his chest heaved.

"*Woof-woof!*" Maggie barked.

With a glance at Maggie, Andrea wiggled. "We'll have to take this into the bedroom."

Rory nodded; yet, his gaze was fixed on her.

Backing up slowly, she gave him her best come-hither look and sashayed the few meters to his room. Frigid air hit her in the face when she opened the door. "Fuck! It's a frickin' freezer in here." She glanced around and noted the open window opposite.

He must've opened it after their shower.

With a chuckle, Rory closed the door and advanced. "Ye'll no' say that in a moment."

"Rory. It's like forty or four below, or something, outside! And you left the window open."

He hauled her up, one arm snug under her butt and caged her against the wall. "'Tis refreshing, but I'll warm ye." He buried his face in her full breasts, drawing a giggle then a moan from her lips and tugged her pants and panties down, gliding a rough hand along her skin.

She pushed his thick flannel off and unfastened his pants, feeling his erection pressing against the buttons and her own desire flaming.

Tilting her head up, he captured her lips, lacing her tongue with his, while gripping her ass with his right hand. When he drew back, he drew his tongue across her collar bone and teased her neck with his soft, scruffy beard.

She was on fire—a molten fire ball blazing in the frigid night. And all she wanted was Rory.

Grasping her right leg, Rory lifted her higher, then

wrenched the side table's drawer open. A wrapper crackled, and the next moment, he filled her.

"*Mmm,* " she moaned, relishing the feel of Rory. But then he was thrusting and taking, driving and propelling them both at a merciless rhythm. She held on as pleasure coursed through her, building and swelling, then bursting inside her.

But he didn't stop.

She gripped his shoulders as he took her further and further. She didn't know if she had more to give. But he showed her she could, urging her higher and higher, until they were ablaze together.

Chapter Forty-Five

THE FOLLOWING DAY, THE DESIGN HOVERED IN Rory's mind. He selected a piece of graph paper and a pencil and sketched with quick, sure strokes, then shaded rippling detail to catch prisms of light like Andrea's curls in the sun. After he finished the initial sketch, he drew another to show the side profile and interior of the design. The fine waterfall hammering exterior paired with the smooth interior would create an exquisite piece once finished with the center stone. Three sketches of the same piece stared back at him. But only one lass would wear the ring. A grin tugged at his lips.

Scrubbing a hand through his beard, he surveyed the design a final time. The ring would be the first of its kind, albeit a challenge like the rocky relationship he'd begun with Andrea. He'd incorporated gold-and-silver-plated metal in sword designs prior, though a ring was something different all together. Still, he never shied away from a task. He'd see the design through just as he planned to see through his proposal to Andrea. Last night, she discussed returning to her job in America with displeasure. Yet, when she mentioned she'd return to Scotland, her bonnie brown eyes sparkled. She could make a life here—cooking and creating—with him.

A few hours earlier, he'd awoken with her tangle of curls spilling over his bare forearm. Andrea snuggled close to his chest in his flannel like a nightdress with the vibrant cross-weave of emerald-green, blue-cobalt, and rust-red, similar to his clan's tartan. He twirled a finger in a ringlet, feeling the delicate swirl and then watched the curl bounce back into the rounded coil as soon as he released the strand. The curl matched Andrea—strong and full of her own vivacious spirit. Watching her sleep peacefully, he knew two things: she would wake up momentarily with a sexy up tip of her lip, and he wanted to wake up with her by his side for the rest of his life.

Now, staring at the silver and white gold, Rory planned. He'd hand forge the shank first, then create the bezel setting to encircle the stone he'd been left by his Nana. The aged gold setting was worn; yet, it held memories of his beloved grand-parents. He remembered the way Nana would prepare food for the masses, including pots of porridge for breakfast and loaves of bread to go with supper. And the way she'd march out into the forge when his grandad was a few minutes late to dinner, hands fisted on her hips, a myriad of silvery-white curls spiraling all over her head. At the sight of his fair wife, Grandad would turn off the forge and finalize what he was working on.

He imagined Andrea's zeal for all things cooking reminded him of his Nana, as well as her spirit. Rory wanted to build his own memories with Andrea—grand ones. Everything was falling into place, and he was ready to take the future into his hands.

* * *

In the late afternoon on New Year's Eve, Andrea towel-dried her hair. Her feet were sore, her ankle smarted, her shoulders and lower back ached, and she was almost positive she still smelled like garlic, even with the second lather of body soap, but she'd do it again in a heartbeat. Prepping food and getting ready for the Hogmanay gala four-course meal with the Murrays and staff was pure bliss. In two days, she'd be back to reality, but the last eight hours were full of fun, flavors, and fire. She'd meant to stay only a few hours—that's what she'd told Sarah—yet, she became completely immersed. She cleaned and prepped an array of colorful vegetables, peeled potatoes, and helped prepare broths including a rich crab broth for the *Partan Bree*, crab bisque, after chopping and baking crab shells. She might've even snacked on a piece of crab or two during break with Sarah. Her ankle had healed. She had a kick-ass, fire-engine-red dress ready to slip into and a sexy Scottish date. What could be better? Bring on the New Year's celebration!

Arriving at a narrow driveway with a rusty metal gate was not Andrea's vision of the director's cottage-mansion that Brie raved about a few hours prior. She craned her head. "Are you lost?"

"No." Rolling down the window, Rory punched in a code. The gate retracted, *clinking* and *grinding* gears.

"Rory, what are we doing here?" She swiveled. "Is this where I find out you're a—"

"Just wait a wee moment."

She harrumphed. Glancing down at her red off-the-shoulder dress and ample cleavage, she felt annoyance bubble. She didn't know what the heck was going on. And, she was dressed to impress!

Rory drove through the gate and pulled around the side lot.

A bunch of older trucks and vehicles lined the lot. "Okay. What the hell's going on? If this is your idea of sightseeing in Glasgow, you're mistaken."

Rory gazed with steel-gray eyes set.

She sucked in a breath as a pit formed in her stomach. She knew that oh-so-serious look.

"I wanted to surprise ye with an early New Year's present." He rubbed a hand over his left jacket pocket, then glanced at her.

She eyed him cautiously. Something was up. Andrea felt it like a sixth sense. Similar to the time she'd accidentally dumped cinnamon in nearly-there mashed potatoes in her early twenties. Though she smelled the spice immediately, the moment she shook the jar, she knew what she'd done—she'd gone and ruined the mashed potatoes. Her stomach bunched.

"I've secured a food van"—he pointed to a faded tan truck in need of an overhaul and loads of TLC—"so ye can start yer own business from the ground up. Ye can plan yer own menu and cook from yer heart."

Her mouth flopped open. Then, she shook her head. "Wait, what? Who said I wanted a food truck?"

"I—"

"You didn't think to check with me first? Oh, sure, you just think all this through in your head and then BAM!" She flicked her hands in the air. "Surprise. Oh, by the way Andrea, I secured you a food truck. What if I can't pay for it or don't want to? Did you ever think of that?"

"Ye don't need to lass. I've taken care of it for ye."

"Oh? Oh, really?" She pressed her lips tight as fury swirled within like a blazing bonfire. "You'll just buy me some dilapidated roach coach to drive around Scotland, so I can sell garlic bread to unsuspecting Scots? Fantastic. Fucking fantastic. I can't operate my own food truck." Her mother's words filtered through her brain and out her mouth.

A thick brow arched. "Why?"

"Because it's insane!"

"Many people have done it with success."

"Well, that doesn't mean I will. So what if a few people liked what I cooked? How does that guarantee a wage? A living? I'll be on the streets in three months or less."

He adjusted, facing her fully. "Now, lass."

"Don't you now lass, me! And who said I was staying in Scotland? I'm leaving, remember? I have a job offer."

He squared his shoulders in the black suit jacket. "Ye, yerself, told me that ye weren't sure going back to yer old role was what suited ye anymore. Ye have a chance to continue something of yer own here—something that sparks yer inner fire."

With a huff, she glanced at the truck. The frame reminded her a tad of the Murrays, but it was…impossible. She couldn't start a business in a foreign country. She didn't even have a work visa. She was an American, for fuck's sake. She spun in the seat. "You're infuriating!"

"Why? Because I've offered ye an option ye didn't think of yerself or one ye were too scared to act on?"

Leaning in, she glared. "I'm not scared."

"Ye are."

"I am not!" She huffed, feeling the heat of fury flash through her again. But oh boy, did she sound like a grumpy child. Shaking her head, she angled away from Rory toward the opposite window where the city lights glistened under the dark starry sky above. "Take me to the gala, or I'm getting out and calling a car."

* * *

New Year's Eve was a time for celebrating, getting drunk, dancing, and kissing a hot guy. Andrea should've been having the time of her life. But no. She seethed. She'd walked in with Rory, or rather, had clomped ahead of Rory once the valet opened the truck door, and sought out a familiar face. She didn't even have time to take in the circular cobblestone driveway lit up with an array of fiery lights or the cottage-mansion's grand entrance, since the little detour made them late to the festivities, and before she knew it, drummers announced the beginning of the *Cèilidh*.

Dancers performed on the opposite side of the grand hall, while a full band in authentic Scottish attire played bagpipes, drums, and violins.

"Happy New Year," Eleana greeted in a shimmering white-and-black, off-the-shoulder gown. Her silky, black hair fell in soft waves down to her waist, while a sparkly clip drew a swoop of hair elegantly to one side.

Pulling her into a quick embrace, Andrea heaved a breath. "You, too."

Drawing away, Eleana searched Andrea's face. "Everything all right?"

"Oh, just dandy." She nabbed a champagne glass from a server and downed the crisp, sweet alcohol. Glancing around the stunning room, she noted the bold-blue, bright-gold, and crisp-white decorations with sparkling star accents and shiny candelabras. Above her, draped string lights, and sheer fabric gave the ceiling an illusion of a starry night. She tried to relax, but her blood still boiled. What was Rory thinking? To spring a food truck on her of all things?

"Come join us on the dance floor!" The band invited guests.

Seeing newcomers move toward the center of the floor, Andrea quickly joined, thankful for a distraction. Grasping a smooth hand, she glanced over and felt the tension in her body immediately ease. Her best friend smiled brightly in a golden, one-shoulder gown. "Brie!"

"I finally found you." Brie gripped her hand. "This is going to be so fun."

Andrea squeezed back and danced, laughed, kicked, clapped, and circled. She tried her best to put what happened earlier out of her mind, but something pestered her like a fly swirling around a kitchen. She saw Rory standing on the outskirts of the dance area, watching all the while. She was still annoyed. But seeing servers circulate with canapés, she was brought back to the kitchen at the studio set, to the commercial space this morning, and finally, to the food truck surrounded by snowy mountains. A deep wanting burrowed in her chest. *Damn him.*

Sinking a spoon into the golden-sheened *Partan bree* an hour later, Andrea closed her eyes, focusing on savoring the sweet and savory crab notes with a sherry bite. Yet, even as delicious as the bisque was, she couldn't push aside the agitation with the man sitting beside her. Stealing a glance at Rory, she gawked when he craned his head at the same moment and met her gaze.

His eyes implored her to speak to him.

But anger still simmered beneath her calm-HR exterior. Setting the spoon aside, she inhaled. She wouldn't make a scene—not here.

Rory angled toward his plate. With a heave of his broad chest, he rubbed his jacket pocket with a bear claw once, then twice. She stilled. *What is he doing?* With a dip of his hand into the pocket, he appeared to grasp something and then release it, patting the pouch.

Was there something in his pocket? Her pulse quickened.

"Beautiful starter, isn't it?" Eleana asked.

"Uh-huh." Andrea flashed a smile, then ducked under the table, inhaling oxygen. "He's not going to do what I think he's going to do?" She gulped one mouthful of air at a time, but she couldn't control the hammering in her chest. Was he trying to trap her? First, with a food truck and second, a proposal? As the subtle notes of pine wafted toward her, she tilted her head and came eye to eye with Rory near the table leg.

"What're ye doin' down here?"

"Checking"—she dashed her gaze around—"the...linen quality. You never know when you need a good linen." She tossed the fabric that brushed the floor. A white tag flashed in the folds. "Yup, just as I thought." Straightening the fabric, she rose.

Rory cleared his throat. "I need to talk to ye. Would ye—"

She jumped up. "Excuse me. I'll...be right back." And she got the hell out of there. Although to be fair, she didn't go very far. She didn't have keys or a getaway car. She wasn't even sure if she wanted to leave. This was supposed to be a fun night. *Fun*. Nothing formal, no surprises or announcements, and no embarrassments in front of a crowd of people. Rory had already surprised her with a truck and that went as well as undercooked noodles in mac and cheese. She skirted past the band toward the bathroom where performers filled the hallway and entrance in blue-and-white dancing kilts, royal-blue waist coats, and pearl-white blouses. Her pulse beat so rapidly, she felt the thump in her neck and swallowed thickly. Spotting a swinging kitchen entry about twenty feet away, she beelined, swung through, and plastered herself inside the door. "Shit! Shit! Shit!"

"Andrea?" Sarah Murray's voice asked sharply.

Swiveling, she stared at Sarah, Finn, and a half dozen sous chefs in a double line plating the final courses. Meaty, rich aromas filled her senses, and she breathed deep, while the musical *clink-clink-clink* of plates sliding down the stainless-steel line mingled with voices filling the room. Yet, she didn't move.

"Why are you in here? Go enjoy yourself!" Sarah bellowed.

With hands shaking, she strode forward. "Give me something to do. Anything."

Sarah tilted her head. Yet, she kept up with the fast-paced plating, adding herbal garnishes and sliding plates onto gold-lined serving trays. "Whatever is the matter?"

"I just need to get my hands on something, okay?"

Sarah stared at her briefly, then bobbed her head. "Right. We're plating the final meal before dessert. Not much you can do now, but extra hands are always good."

Andrea nodded, yet she couldn't deny the urge to run—somewhere, anywhere. She flew her gaze around the room.

"You can top the *Cranachan* cups with fresh raspberries." She directed with a sweep of a hand toward the far side of the room where the fridges gleamed. "Just pull out one tray at a time."

She shifted, twisting her hands together. "I might crush them right now."

As servers whisked by with large serving platters in their arms, Sarah said something unintelligible to Finn. She skirted toward her. Stopping briefly along the wall, she picked up an oatmeal lace cookie and handed it to Andrea. "Looks like you need this."

Bobbing her head, Andrea crunched into the buttery cookie and finished it in two bites, while Sarah returned to the line.

Five minutes later, a server brought back two full plates announcing the completion of dinner service.

With a flash of a smile, Sarah angled toward Andrea. "All right, how about the crèm brulée? You can add and crystallize the sugar." She eyed Andrea. "You've made crème brûlée before, right?"

"With Brie. A few times. You don't have to bake it. And you get to use a torch." She motioned with her hand. "Fire. Fire power. Fire would be good right now."

Setting a hand on Andrea's, Sarah searched Andrea's face. "Honey, spill."

She drummed her nails on the steel table. "There's nothing to spill."

"Darlin', when you hang out in the kitchen in a ball gown instead of dancing with your beau, there's definitely something to spill."

Andrea huffed. "I think he's going to propose."

Sarah squealed. "Oh! A—"

Shaking her head, she swished her hands in front of her. "I don't want to talk about it."

Her smile faltered, and she pressed her lips together. "Fair enough."

After washing up and sliding an apron over her dress, she followed Sarah to the opposite end of the kitchen where an air conditioning vent pumped cool air. She felt like a furnace and welcomed the icy blast.

Sarah grabbed a culinary torch from a granite-covered counter and extended the tool. "I'm giving you this on one condition."

Andrea grasped the small handheld torch. "Okay."

She lifted a perfectly, penciled golden brow. "Don't set yourself on fire."

She snorted.

Gesturing toward a canister of sugar and a spoon sitting near a dozen ramekins of creamy custard, Sarah picked up a second torch. "Go ahead and top them one by one with sugar and then torch the crème brûlée." She clicked off a button. "Safety lock." Demonstrating, she clicked and turned on the torch. A four-inch flame of midnight-blue and neon-orange shot out.

Andrea admired the blue flame with golden edges, while her mind veered back toward a fiery forge and the man standing beside it. The *click* of the torch switch brought her back to reality.

"Easy peasy." Sarah set the torch down. With a wink, she jogged back to the other end of the kitchen to join other dessert preparations.

Andrea sprinkled a thin layer of coarse sugar across the ramekin, then turned on the torch and adjusted the setting to medium like Sarah instructed. The flame was loud—like the whirring of a mini-jet engine—and erased her thoughts. She circled the ramekin, torching the sugar crystals until the surface bubbled, wafting sweet buttery notes up her nostrils and darkening into caramel. But she wasn't quick enough. The crystallized sugar looked like a burnt marshmallow.

"Shit." She didn't need to ruin dessert. With an inhale, she slowly grazed the torch over the second creamy sugary custard and exhaled. The sugar crystals glistened, then turned golden. With a grin, she continued topping and toasting the rich desserts.

Soon, the kitchen staff moved like dancers in a perfectly choreographed catering dance with the start of dessert service —whipping cream, swirling designs, plating cookies, and more.

Another sous chef joined Andrea on the opposite end of the table, topping and toasting crème brûlès at a practiced speed.

She froze with the torch in hand, watching him wide-eyed. These were seasoned professionals, and she was a distraction. A last-minute addition. This wasn't her job or her life. She was playing chef just like Gloria had said. Her chest cracked like the glassy sugar-topped surface. Setting the torch down, she stripped off the apron and wandered back to the ballroom. Her heel caught, and she stumbled. Flinging an arm out, she gawked at the men and women dancing in the center of the floor—performers dancing on...swords. The crack in her chest fissured further as the swords brought her mind back to Rory. How could he surprise her like that? Make her believe in something that wasn't possible? Annoyance lingered like the acrid smells of burnt sugar. Scanning the crowd, she strode forward and unceremoniously ran into a woman with a tartan wrap over her dress.

"Yer Rory's lass," the woman said matter of fact.

"I," Andrea began before she was engulfed by the woman and her heaving bosom.

"Marjory Brown, so nice to meet ye! Isn't this grand? With such an event, someone should be getting married."

Andrea's heart beat pounded like the drums in the background.

"Ye'll soon be planning yer own wedding!" She clasped her hands over Andrea's. "Oh, and how Rory's waited patiently for the right woman to come along."

Panic raced up her spine and consumed her. Andrea tugged her hands free, stepping back. *Rory's lass? Marriage?* She couldn't pretend any longer. This wasn't her. She darted a glance at the exit. The glowing, fiery lanterns were luminous beacons. She gathered her dress and weaved through the throng of people as quickly as her heels could carry her. Arriving at her now-empty table, she grabbed her purse and rushed toward the entry for her coat.

Hearing her name, she turned for a moment only to run into someone else.

A strong hand steadied her. "Andrea. There ye are! Brie has been searching for ye," Bryce said.

"I need to get out of here."

His blue gaze held hers. "Everything okay?"

"Yes." She looked everywhere, but at Bryce. "No...I'm leaving."

"There's no—"

She wrapped him in a quick hug, pressing back the sorrow. "Say bye to Brie and the kids for me." Tearing away, she sprinted toward the fiery lanterns.

Chapter Forty-Six

Rory scanned the crowd of revelers. He'd lost sight of Andrea, which was easy to do in such an environment, but he needed to speak with her. He understood her reaction and surprise with the truck, but he thought she'd be open to the idea, especially after her initial success with the Murrays' truck. She had choices—couldn't she see that? As he craned his head, he couldn't quell the ball that had formed in his gut or the way it rotated like a thick, metal round churning. When he heard his name in a familiar feminine tone, he paused.

"Andrea's leaving," Brie said breathless.

Alarm bells clanged in his head. "Leaving?"

"Bryce just told me." Her eyes glossed. "I tried to call her, but she's not answering."

"I'll get her." With large strides, he marched through the hall and into the cool night.

Andrea stood at the edge of the circular driveway.

Waiting for a car no less. He ground his teeth and strode forward. "What's gotten into ye, woman?"

Whipping her head around, she stared with surprise

etched in her glossy brown eyes, then lifted her chin. "I'm leaving."

"There's no reason to—"

"There is!"

He noted the fire in her eyes and told himself to tread carefully. "Because I purchased a food van?"

She shook her head, tossing curls. "It's time for me to go home."

"Yer due to return to America in two days. What's got ye stirred up?"

"I realized something tonight. I have to stop pretending. This isn't my life. My life is back in L.A. I have a job offer and a future in America. Vacation's over, okay?"

He stepped forward, stroking a riotous curl he loved so much. "It doesn't have to be. Ye can stay with me."

"Stay with you? Sure, let me just move in and play house." She stepped back and threw up her arms. "I didn't sign up for this. I came here to clear my head, not date."

He gripped her arms. "If ye think all we have is a few dates, yer lying to yerself, as well as me."

"Don't you get it? I'm not what you need, okay? I can't give you what you want." She spun away.

But he held on.

She glared, eyes darkening like night.

"We're not done yet." Reaching into his pocket, he retrieved the ring. The outdoor lights caught the diamond, and the waterfall metal shimmered orbs across Andrea's beautiful face.

She gasped.

He knelt before her. "Ye've talent and spirit and everything ye need to succeed. I can see it as clear as ye standing in front of me. And ye have me. Ye drive me mad, fill me with pride and passion, and a fierce love I can't temper. I know yer scared, but ye needn't be. We can build a grand life together, side by side. Marry me?"

Her lips trembled; yet, she stuck her chin out.

God, how he loved that fire.

"No."

He felt like he'd been pummeled with a sledge to the chest. "What are ye so afraid of?" Rising, he grasped a hand and prayed she'd accept the truth swimming in her deep eyes. "Yer running scared, but ye can do this. Ye belong here."

She shook her head once more as the flashing lights of a vehicle approached. "No. I don't. Do you remember when I told you that I flew to Italy to meet my family and explore my heritage when I was twenty?"

He nodded.

"Even though I loved it, I realized I didn't belong there, either. I'm not Italian. I'm an American. Hell, do you know women aren't even named Andrea in Italy? It's a man's name."

He continued staring with his heart thumping like a power hammer, ready to burst.

"I have to go back to L.A. To a career I know. To my independence. That's what I want. Not...not this." She backed away.

A silver car idled a few feet away.

She ran toward the car, opened the door, and disappeared into the darkness.

Gripping the ring, he stared at the muted city lights beyond.

* * *

Rory wrenched his truck door open and cranked the engine over. Yet, he stayed there, gazing at the vibrant party inside, the happy revelers, the shiny décor, and celebratory air. He clenched his jaw.

The metal bore a hole in his pocket. He reached inside, then shoved the ring into the glove compartment. He should've known. Andrea had been out of reach since they'd met. He couldn't convince her to stay. She was always keen on going back to America. As a swordsmith, he controlled the sword design from beginning to end. He started with a design, then he shaped it with a close eye, first heating the metal, then strengthening and shaping the iron to meet his vision. He knew the variances of temperature and how to maintain the heat to keep the piece from cracking. He knew how to control one of the hardest substances on earth, but he couldn't control the woman in his life. Hell, he didn't want to control her. He wanted her to stay. He scrubbed his hands roughly over his face. He'd known she was leaving, didn't he? She'd always told him. *But, ye eejit, ye didn't listen.*

He shoved the gearshift in Reverse and checked his mirrors before stomping on the pedal.

Chapter Forty-Seven

Two weeks later, Andrea reviewed a new hire policy under ultra-bright fluorescent lights in her corner office. The pages blended together in one, black-blobby blur. She rubbed her eyes. After hitting the ground running at the start-up, she was roped into identifying talent and more talent. She was all at once the CHRO, recruiter, and talent acquisition queen with the primary focus being talent acquisition—getting people in the door—to help the company thrive. But they had no pay scales, compensation plans, retention and succession planning. Nothing. She was in a start-up-shit-show stressed out with crazy curls looking more like Medusa day-by-day and eating chocolate like the dark concoction was her lifeline. She'd worked every night since her first day, contacting outside legal resources to procure policies or creating draft compensation plans for review, and more. And she had one person in Human Resources besides herself. *One*. But she and Kristy were in no way the dynamic duo. All Kristy was hired to do was orientation. When Andrea approached her to discuss training documentation and other agenda items, she was flabbergasted when Kristy repeated that she was hired to provide the best onboarding experience for new hires, not training.

Andrea gritted her teeth and took the paperwork. At first, she'd been utterly flattered that she was John's first choice as CHRO, but now, she wanted to be anywhere but here. She smashed the stapler, once, twice, three times, but anger and annoyance still swam in her blood.

Hearing male voices arguing through the corridor and then escalate, Andrea shoved the stapler aside. "What now?"

In the middle of the office, the Chief Technology Officer and a new hire argued. "Wash your hands," "disgusting," and "ICE" were thrown around by the CTO with a contorted, angry face.

The technician stared at the CTO with disinterest in his rumpled gray button-down and uncombed hair.

She marched toward them. "Hey, hey, what's going on?"

"He didn't wash his hands." The CTO pointed a finger at the new hire.

"Okay..." Andrea urged him to continue.

"He took a shit, walked out of the stall, and out of the men's room. Then he proceeded to go into the kitchen and get a glass of water where he stuck his shit hands in the ice."

Andrea's eyes widened. "In the ice?"

The new hire shrugged.

"In my office." She directed. "Now."

He shrugged again. "I'm good."

"You're good? Oh, well, that's just great, isn't it? You're good, but the rest of the company isn't, thanks to your disregard for cleanliness. I'll need to call maintenance for the ice machine to be properly disinfected, put a sign up, and send a notice out." Glancing around the office, she noted everyone was standing around, rubbernecking at the commotion. "Scratch that. Everyone heard. Do not use the ice!"

Nodding and conversations resumed.

She gazed at the tech guru. "My office. Now."

After a fifteen-minute conversation about proper hand-washing techniques, code of conduct, and just plain old common sense with the technician, Chad, she flopped into her chair. "Fuck." She yanked a sticky note from a stack and wrote: contact legal to write an Office and Facilities Use Policy. Yet, the to-do list was growing again and from pure idiocy. "You're a grown-ass man. Wash your hands!" she yelled at her closed door. But yelling didn't help. Anger and agitation still bubbled. She rubbed her sternum to help ease the pressure. Since leaving Scotland, she hadn't found her rhythm. She'd rented her old apartment back, which seemed backward and loser-ish, and she'd started her new job. But something was missing. She pushed a curl away from her temple and buried her head in her hands. "This is what you wanted. What you *want*." Her chest constricted. When a meeting notification chimed, she exhaled. Time to get back to the dumpster fire.

* * *

Another week flew by, and Andrea was figuratively kicking herself for leaving Scotland early and taking the first opportunity that came her way. Before her trip, she would've done anything to be in this position, but now, she wondered, what if? Of course, she needed a job. She had pay bills to pay. She had to do something. She couldn't stay at Brie and Bryce's indefinitely. But what if she hadn't said *yes* to John? Would a better offer have come in?

With a huff, she scrolled through a policy, making notes. A subtle aroma drifted into her office from the kitchen, and she inhaled, closing her eyes. "*Mmm*. Tomato soup with basil." An idea sprung to mind. She pushed the policy aside and grabbed a notepad, flicking a page open to a clean canvas. She wrote: *Chicken Cacciatore*. Comfort food. What her *Nona* used to make for Christmas. Then, another aroma swirled into her office. "*Tikka masala*, garlic, and butter rice." *Chicken Cacciatore with Tikka Masala and Buttery Orzo.*

She jotted down a recipe, adding green olives and bay leaves. "Oh, and how about—"

John walked into her office with a blue polo and a quick smile. "Hey, Andrea. How's the talent search coming along?"

Flipping the page over, she quickly closed the notebook. "Better once we get some recruiters and policies aligned. We don't want to have an HR nightmare on our hands."

"Precisely." He grinned, while his temples shined in the overhead lights from a receding hairline. "That's why I hired you."

"I'll need to hire a few more roles, though timing is tough right now. We'll need one recruiter to start, an HR representative, and a content writer responsible for drafting communication throughout the company."

"Sure. Whatever you want." He checked his watch. "Meeting. Keep me posted."

"Of course."

Watching the door close, she blew a curl out of her eyes. "I'll keep you posted all right."

After work, Andrea ventured into the city. Since returning, she'd been working nights and weekends. She needed to immerse herself in life again—in culture, people, and food—and out of that white office. All around her was color—local block-lettered graffiti on one street corner, artwork in a window in a shop, people of all walks of life, and a myriad of smells from Chinese food to pizza to specialty takeout. A fresh, bold chalkboard sign with violet-and-saffron lettering caught her eye, propped up beside the entrance to a small restaurant space. And on the top, *Menu* was scrolled in whimsical lettering. She paused for a moment to read.

The door jingled and out walked a woman with a short,

black ponytail and blue-silk scarf wrapped across her forehead. She looked Andrea up and down. "You're not Bianca," she said more of a statement than a question.

"Nope, I'm Andrea. Andrea Accardi. Is this a pop-up?"

"It is. Marin"—she held out her hand—"Of M&M Mouthfuls."

Andrea flashed a smile. "Cool name. How long is your pop-up up?"

"Just tonight." She glanced at her smart watch. "That is, if my new line cook shows up."

Andrea arched a brow. "Shouldn't that be someone you already know and have vetted?"

The woman cocked a hand on her hip. "Excuse me?"

"Sorry. I come from HR. Human Resources," she added when the woman kept staring. "We hire and fire, amongst other things."

"Well, this was supposed to be my partner and my big night, but she decided she couldn't go through with the pop-up at the last minute—the pressure she said." She made hand quotes. "Now, I've called in favor after favor."

"I'm sorry," Andrea told her.

"Me, too."

"Can I reserve a seat?"

She shook her head. "We're booked."

"Of course." Andrea cast her gaze over the restaurant space with black-and-white decor and bursts of bright-blue touches. "Good luck tonight. I'm sure the line cook will arrive with bells on."

The woman snorted.

With a quick farewell, Andrea strode toward her apartment building. Yet, as she walked, memories of she and Brie cooking together in the Cairngorms, her putting on a dinner party for the Frasers, and more flooded her mind. A thought snuck into her mind, and she followed the thought like an aroma trail. Marching back, she found Marin adding a few more details to the sign. "If your line cook doesn't show, call me. I'd be happy to help." She offered her card.

Marin glanced at the *Lu Cuoca Andrea* card, then tilted her head. "You cook?"

"Damn straight. I've been a home cook for near ten years, hosted dinner parties, and have taken a slew of classes. And, just last month, I catered an event for *Swords of Scotland* with real-deal movie stars, while on a short work hiatus in Scotland."

With a prop of a hand on her hip, Marin quirked a brow. "Are you serious?"

"Super serious." Andrea retrieved her phone and showed Marin a few pictures.

She inclined her head, while a small smile tipped up the corners of her purple-painted mouth. Suddenly, her jaw dropped when she spied a selfie of Andrea with Bryce. She cleared her throat. "All right, I'll think about it." She tucked the card in her pocket.

An hour and a half later, Andrea had her hair up and apron on, while she and Marin tag-teamed the dinner offerings. Although she didn't know the menu, she caught on quickly caramelizing scallops, crusting ahi tuna, and chopping vegetables like no one's business. And when the chef asked if she could slice zucchini *parpadelle* for the pesto, Andrea smiled. "I sure can." She was in the zone, cooking, prepping, and assisting Marin. And she loved every minute. Though sweaty, she felt the stress from the last few weeks melt away like a stick of butter in a hot pan.

"You weren't lying about your talent." Marin tossed a fresh pile of herbs in with the scallops.

Andrea stilled, remembering something Rory had told her. *Ye've talent and spirit. I can see it as clear as ye standing in front of me.* Something within her cracked. She'd been so angry. At Rory. At the situation. At his proposal. *God*. All because she thought she didn't have a choice—that *he* was making the choice for her—when all he was doing was helping her choose. She'd thought about him every now again, but she'd pushed those thoughts aside. Now, at the sound of a chime, she refocused on the dish at hand, thinking of the quiet man.

Chapter Forty-Eight

A HELLA-AMAZING NIGHT CALLED FOR AN incredible breakfast. Andrea was buzzing with energy the following morning, even though she'd been up past midnight. She scanned the fridge and settled on *California Eggs Benedict*. Selecting eggs, an avocado, a lime, tomato, butter, and some leftover baguette, she swiveled toward the counter.

A familiar, upbeat song began playing.

With a glance at her phone, she grinned at the picture and name flashing across the black screen. She danced to it with a baguette in hand. "Hi, Brie!"

"Andrea! I hope I didn't wake you, but I've been waiting to call you. OMG. You cooked? What? When?" Brie sputtered.

"I did!" Andrea waved the baguette. The event went off with a few delays the night before, but all in all, guests enjoyed the food, while others waited in line out the door, hoping to join the pop-up experience. She'd taken a selfie with Marin beside the M&M Mouthfuls sign with guests in the background, tagged the restaurant space, and posted mid-dinner to spread the word. "It was the best I've felt in weeks! It's Saturday. I've worked way too many hours to count, but I feel amazing. Tired, but amazing, you know?"

"That's fantastic!"

"Thanks, Brie. Being in the kitchen again felt so good." She gazed at her hands. She hadn't even had time for a manicure since returning to L.A., and she didn't care. Her nails were trimmed short, void of the polish she'd painted for New Year's. Spreading her fingers, she remembered how she'd artfully rolled fresh ahi in a spicy, seed mixture, plated herb-and-watermelon radish salads with miso dressing, and topped the vibrant-colored dish with toasted, slivered almonds, and more.

"So, are you going back?" Brie asked.

"No." She sighed, setting the bread down and propped a hip on the counter. "It was just a one-time pop-up. The business partners wanted to make sure they could sell and market their food, and one of them didn't even show up. That's where I came in. Marin—the one partner who showed—will have to decide if she's ready to strike out on her own. She could do it—she's creative. I'm sure she'll figure it out." Andrea stood and cranked the fire to medium under the saucepan, then rotated and selected two eggs.

Brie hummed. "You know I stopped by the Murrays' restaurant yesterday with Bryce. They gave us a tour."

Andrea paused, nibbling her lip. "Oh?"

"Yup. It's not finished, but what they've done to the space in such a short time is incredible! They're calling it *Sea to Star*."

With a sigh, Andrea separated the golden yolks. "I can only imagine. Scottish-Texas fusion, huh?"

"That's right. It's going to be a big hit. And guess what? They're hiring."

"Oh, really?" She flicked her gaze over the shiny, red leather, roll-up case on the edge of the counter. She hadn't put her knives away. They rested on the counter like a prize after a night of spectacular cooking.

"Really!"

She wondered who the Murrays would hire—chefs fresh out of cooking school or seasoned cooks from other restaurants? They had their two sous-chefs, but who else were they looking for? A stack of paperwork rested on her kitchen table —more policies to delve through—and she crinkled her nose. *If only the restaurant was nearby, I'd jump at the opportunity to say good-bye to HR once and for all.*

A muffled voice mingled with Brie's soft tone in her ear.

"Everything okay?" Andrea asked, washing her hands.

"Yep. Someone wants to talk to you."

"Auntie A?" Noah's high-pitched voice came on the line.

She smiled and picked up the coffee pot for a refill. "Hey, buddy." Swishing and swooshing sounds carried across the phone as if he were walking to another room.

"How do you know when you're in love?"

Andrea nearly fumbled the coffeepot. She quickly set it down on the awaiting warmer. "In love?"

"Yeah. How do you know?"

Apparently, this was a serious conversation. Andrea puffed a breath of air out. Hell, if she knew. "I'm not sure, buddy." She opened the fridge.

"But don't you love Rory?"

She froze. "Whoa, where did that question come from?"

"Well, do you?"

"Noah..."

"And don't you miss him?"

"Hey, what's with the fifty questions?" She closed the fridge. "What's going on?" She desperately hoped Rory wasn't there, waiting for her to say something.

"I think I'm in love, but I'm not sure." He paused. "Mom said when you're in love you're happy. I'm always happy, so how do you know?"

She sighed. She loved this kid. And right now, Noah was thousands of miles away, hoping she had the answer he needed. A *real* answer. She couldn't disappoint him. Did she love Rory? She hadn't talked to him since New Years' Eve, but she still thought about him, especially last night when she was in her element in the kitchen. He'd been right. She had a gift. A talent, he'd said. When she helped Marin fulfill her slogan of creating delicious mouthfuls, Andrea had displayed her talent and skill. She smiled slowly. And what was so wrong with helping her see that? *Because loving someone never worked out for my family. It always ended. And I'm stubborn and independent, and...*

She could admit that she cared for him, but love...love made her palms sweat. She thought of Brie. She loved her like a sister and wished she was nearby. And she thought of Rory and how he calmed her with his presence alone—his big, quiet presence. She was drawn to him. "When you're in love...you want to be with that person all the time."

"But what does it feel like?"

Thinking, she remembered Rory holding her with a smarting ankle in the mountain cottage. He made her entire being sigh. "It's like a warm feeling all over your body...like when your mom wraps you in a big hug and you hold on tight because it feels so nice and safe there."

After a pause, Noah breathed into the phone. "I'm in love with Caitlin."

Andrea felt a smile form. "You are?"

"Yep," he replied. "She chases me on the playground when we play tag. And she's really smart and nice, too."

"Well, that's great." The kid was six and knew what love was. A sting of envy pelted Andrea in the chest, and she found herself drawn to the modern Glasgow skyline on her wall. The black-and-white print with silvery city buildings pressing sharply into the sky reminded her of swords drawn—reminding her of Rory.

Chapter Forty-Nine

Rory pulled into the familiar yard, noting the old van parked in the driveway, but not Da's truck. Relief flooded him. He came to talk and to move on, but he was glad to bide his time. The forge door was open wide, and he heard the pleasant *snap-snap* from a welder.

Strolling inside, he watched Collin weld stars onto a decorative gate with iron scroll work. He waited patiently, admiring the skill and technique. Collin and he learned the skill of smith beside Da, watching his hands and listening to his suggestions and directions, since they were wee lads. And he was indebted.

Turning, Collin spied Rory and lifted his helmet. Swipes of soot and sweat beaded down his face and colored the light shadow on his beard. "Yer a welcome surprise."

"Brilliant work."

"Thank ye. I'm fashioning an iron patio fence for a new restaurant in Glasgow."

"Oh, aye?" He tipped his head. "Which restaurant?"

"Sea to Star. The owner's a Scot and his wife's American."

Rory rubbed a hand over his beard. "American?" Immediately, he thought of Andrea, and a knife twisted in his gut. He missed her. Weeks had passed, and he still thought of her and the way she stood on Hogmanay panicked and dead set on leaving. Yet, she'd made her decision; nothing he could've done or said would've made her stay. Following her wouldn't change her mind. They didn't want the same things.

"Ye'd know them, I'm sure. Finn and Sarah Murray?"

He nodded. "Aye, I do. Bryce recommend ye?"

"He did."

He crossed his hands over his chest. "Let me know when yer ready to install. I'll lend a hand."

"Oh, ye'll lend a hand all right," a coarse voice said from behind.

"Da." Rory turned, noting the scrunched expression on Da's face. "Let's put this behind us."

"Ye snub yer nose at what I've taught ye, at yer roots, to leave for the shinin' lights of television, and now ye wish to lower yerself?"

He steeled himself. "Da."

His father stood a head shorter than Rory, but with his wide shoulders and stance, he was formidable at sixty-two.

"Ye have it wrong. If not for yer mastery, I wouldna be able to take on the art of swordsmith. It's because of ye that I'm the man I am now, don't ye see it?"

His full brows rose.

"I'm grateful. I should've said it before, but I was sore. With your comments about my art, I thought I embarrassed ye. That's why I moved and, well, for the job. We need to put this behind us. 'Tis time."

"Embarrassed?" Da scowled and dragged a hand over his coarse beard.

"Aye."

"Yer a skilled artist. Always have been."

Rory tilted his head.

"I suppose my pride was bruised, as well. Ye didn't want

what yer granda and I started—then ye went and disappeared and rarely returned."

"I'm remedying that."

"I can see that for myself."

He reached a hand out. "The strength of the swords I fashion are due to the foundation I learned with ye—with the family. I value what ye've built and what we built. My art is an extension of that."

Da gripped his hand and squeezed. "Aye. The Cameron forge is strong."

Rory shook Da's hand, then drew him in for an embrace, breathing in the soapy scent of his father.

When they separated, he glanced around. "I don't see yer lass with ye."

Rory removed his cap and folded the bill in his hands. "No. She's returned to America."

"Whisky?"

He nodded. Walking into his family home, he smiled at his ma.

She rushed over. "Are ye all right, *main don*? I didna know ye were visiting."

"Aye, I am."

She angled her head. "Come inside for some *Cock-a-Leekie*-Soup."

He sat in his family home, eating a familiar, homey dinner with family around him, and he felt better than he had in weeks. Yet, opposite him was where Andrea sat on Christmas day, and a meter away was where she defended him. Shaking his head, he tossed the memories aside and spooned another helping into his bowl. Memories wouldn't bring her back.

* * *

Scrolling through photos from the night before—sweaty, shining, and savoring every moment cooking—Andrea felt her cheeks burning from smiling. After finishing the decadent California Eggs Benedict breakfast, she treated herself to a shopping spree at William Sonoma. She'd spend part of her sign-on bonus and purchased a new cast-iron, traditional deep skillet in cherry-red, a whistling wine-red tea kettle, as well as matching duo of mugs and ceramic mortar and pestle. The first because she loved the way the California Diver Scallops sizzled in the cast-iron pan the night before. The second because she missed Brie and her love of tea, and the third, because she wanted one.

Knock-knock.

Andrea swiveled. She wasn't expecting anyone. Striding to the door, she gazed through the peep hole and, with an exhale, opened the door. "Mom? What are you doing here?"

Gloria stood dressed to the nines in high heels and an *A*-line navy-blue dress and matching blue-and-pearl earrings. "Is that anyway to greet your mother?"

"Hi, Mom. How are you?" She waved a hand into her apartment.

"Not as well as I'd hoped seeing that my daughter has been back in town for some time and couldn't even spare a moment to drop by, especially after you rebuffed both of my holiday invitations."

Andrea opened her mouth and closed it.

Gloria's gaze swept around Andrea's apartment and settled on the counter and the hoard of cooking goods. "What *is* all this?"

"Some new cooking items and tools."

"I saw your social media posts. Why are you playing chef?"

Andrea blinked. "Playing chef?"

She fanned a hand through the air. "You know what I mean. If you want to get this off your chest or whatever it is, I can have Brian invite you to his new restaurant—it's a three-starred Michelin restaurant—and you can watch his chef create masterpieces."

As frustration clawed up her throat, Andrea gazed at the ceiling. Her happy mood instantly soured. Stalking back into the kitchen, she put away her new kitchen toys. "I'm not playing at anything. I can cook. I'm good at it. Just like *Nonna* said. And I've taken more classes and plan to take more because I love cooking."

"Listen to you." Gloria picked non-existent lint off her dress. "You're not thinking clearly." She turned and flashed a smile. "You know what you need?"

"What?"

"A fabulous dinner."

"What?" she repeated.

"Put all this...stuff away. Get changed, and I'll treat you to a wonderful meal at Brian's restaurant. We'll have a few drinks, since it's early, and then he can give us a tour."

Andrea's brain was spinning. "Brian? Who's Brian?"

"Why the love of my life, of course."

With a roll of her eyes, Andrea placed a hand on the counter to steady herself. "Love of your life or you mean, love for right now? Because that's really all they are, right, Mother? Just players in your love game until you get tired of them and toss them aside."

Gloria's eyes darkened. "How dare you talk to me that way!"

Releasing her hand, she straightened. "I'm sorry. I truly am. But you know what? I had a great guy in Scotland. Great. But you couldn't be happy for me. He and his skills meant nothing to you. Well, they do to me." She tapped her chest. "He even bought me a food truck."

With a hand to her mouth, Gloria gasped.

"That's right"—Andrea leaned forward—"A food truck,

roach coach, meals on wheels. Because you know why? I love cooking. Love it. It makes me feel alive. And he saw that. He believed in me." And at that moment, she knew she had to find a way to return to Scotland. She had to chase her dreams and the man she loved. How could she have been so cruel? So heartless? And so blind? Was she so afraid of her own happiness? She didn't believe she could find someone who understood her. But he did. He took the time, just like he did with every piece he fashioned.

With a hand on Gloria's arm, she steered her to the door. "Now, I'm making stuffed shells. It's my day off, and I'll do whatever the hell I please. Enjoy your dinner, Mother." When the door closed, she breathed deeply.

The Chief HRO position and empty apartment were not the life she wanted anymore. She wanted a full life. And that life was with the ones she loved, including Brie and the kids, and a man who loved her—in all her surly and spicy ways. Besides, what good was cooking a magnificent meal if she had no one to share it with? She knew what she had to do. But she had to figure out a way to get herself to Scotland... Suddenly, she had an epiphany. A work visa. That is, if they'd have her. She scrolled through her phone and found Sarah Murray. With her heart skittering, she pressed the icon and called.

Chapter Fifty

"MORE SPICE?" SARAH HELD OUT A SPOON, FILLED TO the brim with a golden liquid three weeks later.

Andrea licked the hot Texas *queso* dip in the *Sea to Star* kitchen surrounded by shining stainless-steel cabinetry with warm wooden accents and family heirlooms including a few iron Texas stars on the walls. The rich and creamy duo of Scottish cheeses, heat from the jalapeño, warm garlic, and fresh tomato were the perfect combination. But one thing was missing—a touch of freshness.

"What about some herbs to top it off with extra color? Like cilantro and green onion?"

"Oh, great idea!"

Andrea tore a small bunch of cilantro leaves from the herb jar and plucked a scallion. With a couple chops, she added the herbs to a few diced tomatoes and sprinkled the mixture on top. Dipping two chili-lime chips into the dip, she handed one to Sarah and the other to the sous-chef, Dallas.

"Mmm. Perfect," Sarah acknowledged.

Dallas crunched the chip with riotous curls bobbing on top of his head and a big, toothy grin. "Brilliant." His short crop of brown curls danced, while his quick smile spread. "'Tis a party in my mouth!"

Andrea laughed. With his witty sense of humor, he and Andrea had gotten along from the start. She dipped a chip herself, then crunched with pleasure. Less than a month ago, she was sitting in a boring, white office, and now she was cooking with amazing chefs and helping confirm menu options for *Sea to Star's* opening in a few weeks. She was in foodie heaven. Of course, she didn't know what Sarah would say when she called her up the day Gloria waltzed into her apartment, but she couldn't have been prepared for the immediate *yes*.

Andrea told the Murrays she'd enroll in a few more classes, but Finn and Sarah requested she train alongside them and their long-time sous-chefs, Dallas and Wendy, before taking any more classes, while the restaurant renovation finished. She quickly agreed and applied for a visa, listing the Murrays' new restaurant as her new employer, and gave her notice. The next phone call was to Brie.

"You're coming back to Scotland? You what?" She had cried and squealed. "I'm not crying, you're crying! And I'm so proud of you."

Andrea swiped happy tears with the back of her hand. "I'll be back in a few weeks. Tell my favorite kids to get ready for some homemade pizza."

"I will!"

"Oh, and Brie?"

"Yep?"

"Don't tell Rory just yet."

Remembering the secret pact she'd made with her bestie that day, Andrea still hadn't seen Rory or figured out what she'd say. She was an idiot? She was angry because he was right? She did love him, but she needed to figure out what she wanted first? Cooking always helped, so as she moved to another prep station to clean Scottish shrimp, she thought of the quiet man by the fiery hearth.

Boom! Boom! Boom!

Andrea jerked, dropping a shrimp. "What the hell?" She and Sarah walked out of the kitchen and toward the front window.

Some of the construction crew along with two other guys with hard hats and flannel jackets were surrounded by a chalky cement cloud as they drilled holes.

"Oh, they're installing the patio fence today. It's going to be amazing with the star-and-laurel detail," Sarah said.

"Good thing we're in here!" Andrea flashed a smile and turned. The mermaid painting by Mimi graced the entry, surrounded by iron Texas stars. The whimsical acrylic captured the mermaid with a mirror in one hand and comb in the other, while green leaves fanned her lower waist above a beautifully textured aquamarine-and-teal mermaid tail. The Murrays mixed Finn's Scottish heritage and clan crest with elements of Texas, and the resulting ambiance was bright and festive.

When she pivoted, she glanced outside once more and nearly stumbled. The chalky cloud receded, and a man with smoky-gray eyes and an auburn beard stared back. "Rory."

* * *

The gates were open when Andrea pulled up to Rory's property that evening. "This better be a good sign." She continued up the road. A moment later, she swung out of the car and glanced at the starry sky, shining through the trees amidst fluffy white clouds that lit the fresh snowfall on the ground like burnt gold. She smelled the pine, snow, and earth, but amidst the natural scents, the scent of burnt metal was the strongest. She gazed at the forge, puffing a white cloud of smoke into the sky. Hanging above, the sign she'd made graced the entrance. She squared her shoulders and strode to the forge. Lights blazed when she entered, and incessant pounding echoed in the air.

A dog barked.

A moment later, Maggie trotted toward her, tail wagging.

"Hi, girl." Andrea bent down to pet her soft head. "Miss me?"

Maggie responded by growling playfully and then wiggling into Andrea's hands full of energy, fluff, and love.

After a quick rubdown, Andrea stood. "I need to talk to Rory."

With a quick yip, Maggie bounded toward the center of the forge.

"Let's hope he's just as excited to see me." As she followed, hot air swirled around her, and she felt the tiny curls along her neck spiral even more. The forge roared with fire, flaming rich-red and orange and yellow flares.

Off to the side, Rory hammered a fiery-tipped sword on an anvil.

She watched him. She'd never allowed herself to dream of forever with someone. Even though she was bound and determined not to, she couldn't deny the quiet man had captured her heart. Once she'd finally peeled back all the anger and resistance, she realized she wasn't angry at Rory, but her own inability to see a better future for herself—and one that included him. She had a chance to be loved by a man as steady as a rock and as stubborn as she and to make a life with him and for herself.

Her future was so clear now—as if the final ingredient fell into place—finishing the recipe of her life. Yet, standing a few feet from him, she pressed a hand on the nerves tangling in her stomach. Brie had told her she hadn't seen Rory since Hogmanay, though Bryce had been over a few times to visit.

Still, neither thought he was seeing anyone. Hope swirled within her.

Staring at his strong back and the way his muscles moved and flexed with exertion under a cobalt sleeve, she admired him—his creativity, grit, and strength. She wasn't even sure if he wanted to see her. He'd never called, never texted, and never tried to come after her. But she told him not to, didn't she? She told him she didn't want what he offered. And now, she had to ask for his forgiveness and win his love once again. But she continued to stand there, twisting her fingers in front of her. She didn't want to startle him. He *was* working on a big-ass knife. And it *was* red hot. So, she gave herself a moment, while she worked up the courage.

And then, he looked up.

Andrea backed into a table, knocking a tool down with a *clang*. She quickly retrieved the piece.

Rory's beard was longer and less tidy, his cheeks rosy from the fire, and his eyes an intense gray like the steel he held in his strong hand. Setting the knife and hammer down, he removed his gloves and protective glasses. "What are ye doing here?"

She stepped toward him. "I returned to L.A. and started my new job. I thought it was everything I wanted, or, at least convinced myself it was. But after the excitement of being home wore off, I realized it wasn't home anymore. I tried to make it work. Believe me"—she leaned forward—"I tried burying myself in my new job and organizing my old apartment, and then I realized, I was so determined not to lose myself in Scotland and give up who I was that I'd actually found the best version of me."

With a nod, he continued gazing at her.

"I love to cook and bring spice and flavor into people's lives. I like to be with my friends and family—Brie, Bryce, the kids, Mimi...and you. And, I like you." She tugged her jacket closer and glanced up at Rory whose gaze hadn't wavered. "More than like you."

Crossing his arms across his broad chest, he settled against the giant anvil.

She lifted a hand to ruffle her curls. "I didn't expect you, okay? You were wonderful to me, and I got scared. My parents screwed me up, and then I messed up what we had. So, I wanted to come back and say, I'm sorry. Truly. And maybe, someday, you can try to like me again."

"Are ye finished?"

She drew a breath. "I have to go back to—"

"No." Rory shoved away from the anvil.

Ash, metal, and woodsy notes filled her nostrils, and her mouth pooled. *Was he always so strong? So male. And so, hot?*

"'Tis my turn. And yer going to sit here and listen to what I've to say."

"If you think—"

"Damn it, woman." He grasped her shoulders. "I love ye. Yer a pain in the arse, uncannily kind when ye don't try, drive me mad, and cook like an angel. We're made for each other just like the swords I fashion and yer food. We burn and argue, but there's no other place I'd rather be than with ye. And if yer not ready"—he slid his arms down and released her—"I can wait."

"For how long?"

Fear dashed across those gray eyes like a windy storm; yet, he stood strong. "I'm a patient man."

"You are." She smiled. "The Murrays sponsored my work visa and hired me at their restaurant—you saw. I needed to make my own way. Don't you see? I needed to make my own way, so I could make my way back to you. And one day, maybe I'll start a pop-up catering business or hell, drive a food van."

His lips twitched. "Ye should."

"So." She smoothed a hand over his rough one. "You love me, huh?"

He reached his other hand out, stroking a curl. "Aye, I do."

"I love you, too." Rising to her toes, she pressed a kiss to his warm mouth, relishing the soft scratch of his beard. While his strong arms wrapped around her, she felt her entire body sigh as she got lost in the kiss—in Rory—yet, she was found. She'd found her happy place. A moment later, she drew away and gazed at him, heart pumping with anticipation. "Ask me again."

With a cock of his head, his eyes sparkled; yet, he didn't say a thing.

"Don't make me repeat myself, Rory Cameron!"

He chuckled and strolled toward the sword cabinet, returning a moment later with a small, blue box. He knelt in front of her. "Andrea Accardi, love of my life and fire to my soul, will ye marry me?"

In his hand, he held a stunning ring with waterfall silver wrapped around a clear diamond. She lifted a hand to her mouth as joy spread to every inch of her body. "You made this...for me?"

"Aye, I did. There have never been any like it before, and there'll never be one after. Just like ye." He removed the ring and gazed from under reddish-brown lashes. "Marry me."

The man before her was not who she was looking for, but he was hers. She'd found him at her lowest, and he accepted her as she was. Just like her friends. But deep down, they were more—her family. And now, Rory wanted to make a future together. She never planned for marriage, but here it was—an offer of forever and a promise forged by hardworking, gentle hands. Hands etched with lovely lines and firm callouses held hers—hands that supported and loved her, while his gray eyes shone like the sun parting stormy rain clouds. "You know I'm not the best marriage material."

His thick brows rose.

She giggled. "I mean, I break can openers."

He chuckled. "Oh, aye?"

"Yes. Dozens a year." She spaced out each word. "I don't know why, but I'm the can-opener killer."

His eyes twinkled. "I think I can live wit' that." He rose and held her hands between his. "Will ye?"

"Yes!" Andrea kissed him square on the mouth. "Hell yes, I'll marry you!"

He slid the ring onto her finger and wrapped her in his big arms, enveloping her.

She sighed, resting her head against his shoulder. She found where she belonged—with her quiet man.

Epilogue

"ARE YOU SURE I'M NOT STEALING YOUR BRIDAL bliss or thunder or whatever?" Andrea asked five weeks later in an off-the-shoulder, sultry fit-and-flair ivory gown. She stood in her dining room, which was now decorated with rich-red flowers and vining greenery, as well as a variety of white candles.

Brie *tsked* in a wine-red, *A*-line gown and slid an arm around Andrea's shoulders. "No. My best friend is getting married. I couldn't be happier."

Touching her temple to Brie's, she sighed. "Thanks. You know if I don't do it today, I never will."

Brie squeezed and released her, then stared into her eyes with those warm green ones. "You're happy. That's what matters most! Plus, you were already my Maid of Honor, but at the celebration, you'll be my Matron of Honor."

Andrea snorted. "Hell no, I'm the MOH. Matron sounds so old, and I'm still younger than you, anyway."

Brie poked her. "Just by a year."

Andrea laughed alongside Brie.

At a knock on the door, Brie skirted across the living room and peeked out. "It's Bryce."

"Good. I'm ready to get this show on the road!"

As Bryce ducked inside wearing a tartan kilt and stone-gray suit jacket, his smile grew wide, spreading across his entire face and crinkling his crystal-blue eyes. "Why, Andrea, yer a beautiful bride."

"Well, thank you! You look dashing yourself."

With a grin, he lifted an arm toward the door. "Someone's here for ye."

She whipped a finger and backed away, glancing behind her for a hiding place. "Don't you dare bring Rory in here! We need all the luck we can get."

"'Tis not Rory." He stepped aside.

Giovanni Accardi strolled in with slicked black hair streaked with gray and a dark-wine Armani suit. "Andrea Sofia."

"Dad," she whispered. Her eyes glossed as she walked into his open arms. She smelled his familiar citrus cologne and felt his warmth through the sleek suit jacket. She never planned to get married, but having her dad there made the wedding feel even more real. "You made it."

"Wouldn't miss it."

Five minutes later, she sashayed down the aisle over red rose petals Phoebe scattered, hand tucked in the crook of her dad's arm, and smiled at Rory, handsome in his clan tartan kilt and stone-gray suit jacket. The Cameron tartan was red—her color—and she'd matched the color scheme to the bright rose blooms she carried and the lipstick on her lips. "Hey, Swordsmith."

Rory grinned wide, eyes shining. "Lass...yer so bonnie." Then, he glanced at Giovanni and extended a hand. "Giovanni."

He shook Rory's hand. "Congratulations to you both." Turning, Giovanni kissed Andrea on the forehead.

"Thanks, Dad."

Rory offered his arm to Andrea. "Are ye ready?"

"Yes!" She tucked her arm in his and strolled to the altar.

They wed at the top of their property, overlooking the loch with fifty of their closest friends and family in attendance. She had a mother-in-law and father-in-law now. She even called Ailes, *Ma*. She couldn't believe it. Gloria had declined the invitation, which was most likely for the best, but her dad made the trip. Those who mattered were there.

Later that evening, they fanned around the cake table with a handmade three-tiered chocolate cake by Brie with her favorite cream-cheese buttercream decorated with greenery, wine-red rose petals, and thistle.

"Ready to do the honors?" Brie lifted the cake cutter.

"Wait!" Andrea dipped and reached under the table where she'd hidden a surprise a few hours earlier.

Rory bent down with an uptick of a lip. "What are ye up to, Mrs. Cameron?"

"Mrs...Cameron." She smiled wide. "I like the sound of that!" Then, she unearthed the sword in its sheath. "This is how you cut a cake."

Chuckling, he snugged an arm around Andrea and removed the sword's sheath with the other.

With his hand atop hers, she raised the sword and sliced into the bottom tier of the cake, a symbol of longevity, and the sword, a symbol of strength and commitment forged by a man who promised to love, protect, and cherish her forever.

Acknowledgments

First and foremost, thank you, reader, for reading *Where the Stars Burn*. This sassy and smart romcom was inspired by Andrea and Rory's very first meeting on the set of *Swords of Scotland* in book 1 of my Scottish Stars series, *The Stars of Scotland*. I could imagine her wielding the heavy claymore, and the electric connection between her and Rory. Thank you so much for picking this book up, believing in love stories, and supporting my author career. I can't wait to share more stories with you!

Where the Stars Burn wouldn't be here without so many incredible people.

To Sam at *Ink and Laurel* for the most beautiful cover I could ever ask for. Thank you for creating my dream cover!

To my husband, thank you for loving me so fully and truly seeing me, and for telling your friends and co—workers that your wife is a romance author with pride. You make my heart soar!

To my kids for cheering me on and remembering my writing evenings and for the biggest hugs, sweetest kisses, and holding my books with love like your favorite toys. I love you so much.

To my sister, thank you for your constant love, Scottish memes, and taking me on my very first trip to Scotland. I can't wait to take you next time! #twinsiesforever. To Mom, my very first reader and constant cheerleader who always tells me to 'keep going' and 'keep writing.' Thank you for always believing in me and in this story! To Dad, thank you for sharing your love of your (our) Scottish roots and supporting me. To my extended family members, especially the Gregory's and my bonus Vasquez family for lifting me up and always asking what I'm working on next. To Shanel for your sweet friendship, endless love for Rory and Andrea's love story, meeting me for weekly writing dates, and for all the hugs. To Madie for your lifelong friendship, silly texts while reading, and always asking when you can read the next book. Love you all!

Thank you to all the incredible writers I'm lucky enough to call friends. Annie Cathryn for all our touch-base phone calls and for talking through the next phase of publishing with me. I'm forever grateful I joined the WFWA and met you. Ashley Detweiler, Elizabeth Webster, Suzy England, and Taylor Hudson for cheering me on and being on this journey with me. To Ciara Blume and G.C. London, thank you for your support, encouragement, and tips to help make this process smooth. You all are such an inspiration!

Last, but not least, thank you God for blessing me on this incredible author journey. Love always wins.

About the Author

Erica Mae is an author, mom, wife, and book lover. Her books are full of swoony romance, big adventures, and slow burns, offering dreamy escapes for the romantics. Her mission is to bring more love into the world, one book at a time, and her greatest hope is that her books fill you with love and sweet possibilities. When she's not writing, you can find her curled up with a book, exploring with her family, on a yoga mat, or cooking up a new recipe.

Visit Erica Mae Online at www.ericamae.net

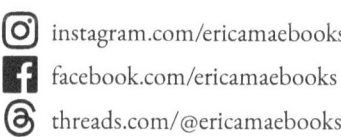

instagram.com/ericamaebooks

facebook.com/ericamaebooks

threads.com/@ericamaebooks

www.ingramcontent.com/pod-product-compliance
Lightning Source LLC
Chambersburg PA
CBHW020543120726
47903CB00001B/104